Killing Beauty

Also by Kim Antieau

Novels

The Blue Tail • *Broken Moon* • *Butch*
Church of the Old Mermaids • *Coyote Cowgirl* • *Deathmark*
The Desert Siren • *The Fish Wife: an Old Mermaids Novel*
The Gaia Websters • *Her Frozen Wild* • *Jewelweed Station*
The Jigsaw Woman • *Mercy, Unbound*
The Monster's Daughter • *Ruby's Imagine*
Swans in Winter • *The Rift*
Whackadoodle Times • *Whackadoodle Times Two*

Nonfiction

Answering the Creative Call
Certified
Counting on Wildflowers
The Old Mermaids Book of Days and Nights
The Old Mermaids Book of Days and Nights: A Year and a Day Journal
An Old Mermaid Journal
The Salmon Mysteries
Under the Tucson Moon

Short Story Collections

Entangled Realities (with Mario Milosevic)
The First Book of Old Mermaids Tales
Tales Fabulous and Fairy
Trudging to Eden

Chapbook

Blossoms

Cartoons

Fun With Vic and Jane

Blog

www.kimantieau.com

Killing Beauty

Kim Antieau

Green Snake
PUBLISHING

Killing Beauty
by Kim Antieau

Copyright © 2019 by Kim Antieau

ISBN-13: 978-1-949644-59-3

A version of part one, *Maternal Instincts*, was originally published in book form by Green Snake Publishing, 2015.

Although this book was inspired by true events, it is a work of fiction.

Cover photo by Philipp Sewing | Unsplash

Thanks to Nancy Milosevic.

Thanks to Lisa Mills Walters.
lisawaltersediting.com

Published by Green Snake Publishing
www.greensnakepublishing.com

For my dad

Part One

Maternal Instincts

One

I didn't hear the girl until she was right behind me and only then because she whispered hoarsely, "Help me. I've been kidnapped."

I had just finished hiking the Mystic Trail and was headed up to the small parking lot, the one away from the trailhead. The creek on my left was heavy with snow melt and louder than usual. Old Doug firs towered over me on all sides, and I felt as though I was still in the wild even as I walked up a paved road; straight above, the sky was clear and milky blue for the first time in weeks. I was giddy to be out of doors without being drenched by Pacific Northwest spring rain—so giddy I wasn't paying much attention to what was going on around me, which was odd because you know the saying, "Once a cop, always a cop."

I quickly turned around and saw a child standing inches from me, female, about eleven years old, white, four and a half feet tall, seventy pounds, with nearly shoulder length blond hair and terrified blue eyes, wearing yellow shorts, red top, white socks, and blue running shoes. She was holding her left hand out to me.

"Please," she said. "Before they come back."

Later I wondered why I did what I did. It was foolish. It was dangerous. I knew my ex would say it was arrogance: I thought because I was a cop I could do anything.

It wasn't that. For one thing, I wasn't a cop any longer. I looked into her eyes. I was a parent. In spite of what my son might think—or even what I might think sometimes—I did have maternal instincts. I knew this girl was terrified, and I had to help her. I had to save her.

So I grabbed her hand, and we ran to my car. I unlocked it, opened the back door, and said, "Get in."

The girl quickly slid into the backseat.

Later when I was questioned about this—and I was questioned, again and again—I was asked, "Didn't it occur to you that you could be charged with kidnapping?"

"No, it didn't," I said. Again and again.

The girl said she was in trouble. What else was I supposed to do?

"Something else," was what my ex said.

So maybe I wasn't thinking. I was running on instinct. Maybe I missed being a cop, missed being able to save people, help people. Missed not thinking about my own crap. Who knows? My heart was racing, my adrenaline was pumping.

"Get down," I said. "Behind the seat."

She did as I instructed. I put the backseat blanket over her and then shut the door. I glanced around. Didn't see anyone. Didn't think anyone from the parking lot could see me.

I noticed a folded sheet of paper on my windshield. I pulled it out from beneath the wiper—it was some kind of religious tract—and tossed it inside the car. Then I got in and started the engine.

"Are they here on the trail?" I asked. "The kidnappers."

"Yes," she said, her voice muffled. "Two men."

"Stay down," I said. "I'm going to drive through the parking lot."

"No!" she said. "We have to leave."

"Don't worry," I said. I leaned over and opened the glove box. My phone was on top of my gun—I couldn't get any service here, but I could take a few pics. I grabbed the phone and then turned the car around and slowly drove into the parking lot. I saw several people coming down the trail toward the lot. A man, a woman, two children. They were laughing and talking. Beyond them, a young man and woman walked together, holding hands. Beyond them were others, but they were too far away for me to discern any features.

I quickly and surreptitiously took photos of the license plates of the cars in the parking lot.

I drove out of the lot, down the road, and out onto I-84, heading east.

"You can get up now," I said. "Put on your seat belt."

In the rearview mirror, I saw the blanket rise, then a small hand pulled it away, and I saw the girl again. She glanced around, clear-eyed and attentive. I heard the seat belt click into place. At first glance, she didn't appear to be overly traumatized. Most children were less accustomed to hiding their emotions than adults, so trauma was usually easier to spot in kids.

Maybe she had gotten away before they could hurt her.

Or something else was going on.

"What's your name?" I asked.

"Danella Green," she said. "My mom said if I was ever in trouble, I should find a woman with bear in her eyes. I could tell you had bear in your whole body. Bears will take care of their cubs no matter what. I knew you'd help me. You'll help me, right? You can take me to my mom."

She said all of this quickly. She was breathing up high in her chest: She was starting to panic. Now that she thought she might be safe, the shock was setting in. I had seen this reaction many times.

"Danella," I said, "your mom was right. You were right. I'll take care of you. Don't worry. Breathe. It's OK. My name is Kate Kelly, by the way."

Her face relaxed a bit.

"I used to be a cop," I said, hoping to reassure her.

She looked panicked again.

"No police," she said, sounding terrified. "They said they'd kill my mom if I contacted the police. Please, take me to our house in Beauty Falls."

We were headed in the right direction.

"Tell me what happened."

"Three days ago, these men came to our house," she said. "They argued with my mother. They wanted her to do something. She said she wouldn't, so they took me. They grabbed me. They said if I didn't come quietly, they'd hurt my mother. Said it would all be over by Wednesday morning."

Today was Saturday.

"What would be all over?" I asked.

"I don't know," Danella said. "The kidnapping, I guess. They said they'd take me back to my mom Wednesday if all went well."

"Where's your mom work?" I asked.

"I don't know," Danella said. "She was at a place in Portland, but then she left. We moved to Beauty Falls a few weeks ago."

"Does she work in Beauty Falls?" I asked.

Danella looked like she was going to cry. Too many questions.

"I don't know," she said. "She hadn't shown me yet. She usually takes me to her work place. Please, can you go to our house?"

I had to take her to the police, whether she liked it or not. I didn't have any choice. I knew the sheriff, Nate Gunderson. He was an old friend. Well, not exactly a *friend,* but we knew one another.

Behind us, I saw a car getting onto the expressway from the Mystic Trail exit.

"What kind of car did your kidnappers have?" I asked.

"Um, I don't know," Danella said.

"Sure, you do," I said. "Get down again."

I saw the renewed panic in her eyes.

"You're OK," I said. "I'm being careful." She disappeared from my sight. "Close your eyes and remember the car."

A moment later, I heard her muffled voice. "Red car. Four doors. It's too big. It creaks when they get into it."

"Good, Danella. Good detail."

The car behind me was blue.

Another car was coming up behind that one, could have come from the Mystic Trail exit, too. We were too far past the exit now for me to know.

It was a red car.

Crap.

Had they seen us?

"Do they have weapons?" I asked.

The red car was coming up fast behind me. Couldn't tell the make or model right away.

"One of them had a gun," she said. "Maybe the other one did, too. I only saw the one in its holster, around his chest."

The car looked like an Impala, mid-90s. Basically it was a cop car painted red. If these were the kidnappers, they apparently weren't worried about laying low. This was a memorable car. A memorable car that was right on my tail.

Normally that would piss me off and I'd tap my brakes. But I didn't do that.

I was tempted to speed up, but my six cylinder Hyundai wasn't going to outrun an eight cylinder Impala. So I maintained my speed.

Suddenly the car swerved left to pass me.

I felt my heart in my throat. That was unusual. I'd been working white collar crime for several years before I left the police force, so I hadn't been in many physically dangerous situations for a while, but still. Had I forgotten how to stay calm?

Naw. My heart had always felt like it was in my throat when I was in danger.

The red car was suddenly beside us. I glanced over. Looked like two people inside. Could only see the man in the passenger seat. Appeared to be in his mid-thirties, wore a dirty baseball cap and a flannel shirt. He looked straight ahead, and he was talking.

I guessed whoever they were they didn't care about me and whatever was in my car.

Good.

My heart went back into my chest.

The car sped past me and was soon out of sight as the highway wound along the curves of the Columbia River.

"You can get up, Danella," I said.

Her head popped up again, visible in my rearview mirror.

I locked all the car doors. Danella wouldn't be able to get out on her own now, in case she decided she didn't like what I was doing.

"Does anyone ever call you Danny or Nellie?" I asked.

Danella nodded.

"Can I call you Danny?"

She nodded again. She had tears in her eyes, but she quickly blinked them away.

"Danny, I gotta take you to the police," I said. "I know the sheriff in Beauty Falls. He's a good guy." OK, he was a jerk I had dated a couple of times when we were teens—including one particular night I didn't want to think about right now. Every time I saw him, I remembered that night. I thought of Amanda, Sylvie, Doug, and Andy. Andy who was still in prison for what he had done to Amanda.

"The police are in on it," Danella said. "Herman and Mitchell weren't worried at all about keeping it a secret because they said they were friends with the police."

"Herman and Mitchell?" I said. "They told you their names?"

"Sure," she said. "I had to call them something. They said they knew the police, and the police wouldn't do anything if I went to them for help."

"Were they talking about any police in particular?" I was trying to figure out details—see if Danella was being truthful or not.

"No," she said. She sounded exasperated.

"Did they hurt you?" I asked. I took the exit for Cascade Locks.

Danella shook her head. "No. They haven't touched me, if that's what you mean. They fed me. They even got me my favorite snack, the Bigfoot Fruit Leathers. They said they were keeping me as security until my mom did something for them."

"Do you know what they wanted her to do?"

Danella shook her head. "Can't you take me to my mother? Then we can all go to the police."

I drove up to the bridge toll booth and gave a ticket to the ticket taker.

"Have a nice day," the ticket taker said, grinning. She waved to Danella. I glanced up and saw a video camera on the top of the booth, aimed directly at us.

Crap, crap, crap. I had forgotten about the cameras.

Now I was on video with a kidnapped child in the backseat.

No matter. I'd be turning her over to the sheriff in about five minutes.

Two

I drove us onto the Bridge of the Gods, the steel-grated cantilever bridge that spanned the Columbia River. The Big River—which acted as a border between Oregon and Washington—reflected the sky today, as if it were a huge lake instead of one of the largest rivers in the United States. My car rattled over the steel grating—I needed to slow down. I glanced in the mirror. No one was behind us. I lightly tapped my brakes.

Beyond the river from us, Hamilton Mountain rose above a forest of Douglas firs. If I turned left, we'd soon reach the entrance to Wanted Lake, where the out-of-town rich people kept summer cabins, and beyond that, the Beautyville Dam. Turning right would take us to Beauty Falls. To the north, the Gifford Pinchot National Forest stretched up to and included Mount Saint Helens and environs.

Once we were across the bridge, I turned right. Hamilton Mountain disappeared as we headed for Beauty Falls on SR 14. I had spent nearly every summer in Beauty Falls when I was a kid, coming out here to get away from Portland on hot summer days. I continued to come back when I was an adult, staying in our family's cottage—which was definitely not on Wanted Lake—until we sold it a few years back. When I left the force eight months ago, I decided to buy a house in Beauty Falls. I wasn't sure why. The town was dying or, at the very least, it was in transition.

I could relate.

Story goes Beauty Falls was named after a tiered waterfall that disappeared when the U.S. Army Corps of Engineers built Beautyville Dam in the 1930s. This explanation never made sense to me because the town of Beauty Falls is miles from Beautyville Dam. I'd heard locals say the falls never existed— the name and the story had been concocted by town officials to get tourist dollars.

When I was a kid, an old Chinook woman came to do a program at the library. She told us the falls did exist, but they were hidden from white folks. This part of the world was flush with waterfalls—there's one at the end of Mystic Trail—so someone could probably point in any direction and say, "The Beauty Falls falls are over there" and somebody would find a beautiful waterfall and believe it to be the "real" Beauty Falls.

Long way of saying, Danella and I didn't see any waterfalls as we drove into Beauty Falls. What we glimpsed was an old logging town trying to come back from near death. It was basically a commuter town now, with most people working in Portland, Oregon, or Vancouver, Washington. Took about an hour from Beauty Falls to get to either of those cities. The main employer in Beauty Falls was the government—either the feds, state, county, or city, although some people worked at Darby's Unmanned Aircraft Systems. Or as the locals called them: Drones Are Us.

I turned off the state highway and headed up Rusty Street hill toward the courthouse.

It was foolish to go to Danella's house if the kidnappers were holding her mother. Or blackmailing her. Whatever they were doing. I had to ignore Danella's distress about going to the police and do what I thought was right and go to the police. Over twenty-five years as a police officer had enabled me to ignore distress when I needed to: mine or someone else's.

I turned into the courthouse parking lot. The courthouse and the adjoining jail filled a cream-colored building that took up half a block. The joke was that the prisoners had the best view in the county since the building looked down at the town and across the river at the tree-covered gorge cliffs. I didn't know if this was true or not: I'd never actually been in this jail. On the other hand, the cops had no view. Their shop was completely windowless. Unless things had changed since I was a kid. I hadn't been inside the building since I was a teen answering questions about Amanda's murder.

"That's the car!" Danella cried, pointing. Then she ducked down. "I told you they knew the police!"

She had pointed to a red Impala parked right in front of the cop shop.

The vehicle appeared empty.

Why would kidnappers go to the sheriff's department?

"Don't let them get me," Danella said.

"I won't."

I had history with Nate Gunderson, but I didn't know enough to say whether he was always the good guy or always the bad guy—could I say that about anyone?—but I didn't think he would knowingly collaborate with kidnappers.

What exactly was going on here?

What the hell had I gotten myself into letting this girl get in my car?

Crap.

I glanced around the lot while driving slowly toward the exit. The red Impala and a sheriff's patrol car were the only vehicles in the lot. I had almost forgotten it was Saturday.

I sighed. The smart thing to do was to take Danella into the police, regardless. I wasn't a cop any longer. I couldn't act like one. I could imagine my ex-husband going on about how I always thought I knew better than other people. And my ex-CO. His lectures always started and ended like this, "You are either a cop who follows procedures and the rules or you aren't, and if you aren't, quit. It would be better for all of us."

I believed in rules. I believed in the law. But sometimes I had to follow my gut. My ex-partner, Don Langley, understood that. Even when my gut—my instincts—got us into trouble.

I drove out of the lot and onto Ontario Street.

"Where do you live?" I asked.

"336 Columbia. Do you know where that is?"

"Yes," I said. "You don't need to cover up, but keep your head down.

I drove up School Street and then turned left and traveled up the hill until I got to Columbia Street. The kid lived only a few blocks from me.

I turned right onto Columbia.

"What color is the house?" I asked. "What kind of car does your mom have?"

"It's light green, the house," Danella said. "We've got a blue Honda. And a dog. Preppy. I hope my mom has been feeding him twice a day. He's got to eat more than once. He's little, but he gets hungry. Maybe that's why he gets hungry." She sounded nervous. Must be a talker when she got nervous. Common trait among criminals. Maybe among people in general.

I saw the green house—Danella's house. 336. A dark blue Chevy van was parked in the unpaved drive. I glanced around. Dark gold Nova parked in front of a yellow house where a man mowed the lawn. The Nova looked familiar. At the house kitty-corner from the green house, a teenage boy was shooting hoops in his drive. Nothing and no one stirred at the green house.

"Whose van is that?" I asked.

I heard Danella rustle behind me as she slowly raised her head and peeked out the window.

"I don't know," she said. "It's not Mom's. Where's Mom's car?"

No garage.

Now what?

I drove to the next cross street and then turned right and went down the road a bit and parked.

"What are we doing?" she asked.

"We aren't doing anything," I said. "What's your mother's name?"

I turned off the engine.

"Maggie Green," Danella said.

"Get back under the blanket," I said. "I'll be right back. Don't leave the car."

"I won't," she said from under the blanket.

I left the windows open a couple inches, and then I grabbed the religious pamphlet and my gun and got out of the car. Locked the car and opened the trunk. I tucked my gun into a hidden pouch near the wheel well. Shut the trunk. Then I straightened my clothes and ran my fingers through my hair.

I flexed my facial muscles and practiced smiling. It seemed like the religious people who knocked on my door were always smiling, and I was about to pretend I was one of them spreading the word. That was my cover in case I needed one.

I strode down the sidewalk until I got to Columbia Street. I turned the corner, looked up the block and saw the backup lights on the blue van come on in Danella's drive. I walked faster. Didn't want to run. Didn't want to spook whoever was in the van.

They were backing out. Could see a figure in the passenger side, but the face was turned away. Short cropped black or dark brown hair. A barber cut. Most likely a man. The figure turned and looked in my direction. It was a man, white, about forty years old. Didn't look at me. Turned away again. The van pulled out onto the street and drove away from me.

I hurried up the street to the house, walked down the drive, then knocked on the front door. The front curtains were open, and I didn't see any activity inside. I started to put my hand on the knob when suddenly the door opened.

"Katie, what are you doing here?"

Debbie North stood on the other side of the door. She was an old acquaintance of mine who cleaned houses for a living. That must be why she was wearing long green gloves. She glanced at the pamphlet in my hand.

I smiled and quickly put it in my pocket. "Someone left it on my car," I said. "Hey, a friend of mine lives here, I think. Is she here?"

Debbie opened the door wider, and I could see the living room. The nondescript furniture reminded me of something I'd see in a hotel room.

"Her name is Maggie Green," I said.

"I'm not sure," Debbie said. "Darby's pays the bills and the tenants usually don't stay long. I've got a memory like a sieve. I only met her once. But whoever she is, she's not here any more."

Debbie turned away from the door, and I came inside and closed the door behind me—using my foot—and then quietly turned the dead bolt to lock it—using my shirt sleeve. If anyone had been watching, they'd probably suspect I was about to commit a crime. Fortunately, Debbie wasn't looking.

She took her gloves off as she walked into the kitchen. I glanced around. I didn't see any personal items anywhere. Danella said they'd only moved to Beauty Falls a few weeks ago. If they hadn't put away any of their belongings, where were the boxes?

"Darby's?" I asked.

"They own this place," she said. "Use it for their new big shot hires some of the time. I come in once a week when someone is living here, but I was on vacation when the last hire moved in. I came on my regular day last week, and she asked me to come back this week." Debbie turned on the kitchen faucet and ran her hands under water.

"So she works at Darby's?" I asked.

"I figured," Debbie said, "but we didn't talk about any of that. She had told me where the key would be if she wasn't here—they won't let me have a key even though I'm here once a week. I thought about telling her Darby's wouldn't like her hiding the key under the stone rabbit in the back where anyone could find it, but, what the hell, none of my beeswax. There's nothing to clean. Her clothes are gone. The kid's, too. I guess they left sometime between then and now."

"I just saw a van here," I said. "Who were they?"

Debbie dried her hands on a dish towel on the fridge handle.

"Just some guys," she said. "Got the wrong house. But I'll have a story to tell at the Timbers tonight." She laughed.

I looked at her.

"Haven't you heard about the men in the blue vans?" she asked.

I shook my head.

"You should come down to the Timbers," she said. "You'd see a lot of old friends."

"And a lot of old drunks," I said.

"I hear that," she said. "But they've got great food now."

"Really?" I said. "I usually walk down to A&J's and get something from the deli."

"Get a social life, woman," she said. "You ain't gonna get that at the grocery store deli."

I laughed.

"Anyway, the men in the blue vans are Beauty Falls' answer to the Men in Black helicopters. Because of the drones. It's probably all paranoid stuff. Although I tell ya, these guys did look like feds. Weren't wearing suits, but they might as well have been. Stiffer than my ex. And I gotta tell ya—"

I put up my hand and laughed. "I don't want to think about Tony and his . . . stiffness."

Debbie laughed. "You should. About the only thing good about the marriage."

"You mind if I look around?" I asked.

"Why? Something up?"

I shrugged. "Just want to poke around."

Debbie looked at me. We had known each other casually for nearly thirty years or more. Finally she said, "Knock yourself out. I've got to do the bathroom. Might as well since I'm here."

Debbie left the room. I took the dish towel from the fridge and used it to open one cupboard door after another—no sense leaving my fingerprints all over. Besides a few plates, bowls, cups, the cupboard was bare.

"Old Mother Hubbard went to the cupboard," I murmured as I leaned over and opened the bottom cupboards. A few pots and pans. Walked to the fridge, opened it. Empty except for a single lemon on the top shelf. I slid open the butter hood. Instead of butter, I found three Bigfoot Fruit Leathers—cherry, apple, and raspberry—flat as bookmarks, shaped like footprints. I took them out of the fridge and slipped them into my back pocket.

I glanced in the plastic garbage can next to the stove. It was empty. I stepped into the living room and called down the hall, "Deb, did you empty the kitchen garbage?"

"No!" she called back. "It was already empty."

Either Maggie Green hadn't left in a hurry, or she—or someone else—had carefully covered her tracks.

I looked around the living room. Didn't find a trace of anything, not even dirt under the couch cushions. Walked down the hall until I came to the open door of a small bedroom. The walls were blue. The floor was covered in the same beige carpet as the rest of the house. Child's bed with mattress. No sheets or pillow. Small dresser, painted blue. I stepped inside the room and opened the dresser. Empty. Closet. Empty.

If Danella had lived here—like she said she had—where were her things?

On my way out of the room, I pressed my fingers on the wall above the light switch. The paint was dry, but my fingers stuck to it, just slightly. I leaned in: couldn't smell anything. Either they used no-VOC paint or else it had been painted long enough ago that it had outgassed.

I walked past the bathroom where Debbie was scrubbing the sink. She glanced at me and then looked back at the sink. "Don't know why I'm doing this," she said. "Place is scrubbed clean."

I walked to the second bedroom. The shades were down so I switched on the light. This room was empty. Didn't have a bed, dresser, piece of lint. Looked like it had just been vacuumed.

Switched the light off and walked back to the bathroom.

"Were their things here when you stopped by last week?" I asked.

Debbie turned around and leaned against the sink. "Yeah,"

she said. "There were a few boxes they hadn't unpacked, but their things were around. Now it looks like no one lived here. Kind of weird. And rude. She didn't even leave a note. Darby's better pay me, that's all I'm saying."

"Did you meet her daughter?" I asked.

She frowned. "Daughter? I thought she had a son." She shrugged. "No, I didn't meet her kid. She didn't show me around since I've been cleaning this place for years. The room is blue. Don't they paint boy's rooms blue and girl's rooms pink? I mean I'm assuming that room was for her kid."

"Anything seem strange about her?" I asked.

"No. She was intense, like all of those engineering types from Darby's. I figured that must be what she is. Either that or Christopher Darby's mistress. I heard he's got an eye for da ladies. Anyway, the engineers think we're all Podunk here, so they barely look at us. Not that she was like that. Maybe she was; maybe she wasn't. I don't know. But she was in a hurry. Why you asking questions? You think something's wrong?"

I shook my head. "You know me," I said. "Old cop habits die hard. I better get going. Might be better if no one knew I was here."

She nodded. "Better for me, too," she said. "They might ask me how I dared to let you in. They're all paranoid at Darby's. They did a background check on me so I could clean some of their rentals. I told them I was bonded, but they wanted to do their own thing. If what they're doing there is so peaceful, why are they so suspicious?"

"Corporate espionage," I said. "Can make or break a business."

"That's right," she said. "You worked white collar for a while. Did you like it? Better than working with whores and drug addicts, eh?"

I laughed. "When I was working white collar, I was still dealing with whores and drug addicts. They just dressed better."

Debbie shook her head. "Of course. What a stupid thing to say. Like I don't know the suits are more crooked than anyone else."

"Yeah, there are good guys and gals everywhere," I said. "I better get going. See you around town."

She nodded and turned back to the sink.

I returned to the kitchen and put the towel back on the handle of the fridge. I hesitated. The towel now had my DNA on it. DNA was better than a fingerprint in court these days. So what? I hadn't done anything wrong. It wasn't like I had kidnapped anyone. Every innocent person said shit like that.

"Idiot." I grabbed the towel again, used it to open the front door, then balled it up in my hand and hurried down the drive and onto the street.

Three

The guy across the road was still mowing. He didn't look over at me. The kid was still playing basketball. He glanced at me, but looked away quickly, finding nothing in his glance to interest him. Good.

When I got to the car again, I unlocked the trunk, threw the towel in, then closed the trunk and unlocked the car. I slid into the driver's seat. Danella quickly sat up.

"Well?" she asked.

"Your mother isn't there," I said. I started the car.

Danella slunk down in the seat without having to be told.

"Where would she be?" Danella asked.

I turned the car around and headed toward my place.

"I don't think she's living there any more," I said. "Your things are gone."

"My things?" she asked. "What do you mean?"

"You must have had clothes and books, or toys, or something. The house is empty."

I saw the panic in her face when I glanced in the rearview mirror.

"They must have taken her because I escaped," she said. "I should go back so they don't hurt her."

"We should go to the police," I said.

"No!" she said. "They swore they would kill us."

"They can't hurt you," I said. "You're with me. I know where your mother works, so we can tell the police and they'll find her."

"They can't hurt me," she said, "but they can hurt my mother! Please, please don't take me to the police."

I rubbed my face. I knew what I should do, but I didn't want to go to the police either. Nate Gunderson had probably never dealt with a kidnapping. I hadn't been primary on any kidnapping either. But I'd been a detective for twenty years. I could protect this kid and figure out what to do.

If I told my ex what I was doing, he'd psychoanalyze me. Suggest it was because our son Scott went to live with him when he was twelve. Scott's choice. I never got over it. Blah, blah, blah. But that wasn't true. I had gotten over it. I was just a sucker for a kid in trouble. I figured I'd want someone to protect Scott if I wasn't around. I wished someone had protected Amanda that night the six of us went out. She'd been a kid. We were all children, really. Andy was the oldest at eighteen, Sylvie the youngest at fifteen. No one had protected us—protected us from each other as it turned out.

I did not want to be thinking about all that old shit.

Didn't like it.

When I'd rescued Danella on the trail, I thought she'd be with me for about ten minutes—long enough for me to drop her off at the sheriff's office.

Now what?

I drove up behind my house and parked the car under the Doug fir, next to my son Scott's old green van. None of my neighbors could see us from here.

"You can get up now," I told Danella.

I turned around so I could see her. She pushed off the blanket and sat up.

"The housecleaner was at your house," I said. "She said she thought Maggie's child was a son."

Danella looked at me. Did she flinch? Did something change?

"No," she said. "I'm obviously a *daughter.* I never met anyone who cleaned the house. *We* cleaned the house. My mom probably called me Danny, so that lady thought she meant I was a boy." She sounded annoyed.

"What color is your room?"

"My room?" she asked. She looked out the window, frowning, as if trying to remember something. "Blue. It's blue. We painted it just before." She looked back at me. "You think I'm lying about all of this?"

"No, no," I said. "I'm trying to figure it all out. Let's go in the house."

We got out of the car, ducked under the overhang, and stood in front of the back door until I unlocked it. Then we walked through the small mud room/laundry room, opened another door, and stepped into the large kitchen. One of the reasons I bought this house was because of this kitchen. The cupboards were tall and white. The floor was hardwood—ridiculous in a kitchen, but I loved it.

Danny was looking around. The kitchen was clean and empty of boxes. The rest of the house was cluttered with boxes I still hadn't unpacked.

"Sit," I said, pointing to the long wooden table. I pulled the Bigfoot Fruit Leathers from my back pocket and dropped them onto the table as she sat in one of the chairs. "You need some water or anything?"

Danella shook her head.

"I'm going to make some calls," I said. "You need the bathroom, it's right down the hall." I pointed. She nodded. She took one of the fruit leathers and began taking off the wrapper.

"I got those at your house," I said. "In the fridge."

"Mom always puts them in the fridge," she said, "even though I don't like them cold." She looked over at me. "See. That proves I live there."

I didn't say anything. I went into the living room, walking along a path between the boxes that I had made when I first moved in. I stepped over to the windows and closed the blinds. Then I sat in the chair by the land line and flipped through the telephone book until I found the number for Darby's.

Crap. It was Saturday. Nobody would be there.

I tried anyway. The phone rang and rang. I was about to hang up when someone answered.

"Darby's, Christopher here." Christopher. Christopher Darby?

In a Southern accent, I said, "Um, could I speak to Maggie Green, please?"

"No one named Maggie here," he said. "No one with the last name Green either."

"I could have sworn this was the number she gave," I said, my accent getting thicker. "You sure you know everybody there? You sound like the man in charge. The man in charge usually doesn't know everybody."

He laughed. "As a matter of fact, I am the one in charge, and I do know everyone. I don't know anyone named Maggie or Margaret who works here. We're a fairly small shop."

"Huh," I said. "This isn't Deirdre's Hair Salon, then?"

"It is not," he said.

"I do apologize. That'll teach you for answering the phone yourself on a Saturday."

"It will indeed," he said. "Have a good one."

Didn't know any big muckety-mucks worked on Saturdays.

I put the phone down. Danny was standing in the archway between the kitchen and the living room.

"She's not there?" she asked.

"Not as far as I can tell," I said.

Danny looked around the cluttered room. "How long you been here? A few days?"

"A few months," I said.

"If my mom left the house, that means she's in trouble, doesn't it?"

"I don't know," I said. "I met you less than thirty minutes ago. I don't know who you are or what is going on."

Suddenly she looked older than her eleven years. "I should have waited," she said. "I shouldn't have run away. I should just go back."

She pulled on a strand of hair and nervously twirled it around her finger. She looked like she was going to throw up.

"Go make yourself a sandwich," I said. "I'm going to talk to the sheriff. I won't tell him anything about you, but I'll find out if he knows Mitchell and Herman."

She nodded again and started to slowly turn around.

"Do you want me to make the sandwich for you?" I asked.

She shook her head. Then she looked back at me.

"Can I call my mom?"

Oh crap. Why hadn't I thought of that?

"Sure," I said. I picked up the receiver—my land line was unlisted. "Give me the number."

She recited it for me, and I pressed in the numbers. "Don't say anything no matter what happens," I said. I pressed the speaker phone button. It rang once. I glanced at Danella. She was biting her little finger. It rang again. Then again.

"Where is she?" Danella asked quietly.

On the fourth ring, the message kicked in, "This is Maggie Green. I can't come to the phone right now. Leave a message." After the beep, I said, "Ms. Green, this is Katherine Smith. I needed to speak to you about a refund check I'm sending out to you. I need to speak with you as soon as possible to make certain I have the right mailing address. Please call me." I recited my phone number, and then I hung up.

"What does that do?" Danella asked.

"Most people will call back if you're offering money," I said. "So if she's OK, she might call back. Even if they're holding her, maybe they'll let her call back. It's about money, after all. It's a shot in the dark. We can call again later. I didn't want you to speak because, for all we know, your kidnappers think you got lost in the forest. Why did they take you on the trail anyway? That seems like a strange thing for kidnappers to do. Where were they keeping you?"

"I don't know where it was," she said. "Some room in some house somewhere. When they took me out of the house they made me wear these sunglasses—they looked like sunglasses— only I couldn't see out of them. I tried looking out, but the Mitchell guy kept telling me to look straight ahead. Inside, there was a living room and a kitchen that I was allowed to go into. There was a TV. No books. That was torture. I slept on the couch. I didn't see where they slept. One of them was always watching me. No phones, except theirs, and no pictures or knick-knacks or anything."

I smiled. "Observing like a cop."

"I was trying to figure out how to get out of there."

"Tell me everything you can remember until you saw me," I said.

"They never opened the windows and it got stuffy in there." She came into the room, moved a box out of the way and sat on the couch. Something about the way she moved reminded me of a deer—almost on her tiptoes. She wasn't afraid, but she was wary. She'd experienced trauma, that was for certain. After Andy killed Amanda, I had walked on tiptoes for days. Months? Took a long time to find my ground.

I was thinking about Amanda again. Thinking about that night thirty some years ago when the six of us went out on a group date and only five of us returned. That sounded so dramatic when I thought about it that way. It wasn't like I'd seen her killed. We paired off. Andy and Amanda set out in one direction, Sylvie and Doug in another, and Nate and I stood by the truck arguing until I stomped away. Literally. I remember stomping. I remember the feel of the hard ground as I kicked the earth, angry with Nate. I walked away, into the near night, off some logging road in the Gifford Pinchot forest. The air had tasted like cedar.

My ex—Peter Smith—told me many times that I had spent my whole adult life trying to save a series of young girls who were stand-ins for Amanda.

I told him that was psychological horseshit. For one thing, I rarely thought about Amanda. For another thing, I tried to save boy children, too.

"Every boy child except your own," Peter said once.

"Because Scott doesn't need saving," I said.

"Sometimes a child needs his mother."

"Fuck off," I told him. It seemed like he was always trying to guilt me about Scott. I never understood why. Scott had chosen to go live with Peter. Not because I was a bad mother or because we didn't get along. Sometimes a boy needed his fucking father.

Or that's what I always told myself.

I rubbed my face.

Didn't want to go to any of these places from the past.

"OK. Then what?" I said. "The house was hot and you ended up at the trailhead?"

"Herman said he had to get out or he'd go crazy," she said. She bent the empty Bigfoot Fruit Leather packaging back and forth as she talked and then wrapped it around her index finger. "Mitchell said he'd heard about this trail. Mystic Trail, I think he called it. He'd always wanted to go on it. He asked me if I wanted to go, and I said sure. Anything to get out of there. I had to promise not to scream or do anything because it would only take seconds to call and have someone hurt my mom. He reminded me that he knew the police anyway, so no one would believe me. Once we crossed the Bridge of the Gods, he let me take off the glasses. We hardly saw anyone on the trail, and we didn't go far, but I kept a lookout for something that would save me. You passed right by us. I knew you were the one who could help. I told them I had to run to the bathroom."

I passed them? I didn't remember seeing her before she said, "Help me."

"By the creek, you know, down from the parking lot," she said.

Oh yeah. I'd been pissed about some barking dog off its leash. I was fantasizing about picking up its owner and throwing him in the water.

Not paying attention in the woods was stupid on so many levels.

"You told them you had to go to the bathroom and they let you go?" I said.

"They didn't have a leash on me," she said. "I pretended I

had to go. They got uncomfortable any time I had to do any girl stuff. That's what they called it. As if boys don't have to pee."

They seemed awfully casual with her for a couple of kidnappers. I'd never heard of a kidnapper taking their kidnapee to the park. Didn't seem very smart. But in my experience, most criminals were none too bright.

"I'm going to talk to the sheriff," I said. "See if I can get some answers. I won't mention your name. Are you old enough to be left home by yourself?"

"I was kidnapped by myself," she said. "I can stay by myself."

I rolled my eyes. Tough kid. Not city tough. Not homeless street kid tough. But she could take care of herself. Up to a point. I had been like that when I was her age, too.

"Make yourself that sandwich," I reminded her as I got out of the chair. Danella stood, too. "Sit at the kitchen table and eat it."

"If I can find it," she said, looking around at the living room filled with boxes.

"Hey, the kitchen is perfectly clear," I said. I saw a sliver of a smile on Danella's lips. She was teasing me. Good. She had some good coping skills. Bad shit happened to everyone. How they coped with the bad shit determined how well they'd survive in the short and long run.

"I'll walk, since it's a couple blocks away," I said. "Keep the door locked and the window blinds closed. Don't answer the door or the phone. Stay inside. Don't touch anything."

She nodded. "OK."

"No one knows you're here," I said, "or even suspects you're here. You'll be OK."

"I know," she said. "You'll find my mom, won't you?"

"Probably not in the next fifteen minutes," I said, "but we'll figure something out."

"You really know the sheriff?" she asked.

"Sure, we dated a bit when we were teens," I said, "and hated each other for a bit after that. We both became cops."

"You said earlier you *used* to be a cop."

"I was," I said. "I retired about eight months ago. Moved to Beauty Falls several months later."

"Retired?" she said. She frowned. "I thought old people retired. I mean people older than you."

I laughed. "Cops usually retire earlier than most people."

Especially when they were asked to retire after they were caught having sex with their confidential informant.

By "they" I mean me.

"So you can find out stuff that most people can't," she said, "because you know people who are still police. You'll be able to find my mom."

"I don't know what I can do," I said. "But I'll do something. Try to be patient."

"Would you be?" she asked. "If someone had taken your mom?"

"No," I said, "but you don't even know if they have her."

"I know she's in trouble," Danella said, "and someone's gotta help her. I hope they don't hurt her because I ran away."

She suddenly looked so vulnerable. She had that wiry skinniness kids of a certain age possess. Like giant Gumbys. Made her look like she could fold and bend and survive almost anything. Until right this second. She was a kid. And she needed her mother.

Maybe I could help with that.

Four

Danella followed me out to the mud porch, staying close, practically stepping on my heels while I locked the back door. Then we walked into the living room again, and I showed her how to lock the front door. Not that she couldn't have figured it out herself.

"Don't answer the door for anyone except me," I said.

"You already said that," she said. She twisted a strand of her hair around her finger, and then she pulled on it to tighten it.

"Don't even say you're here if someone knocks," I said.

"But then they might think no one is home, and they'll break the door down," she said.

I looked at her.

"That's what they say on TV," she said.

"Nobody is going to break down the door," I said.

"I didn't think anyone would kidnap me either," she said.

"Good point. Would you feel better coming with me? I could drive, and you could hide under the blanket again."

"No," she said. "It's too warm for that. Can I watch TV?"

"I don't have TV," I said.

She looked over at the TV on a table in the far corner of the living room.

"OK, I do have a TV, but I don't have any service," I said. "Watch a movie if you like. You'll find some in that box there." I pointed. "Should all be PG. Except the ones that aren't. Don't watch those."

She looked at me.

"No one will knock on the door," I said. "I've never had any-one but Jehovah's Witnesses knock on the door. Once. They asked me if I wanted to be happy, and I told them no. That was pretty much the end of the conversation." I chuckled. Danella still watched me. Wasn't the time for humor, apparently. Or any-thing else. I needed to go to Nate and figure out a way to help this kid and then get back to my life.

I opened the front door, then the screen door. Before I stepped outside, I said, "Don't forget to eat."

Once a mother, always a mother.

She pulled the screen door closed, and I heard her lock it. The front door shut. I hurried down the steps, forcing myself not to look back in case someone was watching.

Not that anyone was.

I jogged across the street and then down the sidewalk past the elementary school. I turned left on Vancouver Street and kept going. When I reached Rusty Street, I looked down the road to the Columbia River at the bottom of the hill. The water was artichoke-green and looked like glass from here. Several white sailboats rode the currents I couldn't see like giant butterflies skimming for a meal. A small flock of seagulls flew above the pier at the end of Rusty Street. Across the wide river, on the Oregon side, rock faces rose up, their visages covered in dark green conifers like giant revolutionaries covered in forest camouflage.

I kept walking down Vancouver, crossed the street, and hurried toward the sheriff's office.

The red Impala was gone.

I hesitated a millisecond before opening the door to the cop shop. Always felt a bit strange seeing Nate Gunderson. We were both members of a gruesome kind of club, I supposed. Had barely seen him in the thirty years since. Maybe once every few years, usually in a drive-by. Then that one time in a Portland bar when my marriage was breaking up.

Nope. Wasn't like me to keep thinking of the past.

I opened the door to the cop shop and went into the waiting room. Or whatever it was called. I stepped up to the window where a dispatcher sat. She opened the sliding glass door.

"Nate Gunderson in?" I asked. I could see the squad room was nearly empty except for a deputy across the room with his back to me. I couldn't see the door to the sheriff's office from here.

She didn't ask who I was. She picked up the phone, pressed a button, and waited. She looked up at me and smiled. Young white girl. Not surprisingly. The county was 93.5 percent white. (I remembered numbers, stats, shit like that. Was a nervous habit when I was a kid, but it turned out to be useful on the job, so I cultivated it.) The woman's shiny silver name tag let me know she was Deputy Sandra Dean. Didn't recognize the last name. She was twenty-five years old, if a day. Dark brown eyes. Black hair pulled back and up. She looked good in khaki color. But then a twenty-five-year-old looked good in anything.

And she was eager to please.

Poor kid. That wasn't going to get her anywhere.

She said something into the phone that I couldn't hear.

Then she set the phone back into its cradle.

"He'll be right with you," she said. She looked at me like she wanted to say something. A talker. Needed to remember that about her in case I wanted to pick her brains at a later date.

A few moments later, a heavy metal door opened, and a man about my age stood on the threshold, dressed in his olive green uniform. Brown hair. No gray. How'd he do that? Hazel eyes. Slight paunch.

"You pick that uniform color?" I said. "It's not very flattering."

"Yeah, well, I can change my uniform," he said, "but apparently you can't change your personality. Still the same after all these years."

"Aw, you remember." I grinned or approximated grinning. I needed to at least pretend we were friends.

We weren't friends. Wasn't sure what we were.

"I wondered when you were going to stop by," he said. "Come on in."

He opened the door a little wider, and I walked past him. I was tempted to pat his belly, but I reminded myself that we weren't that kind of acquaintances. We shared a sordid past—or we shared a tragedy. I glanced at Sandra Dean, and she smiled at me. I winked. Then Nate stepped in front of me, and I followed him to his small office. He closed the door once we were inside. His office was nondescript, reminding me of Maggie Green's living room. The only things on his fake wood laminate desktop were a phone, a computer, one of those calendars you flip over day by day, and a framed photo. I couldn't see who was in the photo.

Nate pointed to the office chair in front of his desk. I sat in it, and then Nate sat in his chair and leaned back in it.

"Wow," I said. "I've never seen a desk so clean."

"Tidy desk, tidy mind," he said.

"What?"

He shook his head. "I don't know. What's up?"

I suddenly realized he was uncomfortable.

Was he thinking of the night of the murder thirty years ago or the awkward get together we had during the last months of my marriage? We had worked together, peripherally over the years when some criminal crossed state lines and came into Washington from Oregon.

"I thought I'd stop in," I said, "now that I'm living here. Say hello. I'm thinking of getting my private investigator's license." Hadn't thought about doing that until that moment, actually. "Wanted to know if you thought I could get work around here."

"You wanted *my* opinion on something?" he asked. "That seems unlikely."

I didn't say anything. We looked at each other.

"You ever hear from Sylvie?" he asked.

I shook my head. "You hear from Doug?"

"Naw," he said. "I heard Sylvie got married not long ago. Some religious guy. They live in Battle Ground, maybe. She has a couple of kids, I think."

"She had a couple of kids *recently?*" I asked. "Little old to be birthing babies, isn't she?"

He chuckled. "Look at you all judgmental."

"I'm just saying. Can't imagine popping one out now myself. Not unless it was full grown and could bring me a beer."

Nate laughed. I cringed. Didn't know why I was talking this way.

"You still married?" I asked. "What was her name? Jennifer. Your high school sweetheart, right?"

Now he cringed. Or flinched.

"No, you were my high school sweetheart," he said.

I laughed. He smiled. "Since we never went to high school together, I don't see how that is possible. But anyway."

"Yes, anyway, I am five years divorced," he said. "They should give a chip for that."

"You in AA?" I asked.

"No, but Jenny thought I should be," he said.

I looked at him. He shrugged. "She drank a little," he said. "Quit when she got pregnant and then thought everyone who drank was an alcoholic."

"Maybe we are," I said.

"I visited Andy in prison not too long ago."

"You're kidding? Why?"

He shrugged. "I've always had questions. Why'd he do it? Did he plan it? All those things."

"You never listened to his confession to the cops?" I asked. "He confessed to Deputy Sheriff Chris Reilly, if I'm remembering correctly."

"Yeah," he said. "I didn't find it very satisfying. You?"

"I read the transcript," I said. "Pretty much what the paper said."

"He said it all like he was talking about going into the woods to pick berries," Nate said. "He was walking along and all of sudden he decided to rape Amanda and then when she said she was going to tell, he killed her." Nate shook his head. "We were friends, you know. Buddies. I thought I knew him."

"Some people say all men are potential rapists," I said.

"Do you believe that?" he asked.

"No," I said. "It's complete horseshit. That's like saying men don't have any control—gives them permission to act like psychopaths. Men know right from wrong just like women, and we can all control our behavior. I don't know what crazy worm got into Andy's brain that night. My guess is he was and is a sociopath, and we just didn't know it."

"You've never been out of control?" he asked. "You've never done anything stupid?"

"I have done many stupid things," I said. "Rape and murder goes beyond stupid."

He nodded.

"Could have been you, you know."

"What?"

"Remember he had a crush on you."

"Like I could fucking forget that, Gunderson," I said.

Crap. I had forgotten why I'd come in here. I had a scared kid waiting for me at home. I had to find out about the men in the red Impala.

"I've been thinking about it a lot lately," he said. "Not sure why. Thirty years this summer. Her parents want to have a ceremony down in the park."

"You keep in touch with her parents?" I asked.

He nodded. "They stayed in town. When I came back, I got in touch with them."

"Why?" I asked. It was like we were summer friends again, and I could ask him anything. That summer when I was seventeen, we had gotten close. For a few weeks, the six of us had done everything together. Went hiking, swimming. Hung out at each other's houses. We never paired up. Not until that night. That night we decided to look for Bigfoot. Legend had it that Sasquatch was some kind of big ape living in our Gifford Pinchot National Forest and environs—and more specifically, the lava beds in our forest. A real live animal. Or a spirit who showed itself when things were out of balance. Loggers and other forest workers occasionally spotted something they thought might be Bigfoot. I didn't think any of us kids believed in a real Bigfoot, but we got a thrill and chill thinking about the possibilities.

We used it as an excuse to wander the woods with other kids, particularly at twilight when Bigfoot was supposed to come out and hunt. We didn't go as far as the lava beds that night. It would be crazy to try to navigate the lava beds at night.

That night—the night Andy killed Amanda—Sylvie, Doug, Andy, and Amanda piled into Doug's truck, and Nate and I got into his. By the time we all arrived at the prearranged spot in the woods, by the time Doug and Nate stopped and parked their trucks and we got out, we had paired up. It wasn't planned, as far as I knew. It just happened.

"Why did I get in touch with Amanda's parents?" Nate repeated my question to him. "Why wouldn't I? We were the last people to see their daughter alive."

"That's not accurate," I said. "Andy was the last person to see their daughter alive—just before he killed her. You and I had already gotten into an argument and were on our way home."

"I can never remember what the hell we argued about," Nate said. "Can you? Sometimes I wonder if we had stuck around maybe none of it would have happened. Don't you?"

"No," I said. "We didn't have anything to do with what happened. Sylvie and Doug waited for them. That didn't stop it from happening. They didn't even know it was happening."

Doug and Sylvie waited until Andy came stumbling out of the woods, crying, scratched up from running through blackberry bushes, he said, screaming that Amanda had wandered away from him and he couldn't find her. Doug called the cops to get help finding her. I didn't know anything about it until early the next morning when Sylvie called to say Amanda was lost in the woods. Could I come and help?

My stomach tightened when I first heard she was lost. I knew right away that something was wrong, something bad had happened, especially when I heard Andy had changed his story and was telling the police that Bigfoot had chased them, and that was how Amanda had gotten lost.

When my dad took me out to the search site, I saw Nate standing around talking with some of his friends, and they were all laughing about Bigfoot. As I stepped out of my dad's truck, I heard one of them say, "Probably just a deer. Andy is such a pussy."

Nate laughed along with the rest of them, but then he turned and saw me. The smile left his face. He knew something was wrong, too. Only he was better at pretending than I was.

It was cold that morning, and steam rose from a slash pile as the sun warmed it. The whole place smelled like earth. That wonderful fecund smell of humus, of the forest ground. Before that day—before that moment—the smell of earth always reminded me of home—of Beauty Falls. After that, for many years, the smell of earth made me sick to my stomach.

A few hours later, Andy confessed to raping and killing Amanda, and he led the police to the place in the woods where he had buried her by covering her with rocks, leaves, and branches.

I had thrown up when I heard the news. Didn't stop for days. Months?

Now I said to Nate, "I don't want to talk about this. Old stuff. Nothing we can do about it now."

"He was fat," Nate said.

"Pardon me?"

"Andy," he said. "He was fat. Obese, actually. They've got him all doped up, I think. He asked about you, Doug, and Sylvie. Talked about the good times. That's what he called them. 'The good times.'"

"That's disgusting," I said.

He nodded. "Not a word about Amanda."

OK. I was done with this conversation.

"So I said to him, 'Why did you do it? What happened to you?'"

I looked away from Nate and closed my eyes briefly. I had a little girl at my house right now who was missing her mother. I had to help her, *help her.*

Amanda was dead and gone.

"Andy looked at me and said, 'What do you mean what happened to me? Nothing happened. I'm the same person I ever was.' I said, 'You killed her, man. Why'd you do it?'"

Nate stopped talking. I glanced at him. Didn't seem to hardly know I was there.

I couldn't help myself: I asked, "So what did he say?"

"He just looked at me. For a moment I thought he was going to tell me. But he said, 'You know, dude, I can hardly remember any more. Gotta put the past behind.' He called me dude. Like we were still kids."

"Gunderson, I could have gone my whole life without hearing that motherfucker's name again," I said. "If I ever see you again, can we skip the trip down memory lane?" I could feel myself getting angry. "I swear if I had him in my sights now I would kill him dead."

Nate cleared his throat. "Man," he said. He looked a little stunned. "I haven't even had my first drink of the day. Heard you were fired from the Portland PD."

"I wasn't fired," I said. "I retired."

"That makes me feel old," he said. "Re-tired. Heard something about you being forced out."

Fuck this.

"So what kind of calls do you get on a day like today?" I asked, trying to change the subject.

He laughed. "I can take a hint. OK. Saturdays are often our busiest times," he said. "Someone always getting lost in the woods. Today we had these two guys come in looking for their thirteen-year-old niece, Danella. Probably half an hour ago."

"*Their* niece? They were brothers?"

Nate made a couple of clicks on his keyboard. "A Mitchell Peterson and his friend Herman Johnson. She was Peterson's niece."

"Sound like made up names," I said.

Nate glanced at me and then looked back at the screen. Oops. I had to pretend I didn't know anything.

"They were on the Mystic Trail," he said. "Had taken their niece for a walk. Said she's mentally ill or developmentally challenged."

"Why were they reporting her missing here?" I asked. "The Mystic Trail is across the river in another state."

"I thought that was strange, too," Nate said, "but they didn't know where the police station was there, and they had been staying here and they knew where the sheriff's office was."

"So they left her there, lost in the woods, while they came over here?"

"They thought they saw her get into a car," he said. "They said she does that. Gets into people's cars and then tells them outlandish stories. They wanted to see if she'd shown up here."

"Any of that strike you as odd?" I asked.

"It all struck me as odd," he said. "They didn't look like the type to walk on a trail or take care of a disabled child. I told them I'd give a description to my deputies, and I gave him the number of the Cascade Locks police and the Oregon State police. He didn't seem overly concerned."

"What's she look like?" I asked.

"They said she was slight, blond shoulder length hair, blue eyes. I ran her name. Nothing came up on her. I ran his name. Didn't come up with anything there either except he apparently lives in Tennessee. On vacation, he said."

"Did you run his plates?" I asked.

"No," he said. "I didn't see what he was driving. Besides, he hadn't done anything wrong."

The phone rang. Nate picked it up.

"Yep?" He listened. "Thanks." He hung up the phone.

"Speaking of the devil," he said. "That was Mitchell Peterson. False alarm. He said they found his niece. She had wandered off the trail. All is well. Glad I didn't spend any time on it."

Oh crap.

Danella must have panicked and somehow contacted the kidnappers.

"Nate, I gotta go," I said as I stood. "I remembered something."

Nate stood, too. "Uh. OK. Stop in any time."

I hurried out of the small office and into the squad room. The girl—the Sandra Dean woman—smiled at me.

"Good-bye," she said.

I was already out the door and sprinting toward home.

Five

I don't know why I ran. If Danella had gone back to them, wasn't a thing I could do. And if she was actually their niece and she had made up the whole story, good riddance to her.

Only I didn't think she had made it up. I didn't know what was going on. Maybe Danella was only telling me part of the story, but I knew she had been scared when we first met, and she was still afraid for her mother.

Where was her mother?

Right then I didn't care.

My heart was in my throat. Ridiculous to feel this way about someone I had known less than an hour.

I took my steps two at a time. Then shoved the key in the lock, turned the knob, and pushed the door open and called into the dark living room, "Danella!"

"What?"

Danella stepped into the room from the kitchen, looking like a spot of light in her shorts, shirt, and blond hair.

I shut the door.

Thank god.

"Danella," I said. "Have you told me everything? About the kidnapping, about your mom?"

I put my hand on her back and steered her into the kitchen.

"Sit down and eat," I said. I walked to the sink, grabbed a glass from the rack, and ran water into it. I glanced at the table. Danella already had a glass.

"I told you everything," she said, her mouth full of sandwich.

"I talked to the sheriff," I said. "Herman and Mitchell had been there. They said you were Mitchell's niece and he was taking care of you." I didn't need to tell her the rest of the things they had said about her. "Is Mitchell your uncle?"

"No! Yuck!" she said.

"This isn't some elaborate hoax, is it?"

"What do you mean? What's a hoax?"

"You know what a hoax is," I said.

"You don't believe me any more?" she asked.

I pulled out a chair next to her and sat in it.

"It feels like there's something you're not telling me," I said. "This guy, this Mitchell Peterson, used his real name. He's from Tennessee. He told the police he was related to you. He knows the police can check out these things."

"Did they check it out?" Danella asked.

She was wide-eyed, scared, and defiant all at the same time. Suddenly she reminded me of my son at that age. Same kind of attitude: help me but do it my way. He had been a little older than Danella when he decided he wanted to go live with his father.

"I don't think the sheriff found out if you were related to him or not," I said. "But Mitchell Peterson doesn't have a record."

"I'm not related to him," she said. "He's mean."

"He was mean to you?"

"He kidnapped me."

I almost laughed. She had me there: Kidnapping was pretty mean.

"They said you were thirteen years old," I said.

"See," she said. "That proves they don't know me. I'll be twelve in June."

"What's your birthdate?"

"June 15," she said. She hesitated a bit. "2004."

She *was* only eleven years old! I was grilling her like she was some kind of criminal.

"Can you find my mom or not?" Danella asked.

I looked at the girl as she sat next to me at my kitchen table, her fingers absently pressing into the bread on the little piece of sandwich she hadn't finished. I knew then and there I should go to Nate Gunderson and tell him what was what. If Nate was conspiring with the kidnappers, he wouldn't have told me about them. Not that I had ever actually believed he was in on a kidnapping. But I had never completely trusted Nate.

Actually, I never completely trusted anyone. Which explained a great deal about my private life. Made me a pretty good cop.

Maybe.

I'd tell any civilian in this situation to go to the police. I was now a civilian. I should go to the police.

"What about relatives?" I asked. "Maybe we should call them and see if your mom is there."

"I don't have any relatives," she said.

"What do you mean you don't have any relatives?" I asked. "You had to come from somewhere."

She shrugged. "Mom and I have always been on our own."

"What about your father?"

"I don't have one."

"So the stork brought you?" I asked.

"Artificial insemination." She said the words slowly but correctly.

Hmmm. When someone didn't have any relatives, it most often meant one of two things: They were either on the run or they were in witness protection—which was a form of being on the run. I supposed it could mean one of three things: She could actually be without family. But that was fairly unusual.

"Does this mean you can't find my mom?" Danella asked.

The phone rang. I walked into the living room and looked at the number before I answered it. My son, Scott, calling from Seattle. He rarely phoned. I hoped nothing was wrong.

"Hello," I said after I put the phone to my ear. I held up my index finger to Danella, who was watching me from her perch at the kitchen table. I mouthed to her, "One minute."

"Hi, Mom," Scott said. As usual, he sounded vaguely annoyed with me.

"How are you, Scott?" I said. "Everything OK?"

"Sure," he said. "I'm coming to Portland on Monday. Thought you could come over to Dad's for an early dinner, late lunch. His classes end mid-afternoon Monday. Meet around 3:00?"

Never any small talk with Scott. Of course, everything he said had an underneath to it. The gist of it being: "You were and are a lousy mom, Mom."

I wanted to say, "Has hell frozen over now because I can't remember the last time the three of us broke bread together? Actually I can't remember the last time we did anything together. Or the last time you asked me to do anything with you."

But I didn't say any of that. I was the adult. Why was I feeling bitter? Petulant almost. Maybe because I wasn't in the mood for contemplating my failures as a parent because my twenty-three-year-old son sounded like he disapproved of me. I needed to save this girl. Or her mother. Or at least figure out what the hell was going on.

My interaction with Danella should be wrapped up by Monday.

"Sure. Do you need me to bring anything?"

"Dad said he'll make everything. So just bring yourself."

"You spending the night?" I asked.

"Yup," he answered. I could tell he wanted to get off the phone. "I don't have any classes for a few days."

"You're almost done, aren't you?" I asked.

"Yes, but we can talk about all that later," he said.

"Why? Are you quitting?"

"Why would you ask that?" he said. "I've never quit anything in my life."

"Sorry," I said. I felt like I was always apologizing to him. "I'm surprised that you want to talk to us in person. You're not sick or anything?"

"God, Mom. No. It's nothing bad. Just wait. Have a little patience. Don't interrogate me like I'm one of your perps."

I almost laughed. "Wow. If you think that's an interrogation, you'd be in for a rude surprise if you were ever arrested."

"At least I'd have your attention then," he said.

I did laugh at this. Shouldn't have. I knew immediately that he was embarrassed for blurting out something a child wouldn't even say.

"I don't have any perps any more," I said. "Remember? I'm retired. You have my full attention right now."

"No, I don't," he said. "I can tell you want to get off the phone."

I wanted to argue with him. I wanted to tell him he was the most important person in the world to me and nothing would or could stand in the way of me being there for him. How many times had I said that to him when he was growing up? He hadn't believed me then, and he wouldn't believe me now. Maybe he was right. I did want to get off the phone now. I had done something foolish: I had taken a child into my car and now into my home. *A child.* A child whose parents or guardians were probably sick with worry. Or, if Danella was telling the truth about everything that meant her parent was being held and made to do something against her will.

What could they be forcing her to do?

What was the truth about what was going on?

"I'm sorry, Scotty," I said. "You're right. I am in the middle of something. I should have said. But I will be there for dinner. With bells on."

I often felt like I was groveling when I talked to my son. Did other parents feel that way? I thought kids were always seeking the approval of their parents, not the other way around.

"Scott," he said.

"What?"

"I'm not Scotty," he said. "I haven't been since I was twelve."

Oh good grief.

"All right, Scott," I said, emphasizing the word Scott. I could hear the edge in my voice. "Is there anything else you need?"

"No," he said. "I'll talk to you later."

Then he was gone. Didn't even say good-bye. I looked at the phone.

"Brat," I said. I dropped the phone into its cradle. A little too hard. It slipped out, and I had to settle it in again.

"Who's a brat?" Danella asked.

"My son. Or me. Depending upon who you ask. Do you have a photo of your mom?"

She shook her head.

"Any ID for yourself?"

"No," she said. "I left my driver's license at home."

I looked at her. "Your pilot's license, too?"

"Of course," she said. "I might have my police badge." She patted the pockets of her shorts. "Nope. Left that, too."

I smiled.

"All right," I said. "I get the point. But just so you know, I've seen plenty of kids your age with school IDs and phones with lots of photos of all kinds of things and people, including their parents."

"Mom says I'm too young for a phone," she said. "She doesn't like having her picture taken."

Another indication that Danella and her mother were on the run or in witness protection.

I heard a car going by outside. Engine was running a little loud. I noticed the blinds had been opened slightly. I glanced at Danella.

"It was too dark in here," Danella said. "I felt like I was with the kidnappers again."

I looked out the front window.

A red Impala moved slowly by my house.

"Shit," I said. I motioned to Danella. "Get in the kitchen."

"What's wrong?" she asked.

"The car," I said. I heard her suck in her breath. I glanced over. She was standing still, looking terrified.

"They don't know you're here," I said. She still wasn't relaxing.

"Might not even be them," I said. I glanced outside. The car had continued down the street. I looked back at Danella. I was usually good with kids. Not my own, but with other people's kids. When I was a cop. I knew what to do. What to say. Don't ask too many questions. Remember that they notice everything. They remember everything: even if they remember it wrong. And they need reassurance. Except when they don't.

"Then why would they be driving by here?" she asked.

Perfectly good question.

"It's a small town," I said. "There aren't a lot of places to go, so they're probably driving up and down all the streets."

Would kidnappers drive around a town looking for a girl? Why would they think she was in Beauty Falls, especially since, according to Nate, they had called to say they'd found her? Maybe one of them was the mother's boyfriend? Torturing her by taking her daughter?

I usually had some idea, some hint, some intuition, some sense of what the hell was going on in most situations. I was dealing with adults, mostly, at least at first. But now I was running around getting nothing accomplished. I couldn't continue investigating while the girl was with me—because the men might see us, and I couldn't leave her here while I investigated. If I was still a cop, it would be different. I could go to work and do some digging.

Maybe I should contact my old partner, Don Langley. He could see if anything was up with Mitchell Peterson. Nate said he hadn't found anything, but he'd probably spent about two minutes on it.

I glanced at Danella. She was watching me.

"Danny," I said. "You don't have to worry. I won't let anyone hurt you."

I don't know why I said it. How could she know that I would protect her—that I could protect her? I knew I wouldn't let any harm come to her. One way or another.

"Let's get out of here," I said. I could take her to a place where no one would think of looking for her. Then maybe I could figure things out.

"Where?" she asked.

"Out of town."

She looked afraid again. "But my mom is here," she said.

Maybe not, I thought.

"You want me to find her," I said. "I can't do anything while I'm worrying about you. I need you in a place where you're protected and where those guys can't find you."

"Can I go home first?" she asked.

"I was there," I said. "Your mom is not there."

"Maybe my mom left me a note. We have a secret hiding place."

"Now you tell me," I said. "I'll go look."

She shook her head. "It's too hard to explain."

"Try me," I said. "I'm pretty good at figuring stuff out."

"It's in my closet, in the far left corner, under the carpet," she said. "Mom made it when we first moved in."

"Because?"

"So we could leave each other secret messages," she said. "In case of emergencies."

"What kind of emergencies?" I asked. If they'd been doing this for a while, maybe they'd been in danger for a while. That could mean a psycho boyfriend or husband.

"Emergencies like when I've been kidnapped," she said.

"You're a little bit of a smart ass, aren't you?" I asked.

"I'm not supposed to curse," she said.

"Curse? How is that a curse?" I said.

"You know," she said.

I frowned. Oh. Ass. A curse word. "That's just a description of a body part," I said. "Would you rather I said 'smart buttocks?'"

Danella giggled.

"Did you eat enough?"

She nodded. "Do I have to hide in the back of the car again?"

"Just until we're on the road."

Six

I opened the back door to my house, stepped out, then looked around. Didn't see anyone. Unlocked the car door with my remote. I motioned to Danella, then put my arm around her to shield her face, and hurried to the car. Opened the back door, and Danella slipped in. She was under the blanket almost instantly. I closed the door, then walked around and got in the driver's seat. Locked the doors all around and started the car.

I drove slowly out of the driveway and then down the street. I went around the block and didn't see the red Impala. Didn't see any cars, actually.

"You OK?" I asked.

"Peachy," I heard.

I smiled.

Drove to Columbia Street. Went by Danella's house. No cars there now. No one across the street playing basketball or mowing the lawn either. I parked up the road away from the house.

"I'll be right back," I said. "Stay down, be quiet, and don't let anyone see you."

She didn't say anything.

"Danny?"

"You said to be quiet."

I rolled my eyes and turned off the car.

"You got me there," I said. "I'll be back soon."

"Can you get me some clothes?" Danella asked. "And some books to read. My library books are on my desk."

Guess she had forgotten what I'd told her: The house was empty. No sense reminding her.

"It's not a shopping trip," I said.

I got out of the car, locked it, then hurried down the street toward Danella's house. I glanced around. No one out on this beautiful day. Of course, it was nearly five. People were getting ready for dinner.

I cut across the empty lot next to the house and followed a path around the back of the blackberry bushes which blocked me from anyone's view. Then I ducked behind a stand-alone wooden garage that leaned slightly to the left. Looked like the next east wind would blow it right down.

Glanced around for the stone rabbit Debbie North had mentioned. Saw it to my right, a few feet from the garage, in the backyard. Looked like the lawn had been mowed not too long ago. Couldn't smell it, but the grass wasn't very high. Five days ago it rained. Grass would be calf high by now if it hadn't been mowed. Didn't mean anything though. Maybe Darby's paid someone to mow it whether someone lived here or not.

I walked to the stone rabbit, glanced around again, then squatted and tipped the rabbit over until I spotted the key. Picked it up, put the rabbit back, and walked to the back door. No one could see me from here. The house blocked the neighbors' view, the garage blocked me from anyone on the north side, and a tangle of vine maple and bushes was a veritable privacy screen should anyone east or south be looking my way.

I put the key in the lock and turned it, pushed the door open.

I stepped lightly into the house—the mud room—and closed the door behind me. Opened the door to the kitchen and walked inside. Listened. The house thrummed with quiet. I moved quickly and quietly through the house until I reached Danella's bedroom—or what I assumed was Danella's bedroom. It was dark in the room, but I didn't want to switch on the light.

I went into the closet, got on my knees, and felt around on the floor until I found the edge of the carpet. I lifted it and put it under my knee. I moved my fingers across the hardwood floor until I touched a circle of metal. I pulled on it, and a small door opened.

"Where is everything?"

I practically jumped out of my skin at the sound of Danella's voice.

I turned around. Danella was standing in the doorway, a shadow of a shadow. Couldn't remember the last time someone had snuck up on me undetected.

"I told you to stay in the car," I said.

"No, you said don't let anyone see me," she said. "No one saw me. Where is all of our stuff?" I heard the fear as her words caught in her throat.

"Danny, I told you everything was gone."

She came into the room. "I—I didn't understand. All of our stuff. Where is it? Did my mom leave me?"

"Would your mother leave you?"

She swallowed, or I thought she did, and then she knelt on the carpet next to me. "No, my mom would never leave me."

"Did you lock the door when you came in?" I asked.

"Yes, but you didn't. Not very smart."

I almost laughed. "No. That wasn't smart. I also told you to stay down and be quiet. Did you forget that part?"

"I can't hear everything you say when I'm under the blanket."

She leaned over and reached into the dark hole in the floorboards. She found something, grasped it, and pulled it out. She glanced at it and then reached into the hole again. Then she sat back on her buttocks. I closed the little door and let the carpet fall back.

"What is it?" I asked.

"It's a photo of my mom and me." She scooted over closer to the door where there was more light. I sat next to her and looked at the picture. Danella looked to be about seven, with long blond hair. She was grinning and leaning against her mother whose curly black hair was in contrast to her own. But their wide smiles were alike.

"Is this significant?" I asked. "Finding this?"

"There should be two," she said. "One for me and one for her. If we were ever in trouble, if we had time, we'd take one of the photos each. That way we'd always have a picture of us together, no matter what. If she took one, that's her way of telling me she's in trouble."

"But if she had time to get the photo, wouldn't that mean she's safe?" I asked.

Didn't seem like they had worked out the details of this little treasure hunt very well.

Danella shrugged again. "That's what she always said. If I was in trouble, and I couldn't contact her, I should take one of the photos."

"Have you had to do it before?" I asked.

She shook her head.

"Why would your mom think you might get into trouble?" I asked.

Danella shrugged. "I don't know. Her work, I guess. She said it was secret."

"Danny, I called Darby's here in town," I said. "They're the people who own this house. The man in charge has never heard of your mother. Does she go by another name?"

"Another name?" Even in semidarkness I could see her confusion. "I don't think so. Where are our things? Where is my mom?"

"I don't know," I said. "I'm going to try one more thing. If that doesn't work, I think we have no choice but to go to the police."

Just then, I heard a sound—a creak of wood? Both of us froze. I put my finger to my lips.

We listened.

Someone was trying to turn a doorknob. Sounded like the front door.

I reached for my gun. Which was still in the trunk of my car.

"I'll be right back," I whispered.

She nodded. I thought she might tell me not to leave her, but I knew already she wasn't the clingy type. She may not have grown up hard, but she had grown up smart.

I walked into the hallway. The shades were shut all around the house, so presumably no one could see inside. That also meant I couldn't see outside. I couldn't hear the doorknob being rattled any longer. That could mean whoever was sniffing around was headed to the kitchen door. I glanced into the kitchen from my position at the end of the hallway. I could see the uncurtained kitchen door window. Didn't see or hear anyone at the window.

I hurried across the living room, got out of sight from the kitchen window, and looked through the pinholes in the blinds. A blue van was parked outside.

Who were they? Not the kidnappers. Debbie said people in town thought the men in blue vans worked for the feds. Men in Black types. I couldn't see anyone in the van, but it was a bit of a blur from this vantage point.

I kept my body as close to the wall as I could as I scooted around the living room to the entrance to the kitchen. I had to decide if I should risk going into the kitchen where someone outside might be able to see me if they were looking in. I glanced in. Couldn't see anything, so I ducked down, and walked, bent over, until I got to the wall. I flattened myself near the door. I heard voices. But they weren't at the door. They weren't whispering either, which meant they didn't think anyone was in the house or they felt they had a right to be on the property no matter who was here.

I carefully eased myself close to the window and moved until I could just see out. I was hoping no one was looking in at that moment.

I saw a man—with his back to me—looking at the garage, the stone rabbit at his feet. He was the one talking. Must be on the phone. Maybe I hadn't heard voices, plural. Maybe just his voice. He kicked the rabbit, then walked away from the house. I watched him until he turned the corner. Didn't see anyone else.

I ran into the living room. Looked through the pinholes. Saw the man get into the passenger side of the van. Then the vehicle drove off.

I ran into Danella's room.

"They're gone," I said. "Come on."

She jumped up and followed me out into the hall. "Was it the kidnappers?"

"No," I said. "I don't know who they are. Have you ever seen any men in a blue van?"

"No," she said. "I don't think so."

I had her wait in the hallway while I went into the kitchen. I looked out the window. Didn't see anyone. I motioned her in. Then I opened the door and motioned her out. I closed and locked the door. Then I put the key under the rabbit. Danella and I hurried to the blackberry bushes. Before I let Danella leave the safety of blackberry cover, I walked to the road and looked up and down it. No van, no red Impala. No cars of any kind. I motioned to Danella. She ran up to me, and we continued to walk together until we got to the car.

"Sit up here with me," I said. "You can duck down if I see anyone."

She got in the passenger's side, I got in the driver's side. We both put on our seat belts. Then I looked at her and said, "You asked for my help. If I'm going to continue to help you, you've got to do what I say. It's for your own safety—and mine. I could have talked my way out of being in that house on my own. But with you there, I had to worry about keeping us both safe. No semantic games again. You knew I wanted you to stay put in this car even though I didn't say that specifically. All right?"

She nodded. "Please don't take me to the police."

"I should," I said. "For your own good. For my own good." I started the car. "This is probably one of the stupidest things I've ever done in my life. And I've got a long list of stupid."

"Or one of the smartest things you've ever done," Danella said.

She was trying to work me. I appreciated that. I was somewhat of a con myself. I could usually finagle myself out of trouble. Could usually get things to flow my way. Not always. Had not been able to con my way out of getting retired.

"Time will tell," I said.

I took us out of town. Didn't see a blue van or the Impala. We drove by the courthouse and the cop shop again. Didn't see Nate. Had this urge to tell him what was happening, so he could tell me I wasn't out of my mind.

I took us back over the Bridge of the Gods. If we needed to leave in a hurry, I-84 was a better choice than SR 14, the two-lane state highway on the Washington side. We drove into Oregon, got onto the expressway, and headed toward Portland.

After we got past the Mystic Trail exit, Danella curled up in her seat and fell asleep. I thought about pulling over and putting her in the backseat, but she looked so deeply asleep that I decided not to disturb her.

An hour later, we got to Portland. Got off at the 43rd Avenue exit. Thought about stopping at the Sandy Whole Foods for something to eat, but I was delaying the inevitable. I drove down Cesar Chavez Boulevard for a bit, then turned left. Stopped when I reached a two-story wooden and stone house. I turned off the car and got out. Danella stayed asleep. I stretched and looked around. Nearly every yard was overflowing with flowers and veggies. One veggie-filled lawn had a sign in the middle of it that read, "Keep Portland Weird." I smiled. Like there was any chance that would change.

I glanced at Danella, pushed the remote lock on my keys, then walked up the stone steps and onto the huge stone porch. I went to the door and pushed the bell. I couldn't hear it ring, but I soon heard footsteps. I glanced back down at Danella. Still sleeping. The door opened, and Peter Smith, my ex-husband, stood on the threshold.

He sighed and shook his head. "So what kind of trouble are you in now?" he asked.

I smiled and shrugged. "All kinds."

Seven

Peter stepped outside and looked down at my car. He cocked an eyebrow as he looked at me.

"A long lost daughter?" he asked.

"Funny," I said. "Here's the short and sweet of it. This girl came up to me as I was leaving the Mystic Trail. Said she'd been kidnapped by men who were trying to get her mother to do some kind of work for them. Now I'm trying to help her find her mother who has since disappeared."

"So you've got a child in your car who isn't yours," he said evenly, "without the permission of her parents. She claims she has been kidnapped. If that's true, if they find the girl and you, I imagine they'd call *you* the kidnapper. Have you actually lost your mind this time?"

"What do you mean 'this time'?" I asked. "It's not like I've ever brought you a kidnapped child before. Wait. That didn't come out right. I did not kidnap her."

"And you're here why?" he asked.

"Because I think it was a terrible idea that we ever divorced," I said. "We are so deeply compatible."

"Smart ass," he said. "Bring her in. I was about to start dinner." He turned around and walked back into the house.

I went down the steps again and then gently knocked on the passenger door window. Danella jumped a bit, blinked several times, and looked around. Finally she opened the car door.

"Where are we?" she asked.

"My old homestead."

We walked up the steps together.

"You used to live here?" she asked.

"When I was married," I said, "for a few years. My ex lives here now."

"You're friends with your ex-husband?" she asked. I glanced at her. This concept seemed foreign to her.

"More like frenemies," I said.

"What?"

"Nothing," I said, putting my arm across her shoulder as we stepped onto the porch. "Yes, we're friends. Of a sort."

I opened the door. Danella hung back, so I went in first. The living room was on my right, and I could smell the kitchen on my left, even though I couldn't see it yet. It smelled like freshly baked something with cinnamon. Peter was standing between the kitchen and living room, watching us.

"Peter, this is Danella," I said. "Danella, Peter."

Danella actually stuck out her hand, and the two of them shook hands.

"I just took banana bread out of the oven," Peter said. "You want some?"

"Sure," she said.

"I'm going to make some calls," I said.

They walked toward the kitchen, and I went into the living room, pulled out my cellphone, and called Don Langley, my ex-partner.

"Kelly!" Don shouted into the phone. He didn't like cellphones and still hadn't completely figured them out. "Where the hell you been? I've called you half a dozen times in the last couple of months and you didn't return a single one of them."

"Hey, Don," I said. "Are you sure you were calling me? I don't remember any messages from you."

"Hell, yes, it was you," he said. "What other sumbitch got fired for screwing a lowlife CI, leaving me with some pussy-faced pencil pusher who doesn't know his ass from another ass."

"I appreciate your discretion and compassion, partner," I said. "And what the hell is a pussy-faced pencil pusher."

"I don't know," he said. "His face is all scrunched up all the time like one of those Himalayan Persian cats. And you know how much I hate cats."

"I don't even know what a Himalayan Persian is," I said. "You own four cats, so your creds as a cat-hater are firmly out the window."

"It's only because of Estelle," he said. "If she ever leaves me, she's taking those furballs with her. Except maybe Lucky. It's inspirational watching her get around on her three legs while batting her one blue eye."

I laughed. "You're making all this shit up," I said.

"How you been, Kelly?"

"Pretty good," I said. "Although I do miss you. I thought we were going to meet for coffee a couple times a month. I've seen you once."

"You're the one who keeps canceling," he said. "Estelle asks after you all the time. Thinks of you like our daughter. Obviously, I've kept a lot from her over the years cuz she would have horsewhipped our daughter for doing some of the shit you've done over the years."

"Don," I said, "much as I am enjoying your one man show, I need your help. I know it's your day off, but I need you to run some plates for me."

"You in trouble?"

"No more than usual," I said. I didn't want to give him the details in case it turned out I *was* in trouble. "I'll send you some pics of license plates. I'm particularly interested in the red Impala. But check the other plates, too. Could you see if there's anything out there about a Danella Green?"

"Like what?" he asked.

"An Amber Alert," I said. "A runaway."

"She's a kid?"

"Yes," I said.

"Picking up strays again, Kelly?" he asked.

"I never picked up strays."

"How about the red-haired girl on Burnside puking her guts out?" he said. "I thought you were going to adopt her."

"Because I asked her how she was doing? That ain't a long term commitment."

"You got her a bed. Made sure she was sober. Bet you checked up on her for months."

"Hey," I said, "isn't that what a peace officer does? You were the one who always accused me of being a hard ass. I felt sorry for her."

"And a dozen others," he said.

I groaned. "Don, can we please not do this. I don't need you raggin' on me."

"I was reminiscing," he said. "Can't stand this new guy. Swear he's got a ramrod up his keister."

I chuckled.

"See if there's anything on a Maggie Green."

"Maggie Green?" he said. "There's probably a million Maggie or Margaret Greens."

"Just see if there are any bulletins on one," I said.

"All right," he said. "I'm at a baseball game. Will do what you want on the way home."

"You there with Estelle?" I asked.

"Yeah, Billy's playing," he said. He paused, and then he said, "He's my grandson. Born about twelves years ago."

"I know he's your fucking grandson," I said.

"Just checking," he said. "You didn't notice much outside of work."

"So I've been told," I said. A million times. Usually not by Don. Something about his words today stung.

"I'll get it done, Katie," he said, mildly, as if he realized he had touched a nerve. I had always had a tough hide—or thought I did. When I retired, that changed a bit.

"Thanks, Don," I said. "I'll talk to you later."

"OK, kiddo," he said.

I ended the call, and then I texted him the photos. I put the phone down and breathed deeply. OK. That was done. What next?

I could hear Peter and Danella talking in the kitchen. Heard Danella's soft laughter. Peter had always been good with kids. At least, he was good with our kid. Maybe that was why Scott wanted to live with him. Maybe that was why Scott and I had never gotten along well. Except when he was an infant. For his first four years we were nearly inseparable. I still worked, but I couldn't wait to get home to him. Couldn't wait to hold him in my arms. Couldn't wait to see what new thing he would do that day, that hour, that minute. Felt guilty every moment I was away from him. Not guilty like "gee, I'm a bad mom because I work." It wasn't that. I figured I brought him into this world, and it was up to me to be alive and present for every moment of his life.

Then he drifted away from me. Or I drifted away from him. For a long time I wondered if it was because he was a boy. Maybe he felt more comfortable with males. But it wasn't as if Peter or Scott were particularly macho or even sports-minded. I was probably more macho than they were.

Not probably. *Was.*

None of us were big sports fans. Except we liked baseball. Or used to. When the Seattle Mariners were the closest major league baseball team, it was difficult to remain excited about baseball.

Anyway, when Scott was twelve, he asked if he could go live with his father. Back into the house where he had spent his first four years. Maybe it was the house he had been close to. Maybe he'd never been close to me.

I looked around the living room. It hadn't changed much in the twenty years—give or take—since I had moved Scott and I out. Scott and I had lived in an apartment near Hawthorne until he begged to go back with his father. I was broken-hearted, but I didn't fight him on it. He was old enough to know what he wanted. I saw him on Wednesdays and every other weekend, except for those times when he'd arrange to be with friends or doing something else which made it too much trouble for him to see me.

Then he was a teen. He rebelled by hating me. Or so it seemed. After a while, I started working more and more so I didn't have to be in his presence. Who wants to be around someone who despises you?

"Aren't you coming?" Danella walked out of the kitchen and into the living room.

"Aren't you and Peter having a grand old time?" I asked.

"He seems OK," she said.

"For a boy."

She smiled. "For a boy. And the banana bread is good. I've never had that before. He's making salmon. I've never had salmon before either."

"You've never had salmon?" I put my arm across her shoulders as we walked toward the kitchen. "You live in the Pacific Northwest and you've never had salmon? Are you a vegetarian?"

"No," she said. "My mom doesn't cook a lot."

"Now is a good time to try something you've never had before," I said. "Besides, it's free food."

Her nose crinkled slightly as we walked into the kitchen.

"Come on," I said. "I didn't divorce him because of his cooking skills."

Peter looked over at us from where he stood at the stove. I knew he wanted to say something like, "I divorced *you*," but he didn't.

Danny and I walked to the table in the bay window looking out over the second floor patio and garden. Danella stood at the window and looked out.

"You used to live here?" she asked. "Why did you leave?"

I laughed. "Usually when people divorce, they stop living together. Didn't that happen with your parents?"

Yes, I was fishing for details.

Danella looked over at me and frowned. She whispered, "I already told you that I don't have a father."

Oh yeah: artificial insemination. I hadn't believed it then, and I didn't believe it now.

Peter came over carrying two small plates, both with two slices of banana bread on them.

"I've made tea, too," he said to me. "Come over and get them."

"You want tea?" I asked Danella. "Maybe he's got apple juice or something."

"I'm eleven," Danella said, "not four."

I looked at her. She grinned a bit sheepishly and said, "Tea, please."

I walked to the stove with Peter.

"Get the cups," he said.

"Bossy." I opened several cupboards before I found the cups.

"They are in the same place they've been for twenty years," he said.

I tried to glare at him. I said, through gritted teeth, "I haven't been here that many times in those twenty years, if you'll remember, since we weren't talking for much of that time."

OK, we had sex now and again, but we didn't spend much time talking or in the kitchen.

I found the cups and put them on the counter next to the stove so Peter could pour water into them. I didn't actually drink tea, just hot water. Didn't handle stimulants well.

"I suppose you want to stay here," he said.

"I could go to a hotel, but I thought this would be less stressful for her," I said.

"And you want an accomplice," he said.

"No!"

I frowned. I *could* have gone to a hotel, but I knew Danella would be safe here.

I felt like I would be safe here, too.

I made a noise. That couldn't be it. I certainly didn't feel unsafe when I wasn't here.

I ran my fingers through my hair.

"Do you have to analyze everything?" I asked. My tone was harsh. I hadn't meant it to be.

"I saw her on the trail," I said. "She asked for my help so I helped her. I mean—"

My stomach lurched a bit. This was unlike me.

What if Amanda had seen someone in the woods that night before Andy killed her? What if she'd asked for help and she was turned away?

I glanced at Danella. She was eating the banana bread and staring out the window. She didn't look anything like Amanda. She didn't act anything like her.

I didn't know why I kept thinking of Amanda's murder.

"Katie," Peter said gently. "She isn't Amanda."

"Don't try to shine any light on my mental processes," I said. "It's dark and scary in here, and you could get hurt."

"Don't I know it," he said, looking away from me.

He picked up two of the cups and carried them to the table. I grabbed my cup and a box of tea he'd left on the countertop. Then the three of us sat around the table eating and drinking. Peter asked Danella about school. She talked easily about the teachers she liked and disliked, the kids she hung out with, those she avoided.

As I listened to her, I remembered Scott when he was her age. His answers to any of my questions had become monosyllabic by then.

If I was honest with myself—because I certainly would never tell Scott this—I was relieved when he left. I had no idea how to handle a pre-teen boy. Probably would have ended up as a juvenile delinquent if he had stayed with me.

Danella and Peter started talking about soccer. The more they talked, the more relaxed Danella got. No wonder Scott had picked Peter: He was easy-going and easy to talk to. I was not. When I used to ask Scott about his day, it always sounded more like an interrogation than a conversation. I wanted to know about his friends, who they were, who their parents were, what the kids said, what he and his friends did while on their own. I made him introduce me to all of his friends at school. He was mortified. His friends thought I was cool because I was a cop, so I played that up. Let them know I would hurt anyone who hurt my son.

I hadn't cared then that Scott was mortified. No one had protected Amanda from Andy. No one had protected any of us from him. I wanted to protect Scott from anyone like Andy.

After Andy raped and killed Amanda, I had wondered, for a time, if all teen boys had a ticking time bomb in their brains, a ticking bomb that sometimes went off and sometimes didn't. As Scott got older, I encouraged Peter to talk to him about sex and his sexual feelings. To let him know how he should treat girls and women. Peter told me, "You should talk to him, too."

"Why?" I said. "I don't know what it's like to be a teenage boy."

"So if we had a daughter, you would have taken care of the sex ed talk?"

"Sure," I said.

"I still think we should both talk to him," he said.

"Not a good idea," I had told him. "I can see it now, 'hey, son o' mine, don't rape any girl ever, period. Don't kill any girl ever.' What good would that do?"

Now as twilight began to settle around us, Peter asked Danella, "So where do you think your mom is?"

Danella shrugged. "I don't know."

"What kind of work did your mom do?" he asked.

She shrugged again.

"She never told you?" I asked. "You never asked?"

"She said she couldn't talk about it," Danella said. "It was secret."

Peter and I glanced at one another.

"She worked on the computer a lot," Danella said. "She said she built things."

"Like a carpenter builds a house?" I asked. "Or like an engineer builds a machine?"

"A machine," Danella said.

"A computer engineer?"

Danella nodded.

"Danny," I said. "Why didn't you tell me that in the beginning? You've known this all along?"

Peter picked up our plates and took them to the sink. "Now that I've spoiled your dinner," he said, "it's time to start dinner. Are you staying?"

"Unless you had other plans," I said.

"Would it matter?" Peter asked.

Danella was watching us. Maybe she was wondering if we would suddenly start yelling at one another. That wasn't our way. Some sniping went on, but we tried to keep that to a minimum. Maybe if we had argued, we would still be married. Maybe fighting would have saved us.

I shook my head at the thought. Doubt it. You have to either hate someone or love them to fight. Don't you? I never hated Peter. Not sure I ever loved him, at least not passionately. I loved him the way I loved my son, the way I loved my family. From afar.

I didn't answer Peter. I looked at Danny. "Why couldn't you tell me your mom was a computer engineer?" I asked. "You came to me for help. I'm trying to help you. If it turns out your mother is out there looking for you, I could be in a shit-load of trouble. They might think I was the kidnapper."

"But I'd tell them you weren't," she said. "You didn't have anything to do with the kidnappers." She looked genuinely distressed.

Peter was doing the dishes noisier than necessary—to my way of thinking—but I didn't look over at him. I already knew he heartily disapproved of me scaring this kid.

"You can't get arrested," Danny said. "You've got to find Mom. You've got to figure this out." She looked at Peter. "She can do it, can't she? I picked the right one, didn't I?"

I glanced at Peter. He stopped what he was doing and looked at us.

"If I got into trouble, Mom said to look for a woman with bear in her eyes," Danella said. "That's why I picked Kate. I was right, wasn't I?" She was pleading with Peter. Seemed she was more stressed than she had let on.

Peter glanced at me. Then he looked at Danella, "You picked right, Danella. If anyone can help you, Kate can."

Eight

"**Can we go** outside?" Danny asked.

I'd forgotten she had been cooped up inside for days.

"OK," I said. "Peter, we'll take a walk around the block. Be back in a bit."

I was sure it was safe. It wasn't like the kidnappers had somehow tracked us to Portland.

Danella followed me out of the house and down the steps to the sidewalk. We could hear the distant traffic on the freeway. The sun was setting, and the huge old trees shut out most of the remaining light. I had always loved the big old oaks in this neighborhood. When I walked amongst them, I felt as though I were in a cathedral, only better, since I wasn't fond of churches.

"I would have never left a place like this," Danny said. "I would have stayed married just so I could live here."

I laughed. "A house and neighborhood ain't everything."

"Did you fight?"

I shrugged. "Not really. We weren't compatible. He hated my job, even though I had the job when we married." I could hear a twinge of bitterness in my voice. "I don't think Peter actually liked me. I don't like being around people who tolerate me. Like me or leave me. That's my motto."

Danella nodded. "I know. My friend Jane down in California liked me. She would laugh at all my jokes, even when they weren't funny. Mom is like that, too. She likes me."

"Did your mom ask you to keep her work secret?" I asked.

Danella nodded. "She said we shouldn't tell people what she did. And we couldn't be in contact with any of our relatives. I don't know any of my relatives, though. Mom and I have always lived on our own."

We walked by large houses with huge front porches. Their yards weren't big, but every inch of earth was filled with tall blooming flowers. As we passed by the houses, I occasionally heard the murmur of voices or the sound of distant music. It all felt so cozy.

And mildly cloying.

"You and your mom have been on your own a long time," I said.

She nodded, barely.

"You've had to rely on each other," I said. "I understand. I pretty much rely on myself. But sometimes we need outside help. This is one of those times. Tomorrow, I'm taking you to the police. I'll take you to people I trust."

"But the police are in on it," Danella said. "We saw their car there."

"I don't think so," I said. "I know the sheriff. It's unlikely he'd be involved in something like that."

We turned the corner. Up ahead was a Mom and Pop store, one of the few remaining in the area. I remembered it from when I lived there. Bill & Millie's, they called it. It was so old it still had a pay phone out front. Danella started walking faster when we saw the neon "open" sign.

"Look," she said when we reached the door, her voice bright and sunny, as though she had completely forgotten about her missing mother. "They've got Bigfoot Fruit Leathers!"

I smiled as she pulled open the door and walked into the small crowded store. A kid stood at the cash register, doing something with his phone. He looked up briefly and then down again.

Danny hurried over to the Bigfoot Fruit Leather stand. She glanced at me. "Will you get me some? I'll pay you back."

"Sure," I said. I pulled a twenty from my back jean pocket.

Danny looked at the twenty and then began picking out fruit leathers: cherry, apple, strawberry, raspberry, and peach. Every flavor except apricot.

"No apricot?" I asked.

She shuddered. "Bleck."

I laughed. Danny slapped the leathers down on the counter. The clerk jumped slightly and looked up from his phone. He seemed dazed for a moment. Then he said, "Bigfoot, man. Yeah. My uncle saw Bigfoot once in the Giff. Heady stuff."

He ran the leathers under the scanner.

"It's not one Bigfoot," I said.

The kid clerk looked at me. "What?"

"You said your uncle saw Bigfoot. There isn't one creature called Bigfoot. If your uncle saw anything, he saw *a* Bigfoot."

The young man nodded as I talked, obviously baffled by what I was saying.

Danny was watching me. I handed the boy the twenty. Danny took the leathers and stuffed them into her back pockets.

Then the man smiled. "I hear ya, sister. You are exactly right. And you, little sister." He handed me the change and then looked at Danny. "I hope you enjoy those flavored pieces of Bigfoot." He winked at her.

For an instant, Danny looked mildly alarmed. Then she said, "I once wrestled a shark to shore. I can handle a little ape meat."

The clerk leaned back, grinned, and then laughed. I put my hand on the back of Danella's neck to steer her out of the store. When the door closed behind us, Danny and I looked at each other and laughed.

"Guess he didn't know who he was messing with," I said.

Danny ripped the plastic covering off a strawberry fruit leather. She gave me the plastic and began eating.

"What am I supposed to do with this?" I asked.

She shrugged. "I always give that kind of stuff to my mother."

"Why? Is she your trash can?"

Danny frowned. "No."

I dropped the plastic into the can. I said, "They make these healthy snacks, and then they wrap them in poison? The world is a freaking strange place."

"Poison?" Danny asked. She looked at her fruit leather.

"Uh, sorry," I said. "I'm sure it's fine."

She gave me a look. Then she pulled out a fruit leather from her back pocket and handed it to me. "Prove it."

I took the leather from her, sighed, and pulled off the wrapping—which I then handed to her.

"Am I your trash can?" she asked.

"Guess so."

She dropped the wrapper into the garbage can.

"See," I said. "You do know how to do it."

Then I began eating the strawberry fruit leather. Danny watched me.

"So far so good," I said. Then I started shaking and rolling my eyes up.

"I don't believe you," Danny said.

I stopped shaking and looked at her. She began eating her fruit leather again, and we kept walking.

"Did you grow up in Beauty Falls?" she asked as we headed back to Peter's house.

"In a way," I said. "I spent my summers there."

"Did you ever see Bigfoot?" she said. "Or *a* Bigfoot?"

"Never did," I said. "Saw bears, cougars, bobcats, deer, elk, mountain men. But never an ape-like creature. I heard stories. This one man believed that a female Sasquatch was in love with him. After a while, he kind of looked wild. Smelled wild, too."

"Do you think she was really in love with him?" she asked.

"I have no idea," I said. "There have been worse love mismatches."

"Did you ever look for Bigfoot?"

"We did," I said. "When we were teens."

The night one of us ended up murdered. The murder didn't have anything to do with Bigfoot, but the thrill of the hunt or the thrill of the find kind of vanished after that.

"There are Native American stories about a wild man," I said. "They were called different things. Sasquatch is one of the names. The Indians didn't go looking for a Bigfoot. They didn't want to see one because they viewed it as a kind of spirit who showed up when things were out of balance. It was a bad sign."

Danella nodded. Then she said, "It still would be something to see, wouldn't it? Maybe when you find my mom we can all go to the Giff, the place that guy said, where his uncle saw the Bigfoot."

"He's talking about the Gifford Pinchot National Forest," I said. "It's a pretty big place, but sure, someday maybe we'll go take a hike."

"Is that where you found me?" she asked.

"No, that was on the Oregon side. We're on the Oregon side now. The Giff is on the Washington side, in the same county as Beauty Falls, where I live—where you live, too."

Danny got quiet. She didn't say anything until we were almost at Peter's house. Then she didn't seem to want to go inside, so we sat on his steps, side by side.

"Do you think you can find my mother?" Danella asked. "Or should I go back to the kidnappers?"

"You shouldn't go back to the kidnappers," I said. I didn't tell her that she had no choice in the matter. I wasn't going to let her return to them. "I don't know if I can find your mother on my own, but I'm sure with some help from my friends, we should be able to figure something out."

"Did you like being a police officer?" she asked.

"I did," I said. "I liked being a beat cop. Did that for a long time. Then later I was in vice."

"What's vice?"

"Probably better not to know. Anyway, I didn't stay there long. Hated it. People were always at their worst."

"Aren't they always at their worst when the police are involved?"

I looked down at her. "How did you get so wise?" I asked.

"It started in my ass and just spread," she said.

I laughed. "A wiseass, eh? You make that up?"

"Naw, Mom says it all the time."

I nodded. "I think I'm gonna like your mom."

"What did you like about police work?" she asked.

"I liked helping people," I said. "I liked being able to fix problems. When I was younger, I didn't pay enough attention. I missed things. As a cop you've got to pay attention. I got better at that the longer I was a cop. Paying attention is how I learned to figure things out."

"Like what?"

"People are habitual," I said. "They'll keep trying to do their routines, even when they're on the run or stressed. Being habitual is calming—or something. I was tracking this one guy, and I learned he played the lottery with particular numbers every week. Eventually I found him by talking to store clerks in the area who sold Lotto tickets, and they remembered him and his numbers. Did your kidnappers have any habits like that?"

Danella didn't say anything for a bit. Then she said, "The Mitchell guy. He has curly black hair. He liked that car. The red car. Was always talking about it. The other guy, Herman, he seemed stupid. He wanted to watch cartoons all day. He has thin red hair, and he smelled like cigarettes. In the morning, they had to have coffee. It's like they were drug addicts or something."

"Yeah, a lot of people are like that," I said. "Don't get it myself."

"My mom drinks coffee, but she isn't weird about it."

I laughed. "Anything else your mom does every day?"

"She jogs every morning," Danella said. "She likes to work. She likes to draw. She can look at things and know what their insides are like. Buildings, bridges, things like that. She likes bridges."

"She came to the right part of the world then," I said. "Is she on any kind of medication?"

Danella shook her head. "No. Not my mom. But he was, the other guy. Herman. I don't know what it was, but he took pills in the morning and at night."

"Did he act differently after he took them?"

"You mean like he was high?" she said. "No. They came from a bottle. Like from the doctor."

"People can get high from those kinds of drugs, too," I said. "But that's good, actually. If he wasn't getting high and they weren't drinking, they might be relatively stable."

"No, there was no drinking," she said. "Mitchell wouldn't let Herman drink, and he had to smoke outside."

"Do you remember the brand of cigarettes?"

She squinted and looked ahead. Finally she said, "I don't know. I didn't actually ever see a pack. He'd go outside."

"Good," I said. "Good details. They might be helpful. You'll hear cops say to each other that good police work is often pure dumb luck. But that dumb luck is preceded by years of paying attention. The more I pay attention, the luckier I get."

I heard the front door to Peter's house open. I looked up.

"Dinner," he said.

Danella sprang to her feet, ran up the stairs, and into the house. I laughed, got up, and followed her—although I walked a little slower.

At dinner—salmon with quinoa and a salad—Danella became a little chatterbox. It was as if someone had flipped a switch, and she went from being someone who shared very little information to someone who shared everything. She talked about her classes. She talked about her school down in California. About her friends. Pamela was too bossy. Ellen was funny. Bobby knew a lot about horses. Juanita talked about planes all the time.

"Sounds like you have lots of friends," Peter said. "I didn't have a lot of friends in school when I was a kid. But I had a few good ones."

"I know how to make friends," Danella said. "You listen to them, and do what they want. My mom says we've got to learn to go with the flow—or flow with the go. Instead of sticking out like a sore thumb, lend a hand. She says that, too."

I glanced at Peter. He shrugged almost invisibly.

"Danny, did your mother ever talk about being in something called witness protection?" I asked.

She shook her head. "I know what that is. I've seen it on TV. But we didn't talk a lot about anything in the past. Mom says thinking about the past is like taking a bath in dirty water. Although she doesn't take baths. She showers." Danella stopped. Looked down. Breathed deeply. Batted her eyes. As if it all suddenly hit her again. She looked up. "I'm tired."

I nodded. Kids don't usually own up to being tired. My kid wouldn't even admit he was tired as he was nodding off.

"You can sleep in our son's old room," Peter said. "There are extra toothbrushes in his bathroom. Katie, you can sleep with her or on the couch."

I looked at him. I started to say, "Not with you, darling dearest?" But then I remembered the kid was a kid. Most kids did not get irony or sarcasm, the illegitimate cousin to irony.

"Do you want help with the dishes?" Danella asked Peter.

Peter smiled and shook his head. "You've had a day, Danny girl. You go to bed."

I took Danella to Scott's old bedroom. I switched on the overhead light, and we stepped inside. I hadn't been in this room in years—decades?—and my stomach fluttered a bit. The bunk beds were still there. How had our tall son fit in one of these beds when he was a teen? The desk was bare, along with the walls—except for one poster of photographs of mushrooms. I walked to the small dresser and opened the drawers. They were empty, too.

"Do you want me to wash your clothes while you're sleeping?" I asked.

"No," Danella said. "If the house burned down, I'd have to run outside in my underwear."

I laughed. "I don't think the house is going to burn down."

"I'm just saying."

Danella looked around the room.

"It doesn't have much personality," I said. "I hear ya."

She looked at me. "I didn't say anything."

"Your silence spoke volumes," I said.

"You're weird sometimes," she said.

"All the times," I said. "My son is a mycologist—they study fungi. Like mushrooms. He's working on his doctorate."

"He'll be a mushroom doctor?" she asked, walking to the beds. "Does he have a tiny stethoscope when he has to listen to a mushroom's heart?"

I glanced at her. She gave me a deadpan look. I laughed.

"You want me to stay here with you or on the couch?" I asked.

She shrugged.

"You gotta tell me, Danny. I can't read minds. Would you prefer me in the room with you?"

"You mean because I'm scared or something? No. I'm not scared."

"OK," I said. "Then I'll probably sleep on the couch. Let the TV lull me to sleep."

Danella nodded as she sat on the bed.

"I'll see you in the morning," I said. "We'll figure everything out then."

She looked up at me. "Thanks for trying to help me."

"It ain't over," I said. "We will figure it out." I walked to the door. "See you in the morning."

As I walked away, I heard the door close behind me. I glanced back. I felt like I was missing something, but I didn't know what.

Nine

Peter and I barely said a word to one another as we cleaned up the kitchen. Then we went into the living room. When I sat next to him on the couch, he moved away slightly.

"Ouch," I said. "Didn't know you found me so repulsive."

"What are you doing here?" Peter asked. "How could you put me in such a position? You show up here out of the blue. I haven't seen you in months."

"I couldn't think of where else to go," I said.

"Anywhere else," he said.

He sounded pissed.

"You didn't seem to mind last time I showed up," I said.

"Oh, yes, how flattering it is when you come over here to get fucked," he said.

"I prefer to think of it as getting laid," I said.

"At the time you failed to tell me you were sleeping with one of your scumbags," he said.

I moved to the other end of the couch and sat cross-legged, facing him.

"He wasn't a scumbag," I said. "He's not a scumbag. He was an informant. He was doing his duty as a good citizen."

That sounded lame even to me.

Peter made a noise.

"It's not like I asked you who you were sleeping with," I said. "It's only us when we're together. No one else matters."

Peter shook his head. "Unless he gave you some disease. Then we'd all be in it together."

"I'm always safe, Peter," I said. "You know that."

"I don't know that!" he said. "You came to my home with a child that may or may not have been kidnapped. The police could show up any minute. That doesn't sound safe."

"The police aren't going to show up," I said. "Besides, I've talked to the police. I talked to Nate Gunderson in Beauty Falls, and I called Don. We're figuring it out."

"I'm not doing this," Peter said. "We have to know each other because of Scott, but this bullshit has got to stop."

I held up my hand. "I promise I won't bring another kidnapped child to the house."

"It's not funny. You know what the fuck I'm talking about."

I put my hand down. I didn't know what the fuck he was talking about. I frowned. "I don't understand this hostility," I said. "Besides me bringing the kid here, what have I done wrong?"

"You're cold," he said. "You always have been. I don't know if you care about anything or anyone else except yourself."

I chewed on my upper lip. Now he was pissing me off.

"Just because I don't wear every emotion on my sleeve—or whatever that expression is—doesn't mean I don't care. I care about you. I care about Scott."

"You never call him."

"How the fuck do you know?" I said, keeping my voice low. I felt my face turning red. I wanted to leave. I did not want to have this conversation.

"For one thing, when I do call," I said, "I get some version of the speech about what a bad fucking mother I was and am. He's old enough to understand things. You wanted the divorce. He wanted to live with you. What wrong did I do? I gave you both what you wanted."

"You let us go," Peter said.

The refrigerator thrummed. Everything else was silent. Even us.

I finally said, "Peter, you didn't like my work. You didn't seem to like *me*. Why would I want to try and keep you in a relationship that was clearly distressing to you?"

"You could have quit."

I rolled my eyes. "So you want to have *this* conversation again? I was good at my job. I wasn't good at much else."

"You gave it up for the scumbag," he said.

"What are you talking about?" I said. "I didn't give up anything for him. I was forced to retire. It was political. They were trying to get rid of me, trying to thin the herd of the oldies but moldies. I wasn't the first to be caught with my pants down."

"Why didn't you fight it?"

I shrugged. "My union rep didn't think I had much chance, since I confessed."

"Should have kept your mouth shut," he said.

"Yeah, but I've never been good at that. Didn't make any difference, me having sex with him. I still got the bad guys."

"The prosecution was still able to use his testimony?"

"The bad guys confessed. We were both off the hook. So I didn't give up anything for him. At least, not on purpose."

"But you must have had feelings for him to be so reckless?"

I looked at Peter. What was he getting at?

"Of course I have feelings," I said. "Is that what you're asking? Or are you asking if I was obsessed with this man? No. I wasn't obsessed. I'm not obsessed. He is just a man. I've done lots of stupid things, and I'll do many more stupid things. This time I got caught, I guess. You're killing the mood, Peter."

We looked at each other. He started laughing.

"Killing the mood?" he said, shaking his head. "Gawd, Katie. You are a piece of work."

"What's this all about?" I asked. "You got a new *chicka?* She doesn't want you sleeping with your ex? I can understand that." He had been in various relationships over the years. Some of them lasted longer than others. Some I met because they were involved in Scott's life. Some I didn't.

"No, that's not what it's about," he said. "It's weird."

"Danny said I was weird, too," I said. "I think I'm perfectly normal."

"Don't you ever want to settle down?" he asked. "Be with one person? We're not getting any younger."

"Did you really say we're not getting any younger?" I made a noise. "Yes, I did want to settle down. With *you.* I married *you.* I had a kid with *you,* Peter Smith. But it didn't work out so I moved on."

"Did you?" he asked. "Did *we?* We're still sleeping with each other."

"That's a testament to what a good relationship we've forged."

Peter rolled his eyes. "I can't believe you said *that.* We've had sex together even when we hated one another."

"I never hated you," I said.

"Sure you did," he said. "And I hated you."

"You're wrong," I said. "I don't hate many people. There are exceptions. I hate the guy who killed Amanda. Some of the criminals I've met over the years. Some of the cops I met in white collar. But generally speaking, I don't hate."

"Those are a lot of exceptions to your 'I don't hate anyone proclamation.'"

"I hate this conversation," I said. "Are we going to go fuck or what?"

I got up and held my hand out to Peter.

He shook his head and grabbed my hand. I pulled him up.

"Or what," he said.

We got naked together. It felt familiar and pleasant. The thing about Peter was this: He knew my body, and unlike other men his age (and younger) he got hard and stayed hard. A woman appreciates that. It ain't the size (most of the time) but a guy has got to have some rock to his geology—and Peter did.

We fell asleep with our arms wrapped around one another. That didn't last. Soon enough, I woke up, wriggled my way out of Peter's embrace, and got out of bed. I looked down at the sleeping Peter, who I could barely see in the dark. What did I feel for him? Did I love him? Wasn't sure what that felt like. I loved Scott, but that was not the same. I felt affection for Peter. Would probably take a bullet for him. But beyond that? I didn't know. I didn't know how I felt about so many things lately. It was ridiculous standing here in the dark trying to figure it out.

I took a quick shower, then got dressed again. I went out to the couch, curled up on it, and turned on the TV—and the timer. Found some old show and fell asleep watching it.

When I awakened again, it was barely dawn. I sat up slowly and rubbed my face. I felt slightly icky. Like maybe I had talked

Peter into doing something he hadn't wanted to do. Maybe he was right: Our relationship was weird.

I didn't hear anyone else stirring. I didn't drink coffee, but Peter did. I got up and went into the kitchen. I'd make a pot for him. When it was a decent hour, I'd call Don and see if he'd found out anything about Danella and her mom.

I switched on the kitchen light and made my way to the stove. I noticed a piece of paper on the island countertop. I picked it up. It was a note from Danella.

"Dear Kate: I'm going to call them from the pay phone to pick me up. I memorized Mitchell's number. I lied. He is my uncle, and I was staying with him while my mom was working. And I am thirteen years old. Don't try to find me. Danella."

I dropped the note, hurried to the door, put on my shoes, and then ran out into the early morning light.

The nearest pay phone Danella knew about was at Bill & Millie's. I ran down the street toward the store. The lights were still on. Or on again.

I was out of breath by the time I reached the store. I hurried inside. That same kid was at the counter. He grinned at me. "Back for more Bigfoot stories?"

I shook my head while I tried to catch my breath.

"The girl I was with, have you seen her?"

"I just opened up about ten minutes ago," he said. "But I did see her last night."

"With me?"

"No later, around eleven," he said. "She used the pay phone. Seemed kind of late to be out. I went to see if she was OK. Tell her she should be careful. But I didn't see her anywhere. About an hour later, I saw her again. She was getting into a car. Figured she'd called you or someone to get her. Must have been hiding that whole time while she waited. Felt sorry for her. You guys have a fight?"

"What? No." This wasn't soap opera 101. "What kind of car was it?"

"Red," he said. "Some old guy's car. I don't know cars much. Ask me about bikes. I can tell you about bikes."

I sighed. "Was he on a bike?"

"No."

"Then I don't give a shit about any bikes," I said.

He frowned. "Pretty hostile so early in the morning."

At this point, I'd usually flash my badge. That always won the argument. Almost always. Couldn't do that now.

"Sorry," I said. "Did you see anyone in the car?"

He shook his head. "Is she OK? I mean, I saw her open the car and get in so I figured it was OK."

"Everything's fine," I said. "Don't worry about it."

I left the store and headed back to Peter's house. I slowly walked up the steps. Now what was I going to do?

Crap, crap, crap.

I walked into the house. Peter was standing in the kitchen in his bathrobe holding the note.

"I looked in Scott's room," he said. "Can't even tell she was there. Do you think it's true?" He held up the note.

"I don't know. No, I don't think it's true. If it was true, why didn't she call from here? She was protecting us from them. She trusted me, Peter, and I let her down. She got scared because I said I had to take her to the police."

"You should have taken her yesterday," he said. "What now?"

I shrugged. "I guess it's out of my hands."

He started to come toward me, to comfort me, I'm sure. But then he must have remembered who I was—and who we were together. He stopped.

"You want breakfast?" he asked.

I nodded.

We cooked and ate in nearly complete silence. I knew he wanted to talk to me, but he also knew I wouldn't say much. I could feel myself withdrawing, from him—from everything. That girl was now out there alone, in danger, because of me. Because I hadn't saved her.

Motherfuck. It was my fucking job to protect and serve. I wanted to scream.

At least if I had been even mildly self-aware, I would have wanted to scream.

Instead I wanted to be alone.

Fuck. Fuck. Fuck.

I also wanted to throw up.

"What's wrong?" Peter asked.

"I don't know. Sick to my stomach."

"She's not Amanda," Peter said. "She's not dead, and she's not going to be dead."

I looked at him, sitting across the table from me, all disheveled and looking vulnerable in his robe and skivvies. Suddenly I hated him.

"What the fuck are you talking about?" I asked.

"Katie, come on. Every June 25 you get the flu."

"What's that got to do with anything?" I pushed my plate away. It slid a bit and hit Peter's plate with a glassy click. "I just said I was sick to my stomach." Should have kept my mouth shut. "Don't analyze me, Peter."

"I was trying to reassure you," he said.

I looked at him.

"Yeah, look who I'm talking to," he said. "Sorry I was acting like a human being reaching out to another human being."

I pushed away from the table and got up, my chair scraping noisily across the wooden floor. I was tempted to pick up my plate and hurl it across the room. But I didn't. Wasn't my way. Instead I grabbed my phone from the counter. Left the house.

Without a backward glance. Peter called after me. Didn't care. Motherfucker. Felt almost blind. Or drunk. Got in my car. Drove away. Maybe a block. Then I stopped. Put the car in park.

Then I screamed and pounded the steering wheel.

"Fuck you, Peter Smith! Fuck you, fuck you, fuck you!"

I was so angry I could have pulled out the steering wheel. Instead, I pounded on it until my hands hurt.

Then I screamed again. The sound reverberated right back at me. I put my hands over my ears.

Peter was right, of course. But I couldn't stand it. Could not bear the idea that Amanda's murder still haunted me all these years later. Especially given all I had seen and experienced since that night.

And now Danella was gone. She said she had lied to me: It had all been a big hoax.

I shook my head.

Bullshit.

It had taken Mitchell Peterson an hour to get to Danella after she called him. That probably meant they were still based in Beauty Falls.

I started up the car again and headed toward home, to Beauty Falls.

Ten

I hadn't even gotten to the expressway when my phone rang. I pulled off to the side of the road and looked at the phone. Langley.

"Don," I said. "What'd you learn?"

"Good morning to you, too, sister," he said. He coughed and cleared his throat. "Guy owns the Impala is Mitchell Peterson out of Tennessee. Nothing on him. Doesn't have a record. Not even a sealed record. Works as a used car broker, in Nashville. Not married, no kids, as far as I can tell. I got no pings on any of the other cars in the parking lot."

"That's it?" I asked.

"Far as I can tell," he said. "The guy is in his forties. A little late to be starting a life of crime."

"Gotta start sometime," I murmured. "What about Maggie Green?"

Don made a noise.

"Too many Maggie Greens?"

"You have no idea," he said. "And without something else to go on, I can't narrow it down."

"OK. She's probably in her thirties or forties, I imagine. She might be a computer engineer. I saw a photo from about five years ago, and she had short, curly black hair. She's got an eleven-year-old daughter named Danella. Or a thirteen-year-old. Not sure. Last known address: Beauty Falls, Washington state."

"That's a little more specific," he said. "What's going on, kiddo?"

"I have no fucking idea. Thanks, Don. When I know more, I'll call you."

"Be careful," he said. "It ain't all ice cream and lollipops out there."

I laughed. That's what he used to say to me when I first started in the white collar division.

"That combination of ice cream and lollipops always made me a bit nauseated."

"Then my work is done," he said. "If I find out anything, I'll call you."

"Call even if you don't find anything. Love to Estelle. Thanks, Don."

"Anything for you, kiddo," he said.

I dropped the phone to the passenger seat. Crap, crap, crap. I had hoped Don would find something that would justify me continuing this—this what? What *was* I doing? Some kid told me she had been kidnapped, and then she told me she hadn't been.

What was going on?

And what should I do?

Was I being played by an eleven-year-old girl? And to what end? Maybe it had started out as a practical joke—on me—and then she hadn't been able to get out of it. I had seen that happen one too many times over the years. Some fool starts something foolhardy but can't own up to his lie or her fabrication and it all keeps getting worse.

Used to be I could spot a liar a mile away.

Or I thought I could.

I waited until traffic cleared, and then I turned the car around. I headed to the other side of Portland. The trees thinned out. The houses got smaller, the landscape sparser. I pulled into an apartment building parking lot. Got out and locked the car. Sprinted up the stairs and walked down an open corridor until I got to 201C. Pushed the doorbell.

Heard stirring inside. My stomach fluttered a bit. "Stop that," I whispered. Then the door opened, and Jay stood there, dressed in jeans only half zipped, wearing a white shirt which was unbuttoned, exposing his dark hairy chest.

He grinned when he saw me.

Gotta love it when a man smiled when he saw me.

I reached for Jay at the same time he grabbed me and pulled me into the apartment. Clothes came off. We made it to the couch. Barely. He worked his way up me. Burying his face in my breasts for a moment, breathing deeply, noisily, whistling. "Gawd, Nothing better." I made him stop to put on a condom, and that wasn't easy to do—didn't want to stop. Wanted to keep going, going, gone. He would have been fine with it. He was younger and stupider—and he thought he was invulnerable. I knew better. Didn't interrupt the flow much anyhow. The whole world seemed to disappear—including Jay, including everything but this glorious body pressed up against mine. Until he collapsed on top of me, and we laughed and said hello to one another.

The first time I'd come to his place—the first time Jay had come close to me and reached up to unbutton my shirt, I had said, "This could get us both in trouble." I might have said more, but he kissed me and put his hand down my pants.

That had been the beginning of the end of my career.

It was sexist bullshit. I knew more guys who had fucked more witnesses, informants, criminals than I could shake a stick at. Well, bad analogy, but you get the idea. Someone ratted me out. I had no idea who did it because no one was supposed to know about me and Jay. But pretty soon I was up for disciplinary action. My CO brought up past incidents involving me going off the reservation, so to speak. He suggested I retire before the board figured out how to take away my pension.

So just like that, I was an ex-Portland police officer.

It had been a good time to leave. I was burned out. I was tired of the petty bullshit we had to tolerate: constant wage freezes, paperwork, heavy workloads. Plus the constant threat of being shot to death. Never liked that part much.

I thought of all this as Jay and I lay together now, our sweat becoming a strange adhesive keeping us together.

Jay finally got up and went to take care of business. He returned a few moments later, pulled me up, and took me into the shower with him.

"I missed you," he said as he lathered up his hair. "Where you been?"

I shrugged and let the hot water run down my back. "Licking my wounds, I suppose. You been able to find another accounting job?" He was the best-looking accountant I had ever seen. Of course, I hadn't realized this until I came to his home one day and saw him out of his suit and in jeans and a T-shirt.

"No jobs," he said. "Gonna start looking in Seattle and San Francisco. Still working at the bar, though. Pretty good tips."

I moved out of the way so he could wash the lather out of his hair.

"Sorry, Jay. I wish doing the right thing made life better. But it ain't always so."

"No shit, Sherlock." He grinned. "Ready to go again?"

I looked down. "Apparently you are. Not here, though. We'll break our necks."

"You sound like my mother," he said.

"Oh, thank you for that," I said, slapping his wet arm.

He laughed. "I am very close to my mother."

"Jay!"

He grinned, picked me up, and carried me out of the shower, dripping wet.

I can't remember which of us turned off the water.

Later I told him about Danella. The whole thing. We sat at his kitchen table, him drinking coffee, me drinking hot water.

"Jesus," he said when I finished. "What are you going to do?"

"I don't know." I looked at him. It wasn't like I was going to ask his opinion. What would he know? He was a civilian, after all.

But then, so was I.

"I still don't know if she was lying or not," I said.

"Trust your instincts," he said.

"Sounds like a greeting card," I said. I smiled. I wasn't trying to be cruel.

"Maybe," he said. "But whenever I talked to other cops about you and about the whole insurance fraud thing, they said, 'Trust Kelly. Katie Kelly has the best instincts in the business.'"

Hard to imagine anyone saying anything good about me these days.

"That must have been before everyone knew I was sleeping with you," I said.

"I guess," he said. "Although I still don't get the big deal. So what?"

"The 'so what' is that I could be accused of getting you to lie in exchange for sexual favors," I said. "Besides, it was inappropriate."

"Why'd you do it then?" he asked. "Other witnesses or CIs or whatever you called me must have made moves on you before. And you turned them down."

I frowned. Actually, I couldn't remember anyone seriously hitting on me while I was on the job. I wouldn't have tolerated it. Would have pulled my gun. Or threatened to.

I customarily made the first move, on or off the job.

I didn't know why I had chosen to have an affair with this CI. The last couple of years I'd started to feel . . . nothing. Not for any particular reason I could pinpoint. Just time? Feeling older? I didn't know.

I had been monogamous when I was married. And relieved to be so. After Peter dumped me, I figured sex was like eating: fun and good for me, as long as I didn't overindulge.

It took me a long time to actually have sex for the first time. I was terrified, although I didn't admit that to anyone. I never understood what had happened between Amanda and Andy. How could a so-called normal boy suddenly have the urge to rape and murder his friend. For a long time, I wondered if all boys were potential rapists. It wasn't until I was in the police academy that I decided I couldn't be a freak about sex forever. I told myself that what had happened to Amanda wasn't going to happen to me, and I didn't want to be celibate for the rest of my life.

So I picked a young man about my size, good looking, tough but smart. He didn't bring his gun with him when we got together, but mine was nearby. Neither of us needed our guns, of course. All went well. Then, as far as I could tell, my fear of having sex was gone.

Sometimes I dreamed of shooting Andy. Shooting him dead. Killing him long before that night. Long before he killed Amanda.

But that didn't have anything to do with sex. What Andy had done to Amanda was crazy.

Jay was talking to me. I had to pay attention. I was sick of these morbid trips into the past.

"If you believe this kid was telling the truth," Jay said, "don't you have to do something? That's what you used to tell me. You said if I knew the truth, I had to act."

"I don't know the truth," I said.

He shrugged. "What do you have to lose?"

I laughed. "If you put it that way. I better get going then."

"Another one for the road?"

"Good grief, no," I said. "What do you think I am?"

He grinned. "A love machine."

I got up from the table and leaned down and kissed him. Then I left, without looking back, just in case I was tempted to stay.

Eleven

I headed home, driving east through the Columbia River Gorge. The old dark rock faces rose up on my right, their visages dotted with green Doug fir whiskers. To my left, when the tall cottonwoods thinned a bit, I could see the mighty Columbia River winding east and west like a giant watery python, silver green on this partly cloudy day.

I wished the landscape could help me figure out what was going on with Danella. Why would someone kidnap Maggie Green's daughter in order to blackmail her? Blackmail her into doing what? Maybe she was in witness protection. Or maybe she was rich and they wanted her money. But why wait until Tuesday or Wednesday? What was happening then? Did it have something to do with her job, if she was a computer engineer at Darby's?

Maybe she was working on a secret project.

Seemed most likely the kidnap/blackmail scheme was all part of some kind of industrial espionage. Maybe they were trying to force Maggie Green to turn over plans for a drone project. But again: Why was it all going to be over by Tuesday or Wednesday? Maybe the local peace group had gone rogue and decided to kidnap a drone engineer. Give peace a chance, babies.

I sped down the highway. That sounded ludicrous. I knew nothing; I had no idea what was going on. Maybe it was all some kind of prank on me.

It was Sunday. Who could I talk to today? Lisa Long, one of my friends from those youthful summers I spent in Beauty Falls, now lived in Hood River, and she was in the local peace group. When I became a cop, she had teased me about becoming a tool for the police state. She'd always been a hippie type, even though she was too young to actually be a hippie. We had remained friends, seeing each other occasionally over the years. "Hey, I'm not against peace," I told her once. "I am a freaking *peace* officer."

When I got home, I hurried inside to get Lisa's phone number—it wasn't on my phone. Fortunately, it was in the phone book. As I pressed in the numbers, I looked outside at the clear blue day—another rainless day in May?—and suddenly it was difficult to imagine a kidnapping had taken place in this town. *This* town. I still thought of it as *this* town, not *my* town. Of course, I knew better than most that horrible things could happen in any town. After all, Amanda had been murdered in this small town on a spectacularly beautiful summer night.

"Hello!" Lisa sounded so happy as she answered the phone.

"Lisa," I said. "It's Kate Kelly."

"Katie Kelly! Wow! Where are you? What's up?"

I smiled. "I'm in Beauty Falls. I live here. Retired." I practically choked on the word "retired."

"Retired? What the? You're younger than I am."

"You know cops. We burn out quicker. Hey, Lisa, I've got something I need to talk to you about. Do you have a few minutes?"

"Actually, right now, no. I just got an SOS call from Mattie. The restaurant is busier than hell. Why aren't all these churchgoers home on Sunday? Or in church!" She laughed. "Why don't you come down and we can talk in-between customers. Better than the phone anyway."

I shrugged. Why not? "OK. Where?"

"Peace City Grinds, man," she said. "Haven't you been? A percentage of our profits goes to the peace group, but we're the owners, Mattie and I. We are officially a part of the capitalist machine." She laughed again. "Oak and 5th. See ya soon!"

Then she was gone. Never met a person who moved so fast and did so much. Raised children, was part of practically every civic organization, active in the peace group and any and all environmental groups, now running a business. Thinking about all she did made me tired. At the same time, she was inspiring. If I hadn't been a gun-totin' peace lovin' poe-lease officer for most of the years I had known her, I might have felt inadequate next to her.

I left the house again, got in the car, and headed down the gorge, crossing the Bridge of the Gods—traveling east this time—toward Hood River, toward the mountains. Thirty minutes later, I glimpsed Mount Adams to the north and then soon after, Mount Hood to the south. I always felt like I was at the heart of the world here.

A few minutes later, I was in Hood River, walking into a small coffee shop on the corner of Oak and 5th. It smelled vaguely of cinnamon and a lot like coffee, which was not my favorite beverage, and it was packed full. Several people waited in line at the counter. Lisa was at the cash register taking orders, talking, and laughing. She waved when she saw me, and I nodded.

I looked around. Large framed photographs of various peace activists adorned the walls. I walked to one wall to get a closer look. Gandhi, of course. Next to him, the Peace Pilgrim. I only knew who she was because she was wearing a shirt that read "peace pilgrim," and her name was on the wall below the photograph. I had heard of her actually; she'd walked all over the country for years, promoting peace. Next to her was Noam Chomsky. And then Emma Goldman. Wasn't she the one who wanted to dance the revolution?

"She did so much to try to stop war," Lisa said, as she came up beside me and put her arm around my waist. "But she also plotted to kill someone once—I forgot who it was—so I was a little hesitant to put her up here. But she was so reviled by the American government because of her politics, so I decided she deserved a place. She was deported to Russia even though she was an American citizen—the government didn't like her peace politics. Among other things. You look good. You want some coffee? A beer?"

"No," I said. I looked around. "You can talk now? Still looks busy."

"This ain't nothing," she said. "Come on. Let's sit here under Rigoberta Menchú. She's a Guatemalan activist. Won the Nobel Peace Prize."

"I feel like I'm in school," I said.

"You wouldn't learn this in any school," Lisa said. "Unfortunately. At least not in any of these worker mills they call schools that they've got around here—around the whole country."

We sat on the stools at the counter and looked out the window toward the main street.

"Where'd you send your kids?" I asked.

"To the worker mills," she said. She laughed, throwing her head back. "I tried homeschooling, but I about lost my mind. There was no peace in my house then, no how. But enough of my revolutionary rhetoric. What do you need?"

"What can you tell me about Darby's?" I asked.

She frowned. "Darby's. What can I say? I mean, they're nice people, but they're scumbags. They're our neighbors, though, so we're trying to live in harmony with them. They started out designing drones for reconnaissance work for non-government agencies. To help out in disasters and the like."

"Not anymore?" I asked.

"No, now they design drones to be used in war zones," she said. "Mostly in the Middle East. They've got a shop in Beauty Falls now. That makes your little town a target, too, should some country or some terrorist group decide to take it out."

A young woman with red hair pulled back into a ponytail walked up to us. The line at the cash register was gone. They worked quickly at this little peace cafe.

"You want some coffee?" Lisa asked me again, before the girl had a chance to say anything. "It's organic and it's better than fair trade. It's direct trade. Straight from the grower."

"No, thanks."

"No coffee? It's the best in the world. No exaggeration."

I laughed. "I hate to tell you this, but I loathe the taste of coffee. No tea either. Stimulants and I don't mix well."

"You've become a nun or something?" Lisa asked.

"Mom, leave her alone. She can eat or not eat whatever she wants."

"This is your daughter?" I asked. "Wow. I haven't seen you

for a long time. You grew up good. I don't remember the red hair."

"How could you forget her hair?" Lisa said. "Essy, this is Katie Kelly. When you knew her, she was a cop."

"It's not like I walked around in my uniform all the time," I said.

"I remember," Essy said. "You and your son Scott came to one of our UU picnics. I liked him. I think I had a crush on him. I was about eight, and he was close by."

I laughed. "Wow. What a memory." I had no clue.

"Essy's boyfriend works at Darby's," Lisa said. "It's the great shame of our family."

"He's a chef," Essy said. "At the Little Salmon plant across the river. Can you believe that? I think that's very progressive. He feeds them good organic whole food meals."

"While they plot the destruction of our world," Lisa said.

"Mom," she said. "Can we cool it with the hyperbole? It upsets Tim."

"Evil prevails where good people do nothing," Lisa said.

I looked at Lisa.

"Edmund Burke," she said.

"Yeah, I know, Lisa."

"Don't be offended," Essy said. "She treats everyone like they don't know anything."

"Get her something good to eat," Lisa said. "A Love Muffin." She looked at me. "It's a blueberry muffin. Later in the season it'll be a huckleberry muffin."

"And a cup of hot water," I said.

Essy nodded, then turned and walked away.

"She looks just like Mattie," I said, "except for the hair."

"Yes, I know," Lisa said. "She's beautiful. Timothy is a good kid. Great chef. Wish we needed a chef here. They pay him pretty well. I imagine Hitler had chefs, too."

"They're that bad at Darby's?"

Lisa shook her head. "No. I'm sorry. I try not to bring up the Nazis in these situations. It's too easy, and it's not right. I apologize. They are pretty good neighbors. No pollution that we know about. They pay their workers fairly. I mean, they are a business. They're completely owned by Boaring Company though. You know: war central."

"Doesn't Boaring make planes?"

"Come on, Katie," she said. "They're war profiteers."

Another young woman—not Essy—brought us muffins, coffee for Lisa, and hot water for me. I fleetingly wondered what Danella was eating. Or was she eating at all? She had taken her Bigfoot Fruit Leathers with her.

"Of the top ten war profiteers in the world, Boaring is number three," Lisa said. "A few years ago they were the largest arms producer in the world. *In the world!*"

"So what I'm gathering is you're not pleased Darby's is here," I said. "Is this true of the peace group as a whole?"

"Yes," Lisa said. "We don't want Boaring here. We're sure they're either already building a weaponized drone at Darby's or will be soon. Besides that, they're using non-weaponized drones to spy domestically. The FBI admitted it!"

"I think they're spying on drug dealers," I said. "Or trying to find someone who's kidnapped. Aren't they?"

"The public has no way of knowing for sure," Lisa said. "They won't say what they're using the drones for. And they say they don't have to ask permission from any courts. It's warrantless searches. That's about as anti-American as you can get. Except nowadays so many Americans are willing to trade security for their freedom. It's a false security anyway. Remember what Benjamin Franklin said, "Those who surrender freedom for security will not have, nor do they deserve, either one."" She looked at me. "Or have your years on a police force changed your mind on the need for warrants in our democracy?"

She didn't sound combative. She sounded like she was asking a question.

So I answered her.

"I took an oath to support and defend the constitution of the United States," I said. "And I hold to that oath to this day."

"That begs the question," Lisa said.

I smiled. "This isn't about me, Lisa. I didn't come here for a political standoff." I'd had hundreds of criminals—or accused criminals—try to get my goat. And my goat had never been gotten. At least not within the confines of an interrogation room or even in someone's living space. I didn't get pissed off. I didn't get offended. Not easily.

"Come on, Lise," I said. "I came to you because I figured you know everything that's going on in the gorge."

She smiled. "Flattering me now, eh? I am familiar with interrogation tactics." She laughed. "Katie, I'm yanking your chain. Look, I'll tell you whatever I know. I want to help."

"Has the peace group demonstrated against Darby's?" I asked.

"When the governor was here a couple years ago," she said, "we had an anti-war demonstration. No one from Boaring or Darby's talked to us, but the governor did. She said she admired our tenacity. I didn't care what she admired. I wanted to know if she was going to do anything. But they never do anything. Politicians pass the buck."

"Is anyone in the group openly hostile to Darby's?" I asked. "I mean, has anyone advocated doing anything more serious than demonstrating?"

Lisa leaned back in her chair. "What's going on?" she asked.

"I'm not working for the police. I'm looking for a woman

who may be in trouble, and she might have worked at Darby's. I'm trying to figure some things out."

Lisa shook her head. "No, no one is violent, if that's what you're getting at. It's a freaking peace group. We're *anti*-violence. Or *for* peace if you're one of those word-Nazis and you want everything *positive*. Christ, I can't stand that. Oh double-Christ. I used the Nazis again. I'm worse than Hollywood."

I couldn't help but laugh. "It's good to see that you've mellowed over the years."

Lisa smiled. "Of course. Bet you have, too. Why'd you retire?"

"Politics," I said. "I didn't want to wear a gun."

Lisa's expression brightened. "Really?"

I laughed. "I had sex with a witness. So they fired me."

"A good man, at least?"

"A good man is hard to find," I said.

"A hard man is good to find," she said. "And boy does that get more relevant as time goes by."

We laughed. Essy came by and shushed us.

"I don't know any one of us who would be violent," Lisa said. "Bob Burgess sometimes talks about a bloody revolution, but it's only talk. I've known him for thirty years. He's cranky."

"You said Emma Goldman once plotted to kill someone," I said. "Peaceful people can be pushed."

"Agreed," Lisa said. "I'll think about it, and I'll ask Matt. Maybe he knows something I don't."

"Do you know any of the engineers who work at Darby's?" I asked. "Someone I could talk to about their employees? I'm trying to find a woman named Maggie Green. I talked to Christopher Darby and asked if anyone by that name worked there. He said no."

"If you know Christopher Darby, why would you need to talk to anyone else?"

"I don't know him," I said. "I pretended I was someone else. Long story."

"Essy!" Lisa called out loudly. Seemed like everyone in the place turned to look at us. Lisa smiled. "Oh, like any of you haven't heard me yell before."

Several people gave her a thumb's up.

Essy hurried over to us. "Mom, this is a place of business. Not a hangout for radicals. Quit shouting."

"We're not radical," Lisa said. "We're decidedly mainstream. And yes, it is a hangout and a place of business. Essy, does Tim know any of the engineers at Darby's?"

"He knows everyone there," Essy said, "but he doesn't talk about it. It's classified."

"Whether he knows someone or not is classified?" Lisa asked.

She nodded. "Everything that happens there is classified."

Lisa looked at me. "See. Doesn't that tell you something? If it was all peace and puppies, why would everything be classified? You never told me this, Essy."

Essy shook her head. "Like I'm going to tell you anything about Darby's. Besides, Tim doesn't tell me anything. He doesn't even tell me what he cooks."

"The menu is classified?" Lisa asked.

"Probably not," Essy said. "But I don't ask."

Lisa made a noise.

"Essy, have you heard of anything big going on this week?" I asked. "Particularly on Tuesday or Wednesday?"

Essy shook her head. "But I wouldn't know."

"Tim hasn't told you he has to come in early or work late or anything?" I asked.

"No," she said. She glanced at her mother. "Why?"

I shrugged. "Just wondering. If you hear of anything, can you let me know?"

She frowned. "Aren't you with the police? Can't you just go ask someone at Darby's?"

"I'm not a police officer," I said.

"She's trying to help someone in trouble," Lisa said.

"Anyway, Essy, even if I were still a cop, I could go and ask, but they wouldn't be obligated to answer me. Unless they were legally compelled to do so. By a federal judge, most likely."

"I don't know anything," Essy said. "Sorry."

I couldn't tell if she was actually sorry. She smiled, turned, and walked away.

"I'll ask around," Lisa said. "See if anything is up with Wednesday."

"Thanks." I finished my muffin. Pretty good stuff.

"You OK?" Lisa asked. "You loved being a cop. You still with the guy they fired you over?"

"I'm OK," I said. "Haven't adjusted to civilian life yet. And no, I'm not still with him. I was never with him. I was having sex with him."

Lisa laughed. "I hear ya. I'm still not sure I'm with Mattie. Or he's with me."

"You two seem inseparable."

"It comes and goes," Lisa said. "Speaking of such things, I heard Christopher Darby is quite the ladies' man."

"Someone else told me the same thing. Is he married?"

"I don't know," Lisa said. "Suppose I shouldn't be spreading gossip. But you and I are old buds. You won't tell anyone." She shrugged. "Besides, I don't care. But don't tell anyone." She laughed. "Shit, you know sometimes it's difficult to tell what's right and what's wrong."

"I can generally tell," I said.

She looked at me. Then she nodded. "Yeah, you're right. Fuck it. Sometimes I get tired of being on the losing side. I mean, we're going to hell in a fucking unraveling hand basket. I got kids. I got grandkids. I want a better world for them. Tired of fighting everything all the time."

"I figure we do one thing at a time," I said. "Right?"

"Put out one fire at a time," she said. "Save one kid at a time?"

I nodded.

"It's thirty years since Amanda was killed," Lisa said. "Thirty years this summer."

"Nate reminded me of that," I said. "I went to see him yesterday."

"I haven't seen Nate in years. Still good looking?"

I shrugged. "In an ass-holey way."

Lisa laughed. "Whatever that means. Could never tell if you two were friends or enemies."

"Neither could we," I said. "He told me he went to see Andy."

"Did he learn anything?"

"I don't know. I think I was so freaked out when he started talking about Andy that I forgot to ask. The whole conversation is a blur."

"I bet," Lisa said. "I can't imagine what it must have been like for the four of you. I heard Doug is happily married. Has a big family. Lives in California, I think. I haven't seen Sylvie for too many years. I'm sure I wouldn't know her if I saw her."

This was excruciating.

I didn't want to talk about any of this. I didn't want to think about any of this.

I had a young girl to save. A mother to rescue.

Or something.

"Lisa, thanks for seeing me on such short notice," I said. "But I better get going."

"Sure," Lisa said. We both stood. She put her arms around me. After a few seconds, I returned the embrace.

"Your number was blocked when you called," she said. "So you better give it to me in case I hear anything." She pulled out paper and pencil from her apron and handed them to me. I wrote out my numbers.

"Don't be such a stranger," Lisa said. "Next time no politics. We can talk about sex and clothes or something."

"Ugh," I said.

She laughed and patted me on the back.

"I owe you anything?" I asked.

She shook her head. "Not a thing."

I nodded.

I was soon out the door.

I hadn't learned much.

And the clock was ticking down.

Twelve

I decided to drive home via SR 14 on the Washington side, so I crossed the Columbia on the Hood River Bridge. At the red light at the end of the bridge, I debated going left toward Beauty Falls or turning right to go to Little Salmon and check out Darby's headquarters.

I turned right. Slowed down as I headed into the tiny town of Little Salmon.

Darby's headquarters building took up most of a block, on the south side of 14, with the shipyard and the river in its backyard. I vaguely remembered a time when it was a tiny mall with small stores inside. No high wire fences surrounding it now.

Didn't see any guards. Nothing to indicate it was a high security building. To the left of what looked like a main door was a small sign with the initials DUAS on it.

No vehicles in the parking spaces out front. I drove a little further down the road. Saw the driveway. A locked gate there. I glanced around. Cameras at all the corners of the building.

I kept driving and then did a U-turn and headed away from Little Salmon toward Beauty Falls.

I never tired of this drive. The two lane highway followed the course of the Columbia River, so I had a view of the river and the majestic rock faces across the river the entire way. On my right, to the north, cliffs, hills, small mountains, and trees rose and fell, rose and fell. Hardly anyone was on the road today, which was surprising, given it was Sunday. Maybe the drizzle had scared tourists into staying home.

The river was green and white where it capped into tiny waves stirred up by the wind. Several fishing boats bobbed in the rocky water. A train suddenly went by, blocking my view of the river and startling me. I looked back at the road in front of me and then in my rearview mirror.

A car or van was coming up quickly behind me. Newbies to the area often drove recklessly on this road, and too many of them ended up as road kill. Locals often drove recklessly on this road, too, lulled by the familiarity of the place, and too many of them ended up as road kill.

The train passed.

I glanced in the rearview mirror again. It wasn't a car. It was a blue van, and it was too close to my rear bumper. The front window tinting was so dark I couldn't see who was driving. If I were still a cop, I'd give them a ticket for that.

"Too close, buddy," I said. I couldn't move to the right. The shoulder was too narrow. Besides, I didn't want to move over. I tapped my brakes lightly.

The van got closer.

"Asshole," I said.

The van lights flashed.

"I'm not speeding up," I said. "I'm not killing myself because you're in a hurry."

Suddenly the van was way too close. He was going to hit me.

"What the fuck?" I said.

Some guy with instant road rage?

Or could this be the same van I'd seen at Danella's house?

The road curved. The van started to pass me. Around a freaking curve. Only now there wasn't a shoulder big enough for me to do anything. It was a rock face.

I drove around the curve. A car was coming from the other direction. The blue van was next to me, only he wasn't trying to get into the other lane to pass me. He was trying to get into my lane. He moved closer, and closer. In another instant the van was going to sideswipe me, traveling at fifty-five miles per hour.

This was going to be bad.

"What are you doing?" I screamed.

He was trying to run me off the road.

I glanced in the rearview.

No one behind me.

"Just stop, Kate. Stop."

I braked.

The van slipped into the right lane ahead of me and raced away.

The car going in the other direction drove by. I saw the driver's terrified face.

The shoulder widened then, so I quickly pulled off to the side of the road. My heart was beating so fast and loud I could barely think.

I looked down the road. No one else was coming. I pulled the car back onto the road and sped toward Beauty Falls, hoping to catch up with the van. If it was just someone being a jerk, that was one thing. But if it was the same blue van, I needed to know what the hell was going on.

I didn't see it ahead of me. Couldn't see anything ahead except windy road.

I was driving too fast.

I was going to end up as a bloody spot on the pavement if I wasn't careful.

I slowed down.

"You're not a cop," I said aloud. Not that I had participated in any high speed chases when I was a cop.

I continued home, traveling at the posted speed limit. I didn't see any blue vans or red Impalas.

At home, I parked in front. I got my gun from the trunk—via the backseat—and put it in the glove compartment again. Debated about taking it into the house, but I figured I'd be leaving again soon.

I went into my house and stopped in the living room and looked around at the boxes. The house seemed strangely empty without Danella there. I rubbed my face. Too many damn boxes.

Crap. I hadn't gotten the license number of the van any of the times I'd seen it, and I should have taken the photo of her mom from Danella so that I could show it around. Besides that, I had allowed Danella to escape. No, not escape. I hadn't been holding her prisoner. Still: She was missing now and at the mercy of dangerous kidnappers.

Or she had been lying to me all along, and I was some kind of fool.

"Fuck me," I said.

I didn't feel like cooking, and I was hungry. I didn't know what to do next. How was I ever going to find this kid and her mother? It was actually none of my business. Out of my hands, out of my responsibility.

I grabbed my jacket and walked out the front door. I hurried across the street and down the hill a bit to the center of our little town, to the Timbers, a local bar. Even though it wasn't night yet, the bar was dark inside. It took my eyes a moment to adjust. I nodded to the bartender—didn't recognize him—and looked around the room. Three of the six tables had people around them. Two of the five booths had couples in them. Music played in the background. Couldn't tell what it was. I hadn't been here since I'd moved to Beauty Falls. Looked like about every other bar I'd ever been in.

I saw a hand waving in the dim light. It was Debbie North. I walked to her table where she was sitting with her ex-husband, Tony North, and a man I didn't recognize—a man in his forties or fifties, graying hair and a salt and pepper beard.

"Hey, Deb," I said. "Tony, long time." Tony and I shook hands.

"Sit with us," Debbie said.

I pulled out a chair and sat at the table. I glanced around the bar, memorizing where the exits were. Bars always made me a little more careful.

"This is Gerald Carson," Deb said. "An old friend. Gerald, Katie used to come here with her family during the summers and now she's moved here."

Gerald and I nodded to one another, neither of us eager to shake the other's hand. He looked like a hard drinker, although the three of them had one beer each in front of them. But he had the ruddy complexion, and his hands had a slight tremor. I sighed. I had to stop sizing people up like they were criminals. I did it more now than I had when I was on the force.

"Yep," I said. "I'm officially a townie."

"Did you ever find your friend?" Debbie asked. "What was her name? Maggie Green?"

"Not yet," I said.

A waitress brought over three baskets of burgers and fries and put them on the table. She glanced at me and asked, "You know what you want?" She looked like she was about thirteen years old. Her blond with five-inch black roots hair was pulled back into a pony tail. She wore a T-shirt and a pair of tight short shorts that didn't leave much to the imagination.

"You got anything besides burgers?" I asked.

She pointed to the chalk board hanging over the bar.

Like I could read that.

I looked back at her. She sighed and walked away. My table companions were digging into their food like they'd never eaten before.

Debbie paused to say, "Mimi bought this place, and she's the chef."

"This place has a chef?" I remembered Mimi's Bar and Grill. She had the best food in town.

"I thought she was long gone," I said.

Debbie shrugged. "Now that there are more commuters, people are willing to pay for what she's selling."

The waitress brought a menu. Burgers. Nachos. Soup. Salad. Seemed standard fare.

"The soup is amazing," Gerald said. "Best stuff."

I'd never heard a man say that about soup.

"Her salads are excellent, too," Tony said.

"Beef is grass-fed, organic," Debbie said. "Not that I give a shit, but you lived in Portland most of your life, so you probably do. Nachos are the best I've ever had anywhere. Organic everything."

"OK," I said. "Give me the nachos. With shredded chicken. And a beer."

"What kind?" the waitress asked. "We've got microbrews on tap. And—"

I held up my hand. "Surprise me," I said. I didn't drink beer for the taste.

The waitress started to say something, but she apparently thought better of it. She left us again.

Debbie laughed. "You still have that cop stare. Must have scared the shit out of people."

Gerald looked at me. "You're police?"

I couldn't tell if he thought that was a good or a bad thing.

"I was," I said. "I'm retired."

I could see he wanted to ask why I was retired, but I didn't want to tell the story, so I quickly said, "Hey, Deb, remember I asked you about the blue van? Well, I've seen them again. They tried to run me off the road."

Gerald and Tony leaned forward and chewed their burgers more slowly.

"Who the hell are they?" I asked.

"It's all paranoid bullshit," Tony said.

"I'm not paranoid," I said. "They did try to run me off the road."

"They started showing up a few years ago," Gerald said. He seemed eager to tell this tale. "If someone was hanging around Darby's and they didn't belong there, they'd soon have a blue van following them. Or when someone was fired, they'd see the blue van for days afterward."

"It's not one blue van," Debbie said. "It can't be. Just like there's not one Bigfoot."

I smiled, remembering my absurd conversation with the store clerk.

"Not that I'm saying there are actually Bigfoots—Bigfeets?" Debbie said. "But the blue vans. Those are rumors, I think. Have you been at Darby's? I mean, why would they be following you?"

"Who would the 'they' be?" I asked.

Gerald said, "Feds, of course. Now that Boaring owns Darby's, they've got to protect their investment."

"Has anyone ever talked to the drivers of these vans?" I asked.

"Sure," Gerald said. "And then no one sees them again."

I laughed. He wasn't smiling.

"Oh, you're serious."

He nodded. I glanced at Debbie and Tony. Their expressions were noncommittal.

I wasn't much for conspiracy theories.

"Could it be that there are a lot of blue vans in this town?" I asked.

"That's what I think," Tony said.

"Everything changed when Darby's came to town," Gerald said. "Used to be a nice logging town. No more. Now we've got a target painted on us."

Beauty Falls hadn't been a logging town for decades.

The waitress brought my nachos and a mug of beer. Didn't know what kind of beer it was. I didn't care.

The bar was filling up. Soon it was so noisy we could barely hear each other talk.

Which might have been a good thing.

I leaned over to Debbie and said, "I thought you two got divorced."

"We did," she said. "But small town, not a lot of choices. Don't want to live with him, but ya know, the sex is good. You and your ex on good terms?"

"Depends on the phase of the moon," I said. "But yeah, the sex is good."

We laughed.

I looked up as Nate Gunderson came into the bar. Out of uniform. He was even better looking in jeans and T-shirt. Debbie waved to him. He was smiling until he saw me. Then he grinned and walked over to us.

"Pull up a chair," Debbie said. "We're talking about little green men and blue vans."

"Little green men?" I said. "I missed that."

"Who do you think is driving the blue vans?" Tony said.

We laughed. Nate found an empty chair and dragged it over. He sat between me and Gerald. That was fine with me.

The waitress was there in a flash. Nate ordered a burger and coffee.

"Oh, man," Nate said to us. "Don't get me started on those blue vans."

"So they do exist," Gerald said. "I knew it."

"Of course they exist," I said. "One ran me off the road today. I was wondering if it was road rage, or is something else going on?"

"Someone ran you off the road?" Nate looked at me. He was frowning.

"You ever heard of the blue van guys doing anything like that?" Debbie asked.

Nate said, "Let's see. I've heard they've kidnapped people and probed them. Speaking of little green men. Um, they've followed people. They've put nails in people's tires. Any crappy thing that happens in this town is blamed on the blue vans. No one has ever given me a license plate number. I see blue vans in town sometimes, like I see hundreds of other vans. They ain't doing anything wrong as far as I can tell. Of course, I mostly hear about these vans from nut cases. No offense, Gerald."

Gerald shook his head. "None taken."

"But you say you got run off?" Nate asked me.

"I was coming back from Hood River," I said. "Got right up on my bumper and then passed me. If I hadn't slammed on my brakes, I'm not sure what would have happened."

"License plate?" Nate asked.

"No."

"So another tall tale," he said. The waitress brought Nate coffee.

"Yep," I said. "I made it all up."

He looked at me and laughed.

Soon enough people I didn't know came over and sat around our table. I moved away from the chatter and was somehow closer to Nate.

"You think they did it on purpose?" Nate asked, leaning in so I could hear him. I could feel his breath on my ear. This was disconcerting.

I tried to move away but be close enough so we could hear one another.

"Seemed like it," I said.

"Why'd you really come in yesterday to see me?" Nate asked.

I shrugged. "Couldn't I be visiting an old friend?"

"We were never friends, old or new," Nate said.

I didn't say anything. I leaned back, looked around, and drank my beer. When the waitress brought Nate's burger, I ordered another beer. Hell, I wasn't driving.

The waitress brought the beer. I drank it. Debbie and Tony went to another table to talk to friends. Gerald wandered away. The other people at the table talked and laughed together. Every once in a while, one of them would say something to Nate. He'd nod and smile and drink his coffee.

"I thought you said you weren't an alcoholic," I said. I was starting to feel tipsy. I was not used to drinking. "Why the coffee?"

He shrugged. "It's more interesting watching people when you're not drunk."

"OK."

"Why do I piss you off so much?" Nate asked. "I've always wondered."

"What?" I said. "I thought I pissed you off. Maybe we mutually piss each other off." I felt like giggling. Thank God I didn't.

The other people at the table left. Nate and I were alone. I looked at him. Having sex with three men in twenty-four hours was not something I aspired to do. Not that I was actually contemplating having sex with Nate.

Bleck.

Suddenly a man was standing next to Nate, smiling, holding out his hand. He had a 100-watt smile and blond hair that was a little too long. Early forties, late thirties. Shirt and slacks, casual but not as casual as everyone else.

His hands were gorgeous. Nails appeared manicured.

He looked over at me with his baby blues.

I was not partial to blonds, but this one was pretty.

"Katie," Nate said. "This is Christopher Darby. Chris, this is Katie Kelly."

Darby held out his hand, and I shook it.

Darby pulled out a chair and sat next to Nate.

"You two friends?" I asked. I tried to blink away the effects of the alcohol.

"He was friends with my youngest brother," Nate said.

"I remember you," Darby said.

"Me?" I said. "How?"

"Uh, from the news," he said. "When Amanda Stenson was killed."

"Oh." Sorry I asked. "I don't remember any family named Darby. Not that I knew everyone, by any means. But I thought Darby's was started by someone from Seattle."

"I'm Chris Reilly's son," Darby said.

Deputy Chris Reilly, the officer who had found Amanda's remains—the one who interviewed Andy and got him to take the police to her body. Deputy Reilly had killed himself a year after Amanda's murder. Walked into the lava beds and shot himself.

"How are you Reilly's son?" I asked. It was the only thing I could think of to say.

"My mom remarried," Christopher said. "I was only ten at the time, and David Darby wanted to adopt me and my sister, who was six. Who were we to argue? I've thought about going back to my birth name. When my dad killed himself, my whole family was so embarrassed. Ashamed, I guess. What a strange reaction, eh?" He shrugged.

"Did he do it because of the murder?" I asked. Nate gave me a look. I couldn't believe I'd said it either.

Christopher Darby didn't miss a beat. "Of course. It haunted him. Couldn't shake it. We should have left this town. But he had his job."

"You moved away after your mom remarried?" I asked.

He nodded. "A few years later. I figured I'd come back. I loved it here. Dad may have been haunted, but I wasn't. Thank God I didn't see what he saw, and I didn't have to listen to that psycho confess."

Nate and I were sitting inches from one another, and I had felt him change as Darby talked. It seemed he stiffened, or his breathing became shallow.

Or was I projecting? I wanted Darby to stop talking.

Yet I wanted to hear everything he had to say. I had not forgotten Deputy Reilly. It had been years since I heard his name, however. Here I was sitting across from his son. Deputy Reilly had spoken to both Nate and me when we drove out to the forest again, after we heard that Amanda was missing.

I suddenly flashed on his face. Looked just like Christopher. I could smell the forest. That morning it had smelled like cut wood. The sun had been too bright. Mist rose from a slash pile, like wisps of smoke from a fire.

"When did you last see her?" Deputy Reilly had asked us.

"Kate." Someone was saying my name. "Katie. Katie. That hurts."

I blinked. The forest disappeared.

Fuck.

I looked over. Nate. Glanced down. I was gripping his arm. He put the fingers of his right hand over my hand, lightly, barely brushing me.

I let go of him. We gazed into each other's eyes for just a moment.

Then he rubbed his arm.

"Hey, Chris, any truth to the stories about the blue vans?" Nate asked.

Christopher laughed. I could still see his father in his eyes. "I don't know anything about any blue vans," he said. "I can tell you that much."

I waited a few minutes, and then I excused myself. I felt sick. It was the beer, I supposed. I paid my tab, and then I left the bar, without a backward glance.

I hurried home.

Thirteen

Once I got home, I didn't think about nothing or nobody, except those stupid boxes I kept tripping over. I stripped off my jeans, shirt, and socks and got under the covers. That was it.

Until a noise woke me up.

My eyes opened to pitch darkness. I listened. Couldn't tell if it was inside or out. I quickly sat up. Too quickly. I was still a little bit drunk.

Were those voices? I reached for the drawer on my night-stand and then remembered my gun was still in the car.

Crap.

I quietly pulled on my jeans, and then I stealthily left the room and headed down the short hallway to the living room. I immediately stubbed my toe on a box full of something very hard. I swore under my breath.

Then I heard voices again. Definitely outside. Maybe someone coming home from the bar.

"Shit, Mike!" "Come on, come on!" Desperate sounding male voices.

Someone was up to no good.

I opened the front door.

Saw two figures running into the shadows before I could get a good look. Down the street a truck travelled, lights off.

I hurried down the steps and into the street.

I looked at my car. The two back wheels were gone. The entire wheels: tires and rims.

"Hey!" I shouted.

But the street was empty, except for me and my wheel-less car.

"Crap, crap, crap."

I got my gun from the car and put it inside the house, in the drawer of my nightstand, and then I called the police.

I sat on my front porch, under the light, and waited.

Nate Gunderson drove up in his squad car five minutes later.

"You could have walked," I said.

"I've got Deputy Hill driving around looking for a truck with tires in the back."

"I don't think you've got enough probable cause to search any truck," I said.

"Let me worry about that," he said.

Nate came up the first set of steps and took out his pad.

"You working the late shift?" I asked. "Didn't I just leave you at the bar?"

He shrugged. "The wife of one of my deputies went into labor. So I came in. You want to tell me what happened?"

"Hell if I know," I said. "I went to sleep. Heard a noise and woke up. I came out and saw two figures running away in that direction—" I pointed. "—and a truck was heading down the street in the same direction. Then I saw my two back wheels were gone."

Nate wrote in his pad as I talked.

"Any description of the figures or the truck?"

"No," I said. "Nothing. Couldn't even tell if they were male or female, although I distinctly heard two male voices before I came outside. One said, 'Shit, Mike,' and the other said, 'Come on, come on.'"

I got up from the steps. I realized then I was chilly because I was dressed only in my jeans and camisole.

"Crap," I said. "You could have told me I was half-naked."

Nate shrugged. "Didn't notice, ma'am."

"Don't ma'am me," I said. I ran up the steps—ugh, too soon to be running—and reached inside the door to grab my jacket off the hook. I put it on, and Nate and I walked down the steps together to stand near my car, which was parked under a street light.

"Does this happen a lot in this town?" I asked.

"It happens," he said. "We've got quite a few meth heads. Plus there's a young guy—heroin addict—named Mike who doesn't live far from here. But I'm a little surprised they stole these wheels."

"What the hell's wrong with my wheels?"

"Nothing personal, Katie. But they usually steal Honda wheels. This ain't a Honda."

"Yeah, right," I said. I rubbed my face. "Man, two beers and I'm knocked on my ass. Must be getting old."

"You never were much of a drinker," Nate said.

I looked at him. "How could you possibly know that?" I asked. "I've hardly seen you in the last thirty years."

"True. I was thinking when we were kids you didn't drink at all. The one time I saw you at that bar in Portland—"

"Oh man," I said. "Please, let's forget that. Forever."

"I'm saying that you were drinking then, and you told me you didn't drink very often."

"How can you remember that?" I asked. "That was twenty years ago."

He shrugged. "You're memorable. You don't exactly tiptoe into a room. When you're somewhere, you're there."

I looked at him. What the hell was he talking about?

"Can we get back to business?" I asked. "What can you do for me? Can you get prints off my car or something?"

"We don't have the manpower for something like that," he said. "Besides, it's probably some skell needing drug money."

"That's your idea of police work?" I said. "Did it ever occur to you that maybe this was on purpose? First I get run off the road and now someone steals my fucking wheels. Maybe I'm being targeted."

"By whom?" he asked. "Who would be after you? Are you involved in something I need to know about? Do you have some intel that says someone might be after you?"

Should I tell him about Danella? He looked at me. I looked away. "I don't believe in coincidence," I said.

"Sure you do," he said. "Coincidences happen every day."

I had to do it. "Look," I said. "This eleven-year-old kid came up to me at the Mystic Trail on Saturday and said she'd been kidnapped. I put her in my car and I was going to bring her to you, to the sheriff's office, but the guys she said kidnapped her were parked at the shop. They were Mitchell Peterson and Herman Johnson. She told me they'd been holding her hostage for several days while they blackmailed her mother into doing something. She was terrified about going to the police, and when she saw their car at the sheriff's department, she thought you might be involved. So I took her to Peter's house. She ran away in the night. Left a note saying it was all a hoax, and Mitchell Peterson was actually her uncle. But I don't believe it. I think something is going on."

Nate didn't say anything at first. Then he started laughing.

I could have slugged him.

"You think this is funny?"

"Kate, you got punked," he said. "I checked the guy out. Nothing was going on with him."

"Yeah, I had my ex-partner check him out, too," I said. "But that doesn't mean anything. The girl and her mother were supposedly living in this house paid for by Darby's and now it's completely empty, like they were never there."

"Maybe they were never there," he said.

"I went to the house," I said, "and I found a photo of the girl and her mother."

"You have it?" he asked.

"No," I said.

"Maybe they lived there at one time. The kid still punked you."

"Why are you so sure?"

"I told you," he said. "I talked to the guy. He said his niece was prone to storytelling. He was trying to be polite, but he was saying she was a little liar. Kids lie. My daughter used to lie practically every time she opened her mouth when she was that age. She used to lie about what time it was or what the color of her dress was."

"I know kids lie," I said, "but I don't think this girl was lying. And maybe you should have sent your kid to a shrink."

"Hey, I could be wrong." He shrugged. "What would you have me do? I've got a list of crimes I know are real, some of them happening even while we speak. So tell me what do you want me to do?"

"Find my damn wheels," I said.

I turned away from him and started walking toward the house.

"Katie," Nate said.

I put up my hand. Then I walked in the house and closed the door.

In the morning, my head hurt. I drank lots of water and then took a shower. After I was dressed and ready to face the world, I went outside and stood on my porch. Yep, the rear wheels were still gone from my car.

Inside the house again, I called my insurance company. Said they couldn't get anyone to come out and tow the car into Gresham—closest place where I could get wheels—until later in the day. Reminded me I needed a police report. I promised to email the insurance company the number on the police report as soon as I got it.

"I'll leave the keys under the mat on the driver's side," I said, "in case I'm gone."

Then I had to call the sheriff's office to get the number of the police report. If I hadn't run off in a snit last night, I could have gotten it then.

Fortunately, Deputy Sandra Dean answered the phone.

"Good morning," I said. "This is Kate Kelly. I was in there Saturday to see Sheriff Gunderson."

"Hi!" she said. I was suspicious of enthusiastic people, but I was hoping to use Dean's bubbly personality for my benefit this morning.

"Do you like to be called Sandra or Sandy?" I asked. "Or Deputy Dean?"

"Sandy is fine," she said.

"Sandy, I had the wheels of my car stolen last night," I said. "I forgot to get the number of the police report from Sheriff Gunderson. Do you think you could get that and email it to me?"

"Nothing easier," she said.

"That's great!" Now I was enthusiastic. I gave her my email address. Then I said, "You've been lots of help. Thank you, Sandy."

"By the way," she said, lowering her voice. "Someone was in here this morning asking about you. He was talking to the sheriff, and I heard him mention your name. I didn't recognize him right away, but I heard the sheriff call him Chris. I think he's the guy who owns Darby's. I don't normally tell anyone what's going on in the shop, but I figure you have a right to know who's asking after you. And you're a cop. So it can't hurt." I didn't correct her. "Honestly, he's so cute. I'd want to know if someone like him wanted to get in touch with me."

She laughed. Giggled, more like it. She was being quite indiscreet, but I didn't care. I was getting what I needed from her. But, yeah, she could get fired.

"Thanks, Sandy," I said.

I dealt with the insurance company, the tow-truck company, and the repair place. Before I could get new wheels, they had to inspect the car to make certain no damage had been done to the undercarriage when the burglars dropped it to the ground without wheels.

I hoped my son's old van parked behind my house still worked. Fortunately, the tags and insurance were current even though I couldn't remember the last time I'd taken it out.

I made myself breakfast—oatmeal and fruit—and tried to figure out what to do next. Maybe I should walk into Darby's and see if I could find Maggie Green.

That reminded me: Why the hell had Christopher Darby been asking about me? If he was interested in me for some reason, I could work that to my advantage. I could get information from him while he thought he was getting information from me.

Today was Monday. Whatever was supposed to happen was

going to happen on Tuesday or Wednesday. I had a day and a half if I was lucky. If Danella and her mother were lucky.

The phone rang as I was cleaning up. Nate Gunderson.

"Found my tires?" I asked.

"No," he said. "But I wanted to tell you that Christopher Darby was in here asking about you. Didn't say why. Wondered what you were up to these days—since he hadn't heard anything about you for thirty years."

"What did you tell him?" I asked.

Nate cleared his throat. "I didn't tell him anything."

"Aren't you two buddies?"

"Why would you say that?" he said. "I see him at the gym sometimes, but not much else."

"He came into the bar like he was looking for you," I said. "He sat with us."

"Naw," Nate said. "I've never seen him there before."

I pushed one of my boxes out of the way and sat on the couch. "Nate, what the hell aren't you saying?"

"He's known around town as being kind of a lady killer," Nate said.

"I've heard the term ladies' man," I said.

"Yeah, that's what I meant," he said. "So he might be trolling for a date. Which is none of my business. He wanted your number, but I didn't give it to him. We've got it, of course. But I didn't give it to him."

He was blathering. Wasn't like him. At least, I didn't think it was.

"Good on you, Nate," I said. "You didn't betray your oath and give out private information."

"I'm wondering why he wanted to know about you," he said. "I mean, sure, if he wanted to date you. But you are older than he is, and I've seen the women he usually goes for. They're young and cute. I mean, younger. Cuter. Blond. This isn't coming out right."

He was spooling out the rope to hang himself. No sense me interfering. I could step back and enjoy.

"What I'm trying to say is I wonder if there might be something to you being run off the road yesterday. If those blue vans are associated with Darby's, which everyone believes they are, and now Christopher Darby is asking around about you, then maybe it's all related. Are you telling me everything?"

I was silent for a moment. Then I said, "You know what, Nate. Why don't you give Christopher Darby my number. Wait. Better yet. Tell him I'll be down at the Timbers for lunch at noon. He can ask me all the questions he wants then."

"I'm not your secretary," Nate said.

"Granted," I said. "But you did just call me old and ugly. You owe me."

"I did not call you old and ugly." He sounded embarrassed.

Lord love a duck. Never realized Nate would be fun to tease.

"All right, I'll call him," he said.

"Thank you," I said. "I'll talk to you later."

When it was almost time, I left the house, put the car key under the mat, and then walked down the hill to one of the two real estate offices in town. A woman sitting at the front desk looked up at me when I opened the door and stepped inside. Couldn't tell if she was a real estate agent or a secretary. She had dyed black hair, very red lipstick, and blue eyes. She could have been forty or sixty. I couldn't tell which.

"Hello," I said. "I'm looking for a rental, and I passed by this little green house on Columbia that looked empty. 336 Columbia. Someone thought maybe you managed it."

The woman smiled. "I know you. You're Kate Kelly. You bought your house through our competitors."

Crap. This town was too small. I couldn't bullshit my way into or out of anything. Guess that meant I had to tell some part of the truth.

"That's right," I said. I held out my hand to her. She stood and shook my hand.

"I'm Rebecca," she said. "I knew you a bit when you were a kid. Your mom and my mom hung out in the summers. We lived on Wanted Lake."

I nodded. Yep. Where the rich people lived. Mom knew a few families there—precisely so we could see how the other half (or rather, how the one percent) lived. I squinted. "Becky Hill." I remembered her. She'd been older than I was, and gorgeous. I used to watch her with her friends when I was a tween, wishing I could be as beautiful and sophisticated as they all were.

"You had a brother," I said. I remembered Nate had mentioned a Deputy Hill last night. "David."

I had a crush on her brother one summer. Although I never told him or anyone else.

She smiled. "Yep. He's a cop now. I'm a Norton. Or was. Divorced, but I kept my name since I have a trillion kids."

I laughed. "That many?"

"Four of them," she said. "But when they were teens it sure felt like a trillion. So are you moving?"

"No. I have a friend in Portland who is threatening to move out here. I told her rentals were difficult to come by. But I said I'd look around."

Becky sat at her computer again. "Let me look. Oh, yes, of course. We do manage that property, but it's not available." She frowned. "As far as I can tell, it is occupied."

"Who owns it?"

She looked at me. "You're a cop now, aren't you?"

"Not anymore."

She shrugged. "It's public information, of course. Darby's owns it."

"Do you know who is living there now?" I asked.

She shook her head and then looked up at me. "No. We're only involved when they want to rent it out to a non-Darby's employee, so I assume someone from Darby's is still in it."

I nodded. "Thanks, Becky. It's nice seeing you. How's David doing?"

"He's doing great," she said. "Except for the divorce. Has three great kids. I guess it's hard for cops to stay married."

I shrugged. "Not all of them. My partner—ex-partner—has been married for thirty some years."

"What about you?" she asked.

I laughed. "I divorced about twenty years ago. Never tied the knot again."

"I should tell David," she said.

"I seem to remember he was quite a handful," I said.

"Still is," she said. "But he might settle down for the right woman."

"I don't want anyone settling on me," I said. "If you hear anything about that house in the next few days, will you let me know?" I wrote my phone number on a piece of paper I found on her desk and then handed it to her.

"Sure," she said. "Can I give this number to David?"

I shrugged. "Why not? Could always talk cop shop."

Fourteen

I left the real estate office and walked down to the Timbers and went inside. It was almost noon. When my eyes adjusted, I looked around. Christopher Darby was sitting in one of the booths. He stood when he saw me. I walked over to him.

"Hi, Chris," I said.

"Hello, Katie," he said. "I'm so glad Nate called and told me you were willing to meet."

We shook hands, and then we slid into opposite sides of the booth.

"You want a beer?" he asked.

"Sure," I answered.

He caught the bartender's eye and said, "Two beers on tap. Whatever."

I smiled. He did that easy. Didn't shout. Didn't make a spectacle of himself. But he got what he wanted. Quickly.

"I wanted to apologize for last night," he said. "I didn't mean to bring up a difficult time in your life. Since my father was involved in it all, I think I presumed an intimacy or—" He looked away for a moment and shook his head. "Or something. Since I was a kid, I've been trying to figure out why it all happened, and suddenly you were there, and I had all these questions."

"You don't need to apologize," I said. "You have a perfect right to ask anyone anything about it."

The bartender came over. I looked at him and smiled. He didn't return the smile. I rolled my eyes. I guess a smile would break his face. He put two mugs full of beer in front of us.

"You want lunch?" the bartender asked.

"One of those burgers is good for me," I said. "All the organic glory of fixin's you got. Medium rare."

Chris said, "Sure. Same here."

Bartender nodded, then was gone.

"But I could see I upset you," Chris said. "By talking about it."

I could deny it. I was here to see what *he* knew. I didn't want him to find out anything about *me*. But that was a key to many interviews: Sometimes I got more information when I appeared to be revealing things about myself.

I shrugged. "It's gonna be summer soon. Sometimes as the anniversary gets near, I get a little antsy. I don't like talking about any of it, it's true. But no apologies necessary. I don't think I ever told you how sorry I was to hear about your dad. He was a nice man. He treated me with respect. Some people were accusatory during that period. Thought the four of us might have been in on it. Or thought we could have stopped it. That did haunt me for a long time. Still does, sometimes, wondering what I missed."

Chris shook his head. "Didn't miss anything. No one knew. Except maybe the cops and his neighbors. Lots of bad family stuff going on in that household. Their family had been here since the town was founded. Made their money and a name logging the public forests and then lost everything. Then they became nobodies and nothings like everyone else. Learned that from my mom years later. My dad told her he'd had run-ins with Andy before he killed Amanda. I guess he'd tortured animals. Horrible shit like that. But none of that got in the papers or anything."

"There was no excuse for what Andy did," I said. "Bad family or not."

"Of course not," Chris said. "I'm saying it was likely he wasn't going to turn out well. So it wasn't my father's fault. It wasn't your fault. My mom said my dad did blame himself. Since some of Andy's behavior before, when he was younger, was sociopathic or psychopathic in nature. My dad thought he should have figured that out and done something different."

"I'm sorry about your dad," I said again. I looked around. "Do you come here often? I've never seen you here before yesterday."

I'd been here a total of two times since I'd moved to town, but he didn't need to know that.

He shrugged. "Not often. Been pretty busy. Yesterday was a fluke."

I glanced at him. He was still looking down. Was he lying?

"What's it like bringing this multimillion dollar business back to your home town?" I asked. "Must feel good."

"It feels great," he said. "I originally designed the drones to be deployed during disasters. They could go places where it wasn't safe for people to go. My dad wanted to help people, and he instilled that in us. So I'm proud of the work I've done here."

He sounded like a television ad for Drones Are Us.

"Are the drones still used for disasters?" I asked.

"Boaring bought us a couple years ago," he said, "so most of our drone work is now in war zones. But again, we're able to go places safely and get intel for our warriors."

Intel? Warriors? Sounded like war talk to me.

"Good for you," I said. I smiled. "I've been hearing quite a bit of talk since I got back. About Darby's. The blue vans. About weaponized drones. People are convinced the blue vans are deployed by Darby's or Boaring to spy on the locals."

The bartender came by with our burgers, and then he was gone again.

"I figured it's only talk, right?" I said. "Superstition. Like with Bigfoot."

We took turns putting ketchup and mustard on our burgers. Then we ate in silence for a few minutes.

"I did get a little jolt yesterday or the day before," I said. Which was it? Christ. I was losing track of time. "A blue van ran me off the road when I was coming back from Hood River. Scared the shit out of me."

He looked over at me.

"I know it's all bullshit," I said, "about the blue vans and Darby's, but I wondered what the hell was going on."

"Probably coincidence," he said. "You don't have anything going on that has anything to do with Darby's, do you?"

Nate had asked me almost the same thing.

"Why do you ask?" I said. "If the blue vans have nothing to do with Darby's, why would it matter? Besides, you would know if I was involved with Darby's."

He laughed. It sounded forced—and maybe a bit fearful.

"You got me there," he said. "I don't know why I asked that question. I'm getting as bad as the locals."

"But aren't you a local?" I asked.

He put down his burger and looked at me—and then looked past me.

"I'm not sure how to answer that," he said. "I suppose I was. But now, I look at people and I can almost always tell who is from Beauty Falls and who isn't. Do you know what I mean? When I look in the mirror, I don't feel like I'm from here. You? Are you a local?"

"No, definitely not. I was a visitor. I'll be a visitor forever. It's not my town. I don't know if anywhere is home. I used to think I'd live here forever. Every summer we came here, I never wanted to leave. Until Amanda was killed."

"You gonna stay here?" he asked.

"Probably not," I said. "Just a place to lick my wounds. Then I'll go back to Portland. I guess. We'll see. So far, I haven't done much socializing. Haven't done any loner drinking at home either. If I start doing that, I'm either moving or I'll be forced to go out and talk to people. I don't remember this place as being particularly social when I was a kid, though."

"No," Chris said. "People stay to themselves."

"Whenever I leave here and get to Portland, I feel such relief," I said. "I feel like I can breathe again. It's like climbing out of a canyon. The sky is bluer in Portland. People all around, walking and biking. Yet when I return to the gorge, my heart beats a little faster in anticipation. There's so much . . . nature, all around. We're small in comparison. Terrible things can happen here, it's true, but the terrible things—or the wonderful things—people do here, seem dwarfed by the magnificence, by the encompassing wild. You know?"

He nodded. "I know exactly what you mean."

"And then when I get out into the woods," I said, "and walk

amongst those old trees that have been around for hundreds of years. Wow. I feel like anything is possible. Good things, I mean. Like all the evil in the world doesn't exist. It's only me and nature. There ain't no evil in nature."

"Except the evil men do," he said.

"I suppose." I sighed. I didn't like thinking human beings were separate from nature. Weren't we a part of it?

We were both silent for a few moments.

"Although it's different here than it was when we were kids," I said.

He nodded.

When I drove into the gorge nowadays, I noticed the acres of dead trees clinging to the cliff sides. The great expanses of green were being replaced by swaths of brown as the trees died off. The trees were stressed by climate change, and they couldn't cope with the pine beetles.

"The air is clearer than when we were kids," Chris said. "That's something. Not sure it's cleaner, but at least we can't see what's killing us."

It wasn't funny, but I laughed.

He shrugged. "Who doesn't want to live in a place named after mythical waterfalls?"

"With a mythical great ape," I said, "or whatever Bigfoot is."

"A mythical ape who lives in the lava beds," he said. He smiled sadly. "They didn't find my father's body right away—because he was in the lava beds. He'd written my mom a note, telling her where he was going. For a while—for those few days when he was gone but before they'd found his body—I imagined he'd gone off with Bigfoot, imagined he was living *la vida loca* with a Bigfoot and his family." He shrugged. "You know how kids are."

I nodded. "The night Amanda was killed we were out looking for Bigfoot. As a joke more or less. Or an excuse to be in the woods at night. We had talked about going to the lava beds to look, but I never liked it there. Only a crazy person would go there at night. Oh geez. Your dad didn't go there at night, did he?"

He laughed. "No! My dad was not crazy. Just depressed. There's a difference, I think."

"Anyway," I said.

"Yep, anyway." He looked at me. "It's nice to be able to talk with someone about it. Even laugh about it. Don't think I've ever done that."

"Most cops have a macabre sense of humor," I said. "We laugh about a lot of horrible things. I don't know. I sometimes wonder if kids still go out into the woods looking for Bigfoot, or did Amanda's murder stop all of that—all of that sense of wonder, the sense of living myth."

"The sense of hormones?" he said.

I laughed. "You got that right. I'm sure in the back of our minds some of us were going up there to make out. Couldn't have gone worse. OK. Now I want to talk about the weather or something."

"Sure," he said. "The weather on this side of the booth is fine. How about on your side?"

"I want it to be over," I said. "After all of these years, I want it done and over. But it seems to be getting worse, the memories. I've been thinking a lot about it lately. I wasn't raped. I wasn't killed. I didn't cause her to be raped and murdered. Yet it all haunts me. Sometimes I think it haunts this whole place."

I stopped. Couldn't believe I'd said all that out loud. Normally I didn't talk about it. Just didn't.

"I know," he said. "I think I've come to terms with the idea that it will never be over for my family. When my father stepped into the lava beds, when he put that gun into his mouth—"

I shuddered.

"—the murder and its consequences were branded on our family forever."

"I'm sorry about that," I said. "I mean, you didn't have anything to do with it. Neither did your father, except after the fact."

Chris and I looked at each other.

"So," he said.

"So . . . do you get a lot of military bigwigs coming and going at Darby's?" I asked. "Anything new and big happening?"

"If we had anything new and big in the works, I couldn't tell you. And if I did—"

"—you'd have to kill me," I said. "Yeah. I've heard it before."

Chris laughed. This time it was genuine.

"Did you call Darby's on Saturday?" he asked.

Shit. I nearly spit out my burger. How the fuck could he know that? My number was unlisted.

"Your voice," he said. "I recognized your voice."

"You recognized my voice on Saturday?" I asked.

"No," he said. "When I saw you yesterday. Something about it seemed familiar. Then I remembered the call."

"My voice is not that distinctive," I said.

"I have many talents," he said. "Why did you call?"

Best to stay as close to the truth as possible.

"I heard that an old friend of mine had recently moved here to work at Darby's," I said. "Maggie Green. We'd been out of touch for a long time."

"Why didn't you say that when you called?" he asked.

I shrugged. "I guess it's the cop in me. Want to keep everything secret. Didn't want her to get into trouble for me calling her at work."

"Alarm bells go off for me when someone is trying to find out information about one of my people."

"I hear ya," I said. I casually continued to eat my burger.

"No one named Maggie Green has come to work for us recently," he said. "In fact, we haven't hired anyone new for a bit."

I nodded. Couldn't tell if this was the truth or not. I looked at him and wondered if he could have had something to do with Maggie Green's disappearance.

If she had actually disappeared.

"I wish I could tell you more about your dad," I said. "He was nice to me. Never accused us. Was respectful of Amanda. Never said anything bad about her. Others did. Wondered why we were all out in the woods that late. Figured we had all gone there to have sex, which, of course, wasn't the truth. At least, not as far as I knew. Maybe that had been Andy's plan."

I felt nauseated just saying his name.

"Anyway, your dad was a good man," I said. "I'm sorry for what happened."

He glanced at me and nodded.

"Hey," I said. "You ever have time to hike on the weekdays?"

"Sure," he said.

"I'd love a hiking partner," I said. "I was going to go up to Falling Creek tomorrow. You want to come?"

"I'd love to," he said. "But I can't tomorrow. Another time?"

I nodded. Was that because something was happening at Darby's on Tuesday?

"I could switch to Wednesday," I said.

"Maybe Thursday," he said. "I'll give you a call."

Well, that little ruse hadn't helped me glean any new info from Chris Darby. What kind of detective was I anyway?

A *former* detective for one.

We talked about the town for the rest of the lunch. And townies. Commuters. Wondering if the town was going to die out. Didn't talk about his father again, or the murder, or Darby's.

Somehow almost two hours went by. As we were paying our bills at the cash register, I got a phone call.

It was Lisa. I answered it and said, "Hang on a sec."

"I'll call you," Chris said.

"Nice to see you," I said. He waved as he left. I got my change and went outside. I glanced down the hill and briefly watched Chris walk away. Then I continued up the hill toward home.

"Hey, Lisa," I said. "Sorry about that. What's up?"

"Essy called," Lisa said. "Tim told her he's been told to prepare an afternoon feast at Darby's for some military bigwigs."

"OK," I said. "Thanks for letting me know."

"Be judicious with this information, Katie," Lisa said. "Essy felt bad sharing it with me. She only told me because she knows I trust you and you felt it was important."

"I won't tell anyone," I said. "Thanks. I'll talk to you later."

"Later," Lisa said.

I headed for the sheriff's office. Deputy Sandra Dean let me in. She nodded conspiratorially at me. Almost winked. I caught Nate's eye as I came in, and he motioned me into his office.

I went in and closed the door behind me. Nate sat in his chair and motioned me to the other chair. I sat down, too.

"Nate, I need you to really try and find this girl," I said. "Something big is happening at Darby's on Tuesday, and I think the girl's kidnapping is related to that."

"But you said she told you it was all a joke," he said. "A hoax."

"I didn't believe her. I know you don't believe me, but could you do some investigating? Check out Margaret or Maggie Green. Danella Green. Or better yet, check out those guys."

He shook his head. "It would have been helpful if you'd brought the kid here right away. My guess is we could have cleared this up in minutes. I would have called her uncle, and he would have come and gotten her."

"I understand your viewpoint. You're probably right. There was something about her. I didn't think she was lying. I felt like I had to help her."

"You've never been wrong about that kind of thing?"

I couldn't tell if he was disgusted with or sympathetic to me. Maybe neither.

"When it comes to kids," I said, "I feel—Oh crap." I saw a clock on the wall. It was 2:30. I was supposed to be in Portland at 3:00 for dinner with my son and ex-husband.

"Jesus," I said. "I have to go. Now." I stood. "So you'll look into this? Maybe talk to Chris Darby? Double-check any Amber Alerts? Has there been a BOLO out on anyone like Mitchell Peterson or Danella Green?"

"I'll do what I do." He was standing, too, his hands on his hips. Now he almost looked concerned.

"My kid," I said. "I'm supposed to be meeting my kid."

I practically ran out of the sheriff's office and into the parking lot. I sprinted home. Got to the place on School Street where I could see my house—and the empty place where my car was supposed to be.

I had forgotten about the missing wheels. The car repair place must have come to pick it up.

Now how was I going to get to Portland?

I called Peter, but it went to voice mail.

"Peter, the back wheels on my car were stolen," I said. "I'm going to try to start Scott's old van."

I called Scott's phone, too, and it went to voice mail. "Scott, I'm sorry I'm going to be late. Someone stole the back wheels off my car. I'll try to get there another way."

I texted both of them. No one texted back.

I went around to the back of the house, unlocked the van,

and got inside. It stunk of disuse. I opened the windows, put the key in the ignition, and turned it.

The engine heaved a sigh or coughed up a fur ball or something, but it started. Yes! Of course it hadn't had an oil change in forever.

I didn't care. I put on my seat belt, backed the van up, and drove it out into the street. It hiccupped a bit, but it kept going. I got gas, and then I headed across the Bridge of the Gods and got on the freeway again.

Tried to accelerate on the ramp, but the van chugged along slowly, increasing its speed a bit at a time until it finally reached 45 miles per hour.

It would be a miracle if I made it to Portland without getting a ticket for going too slow.

"Come on," I said. "I've got to get to this on time."

That ship had sailed.

It was a lovely slow trip down the Columbia River Gorge, the silent old rock faces stoic witnesses to my tardiness. Wispy clouds floated alongside the rock faces here and there, like strange balloons as part of an even stranger parade.

I knew my goose was cooked.

I was nearly an hour late by the time I arrived at Peter's house. I ran up the steps and turned the door handle.

It was locked.

I knocked and rang the bell.

After a few moments, the door opened. Scott looked grim-faced. He didn't move out of the way to let me in. Instead he stepped outside and closed the door behind him. I wanted to reach out to him, brush the hair off of his forehead, give him a hug, something.

He looked furious.

"Did you get my message?" I said quickly. "Someone stole my wheels."

Christ that sounded lame. Like I was some kid trying to convince her parents she had a good excuse for fucking up.

"Yeah, I got it," he said, "a few minutes before you were supposed to be here."

"Come on, Scott," I said. "I'm sorry I didn't get here on time, but things happen. You can't blame me for someone stealing my wheels. The car is in the shop so I drove your van, and it doesn't like to go very fast."

Scott had stopped looking at me. He gazed beyond me and said, "Did your wheels get stolen today?"

He knew the answer.

"No," I said, "but I was taking care of things after that. Talking to the police. Calling the insurance company and the car repair place."

Scott looked at me. "It happened in the middle of the night," he said, "and you didn't fucking call us or even text us until two minutes before we were supposed to eat. Because you didn't think about me. It didn't occur to you to call me because you forgot all about me. You fucking forgot!"

He was shaking with rage. For a brief moment, I wondered if he wanted to hit me. I blinked. No. My son had no violence in him. I had never hit him. Children learned that kind of shit from their parents, and neither of us had ever hit him.

I was too accustomed to looking at everyone as a perp. At least, that's what Scott had told me when he was a teen. Maybe he was right.

"Look," I said. "There's a lot going on that you don't know about."

He threw up his hands. "Of course! There always is. And it's always more important than what's going on in your own goddamn family."

"But *you're* safe," I said. "There's this girl—"

"I don't want to hear it, Mom," he said. "I wanted you here

because I wanted to introduce you and Dad to my fiancée. I'm getting married. But you know what? I don't want you to meet her. I don't even want you at the wedding." He was yelling now, his spit speckling my face.

I stepped back from him.

"Oh fucking grow up, Scott!" I said. "You don't want your mother at your wedding because I was late for dinner? That's petty and childish, and you'll regret it for the rest of your life. But hey, you don't want me there, I won't be there. But take responsibility for that decision and your whole damn life. You've blamed me for everything that's wrong in your life for too long. Grow the fuck up! You had a good home, good parents. So what if I was distracted some of the time? Neither of my parents paid any attention to me when I was growing up, and now they call me about once a year. But I don't blame them for anything that isn't working in my life. That's all on me. *Me!* So grow up, Scott. We raised you better."

Then I turned around, went back down the steps, got in my van and drove away.

When I was out of view of the house, I stopped the car and pounded on the steering wheel. I roared. Again.

Nothing was going right.

I stopped somewhere and got something to eat, and then I headed back up the gorge.

Fifteen

By the time I got home, it was dark. I called the sheriff's office, but Nate was gone, and he hadn't left any messages on either of my phones.

I stood in the middle of my living room looking at all the boxes.

What the hell was I doing here? Why had I moved to this dying town? Why had I let them run me out of my job in the first place? Why had I put that girl in my car? Why had I felt responsible for her?

I rubbed my face.

I didn't care about whys. I had done it. End of story. I either trusted my instincts or I didn't.

I sank down onto the couch.

I did not trust my instincts. Not any longer. Wasn't sure when that had happened.

Why didn't I empty these fucking boxes and make this place a home? Or sell the house and move on? Maybe go down to Mexico. Spend some time in the Southwest. That had been my plan. When Peter and I were married, I figured we'd retire to the Southwest. Or Mexico. I wasn't fussy. As long as we were together. After Scott was born, I figured I'd be happy as long as the three of us were together.

But then Peter asked for a divorce, telling me I had left our marriage a long time ago. I never understood what the hell that meant. What I heard was, "You aren't good enough." He moved on so quickly. Some woman he claimed to be madly in love with. That didn't work out very well. Scott never liked her or her kids. I had been gleeful when Peter and the woman broke up. I half expected him to come back to me then. Maybe I had hoped a little bit.

He did not come back. Then I realized I didn't love him. Maybe I never had. I sometimes wondered—back then—if I had ever loved anyone. Besides Scott. I loved him with such a fierceness that sometimes I felt as if it was uncontainable. I didn't want him to be smothered by it—by me. So I held myself back from him.

I sighed. I should have smothered him with love and kisses and hugs. Maybe he'd be different today. Wasn't anything I could do about that now. Wasn't anything I could do to fix our relationship. Not if he was going to act like such a child.

Where the hell was Nate? He should have called.

I was exhausted. I didn't want to think about any of this. Christ.

I closed my eyes. I'd empty those boxes in a minute.

Once again, I fell right asleep. I woke up in darkness, choking and completely disoriented. It took me a second to realize I'd fallen asleep on the couch, sitting up—and the house was filled with smoke. I couldn't see a thing. I pulled my shirt off quickly and put it over my mouth and nose as I got up and headed for the front door. I tripped over a box and almost fell. I reached for the front door, grabbed the door knob, turned it and pulled. It opened a few inches and then wouldn't budge. I felt around. Boxes in front of the door? I hadn't done that.

I could barely breathe. I turned around and felt my way out of the living room to the kitchen, to the back door. It wasn't quite as smoky, but the door wouldn't open. Nothing blocked it, but I pulled and pulled. It was stuck.

"God damn it." I felt around for a jar of pencils I knew was on the shelf near the back door, and I smashed the jar through the window. Glass shattered and scattered. I reached through the broken glass and felt around for the outside door knob. There was a rope or something around the knob holding it closed. I pulled on it as smoke poured out of the broken window. Got it unhooked, and I opened the door and stumbled out into the back, my feet rolling on the driveway gravel so that I almost fell.

I heard sirens. Someone must have called the fire in. I looked at the house, and I didn't see any fire. Didn't hear any flames.

I ran around to the front of the house. The fire truck and EMS van pulled up. The firefighters jumped out.

"Anyone else in there?" one of them asked.

I shook my head.

"Front door unlocked?"

"Yes," I said, "but something's blocking it."

"Where's the fire?" he asked.

"I don't know," I said. "I woke up and the house was full of smoke."

The firefighters ran up the sidewalk and steps, opened the front door easily, and went inside. The paramedics took me to their truck. I sat on the edge of it as they checked my lungs while I breathed oxygen. I'd been around fires before. I knew I was OK.

But what the hell was going on?

A sheriff's SUV pulled up to the house and parked at an angle near the ambulance. The door opened and Nate stepped out. I pulled down the oxygen mask and called, "Now do you believe me that something's going on?"

Nate didn't say anything, but he headed toward the house.

The paramedic put the mask back on me. I looked back at the house. Nate was talking to one of the firefighters. He glanced at me once and then looked back at the fireman.

Soon enough, Nate walked over to me. He nodded to the two paramedics.

"How you doing, Dee, Bobbie? She OK?"

"She seems to be," one of the paramedics said. "Her lungs sound fine. She might want to go to emergency and check it out, though."

Nate nodded. "I need to talk to Kate alone."

Didn't have to tell them twice. The paramedics stepped away. I pulled off the mask and pushed myself off the edge of the truck.

"They didn't take the hose in," I said. "What's going on?"

"Let's wait for Chuck," Nate said.

"Nate—"

He put his hand up. I wanted to slug him. I wasn't a two-year-old.

I saw the firefighters coming out of the house. One of them motioned to wrap it up. Then he came over to us.

Nate said, "Chief Chuck Hoffman, this is Kate Kelly. This is her house."

"Ma'am, we found the source of the smoke," Hoffman said. "There was a fire in a trash receptacle. Started by a cigarette. Did you fall asleep smoking?"

"I don't smoke," I said. "I hate cigarettes. I fell asleep on the couch, nowhere near a garbage can."

Hoffman shrugged. "The fire was contained in the metal trash bin, lucky for you."

"What generated all that smoke?"

"Probably whatever was in the trash."

Nate and Hoffman looked at me. It was strange how they stood there. As though they needed me to say something else.

"Look," I said. "I did not start this. I don't smoke. I never smoked. I think it's a filthy habit. You won't find any evidence of cigarettes anywhere. Go ahead and look."

"We already did, ma'am," Hoffman said. "We found a pack of cigarettes on the nightstand in your bedroom."

"I don't fucking smoke," I said. He better quit calling me ma'am or I was going to punch him. That was how we talked to criminals: ma'am this and sir that. Granted, that was the way we talked to civilians, too, but there was something about his tone I did not like.

"Nate," I said. "I told you someone ran me off the road. Then they stole my tires. And now this. The doors were blocked! Something is going on."

"I don't think you'll even have smoke damage," Hoffman said. "But I'll have a report soon in case you decide to call your insurance company." He reached into his suit and pulled out a card. He held it out to me.

"Look, Mr. Hoffman," I said. "I am a retired cop. I know a set-up when I see one. I do not smoke. Ask anyone who knows me. I did not start this fire. You need to investigate."

"We don't have the personnel for that," Hoffman said. "We're all volunteer. Maybe the sheriff can help you." He held the card out again. I hesitated and then snatched it from him. He returned to the fire truck, and they soon pulled away.

The paramedics came up to us and one of them asked, "You good to go?"

I nodded. "Thank you."

Then they were gone, too, and Nate and I were standing in the road under a street lamp, all alone.

"Someone started that fire," I said. "Someone tried to run me off the road. Someone tried to keep me from leaving the house. Someone is trying to kill me."

"They're not doing a very good job of it," he said.

"What the fuck, Nate?" I said. "What's going on? I don't smoke. I did not start that fire."

"Look, Katie," Nate said. "I haven't seen you in years. I don't really know you. I know you got kicked off the police force. I don't know why. You come in with this cockamamie story about a girl claiming she'd been kidnapped but then she ran away from you, but there might be some big thing happening on Tuesday or Wednesday. Or something. You say you were run off the road. You say someone stole your tires."

"My fucking tires were gone," I said, pointing to the place where my car had been parked. "You saw my car."

"Now you fall asleep and your house fills with smoke, and there's no sign of a break-in."

"How the fuck would you know that?" I asked. "Have you done any investigating? Yeah, you're right. We don't know shit about each other. I presumed we knew something about one another because of—because of fucking history. But I guess not. You think I made all of this up? What about my personality would ever make you think I was capable of something like that? For your information, I was not fired. I did retire. They wanted me gone because I fucked my confidential informant. Nothing crazy. Just good old missionary position fucking. White collar has a nicer looking, nicer smelling bunch of crooks. I liked the look of one." I was so angry I wanted to scream. "Now get the fuck off of my property."

"We're standing in the middle of the street."

"Then get the fuck out of my life," I said. I walked away and went partway up the slope to my house, and then I turned around. "Now I remember why we were fighting that night Amanda was raped and murdered. We were fighting because you're a fucking asshole. If you hadn't been, maybe we would have stayed with the others. Maybe Amanda would be alive now. Did you ever think about that?"

And then I strode away, heading to the back of my house before I could hear his answer.

Fuck, fuck, fuck.

I saw the steel trash bin upside down in the gravel. I couldn't even remember where I had gotten the tall ugly thing. I kicked it, and it rolled away a few feet and then rolled back to me. I put my foot on it to stop it. It was potential evidence. I should be examining it, not kicking it.

It had not been a good day.

Sixteen

I saw the cop car drive away as I walked around the house, looking for evidence of a break-in. Beyond the broken glass near the back door, I didn't find anything suspicious. I went into the house and opened every door and window. It actually didn't smell much worse than times I'd burned something on the stove. I stood outside, anyway, under the back porch light, and called Debbie North. Figured since she was in the cleaning business, she might know who could come into the house and see what was smoke damaged and what wasn't.

"Doesn't sound like you'll have much smoke damage," she said after I told her what happened. "Though it's sometimes hard to tell. Maybe your clothes. I'd call the insurance company either way. They might pay to get your clothes cleaned, etc."

"I can put my jeans and shirts in the washer," I said.

Debbie laughed. "Suit yourself."

"Actually, I've got some stuff going on, so I don't have time to deal with this right now. Could you come over in the morning?"

"Sure," Debbie said. "I can rearrange my schedule. Leave the house open tonight. Put around plates of vinegar and onions, cut onions. They'll absorb a lot of the stink. You got a HEPA filter?"

"Somewhere," I said.

"Good," she said. "See you first thing in the morning."

After I got off the phone, I brought the trash can over to the porch light and looked at it. The inside was scorched, but the outside wasn't even hot. I sniffed inside it. Just smelled like something burnt.

Maybe there hadn't been as much smoke as I'd thought.

Too late to get fingerprints.

Not that I could do that, and the local cop thought I was making this all up.

Asshole, asshole, asshole.

Since I hadn't started the fire, that meant someone else had. How had they gotten inside the house? I hadn't changed the locks since I moved in. Stupid. The previous owners or the real estate company could have keys.

Probably simpler than that. I never locked the deadbolt so any run-of-the-mill crook could have slipped a credit card into the door and jimmied the lock.

But why? Was it the same person or persons who had run me off the road and stolen my wheels? Was this something to do with Danella and her mother? Seemed too coincidental not to have everything to do with them.

Maybe Danella was back in town and she had started the fire. She knew where I lived.

I leaned my head back.

Man. I couldn't sleep here tonight. Too stinky.

Plus I felt a little creeped out: Someone had broken into my house, and now, it didn't feel like mine.

Tomorrow in the light I would deal with it.

I went inside the house, found a couple bowls and poured vinegar in them. I cut up onions and put them around the house. Then I pulled out the HEPA filters and turned them on. I got my computer and a box with my papers in it. I locked the doors, but I left the windows open, even the one I had broken.

Then I got into the van and drove away from Beauty Falls.

Down the gorge once again. How many times had I driven up and down this stretch of road? This winding stretch of road. After Amanda was murdered, we had stayed in Beauty Falls only a few more days, long enough for the police to finish up with me. Long enough for Chris Darby's dad, Deputy Reilly, to ask all the questions he could ask.

I'd often wondered why Deputy Reilly had committed suicide. Chris had said he blamed himself. Why? He hadn't been there. I had been. I didn't blame myself. I *had* wondered if I could have done anything to prevent it. We probably all had. All of us who had survived and weren't the murderer.

Even Nate probably wondered.

I shouldn't have called him an asshole or brought up Amanda. He hadn't had anything to do with her murder either.

I shook myself. I didn't want to think about Amanda's murder. Too much going on. I wanted to find Danella and put it all behind me. And then I needed to put away those damn boxes and make myself a home.

I stopped the van in front of my old house. Peter's house.

I hurried up the stairs and knocked. I heard movement inside, the door opened, and Peter stood on the threshold.

He hesitated, and then he stepped outside and closed the door behind him.

"What are you doing here?" he asked.

"I had a fire in my house tonight," I said.

He frowned. "What?"

"Yeah. Someone broke into my house and tried to set it on fire. Yesterday someone stole my wheels and tried to run me off the road." I said it all at once. No pity. Just the facts.

"What would you like me to do with this information?" he asked.

"Peter, I've been burned out of my house."

OK. Slight exaggeration.

"You want to stay here?"

"Yes," I said. "Take a hint."

"Our son is here, and he is pissed off at you."

"Now is a good time to make up," I said.

"You are unbelievable," he said. "I'm not a hotel. I'm not your friend with benefits. You cannot stay here, especially given the circumstances."

"All right," I said. "I'm sorry I came by." I held up my hand. "I know where I stand. It's been a difficult couple of days."

"That's always your excuse," Peter said.

"My excuse for what?"

"For your lousy behavior! You couldn't be with us because you'd had a bad day because of something some criminal had done. Or because you had to rescue some child, some woman, some man. You couldn't be with us as yourself. You were always a cop."

I started back down the stairs. Then I turned and looked up at him.

"I don't know what you're talking about," I said. "I've never known what you're talking about. You said you wanted me to be with you as myself. Just us as a family. Well, that *was* me. That *is* me. I help people in trouble. You knew that about me. I was a public servant. We fucking serve. What you're actually saying is you wish I had been someone different." I shrugged. "You know what? That's your problem. That's Scott's problem. I loved you both. I brought home a paycheck. I took care of my son. He wanted a different kind of mother and you wanted a different kind of wife. That is not my fucking problem, and I'm not taking the rap for that any more."

I went to the van, without looking back at the house, and I tried to squeal away, but the vehicle just chugged. Gawd. I hoped Peter wasn't watching. Made for a lousy exit.

I drove to Jay's apartment. It was getting late, so I tapped lightly on the door. After a bit, the door opened. Jay stood there in his cream-colored silk pajamas. He was so beautiful it practically took my breath away.

I started to reach for him, and he glanced over his shoulder.

Oh. He must have company.

"Bad time?" I asked.

"Kind of," he said. "Everything OK?"

"Ah, sure," I said. "Sorry."

I hurried away. I heard him say in a loud whisper, "Katie, call me later."

No fucking way, I thought. I'm not going to be your second bootie call for the evening.

Crap.

I thought about getting a room at a motel. Hotel. Something.

Instead I drove home. I parked behind my house. I got into the backseat of the van, pulled my jacket over me, and closed my eyes.

"Fuck you all if you can't take a joke," I whispered.

I fell right asleep.

I awakened with a start. Someone was tapping on the van window. I opened my eyes. It was Debbie North.

I sat up—groaning, I was too old for this shit—and slid open the door and stepped into full on sunlight.

"Good morning," Deb said. "Tie one on last night?"

I laughed. Or groaned again.

"I wish," I said.

"I didn't think you were here," she said. "I waited for a bit, but it's freaking noon, so I got started without you. Just glanced in the van and saw you. You could have crashed at my place."

"I didn't want to impose on anyone," I said.

At least not anyone I didn't have sex with occasionally.

"Anyway," she said, "I dragged some of your boxes outside. The things in them don't smell, as far as I can tell, and I've got a good smeller. You want us to do your laundry, wash your clothes to be sure, clean up everything? It doesn't look like there's any permanent damage. I can't even smell that something was burning. House smells like vinegar and onion."

I rubbed my face.

"If there's no smoke damage," I said, "why would I need someone to clean up?"

Debbie shook her head. "Good grief, Katie. How long have you lived here? It looks like a motel room. The dust is pretty thick. Almost like no one lives there."

"I've cleaned the place," I said. "I'm just not obsessive about it."

"And those boxes," she continued. "You can barely walk from room to room. I can't do it today, but Sammy is my best worker. He could get everything spiffy, even unpack the boxes if you wanted."

"OK, look," I said, "he can come in and wash my clothes, wash anything that needs washing. Clean anything that needs cleaning. But don't open the boxes and put stuff away."

"Haven't decided if you're staying or not, eh?" Debbie said.

I shrugged. "Yeah, I guess."

"What you need is a wife," she said.

"Doesn't everyone," I said. "If you equate being a wife with being someone's maid. Which, of course, I don't."

"Me, neither, of course," Debbie said. She rolled her eyes.

We laughed.

Debbie said. "Anyway, Sammy can be your—"

"Helper," I offered. "What day is today?"

"Tuesday," Debbie said.

Tuesday. It was all supposed to be over by Wednesday. I had to find Danella today. Nobody else was looking for her, so I had to do it.

Somehow.

"Can you take care of this then?" I asked. "I need to be someplace."

Debbie laughed. "Sure. I'll get Sammy started, and then I'll be off. You OK having a stranger in your house?"

"I had a stranger in here last night," I said. "Why not now?" She looked vaguely confused. "Someone broke into my house last night. I'll tell you about it later. Thanks a lot, Deb. I appreciate it. Let me know if there's anything I can ever do for you."

"Get me out of a speeding ticket?"

"Couldn't even do that when I was a real cop," I said.

I got into the van, started it up, and headed out. Wasn't sure where I was going. I drove the short distance to Timbers, got out, and went inside. I waited for my eyes to adjust to the semi-darkness, and then I looked around. Good. Nobody there I knew.

I sat in a booth and ordered a burger, fries, and beer when the bartender came by. Then I sat staring at my phone. My life had been in a complete uproar since Saturday. Since Danella walked into my life. And then walked out of it. Now she was missing, and my son and ex-husband weren't speaking to me.

I suddenly wanted to talk to someone in my family. I seldom called so it would be strange if I contacted them out of the blue. I spoke with my brother Thomas a little more often than I did my parents, unless we were pissed at one another. He lived in New Mexico, lucky dog, and he was a bit more social than I was. He was older, had been away at summer school—summer college—when Amanda was killed.

Not that I measured everything in terms of where people were when Amanda was killed.

Or maybe I did.

Something about this summer was making me think about her more than usual. Wondering who she would have been had she lived. Would we still be friends? Probably not. We were barely friends then. I wasn't still friends with Sylvie. She had been a bit odd. We had not kept in touch after the murder.

I called my mom.

"Hey, Kate," she said when she answered. "How are you?"

"I'm OK, Mom. How are you and Dad? Enjoying the Arizona summer?"

"No!" she said. "Next year we'll come stay with you for the summer."

I laughed.

"I'm not kidding," she said.

I laughed again. "Hey, you're more than welcome."

"How's Scott?"

"Hates me again," I said. "So what else is new?"

"You sound restless." My mom and I weren't close, but she

did know things about me sometimes that other people didn't. "You retired too early, didn't you?"

"Probably," I said. I hadn't told them why I left the force.

"You were such a good police officer," she said.

How could she possibly know whether I was good or bad?

"Why would you say that, Mom?" I asked.

"Because you worked so hard," she said. "You cared so much about the people."

"Scott and Peter never liked that about me," I said. "They thought I put the job before our family. Before our life together. I thought it was *part* of our life together. They didn't feel that way."

"I know, honey," she said. "Some people are made to be wives and mothers, and some are not."

I didn't know why, but this particular statement stung. Not the wife part. I could not give a rat's ass about that. I didn't even know what the word wife meant. But the mother part. I thought I was a good mother.

"I wasn't cut out to be a mom," she said.

"You were a good mom," I said. I didn't believe that. She never seemed present in our lives. Was never sure why. "You and Dad kept us fed; we had a roof over our heads, all that."

"I didn't have the instinct some people have," she said. "Like that night Amanda was killed. I didn't have an instinct or intuition. You did. I think that's why you are a good mother."

Wait.

"What do you mean about me—about Amanda and me—having an instinct or intuition?"

"You remember," she said. "You didn't want to go out that night. You were nervous about going into the woods. You told me so."

"I don't remember anything like that."

"You said you had butterflies in your stomach," she said.

"You didn't want to go. That was about the time you had stopped talking to me about anything so it was remarkable—I remember it. Plus I read it in your diary. I told you to go and have some fun. See. No motherly instinct."

"I wasn't the one who was hurt."

"Sure you were, darlin'," she said.

"You read about this in my diary?" I asked.

"Yes," she said. "I read your diaries when you were a kid, to keep track of what you were doing. Do you still have them?"

"I do," I said. In one of my unpacked boxes. "Mom, I gotta go. But it was great talking to you. Love you both."

"Are you all right?"

"Yes, sure," I said. "Thanks, Mom."

I had to see that diary entry. I practically jumped out of the booth once I ended the call.

"Make it to go," I called to the bartender, "and I'll be back to pick it up."

I paid him, and then I was out the door. I didn't bother to start the van. I ran the rest of the way up the hill and sprinted home.

The front door was wide open.

I went inside. Heard someone humming. A male someone.

"Hello," I called. "Sammy?"

A youngish good-looking kid of about twenty-five came out of my bedroom with an armload of shirts. He smiled when he saw me.

"Is Deb gone already?" I asked.

"Yes," he said. He had a slight accent. Couldn't place it. "I started. That OK?"

"That's great," I said. "Don't let me disturb you. I need to find a box with my journals in them." I glanced around the living room.

I didn't have a clue. I should have marked the boxes before I packed them.

"Is that like a diary?" Sammy asked. "Because there's a box near the closet with books in them called 'record.' I was looking for clothes that might have been in the smoke."

"Hey, I have no secrets," I said. "Except for my entire life."

"Me, too." He kept walking toward the laundry room. How had this young man gotten so comfortable and familiar in my house after a few minutes and I'd been living there for months and I didn't feel at home?

I walked into the bedroom and went to the box Sammy had indicated. I dug around until I found the journal from the same year as when Amanda was murdered. I flipped through it to June 25.

"Supposed to go out to the woods with Nate and Sylvie, Doug, Amanda, and Andy tonight. Hope Andy doesn't hit on me again. Creeps me out. Not sure us all going is a good idea. Something seems different. Amanda is so young. Maybe I'll blow off the whole thing and stay home."

That was the end of the entry. I turned to the next page. It was blank. I flipped to the end of the record book. It was all blank.

The day of Amanda's murder was the last day I wrote in my journal.

Was that the last day of my life that I had been self-aware? I'd been a teenager. I hadn't had time to be self-aware. I had been self-*conscious*.

I stared at my handwriting. It looked so different from mine now. I could actually read it back then.

I closed my eyes. I was starting to remember talking to my mother that day. Saying I wasn't sure I wanted to go.

She had encouraged me. Which was natural. I had a tendency to be a loner. She wanted me to make friends.

But I'd had a feeling about Andy. I hadn't liked him, and I didn't understand why Nate and Doug hung around with him.

Nobody had suspected something was off with him except me, and maybe Deputy Reilly. Reilly had killed himself.

I hadn't.

I hadn't trusted my instincts then. I sure as hell was going to trust them now. It didn't matter if Nate Gunderson and Fire Chief Hoffman thought I was making up shit. Didn't matter if my son and ex-husband weren't speaking to me. None of it mattered: I knew Danella Green had told me the truth. Now she was in trouble, and I had to save her: one way or another.

Seventeen

I got my takeout dinner, and then I drove all over town looking for the red Impala while I ate. Distracted driver. In the old days, I would have pulled over someone who was eating and driving and lectured them on distracted driving. I gave myself a lecture—and kept driving. I didn't find the Impala.

Then I drove to Danella's house. I parked the van a short distance from it again, and then I walked the rest of the way. I saw two or three other people walking around the 'hood, so I wasn't out of place. No cars in the drive or anywhere else. I hurried up the driveway and then went around the house to the back and retrieved the key from the stone rabbit. I unlocked the back door again and went inside. Shut the door quietly behind me and locked it again. Stuffed the key in my back pocket.

The house throbbed with silence. I looked around the kitchen first, again, to see if I'd missed anything before. Opening and shutting empty drawers and cupboard doors. I leaned in to see if anything was written on the inside of the cupboards.

Nothing.

Mother Hubbard's cupboards were bare.

Or something like that.

Went to the living room. I'd already looked under the couch cushions, but I hadn't slid my hand down between the armrest and the springs. Mostly because that was gross.

I sucked it up, threw off the cushions, and pushed my fingers down into that creepy darkness. Felt crumbs and a piece of paper. I pulled out the paper. It was a piece of a wrapping of a Bigfoot Fruit Leather. I smiled. "Danella was here," I said.

I went to the other end of the couch and stuck my fingers down there. More crumbs. Another piece of paper. Bigger than the last one. I pulled it out. It was part of a grocery list: celery, bagels, hummus, cotton balls. On the other side of the paper someone had scribbled Maggie Green. Only whoever it was had started to write another letter before she wrote the G.

I took the paper into the kitchen where the light was better, and I held it up to the window.

It looked like a capital P. But she had crossed it out. Why? Because her middle name started with P? Maggie P. Green.

Wait. Mitchell Peterson said he was Danella's uncle. Maybe he was. Maybe Maggie's maiden name was Peterson. Maybe her real name was Maggie Peterson, and Maggie Green was an alias or a married name.

This was the lead I needed. I straightened the couch cushions. Then I left the house quickly, hurried to the van, and cranked it up. I headed for Darby's. I was more certain now than ever that Maggie Green existed and her daughter had been kidnapped to force her to commit some kind of crime.

I drove to the river and parked in front of the headquarters of Darby's. Looked around for the red Impala. It wasn't there.

I got out of the van, walked up the steps, and then went inside the bare and industrial-looking building.

A woman behind a desk said, "May I help you?"

I smiled my friendliest smile. "Yes, I'm here to see Maggie Peterson." I looked around then, pretending to be perfectly at home.

"I'm sorry, but no Maggie Peterson works here."

I looked back at the receptionist. What? But I was so certain I'd been right. Maggie. Marge. Margaret.

Peggy. I had forgotten that Peggy was a nickname for Margaret.

"I'm sorry," I said. *"Peggy* Peterson. I've called her Maggie since we were kids."

The woman said, "Who may I say is here?"

"Maggie Green," I said. I smiled. "Yes, we're both Margarets."

The receptionist pushed some buttons or typed a message. I looked around and wondered what I'd say if someone called security.

After about a minute, the receptionist stood and said, "Here's a badge. Please wear it until you leave, and don't forget to sign in and out."

I took the badge from her. It read VISITOR. I clipped it to my shirt, and then I signed the ledger, writing carefully: Maggie Green.

"Follow me," she said. She punched a code into a keyboard next to a closed door beside her desk. When the keyboard blinked green, she opened the door. I followed her into a large area with high ceilings and dozens of cubicles made up of gray carpeted walls. An old biplane and what looked to be a small drone hung from the rafters—away from the cubicles.

I followed the receptionist down a carpeted passageway, past several offices and cubicles. The cubicles were all decorated with photographs and postcards. I heard several people on the phone talking animatedly. I didn't look toward the offices. I hoped Chris Darby wasn't around. It would be difficult to explain my presence.

Soon I was standing next to Peggy Peterson's cubicle. I could tell it was hers by the name on the carpeted dividers. The cubicle itself was bare except for a couple of chairs, and a desk with a laptop on it, along with some papers, a phone, and her cell phone. The receptionist smiled at me and then turned and walked away.

The woman at the desk in the bare cubicle turned and looked at me. Yep. She was the woman in the photo Danella had shown me: Maggie Green.

"Who are you?" she asked. "I don't know you." She was a cool cucumber. She didn't look afraid, just perplexed. But people on the run could become adept actors.

"We might want to speak outside," I said.

"I can't," she said. "I've got work to do."

She squinted at me, as though she was trying to figure out who the hell I was.

"I know your daughter, Danella," I said.

She motioned me to the chair near her. I sat in it and moved closer to her.

"I know she's been kidnapped," I said.

"I don't know what you're talking about," she said. "My daughter is in Tennessee with her grandmother."

"I know your brother Mitchell Peterson has taken her, and he is blackmailing you to do something. I haven't figured out what."

"Look," she said. "I don't know who you are. My daughter is fine. I don't have any brothers."

"I know something big is happening this afternoon," I said. "Are they testing a weapon of some kind? Did he have you program it to blow up? If he did, I can help you. I'm a retired cop. I can get you protection."

"This is ridiculous," Peggy/Maggie said. "I couldn't program a drone to blow up if I wanted to. They aren't weaponized."

"I want to speak to her then," I said. "I want to speak to Danella."

The woman rolled her eyes. "Don't scare her," she said. She picked up her phone, pressed a few buttons, and then put it up to her ear.

"Mom, put on Danella," she said. "Someone here wants to speak to her."

She handed the phone to me. I listened. After a couple of seconds, I heard a young girl say, "Hello."

"Hello," I said. "Who is this?"

"This is Danella," she said. "Who is this?"

"I'm a friend of your mother's," I said. "My name is Maggie Green."

"Hello, Maggie Green."

She didn't sound anything like Danella, and she didn't recognize the name Maggie Green.

I handed the phone back to Peggy/Maggie.

"Be good for grandma," she said. "I'll call you later."

She ended the call and looked at me.

"Are you satisfied?" she asked me.

"No," I said. "That is not Danella."

"I think someone has been pulling your leg," she said. "Now could you excuse me? I've got work to do."

She picked up the phone, hit a button, and said, "My visitor is ready to leave."

Once again, I was stumped. Was she lying? Or had Danella been lying?

Had I lost the ability to spot a liar?

I got up. The receptionist—or whatever she was—showed up, and I followed her down the corridor again. I glanced back at Peggy/Maggie, but she was looking at her computer.

How could I call her a liar and save her child without spooking her, causing her to run? I still didn't know what the hell was going on.

We reached the door. The receptionist opened it and waited for me to go through.

"Oh, I left my purse," I said. "I'll be right back."

I turned around before she could say anything, and I hurried down the hall, toward Peggy's cubicle.

When I got there, I stepped out of the receptionist's view, and I opened the bottom drawer of Peggy's desk.

"What are you—"

I pulled out a framed photograph of her and her daughter: my Danella.

I slammed the picture on the desk. "That is the girl I met. The girl who spent the night at my house."

"What?"

I could hear the receptionist coming down the hallway again. The swish, swish of her corduroy slacks.

"You better tell me the truth or when she gets here, I am calling the cops."

Peggy pushed her chair over a bit and leaned back, "It's OK, Rachel. I'll take her out."

The woman nodded, turned around, and headed back.

"I can't talk here," Peggy said.

"Walk me out," I said.

"Sure," she said loudly. "It would be nice to get a breath of fresh air."

I took the photograph. She started to protest, but then she must have thought better of it because she said nothing. Instead she headed down the corridor.

"Hey, Peggy," more than one of her coworkers said.

She smiled and nodded at each of them. She was good at this game, whatever it was.

She opened the door to the reception area, and I stepped through.

"I'll be right back," Peggy said to the receptionist. The two of us headed toward the door.

"Wait," the receptionist called. She looked at me. "You forgot to sign out."

I went over to her clipboard, and I signed out.

Then we stepped outside and went to my van. When we were both inside, Danella's mother looked away from me and said, "Drive and park away from here, with the van facing away from the building. They might be able to read our lips."

I started up the van and drove about a block away, facing the back of the hardware store, where no one could see us unless they were trying.

"Tell me what's going on," I said. "Danella said the kidnappers promised to bring her back tomorrow if all went well. What's happening?"

Peggy shook her head. "I have to do exactly what he says. Or he will hurt her, and he will hurt me. He is a very dangerous man."

"Who is he? The competition? Some kind of terrorist?"

"He's my ex-husband," she said.

"What the fuck?" I said. "What's with Maggie Green and Peggy Peterson?"

She shook her head. "I've been running from him for almost

ten years, but I didn't get my name legally changed. I had to use my real social security number and the name that's on it. So here at work, that's who I had to be. Everywhere else I was Maggie Green, and she was Danella Green. If anyone ever asked, I'd say one was my married name and the other was my maiden name. But no one ever asked. No one ever noticed in big towns. It's been harder here. Anyway, he found me. Found out where I was working. He knew they were working on something new and were up for a big government contract. He wanted me to program a glitch into the new drone, a glitch that would occur during the test early tomorrow morning. They're showing everyone around later on this afternoon, but the test is tomorrow. When it goes awry, then he was going to blackmail them into giving him money to fix it."

"How would that work?"

"I could deprogram it—fix it, if you will—from a remote location."

"Won't they figure out who did it in the first place?"

She shook her head. "I don't think so. When we were younger, I was a pretty good hacker. We made our living that way for a while. Until I grew up. Until I had Danella. He didn't want to go legit. It pissed him off I wouldn't do it anymore. He hit me on occasion. One day he shook Danella, and that was the last straw. I ran."

"Maggie, Peggy, whatever your name is—"

"Maggie."

"This could be considered treason," I said. "Darby's is essentially a government operation now."

She shook her head. "No. No one will get hurt. The new drones just won't work as expected."

"How do you know?" I asked. "Maybe he has another hacker coat-tailing on your hack to do something worse."

"He's never been political," she said. "Just greedy."

"Maybe things have changed in ten years."

"No!" she said. "Besides, hacks don't work that way." The concern on her face belied that statement.

"Who did I talk to on the phone?" I asked.

"My mother," she said. "Since this happened, I've spoken to her a couple of times. First time in years. Trying to figure out what to do. The girl is my niece—in case someone came looking."

"I can help you," I said. "If you know where Danella is, I can get her."

She shook her head. "I have no idea where she is," she said. "After they took her, they came and cleaned everything out of the house, put it in storage, put me up in a hotel. Figured if Danella did escape, she'd have nowhere to go. They never told me she escaped."

"She came to me when I was in the woods," I said. "I was going to take her to the cops, but Mitchell's car was in the parking lot at the sheriff's office, and Danella got scared. So I kept her, trying to figure out what to do. She ran away, called them, and went back to them. She didn't want to put you in danger."

"You had her and you let her go?" Maggie said.

"It never occurred to me she'd run away," I said. "She has a mind of her own."

"You must have seen that right away," she said. "If she thought she was putting me in danger, she'd do anything."

"I told her we had to go to the police, and she was afraid Mitchell would find out. Does she know he is her father?"

"No," Peggy said. "I don't want her to know."

"Would he hurt her?"

"Yes," she said. "I don't know. He would definitely take her from me, and I'd never see her again. I mean, why not? I did it to him. Not that he cared about us in any true sense. But now I've got to get back to work. I haven't finished the hack. You need to leave it alone. You tried to help. It didn't work. The best thing is for me to do what Mitchell wants. If the police get involved, I'll go to jail, and he'll take off with Danella. This isn't your business, so you need to butt out."

"I'm an ex-cop," I said.

"Ex," she said. "And you lost Danella the first time. I don't think I'm going to trust you to find her a second time. Now take me back."

I started up the van again and drove slowly back to Darby's.

"Who are the men in the blue van?" I asked when I stopped the vehicle.

"What?" she asked. "I don't know anything about them. Give me back my photograph."

"No."

"You can't go to the police," she said.

"I should have gone to the police the very first thing," I said. "I'm keeping the photograph."

She opened the door to the van and got out. She looked up at me. "Think about Danella. What's most important is that she gets home safely. Do you think the police can accomplish that?" She didn't wait for an answer. She slammed the door and walked away.

I turned the van around and headed home. I sighed. I didn't think the local police could do anything.

So what should I do?

Almost by rote, I drove to my house. My car was still gone—I needed to call the repair shop—but a blue van was parked outside the house.

I took my van up the drive and around to the back of the house. I retrieved my gun from the glove compartment, double-checked the safety, and then stuffed the gun into the back waistband of my jeans. Then I went into the house through the back door. Sammy was in the kitchen, cleaning and washing dishes.

The house already smelled and looked better, brighter. Freaking happier. It didn't have anything to do with the lack of smoke.

"Will you marry me?" I asked.

Sammy grinned. "We'd have to ask my husband first. He doesn't like to share."

"There's always some wrench thrown in to prevent my ultimate happiness," I said. "How about I hire you instead?"

"I think we can work something out," he said. "You've got friends outside."

"I don't think they're friendly, actually," I said.

"I've heard stories of those blue vans," he said, his accent suddenly thicker. "They take people up in their spacecrafts or something."

I looked at him.

He grinned again. "Naw. I don't think so. I've been in those spacecrafts and them up there are much better dressed."

I smiled.

I hoped he was joking.

"Oh, it will be fun to pull your legs," he said.

"Leg," I said. "Pull my leg."

"Not the way I do it."

I laughed. "I've got to see what these bozos want from me."

As I walked into the living room, Sammy called, "I can help you unpack later if you want!"

I went through the living room and opened the front door. I stepped outside and sat on my porch, waiting. After a minute or more, the van doors opened, and two men emerged, one from the driver's side, one from the passenger side. They were the men I had seen at Danella's house. As they walked up the steps toward the house, I stood so that I was above them, and I said, "That's far enough. What do you want?"

They both took out badges and flashed them. "I'm FBI

Agent Smith," the brown-haired man said, "and this is FBI Agent Jones." He was indicating the darker-haired man.

"You the ones who ran me off the road?" I asked.

"We wanted to talk with you," Smith said.

"Easier ways to do that. I didn't think the FBI made a habit of putting civilians at risk." Then I laughed. "Oh, wait, I forgot. They do."

Jones looked irritated.

"Why steal my tires?" I asked. "Or try to burn down the house?"

Smith shook his head. "I have no idea what you are talking about, ma'am."

"Don't ma'am me," I said. "My entire life has been turned upside down. Now you all show up. My guess is you are behind it all. Tell me what the fuck is going on."

"May we go inside?" Smith asked. He was doing all the talking, so I guessed Jones was short, pale, and wordless.

"No," I said, "not without a fucking warrant."

"You've got to lay off the Peterson case." Smith.

"What are you talking about?"

"We know that Mitchell Peterson has coerced his ex-wife into reprogramming the government drone." Jones this time. So he did have a voice.

"You knew about this?" I said. "And you know how he coerced her?"

"We do," Smith said.

"Do you have Danella then?" I asked. "If you know she's been kidnapped, then you've gotten her back."

"No," Jones said. "He didn't kidnap her. His ex-wife never legally got full custody of her. She could be charged with kidnapping actually."

"But he is a dangerous man," I said.

"We know," Smith said. "But we know where they are. The girl is safe. He is her father, after all."

"That is the stupidest thing I've ever heard a law enforcement officer say," I said.

"You have to stay out of it," Smith said. "We're trying to smoke out the leader of this group. We think he might be working with some terrorist cell."

"Maggie said he was working alone," I said. "She says he is trying to extort money."

"We don't think that's the case," Jones said.

My heart started racing. If Mitchell Peterson was part of a terrorist group, then Danella could be in serious danger.

"You've got to get Danella out of there!"

"We've got them under surveillance," Smith said. "You need to stay away from the girl and the mother. If you don't, we will make certain you lose your pension."

"You can't do that," I said.

"We can," Jones said. "Ever heard of the Patriot Act? Or Homeland Security? Presidents come and go, but we're still here. If we charge you with domestic terrorism or interference with a government operation or both, you will lose everything."

"I never liked you," I said. I looked at Smith. "I cannot believe that your superiors know that a child has been kidnapped, that you know the whereabouts of this child, and that it's acceptable that you are not saving her."

"She has not been kidnapped legally," Smith said. "She is his child."

"She is not a possession, you asshole," I said. How to win friends and influence people. "That man you say is safe beat and tortured his own wife."

The two men stared at me.

"You interfere, we will arrest you," Smith said. "If you go to Darby's again, if you go anywhere near that child, we will arrest you, and you will lose everything. Your son has disowned you. What's going to happen when he finds out you are a terrorist?"

My fingers twitched. I was so tempted to reach for my gun. In my entire time on the police force, I had never felt this kind of anger.

"Get off my property, you motherfuckers," I said. "You make me sick."

"We've told the sheriff the same thing," Jones said. "He's to arrest you on the spot."

"Good for him," I said.

"Be a patriot," Smith said. "Do the right thing."

"You think you're patriots?" I said. "You aren't. You're supposed to be upholding the laws and protecting the constitution. You're not. You are attempting to blackmail and intimidate me."

"Just doing our jobs," Smith said.

"Fuck you," I said. Then I screamed, "Get off my property!"

The two men backed up, turned around, and got into their van. A moment later, they drove away.

Eighteen

I sat on my porch for a long time. I thought about Scott, Peter, Jay, Don. The only one of them who would talk to me was Don, but I didn't want to drag him any further into this, possibly get him fired. And Nate. Apparently he was now part of the long arm of the FBI. Besides, what I'd said to Nate last night—about him being responsible in some way for Amanda's murder—that was pretty unforgivable.

I was on my own. Which was how I usually arranged things. It was easier that way.

Or something.

Sammy called me in for dinner. Couldn't believe it was that

late. He had somehow put together a meal from what I had in the fridge. I ate it, barely noticing, and half-listened while he talked. When we were finished, he took the plates away and did the dishes.

"The house looks great," I said. "You've been a lifesaver today. Is there anything I can do for you?"

"Yes! Go get me dessert so I can go home. I need to finish a few things here, but I love those tiny little cheesecakes from A&J's. One cherry for me, and one raspberry for Martin. And get garbage bags for yourself."

I didn't know what else to do at that point.

"OK."

I usually walked to the store: It was two blocks away. For some reason, I went out the back door, into dusk, and got into the van.

The store seemed too bright. I blinked several times while I tried to get my bearings. Breathed deeply and settled into place. I went to the aisle with the garbage bags, and I picked up a box. Then I went back to the deli and bakery and found the little cheesecakes Sammy was talking about. I headed to the cash register. I got into the line where my friend Thelma was checker. As I stood waiting, I looked around. I noticed the Bigfoot Fruit Leather stand at the end of the aisle near me. It was almost empty. The only flavor left was apricot.

I felt suddenly very calm and excited all at the same time. I recognized this feeling.

The man in front of me moved out of the way. Thelma smiled at me.

"Hiya, Katie."

"Hey, Thelma." I dropped my items on the conveyor belt, and she began ringing them up. "What happened to all the Bigfoot Fruit Leathers?" I asked.

"Joseph Miller stopped by and bought most of them," she

said, "a few hours ago. He's got some folks staying in his cabin up Baker Road, and they had a hankering for the Bigfoot Fruit Leathers, he told me."

I knew that cabin. When my folks were getting our cabin remodeled one summer, we stayed in Baker's place for a few weeks. I grinned. I couldn't help it. Maybe I had spent all those summers here and then returned to this little dying town for this moment in time.

I quickly paid, thanked Thelma, and ran out to the van. I drove home too fast. I ran into the house and gave Sammy the grocery bag.

"Is there a fire?"

"Might be," I said. "Thanks, Sammy. I've got to go. Lock the door behind you when you're finished."

I hurried into my bedroom, stripped off my clothes, and put on black pants, a black shirt, and a black skull cap. I strapped on my holster and gun, grabbed my phone, and left the bedroom.

"I don't think I want to go to whatever nightclub you're headed to," Sammy said. "Be careful!" he shouted as I hurried out the back door. When I got into the van, I called Nate.

"Hello," I said when he answered. "First, I'm sorry about what I said. You are in no way responsible for what Andy did to Amanda."

"I need to apologize to you," he said. "FBI agents were here. Apparently everything you said must be true."

"I guess it must be if the FBI says so," I said. "No, wait, we don't have time for this. Wait ten minutes and then go down to Darby's and make sure Peggy Peterson is there safe and sound and then text me."

"OK," he said.

I ended the call, put the phone on vibrate, and pushed it into my back pocket. Then I started the van. I drove slowly up the hill to Connor Street, one street over from Baker. I didn't see any blue van, red Impala, or any Fed-looking vehicles. I parked in front of the backyard neighbors to the Miller cottage. My brother and I had run through their backyard on our way out dozens of times the summer we stayed at the cottage. Mitchell and Herman wouldn't see my van even if they happened to be looking for it.

I got out of the van and looked around. Several of the houses on the block were lit up, with cars in the driveways. That was good. If I ran into trouble, I could get help—at least someone would call the police.

I cut across the backyard of the house, running in the dark, jumping over the remnants of small blackberry bushes, until I reached the edge of the Miller cottage yard. My eyes had adjusted to the dark, and I didn't see anyone outside. Fortunately, the wind was blowing, so any sound I made would be drowned out. Even so, I moved stealthily and quietly toward the cottage, stepping over branches and roots on the forest floor, as I headed toward a lighted window. When I got there, I carefully flattened myself against the side of the house near a window. I listened. Heard muffled voices. Then slowly, carefully, I moved myself until I could look in the window.

Herman and Mitchell were sitting at the kitchen table with their backs to the window, fortunately, with Danella sitting across from them. Mitchell was the black-haired one, I remembered; Herman had wispy red hair. Looked like they were playing cards. Danella was safe. Yes. Thank god, I wasn't too late. If she looked over, she would be able to see me.

When the two men were looking at each other and not at Danella, I took off my cap and waved it in front of the window

This kid was cool as ice. She saw me and briefly smiled with relief. I mouthed to her, "Stay near the side door."

She frowned, not understanding.

Mitchell and Herman looked at her.

"What's the matter with you?" Mitchell asked. He glanced toward the window, and I quickly stepped back.

"My stomach hurts," I heard her say.

"Again?" It was a different voice. Must be Herman's. "Man. It's your diet. You and those frigging fruit leathers."

My phone vibrated. I pulled it out of my pocket and crouched down. I read a text from Nate: "Peggy safe."

I texted back, "Come to the Miller cottage on Baker in three minutes, sirens blaring."

I turned off the phone and put it back in my pocket. I returned to the window and waited until the men were looking down again. Danella looked at me, and I pointed toward the side door. She nodded. I hoped she understood I wanted her to get to the side door once I distracted the men.

I ducked down and ran quietly to the area near the front door. I found newspapers, a big box of matches, and a bucket. I wadded a couple of the newspapers and stuffed some in the bucket. Then I lit two matches and dropped them onto the paper. They caught fire immediately. I put the bucket near the window where I knew the men would have to see it.

Almost immediately I heard someone yell, "Fire!"

I raced around to the side door. I heard the front door open at the same time the side door opened and Danella came running through it.

I grabbed her. "Your mother is safe. Come with me." I took her hand. "If we get separated for any reason, you run to the nearest house with lights on and call the police."

I heard someone swearing at the front of the house. I held tightly to Danella's hand and looked back through the forest. Coming in it hadn't looked so dark. Hand in hand, we started running through the woods, going back the way I had come.

But suddenly, I heard a man's voice almost in my ear yell, "Danella!"

I quickly pulled her ahead of me and yelled, "Run!"

I heard Danella running, heard the twigs breaking ahead of me, but I couldn't see her yet. I thought about drawing my weapon, but it was too dark. I glanced behind me and saw a figure coming toward me. I ran, keeping myself between Danella and the man. He wasn't going to get her. No matter what. I couldn't let him get ahead of me because then I couldn't draw my gun.

As I ran, I could smell the smoke from the fire I had started, could hear Danella's breath—she was still too close—had she fallen? I could hear the man right behind me. I had to go faster, faster.

"Danella!" Now the man was roaring. He sounded dangerous. The other man was yelling, too, cursing the fire.

I had to get to her. There, I saw her emerging from the woods. She looked back, but she kept running. *Good job. Good job.*

I could hear the man breathing behind me, and I sped up.

Suddenly, my foot caught on a root, and I tripped. Fell flat on my face, onto the forest floor. I landed with a grunt. Could smell the earth, the damp humus. And the man—must be Mitchell—was almost on top of me. He was going to jump right over me and get to Danella again before I could do anything. Should have had the police come sooner.

Suddenly I felt a boot on my back, pushing me into the ground. My hands dug into the ground, flailed around. I couldn't reach my gun. Even if I could, I wasn't in a strong position. He could wrestle it from me and use it on me. I felt around on the ground for something. Anything.

"Who the fuck are you?" the man said.

My fingers found another root. Leaves. Twigs.

I felt the pressure lessen on my back. He was going to keep

going while I was sprawled helpless on this forest floor smelling dirt.

Fuck that.

My fingers found a piece of wood. Couldn't tell what it was but it had heft. In one smooth motion, I grabbed the wood, twisted around, and bashed the man as hard as I could in the legs.

He cried out and dropped to his knees.

I sprang up. He grabbed one of my legs. I swung the piece of wood with both hands and hit him in the side of the face. He screamed and fell forward.

"Mitchell!" the other man cried.

Christ. Didn't want to deal with him.

I heard the sirens now. They were close.

Mitchell groaned. I dropped the piece of wood next to him and said, "Get out of my town."

I ran into the brush, and I kept running until I was in the street. I looked around. I saw Danella on the porch of one of the houses. I ran to her, and we put our arms around one another. An older man and woman were escorting her into the house.

"Katie Kelly," the old man said. "It is nice to see you. Is this your daughter?"

I could see the flashing lights of the cop cars through the woods now.

"Mr. Stevens?" I said. "Mrs. Stevens? Wow. I can't believe you recognize me. I haven't see you since I was a kid. Can you take Danella inside and don't let anyone in except me or Nate Gunderson?"

"No!" Danella said. "Don't leave me!"

"It's OK, honey," I said. "They'll take care of you. It's almost over."

I watched until the three of them went into the house. Then I hurried to my van and drove around the block to the Miller house. I saw two deputies I didn't know putting Mitchell and Herman in separate squad cars.

Nate came out of the house.

"You OK?" he asked. He actually looked concerned.

"Fine," I said. "I have Danella. Can I take her to her mother?"

"Sure," he said. "I had Deputy Dean take her to my office. You're gonna have some questions to answer. So is she."

I nodded. "I know. I know I should have trusted you sooner. Doesn't come easy for me."

He shrugged. "Glad it worked out. Let's go watch the happy ending."

I laughed. "Yep, my favorite part."

I got Danella from the Stevens house. I promised them both I'd come over for tea one of these days. Danella and I got into my van.

"What a piece of crap this is," she said.

I laughed. "It is indeed."

She looked at me. "Is it all over?"

"You're safe," I said. "What will happen with your mom, I don't know, but she's safe from Mitchell and Herman."

"Pretty clever of me getting them to buy all the Bigfoot Fruit Leathers, wasn't it?" she said. "I knew if you saw that, you'd figure out I was still here and you'd find me. I knew it. I knew the first time I saw you that you could save me and my mom."

"Dumb luck," I said.

"The more you pay attention, the luckier you get," Danella said.

"You got that right, kid."

She laughed and relief flooded my body.

"Can I see my mom now?"

"You sure can."

After that, things got crazy. Danella and Maggie were immediately reunited, and Herman and Mitchell were arrested. It was still against the law to blackmail someone even if the blackmail scheme ultimately failed. Which it did. Maggie easily fixed the glitch. Darby's chose not to prosecute her. Instead, they wanted to give her a raise.

We were all in the news for a couple of cycles. How a retired ex-cop saved Darby's and the nation from disaster while also saving a young kidnap victim. I didn't save the nation from disaster—the drones weren't weaponized. Chris Darby hadn't been lying about that.

I didn't see Smith and Jones again, so I couldn't find out if they were the ones who had stolen my tires and set a smoke fire in my house. Mostly I wanted to know why.

In any case, Chris Darby was so happy with me he wanted to hire me as an investigator for Darby's.

"Doesn't the government do all of your investigating?" I asked him.

He shrugged. "They do some, but mostly we vet our own people. How about we keep you on a retainer? I bet it'll beat your police pension. I like you. I like having someone to talk to."

"I'm not much of a talker," I told him.

Still I agreed to work for him, for a while, once I got my investigator's license.

I hired Sammy to come cook and clean for me—at least on occasion.

Maggie Green decided to return to Tennessee with Danella. With Mitchell behind bars, she could go see her family.

Maggie and Danella came over one day to say good-bye.

Danella jumped out of the car and raced toward me. I opened my arms to her, and we embraced one another tightly.

Maggie held out her hand to me when Danella and I parted.

"Thanks again," she said. "I'm glad you didn't listen to me."

"I rarely listen," I said. "Ask anyone."

"I'll leave you two to say good-bye," she said. "Take your time." She smiled, then turned and went back to the car.

Danella and I sat on the front steps together. She leaned against me slightly.

"You saved my life," she said.

"I wish you hadn't run away," I said.

"My mom says I don't listen either," she said.

"But you pay attention," I said. "That's very important. You're good at noticing things, too."

"Did you know Mitchell was my biological father?" Danella asked.

"Your mom told me," I said. "I'm so sorry about that."

She shrugged. "Got nothing to do with me," she said. "A sperm doesn't make him a real father."

"That's for sure," I said.

Another car pulled into the driveway. I squinted. Looked like Peter's car. First the passenger door opened and Scott stepped out. Then the driver's door opened. Peter got out and waved, but he didn't come any closer. He didn't look pissed anymore.

I waved back.

"You remember my ex-husband, Peter," I said quietly to Danella. "And that's my son, Scott."

"He's cute," she said.

"He's way too old for you."

"No lie. I said he was cute. I didn't say I wanted to marry him."

I laughed. We both stood as Scott approached.

"Hi, Mom," he said.

"Hello, Scott."

"This must be Danella Green," he said, holding out his hand to her. "I've seen you on the news." They shook hands.

"You have a great mother," Danella said.

Scott smiled grimly.

Danella put her arms around my waist, and we hugged one another. I looked down at her. "Keep in touch," I said.

We both wiped tears away. Then Danella let me go and ran back to her mother. I waved, they waved, and then Peter had to move his car so they could leave. I looked back at Scott.

"I'm sorry, Mom," he said. "I should have listened to you. I should have understood."

"Why?" I asked. "Because it was on the news? Most of what I did as a cop never showed up on the news. My working didn't have anything to do with how much I cared about you—or your father, for that matter. We all have to make our way in the world, and this is how I do it."

He nodded. "I know. I'm sorry. I'd like us to start again. I hope you will come to the wedding."

"Couldn't keep me away," I said. "Were you two driving through the gorge and you decided to stop by?"

"No, Mom," Scott said. "We came to see you. Dad made a picnic lunch. We thought we could go somewhere and eat it."

"Wish I could," I said, "but Sammy is here—my new friend Sammy—and we're going to unpack the rest of my boxes today and make this place a home. But you're welcome to come in and help."

Nate Gunderson drove up in his cop car.

"Grand Central Station today," I said. "You and your dad go on inside. I'll be there in a second."

I walked down the steps and up to Nate's SUV as Scott went back to the car. Nate got out of his vehicle. I hadn't seen him since the night we saved Danella and her mother, two weeks earlier.

"Hey, Katie," he said."

"Find out who stole my tires or set a fire in my house?"

He shook his head. "No, but I'm sorry I ever doubted you. It won't happen again. It all sounded so strange. I was worried you had suddenly gone crazy. Like Andy."

"Please don't ever put me in any category that includes him," I said. "Ever."

"No, that's not what I meant," he said. "Ever since that night, the night of the murder, I've questioned my judgment about other people. I didn't know—I never guessed he was so bad."

"I did," I said. "I had an instinct about him. I should have paid attention."

"You asked me how I could hang out with someone like Andy back then," Nate said. "I think that's why you and I were fighting that night." He shrugged. "I don't know. Katie, do you think now that it's been thirty years, we can put what happened that night behind us and move on?"

"I'm sure willing," I said. "But I don't think it works like that." I cleared my throat. "You want to come in and have a beer? My son and ex-husband are inside. And Sammy. Man, the testosterone in that house now. I don't know if I can take it."

We walked up the steps together.

"So you finally decided to make this place home after all?" Nate asked.

I stopped and looked around. To the south of Beauty Falls, across the mighty Columbia River, the gorge cliffs rose into the blue summer sky. I felt a breeze, touched with ocean, coming from the west. We'd have rain in a few days. To the north, even though I couldn't see it, was Mount St. Helens and the Gifford Pinchot National Forest. The lava beds and Mount Adams were northeast. I was a speck on this great landscape, amongst these towering giants of nature. I was fine with that.

Beauty Falls and the Columbia River Gorge felt like home, suddenly, after all these years. Maybe I could finally set down roots here.

At least for now. At least until I knew it was all finished.

Part Two

Beauty Falls

One

On the thirtieth anniversary of the rape and murder of Amanda Stenson, a news helicopter flew over Beauty Falls and my house as my phone began ringing. It was Sheriff Nate Gunderson.

"Katie," he said when I answered, "Sylvie Brubaker just walked in and confessed to killing her kids in the woods. She won't talk to anyone but you. She won't tell anyone where the bodies are, except you. She's got blood on her hands. I think it's real. Can you come over?"

I glanced at the time on my phone. 9:00 a.m. Crap. Scott and his fiancé would be here around 9:30—an unexpected but welcome visit. I needed to be back by then or there would be hell to pay. I hesitated, but then I said, "Be right there."

Scott would be pissed if I wasn't back by the time he arrived. But then, he had invited himself over, out of the blue, so maybe he would understand.

I pocketed my phone, grabbed my keys, left the house, and headed toward the cop shop a block and a half away. It was a beautiful dry and sunny June day.

Thirty years earlier, near the end of a day like this, six of us—all teens—had gone into the forest pretending to hunt for Bigfoot. Nate Gunderson and I were part of the group. So was Sylvie Brubaker, the woman who was sitting in the sheriff's office, claiming she had murdered her children.

Sometimes I felt like that night, that crime, would never be over. I needed it to be done. I didn't want to think about it. And now, if Sylvie had really done this terrible thing. . . .

Some new person was at the window at the sheriff's office instead of Sandy Dean, so I had to explain who I was and why I was there. She wasn't getting it. Life had been so much easier when I could flash my badge, and people just let me pass. Finally Deputy Dean saw me through the thick glass window and told the new one to let me in.

I hurried inside. The place smelled like sweat.

"The sheriff told me to watch for you," Sandy said, leading me toward the incident room.

"So now you're a full-fledged deputy, eh?" I said. "Congratulations. What old are you? Two?"

Sandy grinned. "Two and a half. Here we are."

The incident room was filled with people, most of them men, most dressed in beige uniforms. Nate was at the head of the room, standing with his hands on his hips, something he did when he was intent or upset. I grimaced. So now I was so familiar with Nate Gunderson that I knew his gestures and moods?

Most people were seated at long tables. Deputy David Hill stood against the north wall. We nodded to one another. Next to him was Lydia Hernadez from search and rescue. I knew them both from back in the day. I nodded to Lydia when she looked my way. She discreetly grabbed her crotch. I smiled. Yeah, we were definitely surrounded by a lot of men.

I caught Nate's eye. He grimaced in acknowledgment.

"OK," Nate said to the group. "The FBI isn't here yet, but let's get started."

The FBI? I glanced at Sandy, but she was watching Nate.

"Here's the background," Nate said. "A group of people have taken over the Wind River Ranger Station. They're demanding that the government return the Gifford Pinchot National Forest to the people. They've got weapons. We want to deescalate the situation, so I'm going to go out to negotiate with them. In addition, a woman has just come in and claims to have shot her children in the Giff." I heard audible gasps around the room.

"Two young girls ages six months and ten years," Nate continued. "That's about all she would tell us except that she did it somewhere up Stapleton, off Wind River, near where the men have taken over the ranger's station, coincidentally. The Falling Creek wildfire is on the other side of the Lava Beds, in that area, too. If it blows up, all bets are off. Storm is forecast for this afternoon." He looked at his watch and then up at us again. "We've got a call into Darby's in case we want to use one of their drones. Haven't heard back yet. And I've called in retired Portland Detective Kate Kelly. Many of you know her. She lives in Beauty Falls and is acquainted with the woman."

Why wasn't Nate saying Sylvie's name?

Everyone glanced back as Nate nodded toward me. Then they turned to the sheriff again. He looked as though he was going to say more—maybe tell the group about Amanda Stenson's murder and how today was the 30th anniversary of that rape and murder. But then he'd have to tell them the whole thing. About how we—he and I and the others—had all been out together that night. He looked at me and didn't say anything else.

I didn't blame him. I wouldn't want to talk about that night to a group of coworkers. I hadn't talked about it to anyone for years until I came back into Beauty Falls to live. Inevitably, the topic came up when I spoke to Nate. I always tried to nip it in the bud. The past was the past. Except now this: Sylvie claiming she killed her kids. It never seemed to be done and over. That night never seemed to fully recede to the past.

Nate called Deputy Hill up to the head of the room to talk about the details of the takeover of the ranger station and their strategy for backing it down. And then Nate walked over to me, took my elbow, and led me out of the room. I wanted to shake his hand off my arm, but I didn't. He didn't mean anything by it. I could tell he was nervous.

"Where is Sylvie?" I asked as soon as we were out of the room. "In lockup?"

"No," he said as we continued to walk. "I've got her in Interview Room 1. It's crazy, Katie. I felt like I was going to puke when I saw her standing there, blood all over her, like she was some ghost from the past. I mean, what the fuck?"

"Thanks for including me in this mayhem," I said. "I can't tell you how much I appreciate it."

"I didn't include you," he said. "Sylvie insisted. We've called the number on her driver's license, but it's her cell number, and her cell has a password, so we can't get into it and call her husband. She won't tell us the password. She won't tell us anything except that she killed her kids."

"Are these two crimes related?" I asked. "What Sylvie has done and the takeover of the ranger station?"

"Christ. That had not occurred to me. How could they be?"

"Just covering all the bases."

I really did not want to see Sylvie. Did not want to be a part of any of this. But I was good at it. Interviewing. People told me things. Especially criminals. Don used to kid me about it. He said criminals could tell I was a kindred spirit, so they spilled their guts.

I didn't know what he meant by that. I never broke the law. Not because I was afraid to do so. Nope. I believed in the law; I believed in the rules and regulations that protected us. Laws held a civilized society together. Once people decided to do whatever they wanted without regard to other people, well, that was when it all fell apart.

Nate and I reached the interview room. Nate put his hand on the doorknob. "You ready?"

I rolled my eyes. "Nate, open the fucking door."

"I thought we were going to start being nicer to each other."

"This is me," I said. "Being nice."

I bit my lip so I wouldn't say another word.

He opened the door.

A woman with long black hair and pale skin sat inside the small rectangular room at a small metal table. She held a soda can with her left bandaged hand. One of the deputies stood off to the right side of her, her hands behind her back. Nate motioned to her to leave. Then he closed the door behind her. The room smelled vaguely of blood and gun powder.

"Sylvie," Nate said. The woman looked up at him. She had bright blue eyes. I wouldn't have recognized her from Adam. Or Eve.

"I've brought Kate Kelly," he said.

Sylvie stared at him blankly for a moment, and then she looked at me. Her face brightened as she smiled. Now I recognized her. That big child-like smile. I couldn't help but smile back.

"Katie!" she said.

"Hello, Sylvie," I said.

"I would hug you, but they've got me handcuffed to this table." She tried to raise her right hand, but the metal bracelet jangled. "At least they let me wash off the blood."

I pulled out a chair across from her and sat in it. I had done this thousands of times before. I almost always knew the answers to the questions before I asked them. Now I hadn't a clue.

"Sylvie, can you tell me what happened?" I asked.

She glanced at Nate. "Do I have to? In front of him. He's one of them, you know."

"One of them? The police?"

"No. He's a man. This is personal."

"He has to stay here," I said. "I'm no longer a police officer. If you want, you can whisper it to me."

"Do you have him under your control?" she asked.

Under control? I glanced at Nate. He shrugged almost imperceptibly. I looked back at Sylvie.

"Sure," I said. "Nate will do whatever I say. Sylvie, we need your husband's phone number so we can call him."

"I don't want to talk to him," she said.

"You don't have to," I said, "but we need to talk with him. What's the password to get into your phone?"

"It's the name of my daughters," Sylvie said. "Beauty and Joy. No caps, all one word. Beautyandjoy."

Nate pulled out his phone and texted someone.

"Now tell us what happened," I said.

"All right," she said. "God told me my girls were possessed, and the only way I could save them was to kill them and send them to him."

"And what does that mean?"

"It means I had to do what he said. So I told the girls I was taking them on a picnic. We took the dog because we always take the dog. Besides, I thought it would be good for the girls to have a princess in heaven with them. That was the dog's name. Princess."

"Tell us about Beauty and Joy," I said. "What happened to them?" I didn't care about her fucking dog.

"I took them all into the woods," she said. "Far out down Wind River and then off into the forest. Not where Andy killed Amanda. Not that clearcut. But close. Do you remember it? That was such a terrible night. And you don't even know the half of it." She stared at Nate.

I glanced at the clock. 9:15. I could practically hear the tick, tick, ticking of time passing.

"Yes, that was terrible," I said. "But we're talking about to-day. What happened today? Where are your daughters?"

"My daughters are in heaven," she said. "Haven't you been listening? We are talking about today. What happened then changed me forever which brought me to today. Didn't it change you? I was OK before then, broken after. Because of them." She looked at Nate again. "I want to talk to Doug. He has to answer for this, too. He still lives in Beauty Falls, doesn't he?"

"Sylvie, we can't bring in everyone who was around when Amanda died," Nate said. "Can't you just tell us about the girls?"

"We'll try to find Doug," I said. "But what about the girls?"

"I took them to the woods," she said. "Near where I think Beauty Falls is. I've been looking for those falls since I was a kid. If you find them, all your wishes will be granted. And the town will be saved. Not like it is now. My parents still live here, you know. Remember the falls are hidden from white people, but I'm part Indian. Seminole, so I don't know if that counts here. I don't even know if it's true. Me being Seminole or Beauty Falls being hidden from white people. It's difficult to know what's true anymore, isn't it? It used to be easier. Now people just make stuff up. Maybe even God. Maybe God lies, too." She rubbed her eyes. "If that's true, then I've made a horrible mistake."

"The girls," I said. "Tell me about the girls."

"I shot them," Sylvie said. "I put them on the ground next to Princess, and I shot them all. With my husband's shotgun. The dog made the most noise."

"Where?" I asked.

"I can show you," she said. "I don't think I can tell you."

I nodded. Nate motioned to me.

"I'll be right back," I said.

I started to get up. Sylvie grabbed my hand.

"They're with God now," she said. "None of this can hurt them. Andy wrote to me, you know. He wanted me to visit. So I did. He was convincing. He knows so much. He says he was on a mission from God that night he killed Amanda, God his father. He said he used to think God was his father. Not anymore." She shook her head. "I went there because I thought it might help, you know, to put it all to rest."

"We can talk about that later," I said. "First we have to find your daughters."

"They're in heaven," she said. "How many times do I have to say that? There is nothing you can do for them here."

I did not like interviewing mentally ill people. Their delusions were always so unique to them.

"Are you sure the girls are dead?" I asked.

She let my hand go and looked at me. "What do you mean?"

"Maybe they're still alive and we could save them."

She shook her head. "My husband believes in things like that. If you're a godly person, you can bring people back from the dead with your touch. That's nonsense. But you can send people to God. And that's what I did. Even though God is scary. I did what he said. I shot the dog first. Did I say that? Because I thought that would stop the girls from whining. But it made it worse. Beauty started screaming. Or maybe Joy was crying. And the kick on the shotgun was awful. So I shot again. I think."

I glanced at Nate, then looked back at Sylvie.

"Sylvie, this is important," I said. "Did you shoot your daughters?"

Sylvie nodded. "I'm pretty sure. Though Satan was talking loudly in my ear, trying to stop me, so I don't know."

Nate opened the door, told the deputy to come back in, and then we hurried out.

"Just got a text," Nate said. "We took blood samples from Sylvie's hand, and took it down to the clinic. It's positive for human and animal blood. The human blood could be hers and not her children's. She came in bleeding."

"You can't test blood here in your mobile crime lab?" I asked.

"Are you kidding?" he said. "They took away funding for that, along with funding for nearly half my deputies. We have no forensic abilities here."

"Welcome to Mayberry."

Nate gave me a look. "This is still you being nice?"

"Niceness is fucking overrated," I said.

"We checked the shotgun she used. One shell was remaining. It's possible if she was aiming at the dog and the kids weren't close, she missed. They could still be out there, alive, or alive and injured."

"Or she reloaded," I said. "Shot the two kids and then reloaded and shot the dog or vice versa."

"Yeah, that's true," Nate said. "I'm grasping at straws."

"That's what we do half the time," I said. "Grasp at straws. I don't blame you."

"In any case, Deputy Dean called the husband," Nate said, glancing down at his phone, "and the husband confirms the children and the dog are not at home and are supposed to be with their mother. He's coming here from Vancouver."

"We need to get out to the woods," I said.

"Not with those nutcases blocking the road," Nate said.

"When did this all happen?" I asked.

"Sylvie came in about the same time we got reports of a roadblock," he said. "About an hour and a half ago. When shit hits the fan around here, it really hits. I sent my deputies out, and they verified the roadblock, talked to the man in charge, some guy called Elias Johnson and his brother and father. Or his son. I don't know him, but from the licenses on their cars, they're from Idaho and Utah. We're running the plates. My deputies counted ten men and women but there could have been more inside. I don't want this to turn into another Malheur. I need to get out there before it does. I hate these entitled little pricks, outsiders coming here and trying to tell us what to do."

"Would you feel better if they were from Beauty Falls?"

"Actually, yes," he said. "I'd understand it better. All these little towns along the river—well, everywhere—are dying without any work for anyone. I can understand people becoming frustrated. But how is turning the forests over to big business to log and mine even more than they are doing now going to help any of that? Anyway. I don't want to deal with it. But here it is. I gotta keep everyone safe."

I said, "Right now, I don't care about the ranger station situation. I care about those kids, right? If there is any possibility that they're alive, I want to look for them. It's possible the people at the ranger station will let us through to search for the kids. I wonder if they're the ones who called the Portland news. You saw the helicopter, right?"

"Yeah, I saw it," he said. "It's gonna be a clusterfuck if it isn't already. I've got one of my deputies calling the new stations to try to get them to back off."

"Does Sylvie's car have GPS? Then we wouldn't need her to take us there."

"No, we checked," Nate said. "We could track her cellphone, but that'll take too long. We've got to either get her to describe where she was or get her to take us out there."

"Agreed," I said. "By the way, why is she so pissed at you?"

"I haven't any idea," Nate said. "She's delusional."

"Are your deputies bringing in Doug?" I asked.

He nodded. "They've called him. He said he'd come down." Nate rubbed his forehead. "Will that fucking night ever go away?" he asked. "Do we have to pay for it our entire lives?"

"Pay for it?" I asked. "*We're* not paying for it. But Sylvie's girls may have." I slapped Nate on the shoulder. "Come on. We gotta do this."

He didn't say anything. We returned to Interview Room 1. The deputy stepped out; we went in.

"The blood we tested came back as animal and human," Nate said.

Sylvie smiled. "I told you. They're all with God now. I would be, too, if I could have figured out how to shoot myself with a shotgun. I tried. But then I decided I couldn't leave without some kind of reckoning. For me. For Doug. For you." She looked at Nate.

"We need you to take us to your daughters," I said.

"Once Doug gets here," she repeated.

"He's on his way," I said. "Why don't you take us out, and then Doug will be here when you come back? We can all sit down for a chat then."

Sylvie looked at me and smiled. "You think Doug is just going to come here because you asked? Did you tell him I was asking after him?"

I looked at Nate. He nodded.

"He'll never show," she said.

"Why?" I asked.

She pointed at Nate.

"Ask him."

"I don't know why Doug wouldn't show," Nate said. "Except maybe like the rest of us he doesn't like thinking about this day."

"This day?" Sylvie said. "I think about this day every day. All the time. They blamed us, you know. Many people blamed us. Thought we had conspired to kill Amanda. Or thought if we had stayed together she could have been saved."

"Yes, but we didn't conspire to kill her," I said.

"No," Sylvie said. "But what if we had stayed together? Don't you ever wonder?"

"Of course," I said. I sighed. This was why police officers didn't generally interview people they knew. I was feeling increasingly irritated. What if her girls were still alive and were wounded, bleeding out while we tried to tread lightly because of Sylvie's insanity?

"Listen, Sylvie," I said. "What if your daughters aren't dead? Wouldn't that mean that God decided they should stay here? So if you don't try to save them, you would be going against God's will."

Sylvie chewed the inside of her lip. "When will Doug be here?"

Nate left the room.

Sylvie said, "Quick, Katie. Don't let me be alone with Nate. Or any of them. He doesn't want you to know. Not after all of these years."

"Know what?" I asked.

"About Amanda."

"Sylvie, I can't help you if you don't just tell me," I said. "Are you saying Nate had something to do with Amanda's death?"

"No," she said. "But I've kept the rest a secret all these years. Did Andy try to get you to visit him in prison this year, too? He asked me. I know Nate went, too. Do you know if Doug went?"

"I have no idea," I said. "I haven't seen Doug since Andy was arrested. That's thirty years."

Nate opened the door and motioned me to come out. The deputy went inside as I left.

"I sent a deputy out to Doug's house," he said. "Doug is gone. His wife said he packed a bag and told her he didn't know when he was coming back."

"That's odd," I said. "And get this: Sylvie doesn't want to be left alone with you. She feels like she'd be in danger. Why is that?"

"How the hell would I know?" Nate asked. "She's a fucking paranoid schizophrenic off her meds. You're under the mistaken impression that she'll suddenly make sense and tell the truth."

"Whoa," I said. "Where did that come from? I'm just asking questions here."

"I apologize. I feel like I'm just one big button being pushed."

"Is that from the Big Book?" I asked.

"No, I just made it up."

"How do you know she's a paranoid schizophrenic?"

"Her husband told Deputy Hill," he said. "I've put out an Attempt To Locate on Doug, and my deputies are working with his wife to get a hold of him. They assured her that he is not in any kind of trouble."

"Let me try one more thing with Sylvie," I said.

We went back into the interview room.

"I'm tired," Sylvie said.

"I bet your daughters are tired and hungry," I said.

"I told you we were having a picnic with God," she said.

"But they're dead, Katie. That means they don't get hungry any-more. We never had any money, you know. I couldn't work. I tried, but I couldn't be away from the girls. I was sure something bad was going to happen to them. And Bruce's job is crap. We have no money. No prospects. It's crazy-making." She looked up at me and chuckled. "Literally, I guess."

"Nate will make certain Doug gets here. Whatever you have to say to him, you can say when we get back. I give you my word."

"What good is your word?" Sylvie said. "You promised that summer that we would stay in touch. We didn't. I didn't have anyone to talk to about any of it."

I sat across from her again.

"I'm sorry if I promised that," I said.

"I said you did," she said, with an edge to her voice.

"Is that why you wanted to see me?" I asked. "So you could chastise me for not staying in touch?" I leaned back in my chair. "I don't think you were sending those kids back to God. I think you were just pissed off at the world and this was your way to get revenge. Otherwise you'd quit wasting our time with vague accusations and let us retrieve the bodies of your daughters be-fore the wild animals get them."

Sylvie cringed. "I hadn't thought of that." She was quiet for a few moments while she stared off into space. Then she said, "All right. I'll take you. Can I have something to eat? Maybe an apple or something? I'm feeling a little woozy."

"Sure," Nate said. "We'll get that for you. We'll be right back, and then we can go."

I stood again.

"Thank you," Sylvie said. "And Kate, I wanted you here be-cause I thought you could take care of my girls. I saw what you did last month, rescuing that little girl and her mother. I thought,

I thought maybe you could do that for us. I tried to tell you. I tried to get your attention."

"What do you mean?" I asked. "Did you call? I don't remember seeing any numbers I didn't recognize."

"The smoke in your house last month," she said. "That was me. It was really easy getting into your house, you know. I thought you would investigate, like a detective, and you'd figure out it was me and we'd be reunited. You'd arrest me, and everyone would be safe. I wouldn't have to do God's bidding."

I looked at Nate.

"And the wheels," Nate asked. "Did you steal the wheels from Kate's car?"

Sylvie smiled. "That was clever, wasn't it? I hired a couple kids for that. I figured you'd find them easy, and they'd confess that I paid them."

"Sylvie, all you did was make my life miserable," I said.

She shrugged. "I thought it was a good idea at the time. But you failed to pick up the obvious clues. Or maybe it was just a practice run."

"A practice run for what?" Nate asked.

Sylvie glanced at him, then looked back at me.

"What clues?" I asked. I suddenly felt completely off balance. It was Sylvie who had broken into my home and started a fire? She had paid off some kids to steal my wheels?

"I made sure my fingerprints were everywhere," she said. "Remember they took our fingerprints when Amanda was murdered. I thought you'd check fingerprints and find me. Save me. Save the kids. So you see, it's really on you that we're here today." She smiled. "You were the smart one of all of us. If anyone could have seen Andy for what he really was, it should have been you. You could have stopped it all the night Amanda was murdered. You could have listened to me. I wanted to look for Beauty Falls, the actual falls. But you all wanted to look for Bigfoot, who doesn't exist, by the way. It was just an excuse to go our separate ways and make out. An excuse for Andy to rape and murder Amanda." She stopped. "I'd really like something to eat now."

I pushed away from the table and left the room. I was so stunned I could barely think. I was usually good at interrogations. I didn't get upset. No one was ever able to bait me. Any asshole criminal could say anything to me, and I just kept listening, kept drawing them out.

But I couldn't listen to another word Sylvie said.

Nate took a hold of my elbow, led me quickly to his office, and shut the door behind us.

"What the fuck?" I said. "What the fuck?" I started pacing back and forth in front of his desk, in his tiny little office. He stood behind his desk with his hands on his waist.

"That was great, Katie," he said. "She's gonna take us to the kids. I couldn't get her to do that. Hill couldn't do it."

I stopped and looked at him. "Did you hear her? If you had investigated the break-in at my house, if you'd looked for fingerprints, none of this would have happened. None of it! Instead, you didn't believe me."

"I believed you," he said. "Eventually. I didn't know. I couldn't have known."

"You could have done your job as a fucking police officer," I said. "You could have trusted me and known that I wouldn't make shit up, certainly not about someone breaking into my house."

"I know," he said. "I know." He rubbed his face. "It's water under the fucking bridge. We started over. We're starting over. Don't let this crazy woman turn everything upside down again. You live here. We'll probably work together again. We're almost friends. And besides, I don't have the resources to do that kind of investigation. Come on."

"Fuck off," I said. "Gawd. Anyone can take fingerprints. And she says I should have known Andy was a fucking murderer and rapist. How could I have known that? Did you know that?"

"Katie," Nate said. "Focus. We need to either find the bodies of those kids or find the kids alive. We'll leave in ten minutes."

I glanced at the clock. 9:40 a.m. Scott and his fiancé were supposed to be at my house just about now.

"I need to run home," I said. "I'll be right back."

Nate nodded. "Stay focused," he said. "Ten minutes."

"You already said that," I said. "Now fuck off."

Two

I ran home. Scott's white car was parked in the drive. He got out as I hurried up the stairs to my yard. The door opened on the passenger's side of the car, and a young woman stepped out: Scott's fiancé. I had seen pictures of her, but this was the first time we were meeting in person. She smiled and reached her hand out to me as I came toward them.

"Kirti Chadha," she said as we took each other's hand. Her grip was firm. "I'm so happy to finally meet you. Scott has told me so much about you."

I smiled as we let go of each other's hand. "I bet he has," I said. "Mostly the parts about how I ruined his life."

Scott came over and embraced me. "Never said you ruined my life, Mom," he said. "Made my life miserable, but that's a completely different thing. I'm really glad you emailed me to come for a visit. I almost deleted it because it came from an email I didn't recognize."

"I thought you emailed me?" I shook my head. "Who cares? You're here. Come on in." I went up the steps to my tiny front porch and unlocked the front door.

"This is lovely," Kirti said as we walked into the house.

"Yeah," I said. "I've been here about nine months. Just unpacked all my boxes last month."

We stood in the living room. Kirti looked toward my bedroom's open door—where several unpacked boxes were clearly visible.

"OK, I haven't unpacked all the boxes."

"I'm so excited to talk with you," Kirti said. "The life of a police officer must have been so exciting. We've never had a policeman in the family."

"No?" I said. "I suppose we haven't either."

"When I was a little girl I thought it would be fun to be the police," she said. "But my parents wanted us to be doctors or lawyers if we couldn't manage being a doctor. I'm a bit of a scandal because I'm a scientist."

Ah, she was a talker. Good. We needed one of those in our family. I smiled and then said, "My parents didn't really have much to say about what I did for a living. And I never had much to say about Scott's choice of a career."

"And now he's a mycologist," Kirti said, "about to marry another mycologist. We will save the world."

Scott laughed. It was not a comfortable laugh. He had been trying lately to be more understanding of my life, but it was difficult for him. He had to overcome two decades of resentment over my job and my attention to it. It wasn't easy to let it all go.

Despite everything my ex and I had tried to teach him, he was a bit of a privileged entitled grown up white kid, believing the whole world should revolve around him.

"We're looking forward to hiking the Giff," Scott said. "Are we too late? Is it going to be crowded?"

"Here's the thing," I said. "We can't hike there today. In fact, I can't hike with you anywhere. I have to go out."

"What?" he said.

Aw. There is was, that familiar anger. That tone of resentment tinged with "I told you so." He could convey so much with just one word.

When Scott was a kid, I seldom told him anything about what cases I was working on. He wasn't a kid anymore.

"Some militia-like group has taken over the ranger's station at Wind River," I said, "and they're demanding the government turn the forest over to them."

"That's terrible!" Kirti said. "Was anyone hurt?"

"I don't think anyone was there," I said.

"What's that got to do with you?" Scott asked.

"She's probably helping out," Kirti said. "Your mom has an important job."

"Not anymore," Scott said. "She's retired. She's supposed to be taking it easy."

"She's too young to be retired," Kirti said, "or taking it easy."

"That's right," Scott said. His anger was in full force now. "She was kicked off the force for sleeping with her confidential informant."

"Scott!" Kirti said.

"How'd you find out about that?" I asked. "And I was not kicked off. I retired."

"Dad told me," he said. "I asked and he told me. He tells me the truth."

I sighed and looked at my watch. 9:50. I didn't have time for this.

"OK, kid," I said. "I'll tell you the truth now. A woman is claiming she picked up a shotgun, aimed it at her two young daughters, and pulled the trigger, killing them. She was one of the six of us who went into the woods the night Amanda Stenson was murdered. This happened when I was sixteen, Kirti. This woman—Sylvie—is crazy now. For some demented reason, she will only talk to me even though she blames me for her killing her daughters."

"That's crazy," Scott said, regret in his voice.

"Right now she says she'll take us to the bodies," I said. "So I have to go. I'm really sorry, Kirti. I was looking forward to spending the day with you. These things happen. It's nothing personal. It's not because I think this is more important than you or my son, but it's possible those girls are still alive. It's possible I can help."

"But it is more important," Kirti said. "Of course it is. You go. We'll stay here. We'll make something to eat so when you come back, you'll have something. We'll be here."

"I don't know how long it'll be," I said.

"It doesn't matter," Kirti said.

She looked at her fiancé. Scott shook his head. "No, it doesn't matter. We'll be here, Mom."

"Marry her, son," I said, and I hugged Kirti tightly, briefly. It was nice not to have to defend myself.

"It's just that he worries," Kirti said, as she let me go and reached for Scott's hand. "All those years, he kept thinking you'd never come home, that you'd be killed."

I looked at Scott. "Really? I thought you just hated me."

"Mom," he said. "Of course I didn't hate you."

I was momentarily speechless. "We can talk about this later.

I gotta go. I'll try to keep in touch, but I don't know if there will be cell service out there."

I went into my bedroom and closed the door. I quickly pulled off my pants, put on my ankle holster and slipped the gun into it, and then put on a pair of loose fitting slacks. Finally, I dug out a pair of boots that fit a little loosely and pulled them on. I used to wear them and the ankle holster on the rare occasions I went undercover. If the pat-down wasn't thorough, I could usually sneak the gun into wherever I was going. I wasn't sure what would happen once we reached the roadblock today. I wanted to be prepared.

I opened the door again and went into the living room.

"Here are the keys," I said, dropping them into Scott's palm. "If you leave before I get back, just put them in the bowl by the door. Wish me luck."

"Good luck, Miss Kelly," Kirti said.

I laughed. "Call me Katie. Have fun." I didn't know why I said that last part. It was vaguely humiliating to feel like I had to perform the role of the good mother for my son constantly.

Scott gave me an awkward hug. "I don't hate you," he said.

What a declaration.

"That's good to know," I said. "Love you."

And then I was out the door and headed for the cop shop. Two minutes later the newbie let me in. The place was crowded with men and (some) women in uniform. Practically buzzed like a beehive. The smell of sweat and stale cologne gave me a surge of adrenalin. And I felt a twinge of nausea. Wasn't sure I wanted to do this. I could be home with my son and his girlfriend. Or hiking with them. Oblivious to what was happening in the world. I looked back at the closed locked entrance to the cop shop. I didn't really want to go back to my house. I didn't want to be with my son. I would rather be here.

Maybe Scott had been right all these years. I preferred the

job to spending time with him, or with anyone else for that matter.

I glanced toward Nate's office. He was standing inside with another man whose back was to me. The man's shoulders were slumped in grief or dejection. Was it Doug or the husband? Nate saw me and motioned to me to come in.

I walked to Nate's office and opened the door. The man turned toward me. His face was ashen. He wore a faded denim shirt over a black T-shirt with the words "world's greatest dad" on it. His jeans were old and baggy, his black hair short and greasy.

"This is Kate Kelly," Nate said. "She knew Sylvie when they were girls. Katie, this is Sylvie's husband Bruce Smith."

I held out my hand to him. He wiped his hand on his pants.

"Sorry, I was working at my mom's house when I got the news," he said as he shook my hand. His hand barely touched mine, but his palm was sweaty.

"Do you think she really killed my girls?" he asked. He squinted at me, as if he couldn't quite believe he was awake. He looked like he was going to fall over.

"Why don't you sit down," I said.

He slowly sank into the chair across from Nate's desk.

"We showed him the gun," Nate said. "It's his."

"I was always gonna lock it up," he said. "Should have. Just so much going on. I've been trying to get a job. Been working at the church. Not getting paid. I mean, just doing the work of Jesus. I thought everything was getting better. It had been bad for so long. She went off the meds before the baby. She had the baby blues last time, but since she was older now, we thought she'd be OK. She told me she kwas OK. I should have locked up the gun."

I bit my lip. Couldn't judge the man. Not yet. But yes, if his wife was a paranoid schizophrenic he should have locked up his goddamn fucking gun. Or better yet: Not have one!

"Why do you have a gun in the house with a paranoid schizophrenic?" I asked. Just slipped out.

The man looked at me. "I dunno. Just always had one. Sylvie never expressed any interest in it. I didn't even know she knew where it was. The last time she was feeling poorly I said I should lock up the gun, and she said she didn't know where it was. I guess she lied. I don't believe she'd hurt the girls. Or the dog. She wouldn't hurt anyone. She is a God-fearing woman."

"She told us God told her to do it," I said.

He scrunched up his face, as though in pain. "God wouldn't tell her to do that," he said. "She must have misunderstood. Can I see her?"

"She doesn't want to see you," Nate said. "And we don't want to get her upset. We want her to take us out where she said—where she said she—"

"Where she said she killed your girls," I said. "She said it was out where she thinks the falls are, Beauty Falls. Do you know where that is?"

He shook his head. "I'm not from here," he said. "She is. She loved it. That's why she named our first daughter after it. Beauty." He smiled. "I thought that was a lot to live up to. Being called Beauty. Same with Joy. Can you imagine? Having to be joyful all the time just because of your name? I wanted biblical names. But Sylvie can be persistent when she wants to."

"Mr. Smith," I said, "has Sylvie been having a bad episode lately? I mean, has she been particularly paranoid. Hearing voices?"

"I didn't think so," he said. "But she hides things from me. She always has. She has mentioned the anniversary of that girl's murder a few times lately."

"Amanda Stenson?" I asked.

"Was that her name?" he said. "Sylvie seemed almost happy about it. She said after this year she wouldn't have to think about it anymore."

"Why?" Nate asked.

He shrugged. "I don't know."

"You and your wife didn't talk much?" I asked.

"She had the kids," he said. "I was looking for work. And to be honest, I couldn't always follow her train of thought."

"Why'd you get married then?" I asked. What the hell was wrong with me?

"She was pretty," he said. "She was a good Christian woman about my age. She wanted children. She believed in the same things I did."

I looked at Nate. The set of his mouth told me everything. This had been a disaster in the making for a long time.

"We've got to go," Nate said. "If they're alive, we need to get to them ASAP." Nate came around his desk, opened the door, and called to one of his deputies. "Mr. Smith, Deputy Miklashevsky will take you to a waiting room. We'll contact you as soon as we know anything." Nate said a few things to his deputy, out of earshot, and then the deputy and Mr. Smith left the office.

"Anything new on the roadblock?" I asked Nate.

"No, let's just go see if we can get through," he said. "I'm gonna have you, Sylvie, Lydia, and Deputy Dean in one patrol car. I'll be in another. If they're militia, they're probably conservative Christians. They'll figure you womenfolk couldn't do any harm."

"Shit," I said. "Really?"

"Hey, I'm willing to try anything," he said. "Plus if they let you through, Lydia's part of search and rescue, and you and Sandy know how to track, too. We can do this. It's gonna be all right."

"What the fuck, Nate? Are you trying to reassure me? I don't need reassurance. I'm the alpha here. I can take care of myself."

"Oh Christ," he said. "I wasn't trying to reassure you. And even if I was, accept it like a normal person. And that alpha wolf stuff is outdated, you know. I read where the original studies were on captive wolves who weren't related. So they fought a lot, and researchers got the idea of the alpha male. In the wild, wolves live in nuclear families, with parents and pups. There's none of that alpha bullshit."

I looked at him. "We ain't in the wild, Nate. And you actually read? That is stunning news to me."

"Shut the fuck up," he said. As I turned to door to leave, he pushed me gently on the back. "I read. I think it was in the men's room at the bar."

"Gross," I said. "And it figures."

Three

Deputy Sandra Dean drove the squad car, with Lydia Alvarez in the front seat next to her. I was in the back with Sylvie Brubaker Smith who was handcuffed to the back of the driver's seat. I was glad for that. I didn't want to worry about a paranoid schizophrenic going off on me.

Sylvie whistled or hummed under her breath while we raced down SR14 toward Carson, heading east, sirens blaring, following Sheriff Gunderson. The tall Douglas firs were a blur on either side, but the Columbia River—which I could see beyond the trees on my right—seemed calm, as usual, green even though the sky was blue today. The Big River was more lake than river, at least here, pinned in by dam after dam. Less than a hundred years ago, I had been told, the river ran so thick with salmon you could run across the water, from one bank to another, on the backs of the fish. I was also told that it was so thick with salmon the river looked red in spring and fall. That I believed. Now, the river was radioactive because of an ongoing leak at Hanford's nuclear waste dump. And wild salmon were nearly extinct.

"I swam in that river when I was a kid," Sylvie said.

"So did I," I said.

She shrugged. "Maybe that's why we're so fucked up."

I looked at her. "I am not fucked up," I said. I paused and then I added, "I didn't swim in it that often."

"OK," Sylvie said. "So I hear voices and you don't. But you've got problems, too."

"Sylvie," I said, "I haven't seen you in thirty years. How do you know anything about me?"

"Remember," she said. "I broke into your house."

Oh fuck. I had forgotten that.

"What was up with that?" I asked. "Why didn't you just knock on my door and ask me for help?"

"What fun would that have been?" she asked. "Besides, I had to be . . . what is the word? Secretive? Covert? God was telling me to kill my daughters. I didn't want him to know I was trying to stop it. I saw you hadn't put your boxes away. Hadn't unpacked. What are you doing in Beauty Falls, anyway? Why move back to a dying town on a radioactive river? Returning to the scene of the crime?"

Lydia glanced back at me. I gritted my teeth.

We turned down Wind River Road, traveling north now, away from the river. We barely stopped at the stop sign, and then we hurried through the small town of Carson. Soon we were racing down the winding road that would lead us into the Gifford National Forest.

"Or maybe you came back because you wanted to be near Nate," she said.

I laughed. I couldn't help myself. "Um, no," I said. "I wanted to be away from Portland. I always liked Beauty Falls." Except when I didn't. After Amanda's murder, I never wanted to come back.

"Do you ever wonder how the six of us got together?" Sylvie asked. "You know, when we were kids." She spoke barely above a whisper, as if she didn't want anyone else to hear her.

"It was summer," I said. "We got together the way most kids do."

She shook her head. "No," she said. "We all met down by the river. We were watching the windsurfers, separately. Well, Amanda and I were together. You were by yourself. And then we started hanging out. Amanda and I thought you were so cool. Tough and beautiful. Didn't seem like you were afraid of anything."

I squinted and looked out the window. I vaguely remembered being down by the river.

"We liked going down and watching for cute guys," Sylvie said.

I nodded. "Yeah, I remember that."

"Why didn't we windsurf?" Sylvie asked.

I shrugged. "I had no desire," I said. "Did you?"

"I don't know. I don't remember. Then Nate came down and was watching. You asked him if he was watching the cute guys, too."

I laughed. That sounded like me. I looked at Sylvie again. How did she remember this from thirty years ago?

"And then Doug and Andy joined the group. The six of us wandered around together for a few weeks."

"I know," I said. "I remember." *Now* I remembered. I felt

irritated. The car was going too fast. Sylvie was talking too much. I wanted her to shut up. Needed her to shut the fuck up.

I hated going down memory lane. Ever.

"Amanda was so sweet," Sylvie said. "She followed you around like a dog."

I was starting to feel a little car sick.

Crap.

The road was too windy.

I rubbed my face.

"I don't remember much about her," I said.

"Or me, I bet."

"Or you," I said. I didn't remember a lot about any of it. I probably wouldn't remember much of my teen years if Amanda hadn't been raped and murdered. Most people didn't remember much about their teen years, did they?

"Amanda had a crush on Nate," Sylvie said. "So did I, I guess. But we knew Nate only had eyes for you."

"That was a long time ago," I said.

"Not for me," she said. "I never wanted us to separate and go look for Bigfoot that night."

"You already said that."

Sylvie looked at me and bared her teeth. Then she said, "Just wanted to make sure you're listening."

I felt a chill.

Fuck. I was gonna throw up. Just like a kid. Jesus H. Christ.

"Sandy," I said. "Slow down. This windy road is making me sick."

The deputy nodded, and the cruiser slowed a bit. The tall dark trees still whipped past.

"What do you think she was thinking before he killed her, after he raped her?" Sylvie asked. "Have you ever wondered?"

I looked at Sylvie. Why the fuck was she talking about this?

"No, I haven't wondered." Of course I had.

"I've heard that soldiers in battle say 'mother' just before they die," Sylvie said.

"I think that's a myth," I said. "They probably get shot and are about to say 'mother fucker,' but they can't get it all out before they die."

I saw Sandy glance at me in the rearview mirror.

What could I say? I didn't like being stuck in the backseat with a crazy person.

"What did your daughters say when you shot them?" I asked.

Sylvie looked startled. Then she said, "Beauty said 'momma.'" She looked out the window. "Joy is too young. She can't talk yet."

Even though the cruiser wasn't going as fast as it had been, the sun coming through the trees—dark, light, dark, light, dark, light—was giving me a headache. I rarely got sick. I was not a delicate flower. Never had been as far back as I could remember. Sometimes when I thought about what happened to Amanda, I'd get nauseated.

For a long time after her murder, I could not stand the smell of earth. Something about it reminded me of the morning after, as I stood out in the woods near a slash pile, trying to answer Deputy Reilly's questions about the night before. He was kind and persistent. Amanda was missing then. They didn't know she had been murdered. I didn't know. No one knew except Andy. A few hours later, he confessed to raping and killing her. But then, before that, I stood in the clearcut, answering questions, shivering in the cool summer morning.

"What time did you all get here last night?" the deputy had asked. "What were your plans? How come you didn't stay together? Where did Amanda go?"

During all those years as a police officer, I had seen some disturbing things, had been at bloody crime scenes, had dealt with rotten people sometimes, and none of that had fazed me. Yet get me thinking back to that summer night when I was sixteen and I felt sick, or dizzy, ungrounded. Unearthed.

"Pull over, deputy," I said now.

Sandy quickly pulled the cruiser over to the narrow dirt shoulder, on the other side of the road from Wind River. I stumbled out of the car, closed the door behind me, heard my feet rustle the old leaves in the ditch, and promptly threw up. Still bent over, I turned my head and looked up the road, saw the brake lights on Nate's cruiser come on. Crap. Didn't want him to see me like this: vulnerable. I stood, walked back to the car, and got in. Enough of this shit. We had work to do. I had work to do. I had to find those kids.

Soon enough, we turned off Wind River onto Stapleton where the deputies had set up a roadblock, to keep civilians away from the militia people. We drove slowly around the squad cars. A half mile up, we slowed to a stop. I leaned forward to look out the front window.

"Wow," Lydia said. "This just doesn't seem right."

Blocking the road, facing each other, were two pickups. Several armed men stood by the trucks, all white men, all bearded, except one skinny guy. They were dressed in jeans, shirts, and T-shirts. Almost all wore baseball caps. I'd much rather deal with drug dealers, drug users, or white collar criminals than these men. I understood drug dealers, at least on some level. Or maybe I was just accustomed to them. Good old boys doing shit like this? Well, this was way out of my expertise. Deputy Sandy Dean stopped the car, put it in park, opened her window.

"This isn't where I did it," Sylvie said. "We've gotta turn here, and then it's up further, more in the woods. It's nowhere near here." She sounded almost panicked. She tried to pull her hands from the cuffs.

"It's OK," I said. "The sheriff just needs to talk to them about letting us through."

"How'd you get through here this morning?" Sandy asked Sylvie.

"They weren't here when we came," Sylvie said. "When I left, they just waved me through."

Nate and Deputy Hill got out of their squad car and began to cross the road. One of the militia handed his rifle to another man and then he walked toward Nate and Hill. They met each other in the middle of the road.

"Are you and your men ready to go home?" I heard Nate ask. "Been no harm here, no foul. But we can't let you continue to block the road. People are coming and going into the forest from here. It's a beautiful Sunday morning. It's gonna cause problems if you stay here. Let's end this peacefully now."

The man nodded. He looked to be about forty, stocky, his beard tinged with red.

"That's Elias Johnson," Sandy said to me.

"I understand you're doing your job, sheriff," the man said. "And we're doing ours as American citizens. We want to take this land back and give it to the people."

"It already belongs to the people," Deputy Hill said. "It's public land, i.e. the people."

The man smiled slightly. "The people can't log it," he said. "They can't run cattle on it. They can't mine it. The county can't get taxes from it."

"Actually, it is logged," Nate said. "It's mined and cattle run on it. I'm not here to argue land use. For Pete's sake, the Gifford Pinchot forest is over a million acres. You seriously think the federal government is just gonna turn it over to you? This is a state highway, and I need it open. I need all my roads open. If they aren't opened, we will have to come in and arrest you. I don't want to do that."

"You can threaten us all you want," the man said. "We're willing to die for this. We want this land turned over to the people of this county so they can decide what to do with it. Then we'll give you back your road and your ranger station. We don't want to hurt anyone."

Someone else must have said something because the man looked over his shoulder. Then he looked back at Nate and said, "And we want Jake Cooper and the other defendants in his case released from federal detention immediately. They committed no crimes and we want their records sponged."

Yes, he used the word sponged.

"Whatever needs to happen so they don't have federal charges on their record," he said.

Nate put his hands on his hips. He shook his head slightly.

"Do you know who Jake Cooper is?" I asked Sandy.

She nodded. "Yeah. The feds caught him selling old growth maple. He had an entire illegal mill going in the forest. Millions of dollars of old growth felled, stolen, and sold off. He claimed he didn't know it was stolen. The guys caught cutting the trees said he was their mentor and taught them how to do it. Violation of the Lacey Act. They got all of six months detention."

"Lacey Act?" I asked.

"Trafficking in illegal wildlife, including plant wildlife," she said.

"Cooper, Johnson, Dean," Lydia said. "How do you keep them straight? They're so white-bread."

"It's a white-bread county," Sandy said. She glanced over at Alvarez. "Except for those of us who are red-skinned and a few of you who are brown."

"What does that mean, 'red-skinned?'" Sylvie asked. "I've got Seminole blood in my veins. But my skin isn't red. It's not brown. Or white. It's just kind of beige. And my blood is the same color as everyone else's. I've checked. It's the same."

Lydia, Sandy, and I glanced at each other and then looked out the window again.

"I want to speak to the governor about all of this," Elias Johnson said. "Then we can work something out."

Nate looked back at us.

"I agree that we can work something out," Nate said when he turned back to Johnson. "But right now we have an emergency. Two young children are out in the woods possibly seriously wounded. We need to get to them ASAP."

"Where?" Johnson asked. "We didn't hear anything, see anyone."

"I don't know exactly where," Nate said. "It's up the road. We've got the mother. She's going to show us where it happened. Just let us go on, and we'll figure out the rest of this later. First priority is those kids."

"What happened to them?" Johnson asked.

"We don't know yet," Nate said.

Johnson shook his head. "This all sounds fishy to me. Like you're just trying to get past us. I don't know to what end."

"Look," Nate said, "the FBI is going to be here soon. This is my county, my neighborhood. I want to end this pleasantly. But they're not going to let this drag out for weeks like they did at Malheur. The world's a different place now."

"That's right," Johnson said. "It is. People now understand the federal government has overreached. They are trying to stamp out people like us, like you and me."

"You're not from here," Nate said. "And I am not people like you. I follow the law. The law says I can arrest you. But right now, what I care about is finding those kids and seeing if they're OK. Their mother says she shot them."

Johnson stepped back slightly, surprised or revolted.

Then he looked back at the men by the pickups.

"You hear anything on the scanner about kids being shot?" he called to them.

The tall thin man without a beard said, "They've been scrambling about something. I thought it was us."

Nate said. "Why would I make up a story like this? Come on. You've probably got kids. Some of these men have kids. Be a hero. Help us out."

"We'll let one car through," Johnson said. "The mother in that one?" He pointed.

Nate's body stiffened, and then he turned and looked our way. He didn't like this asshole talking to him like he had all the power, but Nate was going to let him do it, to keep things calm, to get us to the scene of the crime. He didn't have a lot of choices now, not if he wanted to get to the children quickly. He could pretend to give away his power now because he understood the situation. Always con the criminal, not yourself, my old partner used to say.

"Danny," Johnson said. "Go check out the squad car."

The tall thin man began walking toward us. Nate put up his hand and shook his head. "He needs to leave his weapon behind."

Johnson nodded to Danny. Danny leaned his rifle up against the truck—probably had another gun around his waist or up his pant leg—and then walked toward us.

"Keep your hands where I can see them," Nate said.

Danny moved his hands away from his body. He looked to be about twenty years old and vaguely bored as he drew near. When he got about three feet from the car, he leaned over slightly and looked inside. Then he stepped closer to the back of the car and looked in.

"Four women inside," Danny said. "One is handcuffed."

"Check the trunk," Johnson called.

Sandy looked over at Nate. He nodded. She popped the

trunk. Danny went around to the back. I couldn't see him with the trunk raised. When he closed it, I saw a line of cop cars behind us.

"Nothing there," he called.

That surprised me. No weapons in the trunk?

Danny walked back to the pickups.

Sylvie was mumbling under her breath. I was inclined to mumble myself right then. I did not relish sitting here in the backseat of a squad car—like a criminal—unable to do anything to expedite the situation. I glanced at my watch. 10:20 a.m. Tick, tick, tick.

"They're in heaven," Sylvie whispered. "Nothing we can do now except bury them. Keep the animals from eating them. Beauty and Joy are dead, Katie, just like Amanda, and there's nothing you can do about it now."

Four

"Danny will follow the ladies," Johnson said, "in case they need help, and he'll escort them out again. If the EMTs are needed, if the kids need help, I'll let them pass, too."

"He needs to leave his weapons here," Nate said.

"He has the constitutional right to carry a weapon," Johnson said. "I'm not going to deprive him of that. He won't use it on the ladies. What if they encounter a bear?"

Lydia laughed. "This guy is a piece of work."

"I'm fairly certain a bear would run from them," Nate said. "Besides, it's not bear season."

"It's bear season if the bear attacks you," Johnson said.

"Why does it sound like they're not actually talking about bears?" I said.

"I don't need my rifle," Danny said. "Let's just get this on the road."

Johnson shot Danny a look. I couldn't see it full on, but I guessed he was annoyed with the younger man.

"All right," Johnson said. "And I won't ask your deputy to surrender her weapon."

"Yeah, cuz she ain't about to do that," Sandy mumbled.

Nate walked toward us as Danny walked to another pickup parked off to the side of the road.

When Nate got to the window, he said, "Keep sharp. Let me know." He patted the side of the car. Sandy put the vehicle into gear and drove toward the pickups blocking the road and then around them. All the men watched us go. Except Danny. He was driving ahead of us. He pulled off to the side of the road once we were past the roadblock.

"Where to now?" Sandy asked, looking back at Sylvie.

"Just keep going a couple miles in. I'll tell you when to turn."

We drove by the ranger station. Pickup trucks littered the small parking lot. A few men with guns walked back and forth in front of the door, as though practicing drills.

"Men with their toys," Lydia said as we drove by. "I sometimes wonder if something biological just drives them to conflict, to war, to killing."

Her words seemed to hang in the air for a moment.

Then Sylvie said, "I'm so glad I didn't have any boys. I think they're all monsters."

The road wound away from the ranger station and into the woods, becoming narrower as we went deeper into the forest, past second and third growth Douglas firs. The trees shut out the majority of light, and I felt mildly claustrophobic.

Behind us, Danny followed too closely in his pickup.

"Asshole doesn't know how to drive," Lydia said, looking beyond us to Danny. "How much farther?"

Sylvie just nodded. "Up. Keep going."

The pavement ended. Sandy slowed the cruiser. We continued going up.

After a while, Sylvie said, "Turn here." Down one of the many access roads in the forest, probably created by loggers or miners. We were near the lava beds.

"Just up there, in that little gravel pit area," Sylvie said. Her voice sounded small.

I was steady now. No physical symptoms of anything. I had a job to do—even if it wasn't my job. Assess the scene. Look over the bodies or save the girls. I rubbed my forehead.

The cruiser stopped twenty feet from the side of the hill where some machine had exposed the gray rock. I couldn't see anything on the ground from here. We were nearly surrounded by Doug firs. Slightly to the left of the gravel pit, the Douglas firs thinned and an occasional alder or lodgepole pine pushed up through jumbled pieces of lava. I suddenly recognized this place.

"Christ, Sylvie," I said. "What were you doing out here?"

"I told you," she said. "This is where Beauty Falls is. Or where I think it is."

"What is this place?" Sandy asked.

"It's where Christopher Reilly killed himself," I said.

Sandy shook her head. "I don't know who that is."

"Deputy Reilly," Lydia said. "He investigated Amanda Stenson's murder. He got Andy to confess."

Sandy radioed Nate that we had arrived. Then the three of us got out of the car. Sandy came to the back of the cruiser and unlocked Sylvie's cuffs, pulled her hands to the back, and locked her up again.

Danny got out of his truck.

"Sir," Sandy said. "I need to ask you to stay here since this is a potential crime scene."

"My dad told me to keep an eye on you," he said.

"Elias Johnson is your father?" I asked.

"Yeah," he said.

"You can watch us from there," Sandy said.

"They're not cops either," Danny said.

"They've been deputized for this," Sandy said. Which wasn't true. "We'll be back." She put her hand on Sylvie's arm, and we began walking toward the gravel pit. It felt strange coming up the rear, glancing back at the militia kid—or whatever he was. Felt strange not to be in charge, to barely be an actor in all of this.

"Where to?" Sandy asked Sylvie. Sylvie walked resolutely forward. As we got closer to the gouge in the hill, I could see what looked like a large blue blanket on the ground. Something was crumpled on it.

Sandy stopped, keeping a hold of Sylvie. She put her hand out to stop us. Sandy looked at me. "Don't let her go anywhere."

I nodded and put my hand on Sylvie's arm to hold her in place.

Sandy walked toward the blanket, her feet crunching over the gravel. A crow called out, and I looked toward the lava fields. I remembered the first time I had gone out to the lava beds when I was a kid. I had imagined a landscape of beautiful bare dark waves of lava frozen in time. Instead, I stood looking at a jumble of broken rocks. It was as though someone had dumped many loads of broken concrete onto the landscape. That was how unnatural it looked—except the broken pieces were dark. Moss or lichen grew on them now.

The first time I came to the lava beds had been with my parents, and we had taken only a few steps into the fields. We had all been warned about hiking the beds. It was too easy to fall and break something and not be able to find a way out. That was why so many people went into the lava beds to kill themselves. Even if they changed their minds about suicide, they probably wouldn't be able to find their way out again. Apparently compasses didn't work well in the beds. Wasn't sure why. Something about the kind of metals in the lava. I didn't know. I'd never tried it because I had taken seriously all the admonishments about hiking the lava beds: don't do it unless you're crazy and suicidal.

I shook myself and turned away from the crow and the lava beds. Sandy was at the blanket, standing between us and whatever was on it.

She looked over at us and motioned us forward. Lydia didn't hesitate. Sylvie pulled away from me a bit. Then she stepped forward. Sandy moved out of the way.

A small dead dog was curled up on the blanket, its fur bloody, with a halo of dark red around the body. Poor thing had somehow gotten in the middle of some crazy human crap. Or just in the way of a crazy human.

"Princess," Sylvie said.

I glanced at her. Lydia was walking around the blanket, looking for tracks, no doubt.

"Where are the girls?" I asked Sylvie.

She looked baffled. "I-I killed them right here," she said. "I'm sure of it. I think I'm sure of it. I stood right here, right where I am now."

"You were pretty close range on the dog," Sandy said.

"She was always barking," Sylvie said. "Always wanting attention. She had to go first because I didn't want her telling them what I had planned. Princess could read minds. And I was tired of her barking. Bruce promised me he would take care of her, just like he promised he would take care of the girls, take care of me, but he didn't. So I was left to it. I had to pick up her shit when we went to the park. Can you imagine? I had to pick up some stupid bitch's shit. What kind of life is that?"

"Sylvie," I said. "You need to focus. Where are the girls? Did you really bring them out here? Are they somewhere else?"

"No," Sylvie said. "Here. They were here. I swung the gun around—" She briefly closed her eyes. "Tried to pull the other trigger. I thought it went off. I can see them falling. Maybe God stopped it, maybe he changed his mind."

In the right corner of the blanket, far from the dead princess, was a small pink knitted baby hat. I wanted to pick it up, but I wasn't wearing gloves and this was a crime scene.

"It was chilly this morning," Sylvie said as she followed my gaze. "I didn't want the girls to catch a cold."

I looked at her. She smiled. "I was a good mom."

I groaned, inwardly, I hoped. What was actually going on here?

"What kind of sick bastard kills a dog?" Danny came up behind us. "Isn't it against the law to murder a dog?"

"You can't murder a dog," I said. "It is against the law to kill a dog for the fun of it. And it's against the law to seize public property, i.e. a ranger station."

"It's public," Danny said. "We're the public. That can't be against the law."

"And yet it is," I said.

"Get back to your truck," Sandy said. Her voice was firm. Hadn't known she had it in her. I shouldn't have teased her about her age. I caught Lydia's eye. She tilted her head slightly, signaling me to come over to her.

"Tracks," she said. "Going into the lava beds. Looks small, like a child's. Can't be sure." She leaned down. "Blood."

I saw a few drops of blood in the dirt.

"Fuck," I said. "If they went into the lava beds and someone got hurt. . . ."

Lydia and I walked over toward the lava fields, stood on the edge of it, looking in at the broken pieces of once-molten lava. It was a completely alien world in there.

"Beauty!" I called out. "Beauty! Are you in there? It's the police. You're safe now!"

We listened. Silence.

"We better go now," Lydia said. "If they're injured, we've got to get to them as soon as possible."

We turned around and went back to the blanket. Sandy stood with one hand on the butt of her gun, the other on her hip. Sylvie was staring at the dog.

"Where are the kids?" Danny asked. "You said there would be kids."

"We think they might be in the lava beds," Lydia said. She pointed.

"What are lava beds?" he asked. "Like in Hawaii?"

"No," I said. "Not like in Hawaii. This is from an eruption from 8,000 years ago, give or take."

Danny looked over at Sylvie. "I think she's pulling your leg. She probably dropped those kids off at a friend's house, and they are just fine. No mother is gonna kill her own kids."

"Your momma should have drowned you in the river the moment you were born," Sylvie said. "I would have."

This was getting out of hand. "Sandy, you can take Sylvie back, and we'll start the search. Bring the others out to help."

"The girls can't be in the lava beds," Sylvie said. "They're dead. I'm sure of it. We've tried going into the lava fields. That's where Beauty Falls is supposed to be. But it's too dangerous. I got lost. If my girls are in there, they be lost. They be wandering for an eternity. I would never get any peace."

Jesus H. Christ. Were the girls dead or alive? Maybe Danny was right: She was playing us.

"No one is searching nothing," Danny said. "You were supposed to come get the children, dead or alive. I don't see no children, just a poor dead dog that some sick motherfucker shot. So now I gotta take you back."

"You don't understand," I said. "One child is ten years old. The other is an infant. We found blood on the gravel. We need to search for them. We need to get every available search and rescue person here, now, to find them, to save them."

Danny shook his head. He looked scared, confused. He ran his fingers through his hair.

"I don't know what to do," he said, "except take you back. I don't see no signs of any child here. There is nothing and nobody to save. So I'm taking you back."

"She may have shot them," I said. "We have to go *now*."

Danny vigorously shook his head. It looked odd. I wondered if we were now dealing with two crazy people.

"What do you care if we stay here or not?" I asked. "We're not fucking armed. We don't care about you and your little revolt. We care about those girls."

Danny turned around and strode to his truck. He looked around in the back and came up with a rifle.

"Fuck," I said.

He held it on us as he was striding back.

"You cannot pull a gun on a police officer," Sandy said.

"Get your hands up," he said. We all raised our hands—except for Sylvie who couldn't. "You—" He pointed at Lydia. "Take her gun and throw it on the ground, far away."

"I'm not taking her gun," Lydia said. "I don't know what you're doing. But we're trying to save lives. Are you threatening ours?"

"Yes, I guess I am," he said. He seemed confused again.

"I'm with search and rescue," Lydia said. "Do you understand what that means? We search for people and try to save them. We don't care about what you're doing."

"Take her gun and put it on the ground!" he said.

"Then she'll have a gun," Sylvie said. "And she could shoot you with it."

Danny glanced at Sylvie. "If she shoots me, I'll shoot her. Mutual destruction."

Big words coming from this kid. I bet he was repeating crap that his daddy had told him all his life.

"And she's an ex-cop," Sylvie said, looking at me. "I bet she has a gun, too."

I glared at Sylvie.

"Is that true?" Danny asked, pointing the gun at me now.

"I'm not a fucking cop," I said. I pulled up my shirt, turned around so he could see my waistband. I patted down my own legs. Maybe he was that stupid. "I got nothing. Just let us go look for the girls."

"Get in the fucking car and get out of here," he said. "My dad said to come back to the roadblock when you figured out what was going on. We figured it out. A dog is dead, and she lied about the girls. Or you lied. Maybe this is some idea to separate us from one another, so that the government can just come in and kill us. Just like Ruby Ridge or Waco."

Oh Christ. Not one of those people.

"That was a tragedy," I said. "And so was Oklahoma City. So who are you trying to be like? Randy Weaver? Timothy McVeigh? Those aren't heroes and things did not end well for them."

"We're not trying to be like anyone," he said. "We don't think the government should own everything. Now get in the car and drive back to the roadblock."

Sandy looked at me. I nodded. We didn't want anyone else

getting hurt. The four of us walked back to the squad car and got inside. I didn't move Sylvie's cuffs to the front. I just strapped her in as she was.

"This is not comfortable," she said.

"I don't imagine it is," I said.

Danny held the gun on us as Sandy started up the car and then pulled back onto the road. Once we were on the road, he got back into his pickup and followed us. None of us said a word all the way back to the roadblock.

We drove by the armed men and joined Nate and the other police officers on the other side of the block. Danny pulled his truck over by his dad. Lydia, Sandy, and I got out of the squad car and met Nate. He looked tired, haggard almost.

"So what'd you find?" he asked.

"A dead dog," Sandy said. "No kids."

"We found an infant's knit hat," I said. "And a few drops of blood in the dirt."

"I'm pretty sure I found tracks of a young person," Lydia said. "Or at least a small person. I didn't follow the tracks all the way, obviously, but they looked like they were going into the lava beds."

"Lava beds?" Nate said. He looked at me.

"Yeah," I said, "it's right near where Deputy Reilly went in to kill himself."

"Fuck," Nate said. He looked up at the sky and then down at us again.

"Do you think the kids are alive?" Nate asked.

"We don't even know if the kids were ever there," Sandy said. "She's crazy. We don't know which part of what she's saying is true."

"I think they're in the lava beds," Lydia said. "I can track them."

"But you don't know for sure?" Nate asked.

"Well, no," Lydia said. "We won't know for sure unless we find them."

"What about dogs?" Nate asked.

Lydia shook her head. "Not in the lava beds. Wouldn't work."

"Kate, you got any opinion?"

"If there's a possibility those girls are hurt and need rescuing we should get on it. But, Sylvie could be lying."

"Fuck. OK. Let me go talk to Johnson."

Nate went toward Johnson, who met him in the middle of the road. Here we were on this side, there they were on the other, all standing around their pickups, holding guns, wearing camo or T-shirt and baseball cap. Looked like some tableau of good ol' boys. Except none of them were that old. I looked back at the squad cars behind us. Too many. This was not going to end well for anyone.

I couldn't hear what the men were saying, but Nate's body was stiff. He leaned his head down to one side, as if cracking his neck. I had seen him do that before when he was annoyed. I did it on the rare occasions I had a headache: trying to release the pain.

After a few minutes, Nate came back to us.

"They will not let us through peacefully," Nate said. "I can't start a war here. At least not until we know for sure those girls are there. Let's go back to the shop. I'll turn this clusterfuck over to the feds, and let's see if we can get more information out of Sylvie."

Fuck. That meant I had to get back in the car with Sylvie. And then back into the interview room with her. I had to get my mind right. I'd only been off the job for nine months, but I felt rusty—or something. I didn't want to be near Sylvie, didn't want to try and figure out what she was talking about. I didn't want any part of this anymore. I'd go look for the girls, sure. But I didn't want to be anywhere near their mother.

Lydia was already in the front seat again, so I was in the back with Sylvie. Sandy turned the car around, and we headed south, down the winding road, not quite so fast as before.

"I thought we were going to get their bodies," Sylvie said.

She didn't even say their names.

I didn't answer her. I was too disgusted.

"Who were those men?" she asked.

"Some kind of militia group or something," I said. "They want the government to give the land back to the people."

"Bullshit," Sylvie said. "They just want to make money off of it. They want to do whatever they want with it. They'll rape and murder the land and fill their pockets with money."

Lydia glanced back at me. I made a face, like "I dunno."

"Your religion believes all that?" Lydia asked Sylvie.

"My religion?" Sylvie said. "I don't know. But I believe it. I lived here most of my life. I know those men. Or ones like them." She looked out the window. "They are bad people."

"Then help us convince them that your girls are there," I said. "They think you're playing some kind of prank on us."

"Prank?" Sylvie said. "Why would I do that?"

"You broke into my house," I said. "You had someone steal my tires. All to send me some kind of weird message. Maybe you're doing the same thing here."

Sylvie shook her head. "The message was for you to stop me from killing my kids. You didn't stop me. They're dead. Maybe some animal dragged their bodies away. Maybe God took them up to heaven. Yes, that must be it. Please take me home. Take me home. I don't want to be here."

She started rocking back and forth, humming some song that sounded like a dirge.

She stopped humming when we went by the sign that read "You are leaving the Gifford Pinchot National Forest."

"Gifford Pinchot was in love with a dead woman," Sylvie said. "Did you know that? He carried on a secret love affair with a ghost for years. Talked to her all the time. In fact, he said he married her. Called her his bride. This went on for years."

"I heard that," Lydia said, talking to Sylvie like she was a normal person who hadn't just shot a dog to death, who hadn't possibly shot and killed her own children. "Crazy guy, for sure."

"Because he talked to a ghost?" Sandy asked. "Half my family talk to dead people. Are they all crazy?"

"Do they *marry* dead people?" Lydia asked. "Do they have visitations from dead people?"

"I've never heard of any of them marrying a ghost," Sandy said. "But sure, they've been visited."

Sylvie leaned toward me slightly and whispered, "They have no idea what crazy is, do they? We know crazy because we knew Andy." She moved away from me and stared out the window. "Or maybe we just knew evil. And it got all over us."

I was tempted to tell her to move her crazy far from me, that no evil had gotten on me. But I realized I would just be engaging in the crazy. That would not be productive. Instead, I had to get her to tell me everything. Sanely. And in order. As soon as we got out of this car. Then we could find those girls, dead or alive.

Five

I was never so glad to get out of a car in my life. Never so glad to stand in the sunshine and breathe the air deeply. The air was slightly moist, so it could have come all the way from the Pacific Ocean. Might mean rain. No, not this late into June. And certainly not tonight, not with those kids still out in the forest perhaps bleeding to death.

I shook myself. Glanced at Sandy leading Sylvie back into the cop shop. Lydia came to stand next to me.

"You know why they call this the cop shop, don't you?" she asked.

I shrugged. "We've always called it that."

"What did you call your police station in Portland?"

"I dunno. Police station. House. The last ten years or so, I called it the office." I shrugged. "Didn't think about it much."

"My granddad told me it's called the cop shop because this was where they'd come shopping for police."

I laughed. "Really?"

She nodded. "Sure. If loggers were out in the woods and someone was moving in on their territory, they'd pay the cops to come and roust them out. Or beat them up. Or if one of the big-wigs in the logging company didn't want to pay the workers, they'd get the cops to run the men off the land so they wouldn't have to pay them."

"You think that's true?"

Lydia shrugged. "Who knows? My grandpa was quite the storyteller. He worked in the woods and on some of the ranches around here. He said the cops ran the Mexicans off whenever the logging companies didn't want to pay them. I'm hoping you can't pay off the cops here any more." She looked around and then back at me. "You think the girls are out there and alive? I've heard you're pretty good at reading people."

"I'm in the weeds here," I said. "I don't know how to deal with crazy. Maybe Sylvie is just trying to get our attention for some reason. What about you?"

"I think someone small definitely went into the lava beds," she said. "I don't know if she's alive. But I think she went that way. And it's possible someone followed her. Maybe Sylvie. I think I saw another set of footprints. But we've got to get back out there."

I nodded. "Yeah."

Nate drove up just then. He got out and came over to Lydia and me. We nodded to him.

"Sylvie say anything to you on the drive back?" Nate asked.

"Not really," I said. "She's fucking crazy, you know. And she's clear as a bell on some things."

Lydia nodded.

"The FBI is here," Nate said, "so I need to coordinate with them. And Doug is here, too. Can you talk to Sylvie and Doug and figure out what's going on?"

"I'll do what I can," I said.

"Lydia," Nate said. "Can you stick around? Or at least be close by in case we do go out tracking?"

She nodded. "Sure. I'll run over to the Timbers. Just call. I can bring back some decent coffee if you like."

"A beer," Nate said. "I'd like a fucking beer."

"It's 11:00 in the morning," Lydia said. "No wonder your ex said you had a drinking problem."

"Hey," Nate said.

"Sorry," Lydia said. "I was just kidding. I never liked her anyway." Lydia winked and then walked in the direction of the Timbers restaurant and bar.

Nate glanced at me. "I was just kidding about the beer."

I put up a hand. "Hey, you don't have to explain anything to me. I'm not your mother or your ex. Have a beer, don't have a beer."

"I tell you," he said, "this fucking day is going to drive me to drink. Don't you ever wonder if we'll ever be able to forget that day. I mean, have it not matter?"

"Of course it matters," I said. "Jesus. If it didn't matter, what would that say about us?"

"I dunno," he said. "I'm just tired of it."

I followed him back into the cop shop. I thought about telling him what Lydia had said about the origins of that name, but I decided against it. He motioned to Sandy Dean. When she came over, he said, "You stay with Kate. I want her to talk to

Doug and Sylvie. Figure out if those kids really are in the woods."

Sandy nodded.

"Keep me apprised," Nate said. "I gotta deal with the FBI."

I followed his gaze. A woman wearing an FBI cap and jacket started walking toward us, followed by two other agents, one male, one female.

"Well, lookie here," I said quietly to Nate. "A woman swinging her ovaries. That is downright hysterical."

"Yeah, OK," he said.

"Sheriff Gunderson?" the woman said, holding out her hand as she got closer. She smiled, sure of herself. She knew what she was doing. Good. We needed a break from assholes.

I nodded to Sandy. "Let's go," I said. I didn't really want a meet and greet with the FBI. My priority was the girls.

Sandy and I went into the room where Sylvie was being held. The deputy watching her left when we came in.

I sat across from her.

"Are you hungry?" I asked. "Can I get you something?"

She shook her head.

"Sylvie," I said, "we want to help you. And that can only happen if you tell us where the girls are."

"I already told you!" she snapped. She looked at Sandy. "Why is she here? She doesn't have anything to do with this. Is Doug here? I want Doug to know what I've done."

"What exactly have you done?" I asked. The room smelled vaguely of metal. Was that from Sylvie? "We found a dead dog. We don't even know if you killed the dog. Maybe you were just walking around the woods, found the dog, and concocted this entire story to get attention."

Sylvie made a face.

"You've been home alone with two kids," I said. "The baby's been fussy. And Beauty has started to have questions, the way ten-year-olds do. Your husband wasn't living up to his fiscal responsibilities. So you decided to do all this."

Sylvie leaned forward, twisting her face into a strange grimace that made her look almost childlike, with her lower lip up and her jaw clenched.

"I loved every minute with those kids," Sylvie said. "Every minute. And my husband doesn't understand any thing." She practically hissed the words "any thing," making certain I understood that "thing" was separate from "any."

She never said her husband's name. So I would.

"What do you mean Bruce doesn't understand anything?" I asked.

She shot me a look and then cracked her neck by tilting her head to the right.

"It's dangerous out there," she said. "They could get sick, catch some disease. Some pedophile could get them. They could be raped. Murdered. Anything could happen. Already Beauty has to watch what she eats. She gets sick if she has any dairy. Poor kid."

I nodded. "OK. But except for that, your girls were doing all right, weren't they?"

"They were," she said. "I stopped taking my meds, you know. They were eating away at my organs. Or at least, that's what they said might happen. I felt better on them. And I felt worse. When I was on them, I never knew what to do, you know, what choices to make. What was the right thing to do? Off of them, the voices came back. I got guidance. I knew what to do. And then I got the letter from Andy. I don't know how he found me. Maybe it's easy because of who he is."

I glanced at Sandy. What did that mean?

I didn't want to talk about Andy, but if it would get me to what happened to the girls, I would listen.

"Everything he said made sense to me," Sylvie said, "which

was scary at first because I hated him for what happened. I hated him for ruining our lives."

Again I had the urge to say, "My life is not ruined," but this was not about me or about me correcting Sylvie. She was mentally ill. My job was to try and glean the truth through all her chaff.

"He wasn't any different," she said, "except he's heavier. But I could see him for who and what he was."

She shook her head.

"I don't want to talk about that," she said. "Is Doug here? I want to talk to Doug. Or I want you to talk to Doug. He knows what happened that night. He needs to pay for it. We all need to pay for it!" She raised her voice, and spittle flew out of her mouth.

"Sylvie," I said quietly. "You need to calm down. Why should we all pay for that night? Andy killed Amanda. He's in prison. That's the end of the story."

"It's not the end of the story!" she said. "God told me to kill my children! That was the beginning of the payment." She ran her hands through her hair. "I didn't want to do it. But he reminded me of Abraham. God asked Abraham to kill his son."

"Is that what happened?" I asked. "Were you ready to sacrifice your daughters but God stopped you, and you sacrificed the dog instead?"

"Wouldn't that have been great?" She shook her head. "No. And then there's Jesus. God sacrificed his son, let his own son die. How could I do any less?"

"So where are your daughters then?"

"You talk to Doug. Let him tell you why he's here, why I'm here, and then I'll tell you where my daughters are."

"What does Doug have to do with any of this?" I asked.

"Everything," she said. "All of us. We all are a part of this. Forever. And we have to pay for it."

"I don't understand you, Sylvie," I said. I was getting pissed again. Couldn't let that happen. She was just someone I was interviewing. I had no stake in any of it. Beyond my desire to find Beauty and Joy. I wanted to find the girls alive. I needed that. We all needed that.

"You will understand," she said. "You need to understand. Talk to Doug, and then Nate. Bring them all here after, and we can exchange hellos. And goodbyes." She smiled at me and looked normal for a moment.

I looked at Sandy. She shrugged. I got up, and Sandy and I left the room as another deputy stepped in.

"Where's Doug?" I asked Sandy. She pointed. "In Interview Room 2." I glanced at Nate's office. Bruce Smith still sat in front of Nate's desk, his shoulders hunched. I wanted to feel sorry for him, but I didn't.

"Who is this Doug guy?" Sandy asked.

I sighed and took a deep breath. Good to get my bearings. "He was one of the six of us who went into the woods that night. Amanda and Andy went one way, Sylvie and Doug went the other. Nate and I had a fight, standing by his truck. I got pissed and walked away."

"So you all paired off?" she asked. "Like a date?"

"No," I said. "We were looking for Bigfoot."

She raised her eyebrows.

"We were kids," I said.

"And you and Nate were an item?" Sandy asked.

"No," I said. "Neither were the others. Although I guess maybe they were. Nate and I liked each other, I guess. But it never went anywhere, especially after that."

"Are you now?" Sandy asked. "Interested in him?"

I looked at her. "Why are you asking? Are you interested in him?"

"Gawd, no," she said. "He's old enough to be my dad. In

fact, he knows my dad. I know his daughter. I was just being nosey. He seems to really value your . . . expertise."

I laughed. "OK. Well, no, Nate and I are just trying to be friends, since we have so much history because of that night."

Christ. Why was I standing here talking about this?

I knew why. I didn't want to go into that room and see Doug. What the fuck was wrong with me today?

"You ready?" I asked Sandy, although I said it more for me than I did for her.

She nodded. She went to the door and opened it. Then we stepped inside. It was a twin to the room Sylvie was in, only no deputy stood with the man sitting at the long metal table drinking coffee out of a paper cup. He was balding, with gray brown hair on the sides. He was shorter than I remembered, and heavier, with his pot belly pushed up against the table. He looked up at me and nervously smiled. He slowly stood and held out his hand.

"Katie Kelly," he said, "as I live and breathe." I took his hand and shook it. Then I indicated he could sit again. I sat across from him. Sandy leaned up against the wall opposite me.

"You don't look any different," Doug said. "How is that possible?"

"Clean living, I guess," I said. "How are you, Doug? Been a few decades."

He nodded. "I've been OK."

"I'm curious as to why you suddenly took off this morning when you found out the police wanted to talk to you."

"I heard you were a cop," he said. "That makes sense. You were always tougher than all of us. And you played by the rules, whatever we did."

I frowned. I couldn't remember us ever playing anything.

"You didn't answer my question," I said.

"It wasn't sudden," he said, looking down at his hands. "I-I just had somewhere to go."

I almost laughed. "Jesus, Doug," I said, "I've been doing this my whole adult life, and you are the worst liar I've ever encountered."

He sighed, puffing out his cheeks as he did so. He looked at me again. "You always were a little mean."

"I wasn't mean," I said. "I could never tolerate assholes. And you were a little bit of an asshole. At least back then. What about now, Doug? Because now we need you to step up. It's very important that you tell me what's going on with you."

"I left because I didn't want to see Sylvie," he said. "She scares me."

"She scares you?" I asked. "Have you seen her since Amanda was murdered?"

"Back then, yeah," he said. "For a while. But not since then."

"'Then?' When? What the fuck, Doug?"

He looked over his shoulder at Sandy and then back at me. "Does she have to be here?"

"Yes, she does," I said. "I'm not a cop anymore. She's here so that I don't beat up anyone. She's here to protect you."

He looked at her and then at me.

"Yeah, I know you're just messing with me," he said.

"Why are you afraid of Sylvie?" I asked. "Why does she want me to talk to you?"

"I went to visit Andy," he said.

They had all gone to see Andy? Why on Earth?

"And?"

"He said Sylvie was going around the bend," Doug said. "Thought she might do something crazy to me."

"Did he say anything about Sylvie's kids?"

Doug shook his head. "No. Why?"

"Sylvie claims she killed her two daughters, Beauty and Joy, out in the Giff. She won't tell us where the bodies are until we talk to you. I want to know why that is."

"Jesus," he said. "That's horrible. But it's got nothing to do with me."

"Then why are you here?" I asked.

"Because the police dragged me here," he said.

"Doug, what happened between you and Sylvie?"

He shrugged. "We dated for a while and then we didn't."

I rubbed my forehead. Then I leaned back. "Let's try this," I said. "Tell me what happened the night Amanda was killed."

He shrugged. "Nothing happened. You and Nate left. Sylvie and I hung around for a while, and then we left. End of story."

I pounded my fist on the table. "It's not the fucking end of the story!" I said. "What happened between you and Sylvie?" Jesus H. Christ. "I don't know if those girls are dead or alive, and you are standing between me and them. So fucking tell me."

"Nothing happened," he said. "Sylvie and I made out for a while." He rubbed his face. "Then we had sex. It was the first time for both of us. We were both kids. It wasn't much fun. We both cried. Then we went home. That's all."

I looked at Sandy. She grimaced.

"That is not all," I said quietly.

He shook his head and looked at his hands. "She misunderstood things. Afterward, she said I raped her. Not right away, but a few days later. But I didn't force her. I swear I didn't."

I nodded. "OK, Dougie. I understand. She had some regrets afterward. But what happened that night? Tell me everything. It'll be good to get it off your chest."

"We were kissing, you know, like kids do. And then we were having sex. It was quick. Wasn't exactly pleasant."

"And then?"

"You and Nate were gone," he said, "and Andy and Amanda

weren't back. So we did it again." He coughed. "I heard something while—you know—while we were doing it."

I felt the hair stand up on the back of my head.

"What?"

He shook his head. "I don't know. Later I wondered if it was Amanda screaming."

"Why did Sylvie say it was rape?" I asked.

"She didn't at the time," he said. "I swear I didn't force her."

"Which leads me to believe you forced her," I said.

"I didn't," he said. "She willingly opened her legs for me."

That was a strange phrase.

"What do you mean?" I asked.

"Remember, we were kids," he said. "So I was cajoling her. Trying to convince her. That's how I thought it was done. I thought girls never wanted to have sex, and you had to convince them to do it. I was young. I was stupid."

"How did you convince her?"

He cleared his throat. "I-I told her if she didn't have sex with me, I would tell everyone at her church that she did have sex with me. But if she did it, I wouldn't tell anyone."

I didn't say anything right away. Then I leaned forward and said, "Those of us in law enforcement call that coercion," I said. "Which constitutes fucking rape. She said you raped her because you did rape her."

"I didn't know!" he said. "I was a kid."

"Don't give me that fucking bullshit," I said. "You knew, you knew it was wrong. Tell me the rest."

"Not if you're fucking judging me," he said.

"Everyone is fucking judging you," I said. "Tell me the rest."

"First she gave me a blow job," he said. "She had had a little too much to drink or something because she threw up."

"We didn't have any alcohol with us," I said. "She threw up because she was disgusted."

"When she felt better, she started to walk away," he said, "like you did. She said she had to get home. But it was dark, and she came back. Then we had intercourse. I thought she was into it."

"Why?" I asked. "Why would you think that?"

"She didn't say anything," he said. "She just hummed a little bit. I figured that meant everything was OK."

"How did you get her to have intercourse with you?" I asked. He shook his head.

"What did you tell her?" I asked.

"I said if Andy came back, he would have sex with her if I hadn't. Who would she rather have sex with, me or him?"

"What the fuck?" I said. "Was that true?"

He shrugged. "Andy said he was going to have sex with someone that night. So it could have been true."

"You are such a fucking asshole," I said. "So while Andy was out there raping and murdering Amanda you were raping and terrorizing Sylvie. What were you thinking?"

"I wasn't thinking!" he said. "I was a boy with raging hormones."

"Give me a fucking break," I said. "You knew what you were doing was wrong. You wanted something and you took it. And you knew Sylvie was afraid of her parents, afraid of what the people in her church would think. She was your fucking prey."

"I didn't look at it like that," he said. "I figured it would be good for both of us. I was stupid."

"You were a fucking criminal," I said, pushing away from the table. "You're lucky the statute of limitations has run out on your particular crime."

I wanted out of this room. I needed to go home. See my own

kid. Get this fucking day and that fucking crime gone from . . . any part of my life.

"Is there more?" Sandy asked.

I looked over at Doug. More? Shit. Yes, I could see: There was more.

He was still staring at his hands. "She got pregnant."

"Oh fuck me," I said.

"She said we had to get married," he said. "I was a kid. I couldn't get married. I told her she had to get an abortion. Or tell her parents about the pregnancy and go on without me. I didn't have any money. I didn't have any access to money."

"So what happened?"

He looked up. "Nate gave me the money. I drove Sylvie to Portland, and she got an abortion."

Fuck, fuck, fuck.

"I never saw her after that," he said.

I rubbed my hands across my face. Good thing I wasn't playing poker today. My feelings were plain to see. I wanted to punch him. Instead I leaned down so that my face was nearly even with his.

"If those children are dead," I said, "you are partially to blame."

I had to get out of there. I quickly left the room. I stood in the corridor looking around. Most of the officers were gone now, the place was nearly empty. I tried to take a deep breath. I couldn't. I felt a tinge of panic. I looked at the closed door of Interview Room 1. I had to talk to Sylvie now. I knew there was more. I was sure of it. Only one shoe had dropped.

Six

I stood outside the door waiting for Sandy.

"You got a deputy to stay with Doug, right?" I asked.

She nodded. She looked pale, or something. I didn't care. She was a deputy now. She had to get used to hearing other people's nightmares.

I opened the door to Interview Room 1. Sylvie still sat at the table. The other deputy left, and Sandy and I stepped inside. I pulled up a chair and sat across from Sylvie.

"Well?" Sylvie asked.

"He told us what he did to you," I said.

She sighed. "Everything?"

"He said he coerced you into having sex," I said.

"He raped me!" she cried.

"Yes," I said. "He raped you. He told us about you getting pregnant."

She sighed again. Her eyes teared. "He admitted it all?"

I nodded. "Yes. He said he paid for the abortion."

"Nate paid for it," she said. "It was blood money. Doug made me do it, you know. I didn't want to. It was against everything I was taught. I couldn't tell my parents. Not unless we got married. I couldn't get the smell of his balls out of my. . . head. My nostrils. I didn't want to marry him." She shook her head. Then she began to sob. She put her head in her hands and cried. Her shoulders shook.

"I am so so sorry that happened to you," I said. "It must have been awful. Especially given what happened to Amanda."

Her sobs lessened. Sandy handed her a box of tissues. Sylvie blew her nose.

"Did it happen to you that night?" Sylvie asked.

"No," I said. "Nate wouldn't have done anything like that."

I wasn't sure why I said that last bit. Except it was what I believed. He wasn't like that, was he?

What a stupid thing to think. What a stupid thing to say out loud.

"All men are like that," Sylvie said.

I didn't believe that, but I wasn't going to argue with her now. I needed to know where her children were.

"You don't believe me?" She smiled. "I blamed myself for a long time. I thought it was because of the voices. I heard them even before the rape, just in case you thought that caused it. It didn't. I thought Doug must have thought it was OK because I was . . . weird. But then I went to see Andy a few months back. And he told me it was no coincidence that I was raped the same night that Amanda was killed."

"What do you mean?"

"He told me that he and Nate and Doug were all part of a club," she said.

"A club?"

I didn't want to hear this.

She smiled, as though she couldn't wait to tell me what was next. Sobbing one moment and gleeful the next.

"When he told me about the club," she said, "the club they invented, I realized the rape and abortion weren't my fault. It had never been my fault. I mean, I was in some way responsible for what happened to Amanda, just as we all were. And we all have to pay for that. To make restitution for the life she never got. But I wasn't responsible for Doug raping me. That happened because of the club."

I sat silently. She wanted me to say, "What club?" I wasn't going to do it.

"Those three boys had a club," she said again. "They called it the rape club."

Oh fuck.

"The plan was to go out and rape three girls," she said. "One each. And we were the three girls. That's why we split up that night into pairs. The boys did that. So the rape club could fulfill its mission."

The room tilted a bit.

I felt like I was going to throw up again.

This could not be true.

I pushed away from the table and left the room, hurried toward Interview Room 2. I heard Sandy behind me.

"Get the sheriff here," I said. "Now."

I opened the door. Doug looked up at me. I glanced at the deputy. Who was it? What was his name? Couldn't remember.

"Get the fuck out," I said to him. He hesitated. "Now!"

The deputy left. I closed the door and stared at Doug. I could hear my heart in my ears.

"Rape club," I finally said. I swallowed. "Was it real?"

"It was just a name," Doug said. "We didn't take it seriously. We didn't even know what rape was back then."

"Apparently at least two of you did," I said, "since you both raped someone that night. What about the murder? Was that part of the club?"

"No! Good gawd, no. It was a joke. Like when you call someone a bitch. It doesn't mean anything. As a boy you say 'I'd like to rape her.' We just meant we wanted to have sex. We didn't know back then."

"Fuck you," I said. "Fuck you. And Nate? Nate was a part of this?"

"They were just words," Doug said. "Just words."

"That night," I said. "You were all going to rape us?"

"No," Doug said. "That can't be right."

The door opened. Sandy was there.

I needed to leave. Had to get out.

"Nate is en route," Sandy said. "The FBI has taken the lead in the occupation of the ranger's station."

I left the room and went back to Sylvie. Sandy followed me, closing the door behind her.

"OK," I said, trying to be as composed and relaxed as possible. Even though I didn't feel composed or relaxed. I wanted to punch someone or something. I eyed the wall. No, that would just break my hand.

"Is there anything else?" I asked Sylvie. "Anything else you need to tell us before you tell us where the girls are?"

Sylvie shook her head. "It's now all out in the open," she said. She grinned. "Finally. I can have some peace. The girls are with my friend Polly. Safe and sound."

Please, let this be true.

"I wouldn't hurt my children in a million years," Sylvie said. "Well, except for the one I aborted. Have you ever had an abortion? Before you had your son. Or after? It's not as bad as you'd think. I thought the gates of hell would open up. But it's not like that. It's just a procedure." She shrugged. "Sometimes I thought she was haunting me, the baby I aborted—she was a girl—like Gifford Pinchot's ghost. My ghost daughter instead of a ghost wife. I am now a ghost wife. How is your son, anyway? I'm sorry I spoiled your day with him."

Felt creepy she knew I had a son. And how did she know I was spending the day with him? Probably when she was vandalizing my house she saw a photo. Or maybe someone we knew in common. Maybe my calendar?

None of that mattered. The girls were alive. She said the girls were alive. I had to find out for sure.

"You can call Polly," Sylvie said. "My husband has her phone number. The girls are just fine."

I hoped she was telling the truth. I wanted this over, and I needed those girls to be safe. Too many horrible things had happened because of that night, because of Andy and his craziness: the lives of those two girls couldn't be lost, too.

I started to leave the room, but Sylvie caught my right hand with her free hand. "We need to get back at them," she said. "Start our own club. Maybe a revenge club or a murder club. I don't care what God thinks. They need to pay for what they did."

I pulled my hand away and left. I went into Nate's office where Bruce Smith was waiting.

"Mr. Smith," I said, "I need you to call your wife's friend Polly. Sylvie says that's where the kids are."

"Oooh," he said, his body trembling as he stood. "Do you think?" He fumbled for the phone in his pocket. "Polly Zweib." With shaking fingers, he scanned his contacts and then pressed call when he reached Polly Zweib. "Oh merciful God." I heard a woman's voice say, "Hello." Mr. Smith turned it on speaker.

Then he said, "Polly. This is Bruce Smith."

"Hello, Bruce." A woman's voice.

"Yes. My wife says the girls are with you?"

"Of course," she said. "The girls are here playing, safe and sound." She said something else I couldn't quite hear, and then she was louder again. "Jason took Beauty and Heather out for ice cream or else I'd put her on the phone."

"That's all right," Bruce said. "Oh, thank you so much. Thank you. We'll talk soon. Goodbye." He almost dropped the phone before he got it back in his pocket. His eyes were filled with tears. "They're OK."

"Who is Heather and Jason?" I asked.

"Heather is Polly's daughter," he said. "Polly and Jason's daughter. She's a friend of Beauty's." He smiled. "They're alive. Everything is OK."

Suddenly he put his arms around me, held me tightly. I patted his back as he trembled, as he cried. Finally he pulled away.

"What will happen now?" Bruce asked. "Can I talk to Sylvie?"

I looked at Sandy who was still dutifully following me from place to place.

"That's up to them," I said. "My job is finished here. I leave you with Deputy Dean."

"Thank you for everything you did," Bruce Smith said.

"I have no idea if I did anything," I said. "I don't really understand what happened, but I do know your wife needs help. And she shouldn't have access to weapons."

"I know, I know," Bruce said. "I promise. I'll watch her."

I nodded to Sandy, and then I walked away from them. Walked away from Doug and Sylvie, too. I was so relieved. This

. . . whatever it was . . . this search had ended better than I thought it would. I opened the steel door and went into sunshine.

I was relieved, but I still had a knot in my stomach. Sylvie had roped me into her little drama. She hadn't been able to face Doug on her own so she brought me into it all to expose it, to bring it to light.

I strode across the parking lot. I wanted to get away before anything else happened. Before I learned anything else about my past that I didn't want to know.

Nate pulled up in the squad car just then. He smiled and waved at me as he got out.

I wanted to punch him.

I turned away and headed in the direction of home.

"Katie," he said. "Wait up."

"I'm trying to protect you," I called back, without looking toward him.

I heard his footsteps behind me. Felt sick to my stomach again. I stopped and turned around. I couldn't see in his face or body the boy he had had once been. That was probably a good thing.

"You did it," Nate said. "You got her to talk. And the kids are safe and sound. Why aren't you leaping with joy?"

"I don't leap for anything," I said. "I'm so pissed at you I can hardly see straight. She told me everything, about Doug, about getting pregnant, about the abortion. You should have told me!"

"Why? What did that have to do with anything?" he asked. "That was thirty years ago."

"Amanda's murder was thirty years ago," I said, "and it still matters. Sylvie kept hinting that you and Doug had done something, and now I know what."

Nate shook his head. "I helped Doug when he got a girl pregnant. So what? That's not why she turned into a psycho!"

"Doug raped Sylvie," I said. "You left out that little detail."

Nate stepped back from me. "What are you talking about? He never told me that."

"Why would he have to?" I asked. "Wasn't that the intention of your little rape club? You found three girls you thought would be vulnerable, would be ripe for the picking, and you took us out into the woods where no one could hear us fucking scream!"

Which was what I was doing right now. A few people in the parking lot looked over at us.

I didn't care.

Nate shook his head. "You can't believe that."

"Sylvie and Doug both copped to it," I said.

"But it's not true," he said. "And how would Sylvie know anything about it?"

"Andy told her," I said.

"Fuck," Nate said.

"What does it matter if it's not true?" I asked.

Nate looked around. Then he rubbed his mouth. "It was something Andy came up with. He called it that. I didn't really even know what it meant. I was a kid."

"You were seventeen years old," I said. "You knew."

He rubbed his eyes. "It was Andy's thing. He joked around about it. It made me uncomfortable. I thought it made Doug uncomfortable, too. But I didn't challenge Andy. He was scary. He hurt animals."

"Then why the fuck did you hang out with him?" I asked. "And why on Earth would you let a young girl walk into the woods alone with him?"

"I don't know why I hung out with him," Nate said. "We'd known each other forever. He was always weird. And don't you think I've wished every day of my life since that night that I had done something to stop him?"

"Sylvie says on that particular night, all three of you intended to rape us. That means you intended to rape me."

"No!" Nate cried. "That is absolutely false."

"How is it that Amanda was raped and killed that night," I said, "and Sylvie was also raped that night."

"I don't know!" Nate said. "This is the first I've heard of . . .of what happened to Sylvie. Christ." He shook his head and rubbed his face again. I almost felt sorry for him. Except I was still angry. And sick to my stomach.

"If they came there that night with the intention of raping Amanda and Sylvie," I said, "and you did nothing to stop it, then you are just as responsible for Amanda's death as Andy is. You are just as responsible for Sylvie's rape as Doug is."

"I didn't rape and murder anyone," Nate said. "I never had any intention of doing anything like that. I didn't know Andy was serious about it. Boys say awful things about girls. Disgusting things. All the time. How could I know that this particular boy was going to follow through on his disgusting talk?"

"He wasn't a boy," I said. "He was a fucking man who murdered a young girl. That could have been me, Gunderson. You've got a daughter. Jesus."

Nate looked at me. He had tears in his eyes. "I have tried every day since then to be a better person. A better man. I swear on the lives of my children that I had no idea what Andy or Doug was going to do. I was not part of any rape club. And God, I wish I had done so many things differently that night."

We stood looking at each other.

Then Nate glanced away. While looking at the tall mistletoe trees across the street that shielded the view of the jail from the elementary school, Nate said, "When I visited Andy, he mentioned the rape club. I had completely forgotten he used to talk about it. He said he should have told the police about it. He said he hadn't said anything because he wanted to protect me and Doug, but now it was time. I told him to go fuck himself. I said I wasn't part of any rape club, so he could say whatever he wanted. He's such an asshole. He thinks he's fucking God. He had a right to rape and kill Amanda because he's God, he said. Or like a god. It all made me sick. I couldn't stay and listen."

"So all three of you have visited him recently," I said. "Upon his request. Why do you think he didn't ask me to visit?"

"I don't know," Nate said. "Maybe he didn't know how to get in touch with you."

"Did he ask you about the rest of us?"

Nate shook his head. Then he looked at me. He pressed his lips together. "You're right. I should have told you today about the pregnancy, about the abortion. I really didn't think it had anything to do with now."

"I gotta go," I said. "My kid is visiting. I'm glad it all turned out. Next time you need help—" I waved a hand, as if in dismissal, and I walked away. I had had enough of Nate, Sylvie, Doug, and the past. I just wanted to see my son—and listen to him berate me for being gone so long. Now that sounded like a good time.

Seven

When I got back to the house, Kirti and Scott were in the kitchen, cooking something. Kirti was stirring the contents of a large soup pot on the stove. Scott chopped vegetables on the cutting board on the kitchen table. The house smelled good—although I couldn't identify what the smell was. They both looked over at me when I came into the kitchen.

"The children?" Kirti asked.

"They're safe and sound," I said, using the same words Sylvie had—and the same words Nate had—to describe the children. Same words Polly Zweib had used.

"I'm glad to hear that, Mom," Scott said.

I walked over to the calendar by the stove and looked at today's date: June 25. I had written in: "Scott coming." Had Sylvie seen it when she broke into my house? No. If she broke in a month ago, Scott wasn't speaking to me, and he wasn't coming over. A month ago I didn't even know Scott was engaged.

Christ. Maybe she had just guessed he was coming over. Maybe she figured I did something every year to keep from thinking about that night. What if she had been in my house again, since then?

What did it matter? We had her in custody, would probably charge her for killing the dog and giving a false police report. She wouldn't be coming anywhere near my house any time soon.

I could forget all about her again.

I felt speechless. Or beat up. I couldn't fully feel relief that the girls were safe because I kept getting flashes of that night, when Amanda was murdered. Was there something I had missed that night, something that would have told me some kind of conspiracy was . . . in place?

"Thanks, Scott," I said. I suddenly felt tired. I pulled out a chair from the kitchen table and sat on it.

"If you're hungry, we've got food," Kirti said. "We gathered up what you had in the fridge and added a few of our own ingredients. Soup. Veggies and hummus. Fruit slices we'd packed for our hike. Be good for you to eat after your ordeal."

I looked over at her. "My ordeal?"

She nodded. "You have ordeal written all over your face."

"Well," I said, "someone please get the eraser."

Kirti smiled. "Food. Food is the eraser."

I felt dazed, not at all like myself. I generally didn't feel dazed after a case. It was my job. I did it well. I could tell when people were lying. Or at least, I knew how to ask questions until I could figure out if they were lying or not. It was experience, that's all. It wasn't like I was some kind of police savant. Especially the last few years when I was doing white collar crime. Sometimes a suspect could lie straight to my face, and I'd believe him. Her. That was when my partner, Don Gallagher, helped. He didn't believe a thing any of them said. He believed the more money someone had, the bigger and better liar they were.

I didn't know if that was true or not, but as the years went on, it seemed as though people had gotten better at lying.

Or else I had gotten worse at figuring out the lies.

Scott began opening my cupboards, looking for plates and bowls. I let him look. I didn't feel like saying anything. I just sat, immobile.

"Are those militia people still at the ranger's station?" Kirti asked.

I blinked. I didn't know. I hadn't even asked. I shrugged. I saw Kirti and Scott exchange looks. I didn't care. I reached down and pulled my gun from my ankle and set it on the table. The noise it made—metal against wood—was too loud. Out of the corner of my eye, I saw Kirti jump. Scott looked at me and then looked at the gun and then at me again.

I got up, grabbed the gun, and took it into my bedroom and put it in the top drawer of the night stand. I stared at my bed for a few moments. It looked so inviting.

I shook myself. What the fuck was wrong with me? It was barely noon.

I went back into the kitchen. Kirti was ladling some of the vegetable soup into three bowls Scott had set on my long wooden kitchen table. I wondered how they had gotten that together from my cupboards and fridge.

"Looks good," I said.

Scott set a platter with vegetables, apple slices, and hummus within reach of all of us.

"And last but not least," Scott said as he brought over a plate piled with sandwiches, "tuna fish sandwiches. Sustainably caught."

"I thought tuna had radiation in it," I said, "from the nuclear plant at Fukushima."

"Depends upon who you talk with," Scott said. "But we got ours from a company who tests for radiation."

"What a fucking world," I said. "Jesus." Scott cleared his throat. I glanced at him as he and Kirti sat at the table, Scott at the end and Kirti next to me.

"Sorry," I said to Kirti.

"You don't have to fucking apologize to me," she said. The word "fucking" sounded strange coming out of her mouth. Not sure why. But it made me smile. Scott had just bitten into a sandwich, and he looked like he was going to choke on it.

I was not hungry, but I couldn't—wouldn't—refuse this bounty. They had said they would be there when I returned, and they had been true to their word.

I picked up my spoon and began eating the soup. It was strangely pleasant. Normal. I sighed. Kirti smiled as she picked up half a sandwich and began eating it. Scott had his elbows on the table as he ate. I remembered how my mother used to tell me to get my elbows off the table—it was impolite, she said. "Why?" I had asked her. "Because it is," she said. That was never good enough for me. I kept my elbows off the table, but I never made Scott keep his elbows off. I told him other people might think it was rude, so when he went to other people's houses he might want to keep his elbows off the table. Especially if he wanted to impress someone.

I often wondered how many things people did just "because." Didn't know why they did it, but because everyone else did. . . .

Why had I hardly talked about Amanda's murder to anyone in thirty years? Because…

"When I was sixteen years old, I went out in the woods with five other teens. The sheriff, Nate Gunderson, was one of the teens." I started talking, in-between bites and sips. "We had become summer friends, me and Sylvie and Amanda. They were a little younger, and they kind of looked up to me, and I liked that. I was not exactly friendly in high school in Portland. I had friends, but . . . I was kind of nothing. Or like clay, you know, the way teens can be. I didn't have any deep thoughts, at least none that I can remember.

"Amanda was such a sweet girl. She imitated me a bit. Since I was older, she tried to style her hair like mine. She dressed like me. I pretty much wore jeans and a T-shirt, but she emulated me. I was probably flattered by that. And we met this boy, Nate Gunderson. He was cute, and he was kind of funny. He'd notice things that we didn't. And then after a while, his two friends came to hang out with us, too. I didn't really like either one of them. No, that's wrong. I didn't dislike Doug, but Andy was kind of creepy. But so were lots of boys my age, and he was a little older."

I took a breath and another bite of tuna. I wondered if the tuna had struggled much before it finally died. Weren't tuna big fish? Fast fish? Predators before they became prey?

"Really, I didn't pay much attention to Andy," I said. "I just wanted to be outside, have fun. Thought it would be fun to be out looking for Bigfoot. That's what we were doing that night when Amanda was murdered. None of us believed in Bigfoot." I paused and closed my eyes. I could see us all out of our vehicles looking at the forest that was darker than everything else. The sky was still pale blue as the sun went down. "Maybe they believed in Bigfoot. I dunno. It was just a joke. Or something. It was a way to be outside at night without our parents making a fuss. Although I guess they should have made a fuss."

I opened my eyes and looked at my son. He looked afraid. Why? Hadn't I ever talked to him the way one adult speaks to another?

"We broke up into couples," I said. "I don't know why. I couldn't imagine Andy with anyone. Yuck. Doug and Sylvie were laughing. No, wait. The four of them went toward the woods together." I squinted. "And then maybe they broke apart. That's what I always thought. Nate and I stood there. We were fighting. I can never remember why. It doesn't matter. He would just say stupid things and get on my nerves. I guess. Maybe he took my hand. In a romantic way. Maybe that pissed me off. Or maybe that's what I wanted. I wish I could remember."

I took another bite of my sandwich. I chewed it. Had to force myself to swallow it.

"Something was off that night," I said. "That's what it was. That's what I've never wanted to say. I didn't like where we were. I didn't like being there at night. I felt like something bad was going to happen and it fucking did. And maybe if I had said something, done something. Maybe, maybe, maybe. Instead, I started walking back, I think. This part always confuses me. I started walking and Nate picked me up or I just got in the truck and told him to take me home. But I felt strange out there. So far from home. Getting dark. I didn't have a vehicle. I had to depend upon Nate to get me out of there. And so he dropped me off at home and I went to sleep while Amanda was getting raped and murdered. And I just found out today that while I was sleeping the other girl—Sylvie—was getting raped too."

"Oh, that's awful," Kirti said.

I nodded. "And it's Sylvie's kids we were looking for today. The next morning, the morning after we were all in the woods, I went out there with my dad to see if we could help find

Amanda—because Andy claimed he had lost her in the woods. But I knew something really bad had happened. I saw Nate there, too. We didn't say anything to each other, but we both knew. Everything was so normal. Steam rose from slash piles. Crows and blue jays called out. The sky was that milky blue it sometimes gets in the morning, during the summer. I suppose it would have been pretty in other circumstances, except for the fact that we were standing in a clearcut. Those always feel so . . . violated. We eventually went home and Andy eventually confessed to raping and murdering Amanda. He led the police to the place where he had buried her in the woods, under some rocks and leaves and branches. He took a plea, and he's been in prison ever since."

We ate quietly for a few minutes.

"I never knew all of that," Scott said. "I knew about the murder and that you were all friends. But I didn't know the rest."

"It's not something you tell your children," I said.

"I'm not a kid anymore, Mom," Scott said.

"It's not really something you tell anyone," I said.

"What about Dad?" he asked. "Did he know?"

"Sure," I said. "Most of it. I'm sure." I shrugged again. "The cop Andy confessed to, Deputy Chris Reilly, interviewed me a couple times. He was always nice. A year after the murder, he went into the lava beds near where we were looking for the girls today. Went into the lava beds and killed himself."

"Oh," Kirti said, her oh becoming a moan. This was why I didn't talk about it. But now, I couldn't seem to stop.

"His son, Christopher Darby, told me last month that his dad always felt like he should have done something before Andy killed Amanda, that somehow he should have known. Christopher owns Darby's—you know, the drone place. Good guy. I think. I don't know, though. Sometimes you just can't know."

"That's who Mom is working for now," Scott said. "Darby's. She does employee background checks."

I shrugged. "I only come in when they're not sure about someone they're thinking of hiring," I said, "and it's only been for a few weeks. I'm not sure I like trying to dig up dirt on people."

"Didn't you do that as a police officer?" Scott asked.

"No," I said. "Or if I did it was because I thought they'd committed a crime. These people at Darby's are just looking for a job."

"A job making drones," Scott said. "Drones that can be used to spy on citizens. Maybe even weaponized drones."

I did not want to have this argument today, now, especially since I hadn't decided how I felt about it.

"Let her eat her lunch," Kirti said gently.

"Sorry, Mom," Scott said. "I didn't mean anything." He looked embarrassed or ashamed.

"I never wanted you to be touched by this terrible thing," I said. "I didn't want it to contaminate you. Or your father. Or anyone. Sometimes . . . sometimes it feels like what happened that night has colored my entire life, no matter how much I try to put it behind me. And then something like this happens today. Sylvie pops up after 30 years and says she's killed her children on the 30th anniversary of Amanda's murder. We got out there and found a dead dog and a baby's cap. But no girls. And now Sylvie says she was raped that night, too, because the boys had something called a rape club."

"What?" Scott gasped. "Were you? Were you—were you?"

He couldn't even say the word.

"Was I raped?" I said. "No. Nate and I argued and he took me home. He claims he was not part of any rape club. Says it was just Andy being crazy. But then today Sylvie tells me she was raped by Doug."

I stopped and rubbed my face.

"Last month, you know when I was helping Danella Green find her kidnapped mother, I had a couple incidents here. One was my house was set on fire. I was sleeping and woke up to the house filled with smoke. They never actually found a fire. And I had the back tires stolen from my car."

"I remember that," Scott said. "That was your excuse for being late the night I was going to tell you I was engaged."

"It wasn't an excuse," I said. "It was a reason." I put my hand up. I was not going to argue about this. "Anyway, it turns out that Sylvie did both things. She said she was trying to get caught, so that I could talk her out of killing her kids."

"That's crazy," Scott said.

"Yeah, I know. It doesn't make a lot of sense."

"She's mentally ill," Kirti said, "right? Often they have their own kind of logic. Their own world view."

"Yes," I said. "You're right. But something about it all still bothers me."

"It's so horrible," Kirti said.

Scott said, "I don't know how you could have chosen to spend your life surrounded by such . . . awfulness."

I looked at my son.

OK. That was enough. I could never make him understand. Maybe because I didn't really understand either.

My ex said I had spent my entire adult life trying to save Amanda's life. That didn't make any sense to me. It wasn't like I could go back in time and prevent it.

I sighed. "Tell me something fun. Something good." I smiled.

"May I ask one more thing?" Kirti said.

"Sure," I said. One last thing.

"You said you found a dead dog and a baby's cap," she said.

"Yeah."

"But you didn't find the children?"

"No," I said.

"So why was the cap there?"

"Maybe to throw us off," I said. "I'm not sure. Now, tell me how the wedding plans go."

Kirti and Scott looked at each other, and then Kirti said, "We're not sure. Maybe next spring."

"That's a long way off," I said. "For some reason, I thought it was sooner. I assume it'll be in Seattle?"

"Actually, my parents live in Portland," she said, "and that's where I grew up, so we're thinking about Portland."

"That would be great," I said. "I never like that drive to Seattle. I feel like someone is always trying to kill me—with their car."

Kirti laughed. Scott scowled.

"Any advice for us?" Kirti asked.

My eyes widened, and I dropped my spoon dramatically. "Advice? Are you asking me for advice? I don't think Scott has ever asked me for advice his entire life."

"He's not asking," Kirti said. "I am."

"Make sure you know each other," I said. "Can't make a marriage out of lust, not one that will last. Talk about expectations: children, job, sex, food, money. Make sure you like each other's jobs."

"Dad hated Mom's job," Scott said.

I nodded. "Same job I had when we got married, same job when we divorced. I didn't understand why he didn't like it."

"Because he was afraid you'd be hurt," Scott said. "That's what I was afraid of, too."

"That would be nice to believe, I suppose. But it wasn't that. He thought I gave too much to it, thought I cared more about the people I worked with—even the people I arrested—than I did for him or for you." I shrugged. "Maybe I was more comfortable around them. But I figured I was making the world safer for you and your dad. That way I wouldn't have to worry about you so much. For so many weeks or months—maybe even years—after Amanda was murdered, I'd wake up in a sweat wondering how to go on, how to be in this world without being terrified for myself and everyone I loved. Being a police officer gave me some control, I thought, and some skills. When you left to go live with your father—he left when he was 12, wanted to go live with his pops—I often parked outside the house, just to make certain you were both OK. That you were safe." I heard my voice break. Felt tears sting my eyes. I blinked.

"I didn't know," Scott said. "I always thought you were glad to see me go."

I looked at him. "What? How could you think that? It broke my heart. It fucking crushed me."

"But you never said. You never asked me to stay."

"You were a twelve-year-old boy who wanted a man in his life," I said. "You were unhappy living with me, and you thought your dad would make you happy. I wasn't going to ask you to stay for my benefit! The job of a parent is to do what's *best* for your kid. One hundred percent of the time."

"Then why didn't you quit your job?" he asked.

"You don't do what your kids want," I said. "You do what's best for them. How would it be good for you if I quit my job just because you wanted more of my attention?"

"I didn't want you dead!"

"Scott," I said, "come on. You wanted me home catering to your every need and want. That's what all kids would like. Unless they have it. Then they want something else."

"I wanted my mother to work," Kirti said. "I wanted her to dress like how I thought an American would dress—like all the other mothers—and I wanted her to have a job so that she wouldn't know every single thing about every part of my life."

"See," I said. "Anecdotal proof. And I wanted my mother to be on this planet. She always seemed so out of it. Like some drug-addicted mother from a Tennessee Williams play."

"Grandma is a drug addict?" Scott asked.

"No. At least not that I know about."

"I wished you had told me all of this before," Scott said.

"Why?" I asked. "So you could criticize me for telling it all to you earlier?"

"I'm not criticizing you," he said.

"That's what it sounds like," Kirti said.

Scott sighed. "I guess—I mean, I should have said that I'm glad we talked about it today. Finally."

I laughed and shook my head. He could not resist getting in that final dig.

"You should watch that passive-aggressive streak you have," I said. "It's not good for you or the people around you."

"Now who's being critical?" Scott asked.

"I am," I said. "And I'm giving you some good advice. Passive-aggressive is just a nice way of saying asshole. So don't be an asshole."

Kirti laughed loudly.

"You're getting way too much pleasure out of this," Scott said to Kirti.

"Yep," she said, nodding.

"This was a great lunch," I said. "I needed it." I breathed deeply. I could let this go. I could. The girls were safe. Sylvie would get help. And…

"It was hard getting anything past Mom," Scott said. "She was really good at telling whether I was lying or not."

I nodded. "Yep. It's a good skill for a parent to have."

"I fooled you sometimes," Scott said.

"Really?" I asked. "When?"

"Sometimes if I told you what you wanted to hear, I could

get something by you. First I'd admit to one thing and then charm you with the next thing. 'Yes, Mom, we went to the arcade after school, but then I went home and did my homework,' even though I hadn't done my homework. But if you were tired or you didn't want a fight, sometimes I could tell, and then I'd just say what you wanted to hear—or what would make you relax."

"Well, you little con," Kirti said.

"Yep, I was one bad boy," he said.

I laughed. "You were not," I said. "Most kids are con artists. Criminals, too. I probably couldn't tell you were lying because you were mine, and I didn't expect it. When I'm interrogating a suspect, my only goal is the truth."

"But you must care about the outcome," Scott said.

"I want the crime solved," I said, "and I want peace for the families. But it's not personal."

"It must have been personal today," Kirti said. "Because you knew her, because she asked for you."

I nodded.

I closed my eyes. I could see Sylvie standing near the blanket in the forest. She looked shocked that the girls weren't there. But she would have known they weren't there—because she didn't kill them.

And yet, she had seemed so certain that she had to kill them, for their own good. I had run into crazy many times before and crazy did have its own logic.

She had been surprised that her girls were not on the blanket next to the dog. Dead.

She thought she had killed them.

Yet later she told us they were safe and sound.

And her friend Polly had confirmed they were safe and sound.

They had used the same phrase.

Oh crap.

No, no, no.

Sylvie had told me exactly what I wanted to hear: the girls were safe and sound.

Fuck.

How stupid could I be?

I put my head in my hands for a moment.

Then I looked at Kirti and Scott. "I don't think the kids are safe. I need to go."

"Of course," Scott said.

I pulled out my phone and called Nate.

"I think she lied to us," I said when I heard his voice.

"What?"

"I think the girls are still out in those woods. Call Polly Zweib or whatever her name is. Demand to speak to Beauty because I don't think she's there."

"I don't understand," Nate said.

"Is Sylvie still at the cop shop?"

"Yes," Nate said. "You've only been gone for a short time."

I wanted to scream, "Don't talk to me about time!" How much time had I wasted by believing a crazy woman?

"I'll be right there," I said. "Don't let her go."

I stood and slipped the phone into my back pocket. I could hear the clock ticking in my head again. I looked at the clock on my stove. Noon. Fucking high noon.

I ran into the bedroom, got my gun and put it in my boot again, and then hurried back to the kitchen.

"Kids, thank you for this talk," I said. "You helped. Now, I've got to see if I can fix my screwup."

"We'll wait for you," Kirti said. She stood. Scott came to stand next to her. He put his arm across her shoulders.

"That's right," Scott said. "We'll be here when you get back, and you can tell us all about it. Or you can say nothing at all. But we'll be here. I'll be here, Mom."

"That's kind of you," I said. "But there's no need. I don't want to keep you. Go out and enjoy the day."

"We'll enjoy the day," Kirti said. "Right here in Beauty Falls. We'll feed you when you get back." She smiled, but she knew everything was not bright and cheery. She knew I was about to walk back into a horror show. Yet she was reminding me that I had another world to come home to.

My son was a lucky man.

"OK," I said. "Once more into the breach, dear kids, once more."

"God for Harry, Beauty Falls, and Saint George!" Kirti cried, raising her fist.

I laughed. "Jesus, Scott, you have got to marry this woman."

Then I stepped out into the blue sky day again.

Eight

Nate came out of the door to the sheriff's department as I was about to go in. He looked me straight in the eye. Now that the truth was out, he wasn't going to avoid it. Or me. I supposed that indicated a core decency in him.

Or maybe he was trying to con me, too.

"You were right," Nate said. "The girls aren't with Sylvie's friend Polly. She told me Sylvie asked her to tell anyone who called that she had the girls and they were safe and sound. Sylvie convinced her she needed time to get out of town and away from her husband."

Nate held the door open for me, and we went inside.

"Yeah, I fucked up," Nate said. "I should have asked the Clark County sheriff's department to go out to that woman's house to make certain the children were there. Christ. I believed Sylvie. I fucking believed her."

"She was trying to buy time," I said, "so that her daughters would die out there."

"We need the truth," Nate said.

"Get someone else to do it," I said. "You and I are too close to the situation. I mean, she fucking lied to us, and we both missed it. Those girls could be dead now because we believed her. I believed her."

"If there's any hope that they're alive, you're the one to find out. We don't have time to get someone else up to speed, to get Sylvie to trust them. You gotta do this, Katie."

Fuck.

Nate pointed to Interview Room 1. I strode to the door, jerked it open, and said, loudly, forcefully, "We know that you're a liar, Sylvie Brubaker Smith. Your daughters are not safe and sound with Polly. Now tell us where they are."

The deputy who had been inside the room with Sylvie left as Nate came in and closed the door behind him. Sylvie looked up at me, shaking her hair out of her eyes. She smiled.

"That was pretty stupid of you," Sylvie said. "I guess you didn't avoid being raped because of your intellectual prowess."

I pulled out a chair and sat across from Sylvie.

"Tell me what happened and where they are," I said.

"Pleasure," Sylvie said. "I have done what God asked of me. Soon we'll all pay the price, and the souls of the children will be saved. We will be saved. The sins of the parents will be visited on the children. Should be visited."

"Sylvie!" I snapped. "Tell us what happened."

"Or what?" she asked. "What are you going to do to me if I don't tell you? Take away my dead children?"

"So your word means nothing?" I said. "We did as you requested. We got Doug here. You got to tell the truth of what happened that night. And now, in turn you lied to us."

"I killed my children," she said. "Do you think I'd actually hesitate to lie to you? What is a lie compared with filicide and infanticide? In any case, I must do as God instructed."

This was going nowhere.

"We're sorry for what happened to you," Nate said, "for what Doug did. There is nothing we can do about the past."

"But there is," she said. "And I am doing it."

Nate sighed.

Sylvie asked, "What time is it?"

"A little after noon," Nate answered.

"I guess it's OK then," she said. She looked at me and smiled as though she was seeing me for the first time . . . again.

"I shot Princess first," she said. "The sound was so loud. It shook me up. The dog didn't make a sound, but Beauty screamed and Joy cried. Some of the buckshot got the girls, I thought. I was sure they'd be dead, too. I was sure I had done God's work. But they weren't dead, unless the dead can cry and scream."

I blinked. Swallowed. I wished I could close my ears and not hear it. But I had to listen to it all, every detail, try to glean the truth from the . . . chaff.

"Then the Devil—using my own voice—told Beauty to run, run, told her to find the Beauty Falls and she'd be safe. Beauty had Joy in her arms and was running when I shot again. The pieces of shot turned into butterflies, black butterflies, who all flew up and away. Beauty went into the lava beds and disappeared. Maybe a door opened in the beds and she went through it. I don't know. I reloaded the gun. Told Beauty to come out and meet her maker. That was me. I was her maker. Get it?" Sylvie smiled. She liked her word play.

"I went in after her," she said, "but I slipped and fell, so I didn't stay long. That's how I hurt my hand. I waited a while, calling to them, but I heard nothing. I hope my voice was the last one they heard as they lay dying."

Fuck, fuck, mother fuck.

Beauty must have been terrified out of her mind.

"Did you shoot them?" Nate asked.

"I aimed at them," Sylvie said. "I thought I had, but who knows. If the shot didn't kill them, the lava beds did. Now, can I get something to eat? I am starving. Maybe literally. It's been days since I've eaten."

I knew she was sick. I knew it wasn't her fault, in the grand scheme of things. But I wanted to scream at her. I wanted to shake her.

"We'll get you something to eat," Nate said. "Sure."

I pushed my chair away from the table. Sylvie looked up at me and smiled.

Nate and I left the room together.

Sylvie called after us, "Nice seeing you again! Enjoy your kids while you can."

I was tempted to yell after her: "I didn't kill my child, so I will enjoy him, thank you."

Something about her made me feel . . . childish.

"Call out search and rescue," I said. "We have to find those kids."

Nate shook his head. "I can't call out search and rescue. That would be putting too many civilians in danger. There are too many militia people in that area."

"Has to be some way around them," I said. "There must be back roads we can go on and then hike over to where Sylvie chased the girls into the lava beds."

Nate said, "If the girl took her baby sister into the lava beds, I don't know if we'll ever find them."

"We've got to try," I said.

Sandy Dean came up to us. "FBI is trying to get a hold of you, sheriff," she said.

"Crap," Nate said. "I left the phone in my office. I'll be right back."

Sandy and I stood quietly for a few seconds. Then she said, "You and Nate good?"

I gave her a look.

"He was a kid," Sandy said. "I bet he had nothing to do with any rape club."

"So he says. But I don't care about that right now. I just want to help find these kids."

"You think they're still alive?"

"I have no idea," I said. "But Sylvie says Beauty ran into the woods with her baby sister, which means they had to be alive then. Maybe she's lying. Nate said the FBI has got the roads all closed now as they're dealing with this militia. But couldn't we go down Wind River, past the ranger station—and past the militia people and then head across and over to get to the lava beds?"

"Lydia would know," Sandy said. "The map is on the wall around the corner. I'll go find her."

I went to the wall on the other side of Nate's office and found a detailed map of the county. I followed State Route 14 with my finger—SR14 was the main road through Beauty Falls—until I got to Wind River Road and then down Wind River Road to the ranger's station. About then Lydia and Sandy were next to me.

"This is where Sylvie said she killed the girls," Lydia said, moving her finger across the map. With her other hand, she followed the course of Wind River Road, stopping when she was almost opposite to where Sylvie had taken us this morning.

"There is a logging road that goes partway in," Lydia said, pointing. "Once we're past the roadblock, we could go up this road, and then hike through the woods. There's a bridge here, on this property. I know the homeowners. They'd let us cross, and the river is pretty low now. And then we could hike down here, skirting the lava beds until we enter at the same place we were this morning."

"How long will that take?" I asked.

"Not long," Lydia said, "depending upon the brush. Maybe an hour if we're going fast. We won't be on an actual trail, and I don't think there's been a fire in that area for awhile. We'll encounter a lot of bushes and or Oregon grape. Hopefully no blackberry bushes are up there." She shook her head. "I really don't know."

I looked at the clock. Coming up on 12:30.

"If we could get there by 1:00, 1:15," I said, "and get to the lava beds by 2:30, we'd still have plenty of daylight."

The sun would go down around 9:00 p.m.

"If gets dark in the lava beds before sunset," Lydia said. "They're surrounded by forest. And the beds curve up into the forest where it's even darker." She shook her head. "Let's just hope we find the kids quickly."

Nate came out of his office. "All right," he said. "Apparently Elias Johnson won't talk to the feds. He says they have no jurisdiction."

"But they've taken over a *federal* facility," Sandy said.

"Yeah, well, they have some convoluted idea or belief or something about the government stealing the land from the county or the state. States' rights and all that. He wants to talk to me, so I need to go out there. I talked to the agent in charge and told her about the kids. They'll let you go past the blockade. You'll just follow me in. Do you have a plan?"

We showed Nate on the map where we were going to start hiking in.

Nate nodded. "All right. I'm assuming the militia people probably have lookouts on Wind River Road, even if we can't see them. I don't want you taking a squad car. That'll make you more of a target."

"We can take my car," Lydia said. "I got everything we need, backpacks including food and water, rope, flashlights."

Nate nodded. "Phones won't work there, you know, or hardly anywhere down Wind River. And your compasses won't be reliable."

"We know, sheriff," Lydia said. "Let's get going."

"I'll be out there in a minute," Nate said.

Lydia and Sandy hurried away. I started to follow them, but Nate took a hold of my arm. I looked down at his hand on my sleeve, and he immediately let go of it.

"Are we good?" he asked.

I looked at him. I felt vaguely sick to my stomach. But that was it. I had a job to do, so nothing else mattered. Time was a wastin'.

"You want to ride with me out to the blockade," he said, "and we can talk?"

"About what? You want to fill me in on all the details of the rape club?"

He cringed and glanced around. "I thought you might want to talk, that's all."

"Hell, no!" I said. I laughed—snorted, more like it. "No. I do not want to be in a car alone with you. Talking. Or doing anything else. We clear?"

Nate grimaced.

"Come on," I said. "You need to lead us out."

Just then, Sylvie's husband came around the corner. His eyes were red, his body rigid even as he strode toward us.

"Mr. Smith," Nate said, "I sent someone to—"

"They told me," he said. "First they said Sylvie may have killed my precious girls. Now they say it's possible they're alive. I don't know what to believe! I have prayed. I have prayed like

I never prayed before." He was shaking as he stopped before us—or shivering, like a dog left out in the cold too long. "I wish I could go back in time and change everything. I would stop this. Somehow. I was so caught up in all of my failures that I never saw this coming. I always thought—even though she was sick—I always thought she was strong, Sylvie, that she could do anything. I never guessed. Never guessed." He shook his head.

It was a lie I had heard many times over the course of my career: "If we had only suspected, we would have done something, anything, to stop it." Most of the time it was not a surprise, even if the family and friends claimed they never saw it coming. That was why Deputy Sheriff Christopher Reilly had walked into the lava beds a year after Amanda was murdered—because he had known Andy since he was a child in grade school. He had heard about him pulling the legs off of bugs. About torturing animals. About scaring his mother with a knife one night. But he hadn't wanted to believe that the child he had seen on the playground with his own son—perhaps—could have grown into such a monster. Monsters aren't born as full grown men or women. They've got to be . . . raised into monsters.

"We're going out now to look for your daughters," I said, interrupting my own thought stream.

Bruce Smith took his wallet from his pocket and then pulled out a photo and handed it to me. In the photo, he sat on a bench next to Sylvie. He held the baby while a young girl stood behind everyone, one hand on her mother's shoulder and the other on her father's. She smiled broadly for the camera. They all did. A happy little family. With the mother wearing an out-of-date long dress, her long hair pulled loosely away from her face. Even in this photo, with Sylvie smiling, I didn't recognize her as the girl who had spent part of the summer with me and Amanda.

"Those are my girls," Bruce said. "Full of life. They deserve a life, one different from ours. Do you think it's possible? Now?

Or is it all lost, all over? No jobs. No good air or water." He shook his head. "Sometimes I think the Rapture has already happened and we were all left behind in this hideousness."

He stared at the photograph he held. "Except these girls. They are not a part of any . . . horror." He looked at me. "Bring them home." He held the photograph out to me. "Please, take it with you, to remind you."

I didn't need any reminder. I knew what my intention was: I wanted to save his daughters. I took the photograph.

He wiped his face across his arm.

"May I see Sylvie now?" he asked.

Nate said, "I think it would be better to wait. I'll have one of the deputies get you something to eat." Nate put his hand on the man's left shoulder. "Come with me. I'll meet you outside, Kate."

Lydia and Sandy were already in the car when I got there, which meant I was going to have to sit in the back again, like some kind of criminal.

Before I had time to be annoyed by that, Nate came out. He handed me a phone. "This is one of those cheap prepaid phones. For some reason, they're more likely to work out in the forest. Just in case you need to get a hold of me. I'll meet you at the lava beds as soon as I can. Who knows? Maybe I'll miraculously convince the militia to go home peacefully. So keep me apprised."

I took the phone and tucked it in one of my boots. A gun in one boot, a phone in another. My idea of a purse.

"Good luck," Nate said.

I didn't know what to say, so I just nodded. We were going out looking for two little girls who could be dead. I had seen dead children on the job before. Two dead in a car accident when I was first starting out. Looked like they were both asleep. Except something was missing. Like finding a dead cat on the side of the road. Only a thousand times worse. And then a boy whose brother had accidentally shot him with their father's gun. That had been . . . obscene. I closed my eyes briefly, trying to wipe that memory away.

Fortunately I had never seen Amanda dead—except in my imagination. That was bad enough.

No, I didn't want to find any dead children today. Or any day.

Nine

Soon enough the four of us were headed out of town again. Nate was alone in his squad car ahead of us. Sandy, Lydia, and I were in Lydia's car, with Sandy driving for some reason. She drove too fast again, but I didn't get sick. Enough of that. I swallowed forcefully and looked out the window as we went through Carson.

We stopped briefly at the new blockade the FBI had set up. Nate talked to someone who came up to his window. I saw him gesturing to us, saw the agent or whatever he was look back at us, and then we were headed down the road again, deeper into the forest. We passed by second growth forests, maybe third growth. I didn't know. And then the road curved again and again, and I knew we were in mixed forest, mostly new growth with some of the old growth that hadn't been burned up in a massive fire that had nearly leveled these forests more than a century ago.

"Did Sylvie give you any more information?" Lydia asked. She glanced back at me. "I figure she must have or we wouldn't be going out again."

"She told us she shot at the children," Sandy said, "as the older one was running into the lava beds. So there's a better chance that they're alive. Maybe. Since before she said she had killed them."

What were we doing? Running after rumors? Ghosts?

"She doesn't sound very reliable," Lydia said.

"We can't tell what is reliable," Sandy said, "and what isn't. Some of the stuff she's told us about the past turned out to be true."

Sandy glanced up in the rearview mirror at me. I looked away. I certainly did not want to discuss the rape club with either of them, at least not now.

Nate slowed his cruiser before he turned down the road where the militia was. We kept going. No other cars were on Wind River Road since the FBI had shut it down in both directions. Or had the militia group closed it down in the north? I didn't know. I didn't care. Just get me on the trail. Find the girls. And then get back to my son. Put this whole awful day behind me. Again. I was sorry Sylvie had been raped. I mean, gawd. It was horrible. But it wasn't an excuse for her craziness.

I bit the inside of my cheek. I didn't know what I was thinking. An *excuse* for her craziness? Of course she had a reason for her craziness. It was probably brain chemistry. And yet, I didn't feel sorry for her. She had already killed her pet. She'd broken into my house. I just wanted her out of my life.

Soon enough, Sandy pulled off the road and onto a turnout. She popped the trunk, and we all got out.

"No smoke," Lydia said. "Last I heard the wind was still sending the fire eastward. Although the storm could change all that."

We did not need a wildfire to deal with on top of everything else.

Lydia took out two backpacks and handed one to each of us. Then she pulled on her own.

"I always keep extra," she said, "for search and rescue. You never know which yahoo will come unprepared."

Sandy laughed. "Yeah, well, I guess that makes us the yahoos."

Lydia shrugged. Then she leaned into the trunk and pulled out a machete longer than her forearm. She held it up and grinned. "My favorite thing from my days in Central America. It was a gift. It's pretty old, but sharp as a—well, as a machete. It was so fucking easy to track in the jungle. Just follow the machete trail. Of course, if we didn't follow it right away, the jungle healed itself and grew right over it all again in hours. Maybe minutes. Like fucking magic."

"You tracked people in Central America?" Sandy asked.

Lydia shut the trunk and locked the car.

"Not on purpose," she said. "I just got lost a few times."

I laughed. Sandy rolled her eyes. Lydia chuckled. "These young uns," she said. "They are gullible."

"Yeah, well, come on, *abuela*," Sandy said, "we're following you."

I looked around the silent forest: trees all around us, the road a gray line winding through it all. Above, a blue sky. Thankfully it wasn't too hot. Even so, I took a swig from the water bottle hanging from my backpack. It tasted . . . warm.

"Is this water from this century?" I asked.

"Beggars and choosers," Lydia said.

Lydia stepped off the gravel side of the road and went down into the ditch and then stepped into the semi-darkness of the forest. Sandy followed, and I was next, all of us heading west. The forest floor was free of bushes this close to the river. Young Doug firs grew around us. We followed a deer or fisher's path through the trees and Oregon grape.

At one point, Lydia stopped to show us the bear marks on an older Douglas fir, where the bear's teeth had dug into the cambium. Teardrop-shaped pale gold exuded through the cuts.

"This happened recently," Lydia said. "Be on the lookout. Make a lot of noise." She picked up a stick and broke it. The sound echoed through the woods. "It's the polite thing to do."

We walked down into a small ravine or trench, up again, and then down through some cottonwoods. The river was near, but I couldn't hear it yet. We walked northwest for a bit, through the young cottonwoods and birch. Soon we were walking alongside the river which was now running shallow and slow. A belted kingfisher flew above the water, low, her rattling call piercing the forest as she flew by us, like some kind of bird school marm scolding us for our intrusion.

"Supposed to be good luck to see a kingfisher," Lydia said. "At least that's what someone told me once."

"Then it must be true," Sandy said.

"You're too young to be such a smart ass," Lydia said.

"Better than being a dumb ass," Sandy said.

Lydia and I both groaned.

"No, wait, I didn't mean you were a dumb ass," she said. "I

meant I was surrounded by boys growing up, and they were always calling me a dumb ass. So I learned to give it back to them."

"Aren't families wonderful?" Lydia asked.

"Speaking for myself," I said, "at least no one in my family ever tried to shoot me."

"Yeah, speak for yourself," Lydia said. "I had a brother and a cousin who tried to shoot me."

"What?" Sandy asked.

Lydia nodded. "They were drunk—and kids. They got hold of my uncle's gun, swore it was a toy, and they were pointing it at me and my sister. Fortunately no one got hurt. Well, my father beat the shit out of my brother when he got home. But I gotta tell ya, I think he deserved it."

I didn't know if I should laugh or be horrified. Lydia laughed. Then we went quiet for a while as we walked.

Eventually Lydia stopped and pointed. "There's the private bridge up there." I saw a small wooden bridge not far from us. If Lydia hadn't pointed it out, I probably would have missed it in the tangle of vines that were taking up real estate around the bridge.

A dog began barking in the near distance, its voice deep and slow, like some kind of drunk hound dog.

"They have a dog?" I asked.

"I guess," Lydia said. "I didn't remember that. I'm sure it's fine."

"I can't tell you how many calls I took where someone was bitten by a dog the owner claimed would never hurt a soul."

"You had to go out on dog calls?" Sandy asked. "We do, too, now that the money was cut for animal control. I hate it."

"Those calls escalated into something worse," I said. "Even though a dog bite is pretty bad in itself."

"I'll see if I can call them." Lydia took out her phone. "Nope. No service. Come on. I've used this bridge many times. Tom and Betsy McIntyre."

"Oh, we're coming on the backside of their property," Sandy said.

"Why does that matter?" I asked as we walked to the stairs that led up to the bridge.

"We've been called out here a few times," Sandy said. "A dog incident a couple years ago, when I first started working dispatch. Then they had some kind of clan meeting our here last month that . . . disturbed the neighbors."

Lydia and I both stopped walking and looked at Sandy.

"As in the ku klux klan?" Lydia asked.

"I didn't see anyone in white robes," Sandy said, "but there were quite a few confederate flags. And lots of guns."

"Everyone and their dog has guns out here," Lydia said.

"And they did not like police," Sandy said. "Except the sheriff. They liked Nate. When some of the . . . guests got belligerent, the sheriff put on his good ol' boy song and dance and charmed them all."

"How?" I asked. "By spewing racist epithets?"

Sandy made a face. "No, he's not like that. He just called them out by name. Like, 'Hi, Billy, saw that great pass your son made at last Friday's game,' and 'You need some help shearing those sheep this year, I'm your man. Remember when we did that as kids for your dad for a buck a day?' Stuff like that. Calmed everyone down, and McIntyre promised to keep the gun play and carousing to a minimum. So I guess they put on their white robes and did all their ceremonies quietly."

I snorted.

"That works?" Lydia said. "Just to remind them that they know you? I'd think familiarity would breed contempt."

"You'd be surprised," I said. "The ability to talk about the weather or sports has saved lots of calls from turning . . . bad."

"Well," Lydia said, "I've never had a bit of trouble with the McIntyres when I've been tracking, and I'm brown. Sandy's red. I guess your lily white ass can save us from trouble, Katie Kelly, should there be any trouble."

I grimaced. "Yeah, thanks, but no thanks. I'll let you go first since you have a rapport with them. I'm not looking for a *Deliverance* moment here."

Sandy looked at me. "What's a deliverance moment?"

I started to explain, and Sandy laughed. "I'm kidding. I've seen that movie. Complete fear mongering about country folk."

"Yeah, just you using the word 'folk' means I gotta watch out for you," I said.

Lydia led the way up the steps to the wooden bridge. The bridge was narrow but seemed sturdy, with a rope safety line to hang on to as we crossed. Cottonwoods lined the banks of the slow-moving stream beneath us. Beyond them, Douglas firs towered, cutting out most of the sunlight. A crow flew above us. We reached the top of the stairs and stepped onto the bridge.

And then I heard the *chk-chk* of a shotgun racking.

Chills ran up and down my spine.

The three of us stopped walking.

I looked around quickly. I saw only trees.

"Mr. McIntyre!" Lydia called. "It's Lydia Alvarez from search and rescue."

A white man dressed in camo stepped out of the green and black on the other side of the bridge. He dropped the muzzle of his shotgun when he saw Lydia.

"My turn to apologize," Lydia said, still not moving forward. "I should have called. We've got a couple of missing girls."

"Come across," he said, waving us forward.

When we stepped off of the bridge onto McIntyre's land, Lydia introduced us to him.

"I apologize," McIntyre said, "but we heard about the militia taking over the ranger's station. I was concerned some of them might be coming this way."

Lydia nodded. "That's why we're hiking through here. The girls are over by the lava beds, maybe in them, off Boot Hill Road, but the militia people wouldn't let us pass. So we're going in the back way, skirting the lava and getting to the point of entry."

McIntyre nodded. "Yep, this is the best way." He pointed west. "There's a trail through there that will get you to where you need to be. Shouldn't run into any more people. But the bears are out."

"I saw sign of them," Lydia said. "Any other day I've be thrilled to track them. But we have other goals."

"Did the girls get lost hiking?"

Lydia shook her head. "It's a long story," she said, "but they're in danger. They're ten and under one."

"Jesus," he said. "I can take out my hounds and come with you."

Sandy said, "They do well in the lava beds?"

He grimaced. "Yeah, probably not. They could track to there, but not inside the lava beds. I better let you girls get going, then."

"Thanks, Mr. McIntyre," Lydia said. "Say hello to your wife."

He nodded. Lydia led us away from McIntyre. When we stepped onto the trail again, I could just see his house and barn in the near distance behind us.

"Welcome to Beauty County," Sandy said quietly as we hurried back into the forest. "Land of the free, home of the armed."

For the next hour, more or less, I followed Lydia and Sandy through the dense forest. It was mostly second growth Doug firs with ferns, Oregon grape, and salal growing close to the trail. I didn't know if we were on U.S. Forest land or someone's property, but I figured Lydia knew what she was doing. The forest was quiet, as it usually was when I hiked it. If we stopped, we'd hear birds after a bit. I knew the forest was filled with creatures—at least I hoped it was—but they were quiet as we passed through. I didn't even hear any birds alarming on us, telling other birds that we were coming by. I felt almost peaceful as we walked. As if nothing could possibly go wrong on this beautiful summer day, certainly not in this peaceful forest. We didn't hear or see another human being. We tried our various cellphones periodically, but none of them got any service. We were alone. Except for all of nature.

And then we travelled up for a time and then down. I wasn't certain how it happened, but we were suddenly there, in the gravel pit: there was the blanket and the lump of something that I knew was a dead dog.

We were still for a moment, staring at the scene of the crime.

"Christ," Sandy said, patting her pockets. "I must have left my phone on that last rock outcropping." The last place we had tried to get phone service. "I'll be right back."

Sandy slipped back into the woods. Lydia and I stood in the gravel pit, about twenty feet from the blanket, looking around: up at the blue sky, around at the Douglas firs surrounding us, anywhere except the gore on the blanket.

I shook off my backpack and dropped it to the ground. Ahhh, that felt good. I breathed deeply and closed my eyes. I almost felt relaxed.

"Beauty," I called out softly but loud enough to be heard.

"Beauty, we're here to help you and your sister. Your mom is in jail. She can't hurt you."

Lydia and I held our breaths for a moment, listening. We heard a blue jay call out. Then the high-pitched whistle of some insect. That was all.

And then I heard a deep male voice say, "Put your hands up where I can see them."

Christ.

I raised my hands and turned around.

Ten

Danny Johnson stood thirty feet away, looking down the barrel of his rifle at us.

"I knew you'd come back here," Danny said. "My daddy is too trusting of cops."

I glanced over at Lydia.

"We're not cops," I said. "We are private citizens trying to save the lives of two little girls."

"Bullshit," Danny said. "Where's the cop?" He looked around.

"What are you talking about?" I asked.

"You came with a cop last time," he said. "I wanna know where she is."

"She's back at the station," I said. "We came out to find the girls. Good Samaritans and all that."

"Cut the crap," he said. "You came here to capture us."

"Yes, just the two of us," I said. "That would have been smart."

I was hoping if we talked long enough, Sandy would hear us, stay back, and maybe get the jump on this guy. Or just stay out of his way. It was better if all three of us weren't caught.

"All we care about are those girls," Lydia said. "They might be hurt."

Danny shook his head. "I don't believe there are any lost or hurt girls. You made that up to fool us."

"We didn't know anything about you when we found out about the girls," Lydia said. "This is what I do. I look for lost people. Let me do it. You can wait right here and watch us go in."

"Go in?" he asked, dropping the rifle slightly. "Go in where?"

"Into the lava beds," Lydia said, inclining her head in the direction of the lava fields.

"Lava beds?" he said. "There's volcanoes around here?"

"Dude," Lydia said, "you're in the Cascades. Mount St. Helens." Lydia pointed north. "Mount Adams." She pointed northeast. "Mount Rainier." Northwest. She pointed south. "Mount Hood. They're all volcanoes."

"Oh, yeah, sure," he said.

"Guess you're not from around here," I said.

"So what?" he said. "I can still have an opinion about what's happening. It's my country, and I want the land to go back to people."

I rolled my eyes.

"If you don't want to wait for us," Lydia said, "you can come with. Help us find the girls. You'll be a hero."

He frowned. Even though he was pointing a gun at us, I wasn't afraid. Not yet. I was more annoyed than anything else. I knew it could all go sideways any second. For one, he was stupid enough that he could shoot us by mistake. But right now, he was an impediment to us finding the girls.

And where the hell was Sandy?

Finally, he shook his head. "No, I'm taking you back to the station. My dad needs to know that the cops are not to be trusted, even the sheriff."

"You think daddy dearest is gonna be glad that you kidnapped two people?" I asked. "So far your group is only guilty of trespassing, I would imagine. You take us, you are raising the stakes in a way that your father may not have intended."

"You have no idea what my dad intends," he said.

I glanced at Lydia. She looked scared. Yeah, that was the proper emotion when one is staring down the wrong end of a gun barrel: fear.

"That's true," I said. "Why don't you call him? Let him know you found us. Give him our side of the story."

That would be better than Danny kidnapping us. Plus, it would give us time for Sandy to come and save the day. Danny seemed to think about it. Then he wiped his eyes on his forearm. The rifle shook slightly. I could have lunged at him then, but I was too far away, would take too long to get to him.

"No," he said. "You don't get to tell me what to do." He switched the gun so he was holding it with one hand and reached into his pocket with the other and pulled out what looked like plastic handcuffs.

Why on earth was this young man carrying plastic handcuffs?

He tossed them on the ground in front of us.

"You," he said, indicating me. "Put those on her. And then she'll put them on you."

I didn't argue with him. I picked up the plastic handcuffs. Lydia held out her hands, wrists pressed together, and I slipped on the cuffs.

"Tighten them," he said.

"I don't want to cut off her circulation," I said. I tightened them slightly.

"Now her you," he said.

I did not want this to happen. I glanced around the woods. No sign of Sandy. Lydia picked up the other handcuffs, gingerly, since her wrists were bound. I held my hands together, thumbs pressed against each other, my fingers balled into fists, while she slipped the cuffs on. She tightened them, but not too much. Once I relaxed my hands, I was hoping there would be enough movement that I could slip the cuffs off.

"Now get in the truck," Danny said. "Go on." He used the gun as a pointer.

"Don't do this," I said. "You're getting yourself into a whole bathtub of hot water. Come on. Where's your mother? Talk to your mother about this if you don't want to speak to your dad. I have a son about your age. I sure wouldn't want him getting into this kind of trouble."

"I'm just protecting what is mine," he said.

"What's yours?" I asked. I looked around.

"This occupation," he said. "That's ours. You're trying to disrupt that. I'm gonna stop you. And don't talk about my mother."

I clenched my teeth. Everything I ever learned, everything I ever experienced, told me I should not get in that truck.

"I'm not going with you," I said. "I don't know what you're going to do with us."

"I won't hurt you," he said. "I wouldn't hurt anyone."

"You're holding us hostage," I said. "You've got a gun on us."

"I said I won't hurt you," he said. "Get in the truck."

"No, we're not going with you."

"Get in the fucking truck!"

I pressed my lips together.

"I won't shoot you," Danny said. "But if you don't get in the truck, I will shoot her." He pointed to Lydia with the barrel of the gun.

"Fuck," I murmured.

"Look, it's just a mile away," he said. "I swear on my mother that I won't hurt either of you."

"Unless I won't get into the truck. In that case, you'll shoot her."

"Jesus," he said. "Just get in the truck."

I glanced at Lydia. She looked terrified. I started walking toward the truck. My hands were bound in front of me. If worse came to worse, maybe I could choke him. Or get my hands out of the cuffs and punch him. I didn't want to do that. That would hurt. Fortunately the idiot had not patted us down or checked for guns. I still had my gun in my boot. And Sandy was out there somewhere.

Danny opened the passenger door. I got in first, and then Lydia sat next to me. The console of the truck was smeared with dirt and oil, and the whole thing smelled like French fries. I kicked away the fast food to-go boxes on the floor to make way for my feet.

Danny set down the gun and then pulled a kerchief from his pocket. He rolled it up and put it across Lydia's eyes and tied it in the back. She was strangely quiet.

"Danny," I said. "What are you doing? You trying to give her an eye infection?"

"I don't want you to see where we're going," he said.

"I thought you said we were going to the station," I said.

He closed the passenger door. Then he opened the driver's door and got in next to me, holding the rifle again. He pulled out another kerchief. I leaned away from him as he tried to put it on.

"This is stupid," I said.

His eyes were starting to glaze over. That wasn't a good sign. I had to get him to feel some empathy for us.

Unless he was a psycho.

Like Andy.

"Would you do this to your mother?" I asked.

"You're not my mother," he said. "And she doesn't understand our fight. Now hold still."

So I did. He put the kerchief over my eyes.

"It's too tight," I said.

He loosened it, and then I could see under it. I heard him put the rifle on the rack behind us. Then he started up the truck. I leaned against Lydia, letting her know we were in this together. She did not respond.

The truck bounced down the rutted dirt road. He turned left, so I figured we were going in the direction of the station. I was fairly confident that if he took us to his father, he would let us go. Even though they all had guns, I figured their beef was with the government, not with us.

Then we were on paved road for a bit, and he slowed the truck. We rode briefly on what felt like a dirt road. Then the truck stopped, and Danny turned off the engine. I heard him grab the gun again. He got out.

"Wait here," he said.

"Well, OK," I said.

I heard him walk away. I leaned down and lifted my kerchief with my bound hands. I squinted and looked around. We were parked behind what looked like a camping trailer. I couldn't see any other buildings, couldn't tell if we were near the station.

"Lydia," I whispered as I pulled down the kerchief again. "You with me?"

"Yes," she said. "I just figure we should do what he says."

"Should never get in a vehicle with the bad guy," I said. "Never."

"But we just did," she said. "We got into the fucking truck."

"Yeah, but we didn't go far," I said. "I don't think this guy is gonna hurt us."

"Not on purpose," Lydia said. "Jesus. This day just keeps getting worse."

"We're gonna get out of this," I said, "and then we're gonna find those girls."

"I didn't sign up for this," Lydia said. "I'm sorry,"

I said. "I will get us out of it. I'll make sure he doesn't hurt us."

I don't know why I said that. I was never one of those cops who believed that my gut was always right. My gut told me Danny wouldn't hurt us, but I could be wrong.

Once I was working an insurance fraud case, and Don and I interviewed the owner of the building that had burned to the ground. I thought he was guilty. Don thought he was innocent. We didn't have any good evidence one way or another.

"Are you sure he's innocent?" I asked Don.

"Yes, I'm sure," he said. "That doesn't mean I'm right."

I've always remembered that. I could be absolutely certain about something *and* I could be wrong.

Right now I needed to get Lydia out of her very normal and natural fear response. If she was going to curl up into a fetal position, she would be no use—and in fact, she would be a detriment to both of us.

I heard footsteps. I felt the urge to pull off the kerchief over my eyes—to see who it was—but I didn't. Better to play the docile captive for a bit.

"Come on," Danny said. "We're going to wait in my trailer until I can talk to my dad. It's getting hot out here, and my trailer has AC."

Crap. Bad to be in the truck. Worse to be in a building with the criminal.

"We don't mind waiting out here," I said. "It feels nice. Open up the windows, we'll be fine."

"I don't care if you're fine," he said. "Breathing this air has given me allergies or something. Be better inside."

He opened the driver's door and said to me. "You first." He grabbed my arm. I wanted to jerk away, but since I couldn't see—except for a sliver under the kerchief—I let him help me out of the truck. Once I was on solid ground again, he led me toward the trailer.

"Step up twice," he said. I put my foot up and forward until I touched metal. I stepped up twice. Danny let go of my arm, and I heard the door open. He led me inside. Stuffy. He told me to sit. I gingerly sat on what felt like a cushioned bench.

"Don't move," he said.

As soon as he was gone, I lifted the kerchief again. I checked the cuffs. They were loose enough for me to remove. But I'd leave them for now. I loosened my boot, and then reached down for my gun.

I heard Danny say "step up" once as my fingers found the metal of my gun.

Then I heard a cry, and the sound of someone falling or being hit.

I jumped up, grabbed the door with my cuffed hands, and jerked it open. Danny was leaning over, trying to lift Lydia up. Blood seemed to pour from a wound on her head.

"She tripped," Danny said, apparently not noticing or not caring that I'd pulled off my kerchief. Danny pressed Lydia's kerchief against her forehead.

"Hold it on the cut," Danny said. He removed his hand as she put her hand on the rag.

Danny half-lifted, half-carried Lydia up the steps. She stumbled into the trailer. This would have been the opportunity to overtake him, but he didn't come into the trailer. Instead, he went back to the truck and got his gun.

Shit.

"You OK?" I whispered to Lydia.

"It's a lot of fucking blood," she said. "I hit on the corner edge on the top step, I guess."

"Hard enough for a concussion?" I asked.

"Naw," she said. "But I can pretend."

Danny came into the small trailer and closed the door. With him and us and his gun, it was close, stuffy, and uncomfortable.

"I think she might really be hurt," I said.

I didn't, but I wanted him to think so. The blood had soaked through the kerchief.

"Do you have a first aid kit?" I asked.

"Naw," he said.

"There's one in my backpack," Lydia said.

Danny went to her and began pulling things out of the backpack while he kept a hold of the gun: snacks, water, then a small first aid kit. He opened the kit.

"What am I looking for?" Danny asked.

"First let's wash it," I said.

"I don't have water here," he said. "Here's an alcohol pad. That'll wash it."

"Are you gonna do it or will you take off these cuffs so I can do it?" I asked.

"You do it," he said. "You can do it with your hands cuffed. I don't like blood. Makes me pass out."

I took the alcohol wipe and went to Lydia. She moved the

kerchief away from the wound. I could see a small triangle wound, about a quarter inch deep.

"This is gonna hurt," I said. I swabbed the blood. Lydia didn't even grimace. She glanced at me. She was back. The fear was gone. The wound was pink for a moment, and then it was bloody again. I dabbed it.

"I need to dress it," I said, "or it'll keep bleeding."

Danny held out the first aid kit to me. It took a little maneuvering with my cuffed hands, but I found a medium-sized sterile piece of gauze. I pressed it against her forehead.

"I need you to tape this while I hold it," I said to Danny.

He hesitated. But then he set the rifle down away from me—I'd have to go through him to get it. He took the tape from the kit and gruffly and quickly taped the dressing onto Lydia's forehead. I wiped the blood from Lydia's face with my sleeve. The gauze got a spot of blood on it, but the bleeding was slowing.

"I thought you said you weren't gonna hurt anyone," I said.

"I didn't hurt her," he said. "She fell. I can't help if she's clumsy."

"I'm not clumsy," she said. "I was fucking blind."

"Hey, watch your language," he said.

"My language? You've kidnapped me! How about watching your criminal behavior? My language ain't hurting anyone."

I sat next to Lydia on the padded bench. She leaned slightly on the table. I squinted. I hoped she really didn't have a serious head injury.

Danny moved away from us and continued looking through Lydia's pack.

"That's my stuff," Lydia said, "which I bought myself for when I go out on search and rescue. I had those snacks in there in case we found the girls."

Danny stuffed the fruit and nut bars into his pockets. Then he pulled out a prescription bottle. "What's this? Drugs?"

"It's a prescription," she said. "Yes, it's drugs. They're antihistamines."

"I could use a couple of these," he said. "I forgot to bring mine. Why do you have a prescription? I just get mine at the pharmacy."

He opened the bottle, shook out two pills, then popped two in his mouth. He took a swig of water from his canteen he got from his waist.

"Be careful," Lydia said. "They can make you sleepy."

"Not me," he said. "They never have. My mom used to give them to my brothers to put them to sleep when they wouldn't calm down. She tried that with me, too." He shrugged. "They made my allergies better but didn't put me to sleep."

"I think she needs to see someone about that fall," I said. "She might have a concussion. That could be dangerous."

He leaned against the wall. Then he pushed aside a gingham curtain and looked out.

"I just wanted to help my dad," he said. "I wanted to help take these forests back."

"Back from whom?" Lydia said. "Are you going to give them back to the Native Americans? If so, which Native Americans?"

"We should be able to run our cattle in these woods," he said. "Or cut trees. Or hunt. It's as if the government has become a forest slum lord. Or like those places in England, where the king or the lord owned all the land and the people were punished if they used it."

"This isn't anything like that," Lydia said. "Your friends, or whoever they are, cut down priceless old growth trees and sold them and lined their own pockets. That's against the law. They essentially stole from you! You are defending them from stealing from you."

Danny sat on the bench opposite of us. He stretched out his long legs and yawned.

"There's nothing for us anymore," he said. "We've got nothing. They make all these laws to protect other people. But what about us? We've got no jobs. We've got no future. We've got nothing."

"Who is 'we?'" Lydia asked. "White men? Ranchers? Christians?"

"All of that," he said. "All of it. We used to be the ones in power. Now we don't have any."

I laughed. I couldn't help it. If I'd been interrogating him maybe I wouldn't have. But this, this I couldn't let pass.

"White men are no longer in power?" I asked. "Where the fuck do you live? White men are still in power everywhere."

Danny rubbed his eyes and yawned again. Then he waved me away without looking at me.

"Shut up," he said. "I've got to get my dad. Show him my trophies. He'll know what to do with you. We never wanted to hurt you. Just keep you and the sheriff occupied while the other stuff was going on."

He put his head in his hands. I glanced at Lydia. She winked. I made a face. What was going on?

"Keep 'you?'" I asked. "Who are you talking about? Keep us occupied while what other stuff was going on?"

"I didn't want this to happen," he murmured. "We all want a place in this world."

In all of my years as a police officer, that was one absolutely true thing I had learned: People wanted to belong. To something, to some place, to someone.

Danny slouched back further. Then he fell over onto his side. His mouth opened, and he began to snore.

"Danny," Lydia said. "Danny!"

The man didn't move.

"Those are pretty strong antihistamines," I said as I quickly pulled my hands out of the plastic cuffs. Then I leaned over Danny and grabbed his rifle.

"Asshole," I murmured.

"They're sleeping pills," Lydia said as I looked around for a knife or scissors. "My husband had a problem for a while with an addiction to some prescription drugs, including sleeping pills. So I hid them in my pack in an antihistamine bottle. Sometimes when I'm tracking I have trouble sleeping."

I found a knife in the tiny kitchen and cut Lydia's cuffs. Danny made a noise. Lydia and I both froze and looked over at him. Then I chuckled. I had the fucking gun. Chances were he couldn't hurt us now. He turned over in his sleep and started snoring again.

"You are a clever woman," I said. "What would happen if your husband needed an antihistamine?"

"Hopefully he wouldn't be looking in my pack," Lydia said. "I was just a little paranoid for a while. Let's find more of those flexi-cuffs."

We quickly ransacked the trailer. Didn't find anything else. Except rope. I tied Danny's feet together and then his hands. He didn't move a bit.

Why were criminals often so stupid?

"How's your head?" I asked.

"I've got a headache," she said.

"Let me see your eyes," I said. She looked at me, eyes opened wide. I looked at her pupils. They were both the same size. I nodded. "They look fine. Still, you should see someone."

"Let's get out of here," Lydia said.

"Keys," I said. "We don't want him coming after us."

I looked around for keys and a cell phone. I didn't find either. I reluctantly patted Danny's pockets. No phone, but I did find what felt like keys. I reached into his front right pocket and pulled them out. Then I grabbed the gun again, and we hurried out of the trailer and almost ran smack dab into Sandy.

"I'm so glad to see you!" Sandy said. "I got to the picnic area just as he was taking you away. I practically ran all the way here—while looking for phone service. You OK? Where is he? What happened? Did he attack you?"

"I fell," Lydia said. "He's in there, passed out. We've got his keys."

"I think she needs to see a doctor," I said.

"Can I try the phone?" I asked. Sandy handed me the phone, and I tried calling the sheriff. It worked.

"Gunderson here," Nate said.

"Where are you?" I asked.

"I'm just getting to the checkpoint," he said. "We had some problems with Sylvie, so I had to get back. Where are you? Have you found the girls?"

"That little peckerwood Danny took Lydia and I hostage," I said. "We got away. I don't know where we are." I looked around. "You two know where?"

"About a quarter mile from the ranger's station," Lydia said. "The campground is over that way." She nodded, indicating the direction.

"Little motherfucker," Nate said. "Are you all right?"

"Lydia fell and she's got a gash on her head," I said. "It's probably fine, but it is bleeding through the gauze. I think she should at least see a paramedic. Might need stitches."

"Fuck," Nate said. "This is just gonna complicate the hell out of everything."

"No shit," I said. "I still want to look for the girls. Did Sylvie tell you anything else?"

"No," he said. "She was ranting about this being the end of everything as we knew it. Where's Danny?"

"He's tied up in his trailer," I said.

"Let me see if I can negotiate getting in there," he said, "and then you and Lydia can drive out in my cruiser while Sandy and I go look for the girls."

"No fucking way," I said. "Sandy can take Lydia. Or you can take Lydia. I'm going in. Whoever has the most tracking experience should come with me."

"Tracking experience won't make a whit of difference in the lava beds," he said.

"I'm not going back," I said.

"Why do you have to argue with me every fucking step of every way?" Nate asked.

"I'm taking the truck to where Sylvie shot the dog," I said. "Sandy and Lydia will wait here for you. I'll wait ten minutes and then I'm going in. Too much time has already passed."

"You can't go in the lava beds by yourself," he said. "You might never come out."

"Those girls are in there alone," I said. "And these assholes are so intent on hanging onto their power that they don't give a shit about them or anyone else. I'm not going to let them fuck this up any longer."

"No, instead *you're* gonna fuck it up," he said.

I growled and punched the off button and then tossed the phone to Sandy.

"You OK until Nate gets to you?" I asked Lydia. Sandy turned away from us as she put the phone to her ear.

Lydia nodded. "If it wasn't the lava beds, I'd say I'd be good to go, but you need everyone to be a hundred percent. I'll wait here. I'll be fine."

Sandy turned around. "They're letting Nate through. I swear he could charm the skin off a snake."

I stared at her. Charm? I couldn't imagine Nate having any charm.

"Well, maybe that's the wrong word," Sandy said. "But he's

good at keeping his cool and getting people to do the right thing."

"OK, then he'll be here soon," I said. "I'll wait for him at the blanket, at the lava beds."

I went to Danny's truck and got in the driver's seat. It smelled like sweat and grease. I felt a tinge of anxiety and wasn't sure why. I glanced over at Lydia and Sandy. They nodded, letting me know it was all right: I could leave them there. I started the engine and then drove away.

"Hang on, Beauty and Joy," I said. "I'm on my way."

Eleven

I parked the pickup out of the way, under a couple of young Douglas firs, and then I got out and walked up toward the gravel pit and the picnic area, to the place where the dog still lay dead on the pink blanket. The place looked like some kind of tableau as I walked toward it, or like a set on a theater stage, waiting for the actors. Now it was almost completely in shade and was so quiet, I could have heard a pin drop. I listened so hard my ears throbbed.

"Beauty," I finally said. My voice cracked. I cleared my throat and called her name again, not too loudly. "Beauty, my name is Kate Kelly. Katie. We know what your mother did. We can protect you. I'm here to help."

I listened. In the distance I heard some kind of bird call out. But it was too far away: I couldn't tell what it was.

I walked around the area again—avoided looking at the dog —and stopped at the edge of the lava beds. I stood on the threshold looking in. I could see rectangular moss-covered pieces of lava strewn everywhere. They made up the ground. They were the ground, so uneven and treacherous that only the occasional lodgepole pine or alder poked up in and around them, clinging to dear life in these ancient beds where lava once flowed.

Nate was right. It would be foolish to try and navigate the lava fields by myself. Suicidal. I blinked. I wouldn't even know how to describe this place to anyone. Until I came here decades ago, I had always imagined lava beds were smooth, like glass, or like gorgeous black perfectly still waves. I had seen places like that, closer to Mount St. Helens. These fields were almost the opposite of that. Nothing beautiful about them except for their utter wildness. Even the ground was wild. It was as if some giant had crushed the lava flow into a million pieces and then this same giant had thrown them up into the air to see where they landed. Maybe the giant was using the pieces of lava to divine the future. Lava divination instead of stick divination. I wondered what the giant had seen, looking down at the lava from above. What had the chaos told her?

I shook myself and stepped back. That was a little fanciful for me. I didn't believe in divination, fictional or otherwise. Life happened. We couldn't know the future, but we could guess it if we did something wrong, something illegal, something cruel. Then it was my job to bring about retribution for this wrong. I turned away from the ancient lava flow. No, not retribution. Justice. That was what I had worked for all of my life. Fucking justice.

If those children were dead . . . how could that ever be made right?

It couldn't be. Just as Amanda's murder was never set right, except that Andy was punished for it. But that hadn't brought Amanda back. Some acts defied justice.

This place made my mind wander—or speculate. Some biologists have theorized that if Bigfoot was an actual animal species, it was possible they lived in the lava fields, safe from human interference, munching on berries and pikas. If we had been looking for Bigfoot out here instead of in another part of the forest that night, would Amanda still be alive? Would Sylvie be sane?

Of course, the purpose hadn't been to look for Bigfoot. Not really. It had been an excuse to be together. A bunch of kids having fun in the woods. That was what I thought—what Amanda had thought.

Instead, it seemed, the boys had some kind of rape club.

And murder club?

"Ugh." I shook myself. Jesus. None of that mattered now. The only thing that mattered was finding the girls.

I dug the phone out of my boot, had to think a minute to recall the number, and then I called my son.

"Hello," he answered.

"Scott, it's Mom," I said.

"I didn't recognize the phone," he said.

"Yeah, how are you two doing?" I asked. "I'm really sorry this is taking so long." I walked away from the lava beds and the dead dog.

"Don't worry about it," he said. "We're fine. We walked around town. And we've watched some of it on the news."

"It's on the news?" I asked.

"The part about the militia," he said. "Or whatever they are. Not the rest."

I nodded. "Good, good. We had to hike in so it's taking longer. What are they saying about the group?"

"That they believe the federal government has too much power, and the guys who cut down the old growth maple shouldn't be in jail. They're not leaving until the men are released."

"Yeah, like that's gonna happen," I said. "Look, Scott, I haven't found the girls yet, and I want to keep looking. I know I promised you I'd be there. I know you were expecting this all to go away once I was off the force."

"No, I didn't, Mom," he said. "I know you. You'll always be trying to save every kid in the world."

I didn't detect a hint of bitterness in his voice. Perhaps my son was growing up.

"Not every kid," I said. "Just the ones who are close by."

"I'm glad those kids have you," he said. "If anyone can find them, it's you, Mom."

"Did pods come while I was gone and take my son?" I asked.

"Funny," he said. "Kirti wants to talk to you."

A pause. "Hi!" She sounded so perky. I smiled. I couldn't help it. What a nice fresh breeze she was to our family.

"How are you?" she asked. "Do you need anything?"

I almost laughed. What on earth could she do for me? I shook my head. It's the thought, I told myself. It is the god damn fucking thought. Shut up and say thank you.

"Thank you," I said. "But no. This might go into the night. You and Scott should think about going back to Portland. I'm so sorry."

"Actually, we have tomorrow off," she said, "so we were thinking of staying here. We could find a hotel and then meet you in the morning. Or we could just wait here and have something made for you to eat when it's all over."

We had two hotels in town. One was a dive. The other was an overpriced "lodge."

"You're welcome to sleep in my room," I said. "When I get home I'll just take the couch."

"We couldn't do that," she said.

"Sure you could," I said. "I don't know when I'll be back. Better someone gets some rest."

"OK," she said. "We walked around Beauty Falls today, and we're thinking of maybe getting married here, if that would be all right with you."

"Of course," I said. "I would love that. Will it be too far for your family to travel?"

"No!" she said. "They'll think of it as an adventure. Traveling to rural America to sightsee and go to a wedding." She laughed. Her voice sounded tinny in my ear. A hawk called out far above me. I looked up to see it circling.

"By the way," Kirti said, "a guy from the gas company was here."

"I don't have gas," I said.

"Well, we didn't let him in," she said. "Scott nixed that."

"What'd the guy look like?"

"Just some schmo," she said. She said the word "schmo" awkwardly, as though she'd never said it out loud before. I could hear Scott in the background saying something. Kirti repeated for me. "Um, 5'8". White. Brown hair, balding. Pot belly. Pale blue uniform with Vista Gas on the back. Eric on the name tag. Pale blue van with Vista Gas on it, too."

I nodded. I had taught my son well.

"Tell Scott good job," I said. "It sounds like the guy was legit. What'd he want?"

"Something about a complaint of a gas leak," she said. "Must have gotten the address wrong."

Right now a gas leak sounded . . . normal.

"I'll call them tomorrow and see what's up," I said.

"OK," she said. "But we're having a good time."

I shrugged. Probably a better time without me there getting on Scott's nerves.

"I hope you find the kids," she said.

"Me, too."

"Bye, Mom!" I heard my son call. For some reason, that choked me up a bit. Sounded like he was a 10 year old boy again, back when he still liked his mom, still said hello and goodbye when he saw me. I didn't want the call to end. I wanted to listen to his voice forever. He could talk about anything right now; I didn't care.

Just talk to me. Tell me your dreams. Your disappointments. Tell me I didn't fuck up your whole life, not really. Tell me you love me. Tell me you hate me. Just keep talking. . . .

I didn't have time for nostalgia. Nate drove up in his cruiser just then.

"I love you!" I called, hoping Scott would hear.

Kirti said, "We love you, too."

I smiled. She didn't even ask how on Earth I could love her when I had known her only a few hours. But she loved my son. She was kind to me.

Goddamn it. I loved her.

"Bye," I said and ended the conversation.

Nate got out of his cruiser and walked toward me. I felt a wave of nausea as I looked at him. I had almost forgotten all about the rape club. I squinted. He was alone.

"What the hell?" I asked. "We need help to find those girls."

Nate shrugged. "I dunno what to tell you. Johnson let Lydia and Sandy through so Lydia can see a doctor, promised to horse-whip his son, and then said I could come help you. He'll wait on negotiations until we find the children, but he won't let anyone else in."

"I don't understand this guy," I said. "Why does he trust you? Do you know him and not remember? Was he part of your rape club?"

Fuck. It just . . . slipped out.

"Jesus, Katie!" he said. "There was no fucking rape club."

"Then how come two out of three of us womenfolk got raped that night?" I asked. "Sounds like something close to a club. Or in our business, I think they'd call that a conspiracy."

"Andy was a crazy mother fucker," Nate said.

"A crazy person who was your friend. You knew he was crazy, and you brought us all out to those woods."

Nate shook his head and looked around, as though he could find the answers in these woods. His gaze stopped at the blanket, where it lingered for a moment. Then he looked at me.

"I don't know Elias Johnson. I don't know why he's letting me look for the girls. But I'm not going to worry about that now. We can arrest them or do whatever later. Right now we're burning daylight. Let's go find the girls."

"What about Sylvie?" I said. "Did she say anything else?"

"Naw," he said. "And she seems to be getting crazier. She wanted to call Andy."

"What? Why?"

"I don't know," he said. "She said she was mixed up about the date. When I asked her what date, she wouldn't tell me. When I wouldn't call Andy, she pretty much stopped talking. And her husband just wrings his hands. Cries. I had to let Doug go." He shrugged. "I mean, I couldn't hold him. His wife called, upset over something with their kid, so I cut him loose. If he did rape Sylvie, the statute of limitations is long over.

"This is a strange day," I said.

"Understatement of the century," he said. "I've got Sandy's backpack in the cruiser, along with my own."

I nodded. We got the packs, put them on, and then walked

around the blanket and up the hill a bit. We stood on the threshold, on the unseen beach of what had been a river of lava at one time. Now it was thick with scraggly trees. Beyond the trees were the broken pieces of fire.

"This is crazy," Nate said.

"No shit, Sherlock."

"Maybe she made it all up," Nate said, "just to get us here, hoping we'd fall and die."

I glanced back at the blanket. "That dog is pretty dead." I took a step. "Stay close."

"Never closer," he said.

Twelve

We walked slowly and very carefully over the huge lava pieces. It wasn't like walking through a boulder-strewn field. It was more like walking on a mountain of giant Lego pieces, without any ground apparent—unless one fell through one of the many pockets spread randomly throughout the field. We both looked at the "ground," at the pieces we walked on, trying to track, trying to find some trace of the girls. It took us several minutes just to go a few feet. I tripped twice, once over an above ground root, once over who knows what. Fortunately I was able to grab a tree to steady myself.

"How far you been into a lava bed before?" I asked.

"About three feet," Nate said. "You?"

"Farther than that," I said, "but not by much."

I stopped and looked around. "Beauty! Beauty!" I called. "We're trying to find you! You're safe. We won't hurt you."

We both held our breaths and listened. Heard only throbbing silence.

We walked up one hill of Lego-like pieces of lava, carefully crawling over some, making certain they stayed in place, while watching out for rattlesnakes and scorpions. The sun beat down on us. We walked past caves made by the lava boulders. Nate flashed a light in each one. They were all empty.

"Do bears even live out here?" Nate asked.

"I dunno," I said. "You're the country boy. My guess is everything can live out here except humans and anything with hooves."

Every few minutes, we stopped and called out. "Beauty! Beauty!"

We never heard a response.

"Sylvie said she picked this spot because she thinks Beauty Falls is somewhere near here," I said. "Have you ever heard that?"

"Yeah," Nate said. "But we won't find it. No non-Indian person will. And since all the white people get lost in the lava beds, people think it must be somewhere in them. Logical. For a crazy person." He chuckled. I glanced at him, and he stopped laughing. "But yeah, I've heard that rumor. I think it's all bullshit anyway. I like the stories, though. You can tell by the story what's important to each person. If they say there's buried treasure under the falls, then money is their desire or need. If they talk about the water from Beauty Falls being a healing elixir, they need physical or emotional healing."

I stopped as we came upon a bouldered hill and looked back at him.

"Really?" I said. "You've thought about all this?"

"Well, sure," he said. "This is my home. Don't you wonder why our town is named after waterfalls that don't seem to exist except in the imagination?"

"Maybe it wasn't named after any waterfalls," I said. "Maybe it's a warning. Or a declaration of what this place really is: Where beauty comes to fall, or die."

Nate raised his eyebrows. "I never thought of that," he said. He shook his head. "Naw. I like the idea of finding a waterfall that brings peace to everyone who visits it."

"I guess we know what's important to you," I said.

"Damn straight," he said.

We stood in the hot sun looking around for any sign of Beauty. I looked down and saw what appeared to be a very narrow trail running alongside the boulder hill. I pointed. Nate nodded. We climbed down to the trail which turned out to be an animal path.

We walked this trail for a while. It was so narrow in some places we had to walk sideways to get between rocks. Often we had to hug the rocks to keep from falling off a ledge. We detected no signs of the fire or a storm.

"Jesus H. Christ," Nate said. "We're getting further and further away, and I see no signs of the kids."

Just then a slight breeze rattled the leaves on the few trees around us. Something caught the light on one of the bushes growing near a lodgepole pine. At first I thought it was a spider web. A gold spider web. It was right off the trail, so I climbed up to look.

When I got to the webbing, I leaned over, reached out my fingers and touched two golden strands . . . of human hair.

"It's hair," I said. "It could be Beauty's."

Nate came up next to me, pulled out a plastic bag, and opened it. I carefully pulled the hair off the shiny leaves and dropped it into the bag. He closed the bag and put it in his shirt pocket. We both knew he might need to test any DNA on it, in case we never found the girls.

"This could mean we're on the right track," Nate said.

"Or a bird dropped it," I said. "Or it's been here a while."

"There's no dew on it," Nate said. "So it probably wasn't here all night. We had low clouds last night."

I nodded. "All right then. Let's go."

We continued on the trail that was less a trail than maybe a path squirrels had made. If Beauty had come this way, she most likely would have followed this trail. At least I hoped so.

We walked up toward a copse of lodgepole pines, their skinny tall trunks ending up in a mop of green branches, reminding me of a gathering of unruly teenagers. I hurried toward the trees, longing for shade. When I got to them, I took off my hat, wiped my forehead, and looked behind me.

Nate wasn't there.

Maybe he'd stepped off the path to take a leak?

No. He'd be stepping off to oblivion.

I looked down the hill and saw only a tumble of lava blocks. How had we managed to come up them, let alone see some semblance of a trail was beyond me.

"Gunderson!" I called.

I listened. Trees creaked slightly in the wind.

Fuck.

"Gunderson!" I cried.

Nothing.

I hurried—as best as I could—back down the hill, calling Nate's name and then listening for a call back.

Finally I heard a faint, "Katie."

I stopped and looked around. Trees behind me. Slabs of concrete-like lava beside me and before me. I looked off to the side of the trail where it dropped down ten feet more or less. Nate lay crumbled at the bottom of a kind of cave created by the tumult.

"Oh fuck, Nate," I said. "Are you all right?"

He shook his head. "No."

"Did you hit your head?" I asked as I looked around, trying to figure out how to get him out. Could I climb down?

"No," he said. He tried to push himself into a sitting position. "Aw, fuck. Something is wrong with my leg."

"Is it broken?"

He gingerly felt his right leg with his hands. "I don't think so."

"Can you stand up on your own?" I asked.

He tried to push himself up to a standing position, but he couldn't find a way to stay up because the rocks were at an angle.

I remembered Lydia had put rope in the backpacks. I took mine off, opened it, and pulled out a roll of nylon rope.

"I've got rope," I said.

Nate looked up at me. "So I can hang myself? You can't pull me up."

"You don't know," I said.

He made a face.

"If you weren't this big ass Swede or Norwegian or whatever the fuck you are, I could haul your ass up. If you can help, maybe we can do it together. You can't stay in there for very long. The sun is right on you."

"I'm not planning on setting up a camp," he said.

"What happened, anyway?" I asked. "How'd you end up in there?"

He looked up at me. "Jesus, Katie. Obviously I zigged when I should have zagged."

I couldn't help it. That made me laugh.

"Yeah, stupid question," I said. "Sorry. We'll figure something out."

"Try calling for help," he said.

I looked around until I found a nearby pine that was half grown-up, half sapling, and I tied the rope around it. Then I tossed the rest of it down to Nate.

"Tie it under your arms," I said. I pulled out the phone that was still in my boot. I called the police station. No connection. No bars. I tried 911. Nothing.

I looked around the cave Nate had fallen into, trying to figure out the best way to pull him up. Straight below me, it was just sheer rock. Behind Nate, jagged rocks went up higher into more jagged rocks. To his left, the rocks were stacked more evenly. In fact, if he could walk, he could use them as steps and walk right out.

"Nate," I said, pointing. "Can you get over there?"

"I just see rocks."

"They're like steps," I said. "If you could walk—"

Nate had pulled himself up to a standing position. He tried putting his weight on his leg. He grimaced and chewed his lip.

"OK," I said. "I could come down and act as your crutch, and we could come up together."

"Or get trapped down here forever," Nate said.

"No, I'm not hurt. I could climb out even if I couldn't get you out."

"Unless you fell and got hurt."

"Nate—"

"Don't argue with me," he said.

"I will fucking well argue with you if I want," I said. "Who the fuck are you?"

"I'm the one who is hurt," he said, his voice calm as he looked up at me. "And we still need to find those girls. I've done lots of rescue work in the wilderness. You have not. Let me tell you. The number one thing is to not put any other people in danger."

Ah crap.

"You're gonna have to trust me," he said.

I gritted my teeth.

"About this one particular thing," he added.

"OK. What should I do?"

"I see what you're calling steps," he said. "I think that is a good idea. If I had a crutch. Maybe up by the trees you could find a fallen branch, something sturdy enough to hold me and not slip out from under me."

"All right," I said. "Drink some water. I'll be back."

Man, it was getting hot. I was starting to feel it. Exhaustion. Just from being in this catywampus place.

I hurried up to the trees—although "hurry" was a relative term. Fortunately, the ground beneath the grove of trees was bare of lava—at least bare of broken lava. I was able to stand still on solid earth for a moment and get my bearings. I looked around. A crutch. I needed something that would act as a crutch. I picked up a fallen branch, leaned on it, and it snapped. I did this several times. None of them would hold Nate. I kept walking through the trees until I came to the end of them. The lava beds sloped down from here, seeming to go in all directions. Except to the north, a line of trees hugged the beds. Maybe it was more woods than lava. Beauty could have gone that way.

I saw something beige near one of the boulders, and I crouched down. It was a stick, about two inches in diameter. I pulled it up and out from between two rocks. It was taller than my armpits, so it might work for Nate. I leaned on it, hard. It didn't waver. I wondered how it had gotten here. It looked like someone's walking stick—but it had been there a while. Moss was growing on it.

I saw a flash of something where the stick had been. I

crouched down again. Between the rocks, in the dark, was a tiny puddle of water. I glanced around. Where had that come from?

Didn't matter right now. Had to get Nate out.

I went back to Nate.

"I found something," I said. I pulled off my shirt and tied it to the top of the stick, to give him some padding. Then I held out the stick to him.

He took it, put it under his arm, and gingerly limped over to the lava steps. I took up the slack on the rope and followed him the few feet to the other side of his strange cave. I sat on the ground, put my feet against rock, and held onto the rope.

"I'll try to keep you steady," I said, "in case you slip."

He nodded. He was pale and sweaty. Not a good sign.

Slowly, he put one foot on the step and then the crutch and then his foot. It was difficult to watch. I thought he was going to slip and fall every time he moved. It took a while, but he was finally close enough that I could pull him all the way up, and he could lean on me instead of the stick.

He was heavy, but I let him lean while I untied the rope from his waist.

"Let's go up here," I said. "There's shade."

He dropped the stick. I heard it clatter on the rocks. I needed to get it again—for my shirt. Later. Now we went up toward the trees, our arms wrapped around each other as I became his human crutch. I'm not certain how we did it. He was bigger than me, weightier, and the trail was narrow. We were both breathing hard and sweaty as hell.

I got him under the trees, sitting with his back against a trunk of one of the trees. I pulled off his backpack and handed it to him. He opened it to see what had been damaged or destroyed in the fall. I took off his right shoe and sock as he grimaced.

His ankle and part of his foot had started to swell and turn colors.

I said, "Why don't you scoot around here so that you can rest your leg on an incline."

Nate did as I suggested. I gently felt his foot. He gave me a dirty look. "That hurts," he said. "But it's not broken. I don't think."

He pulled out his phone and tried calling out.

"Nothing," he said. "Goddamn it."

"I need to check to see if you're hurt anywhere else," I said.

"Everywhere hurts," he said.

He lifted his shirt. I didn't see any bruising. I went to the other side and pulled up his shirt. His back looked OK, too.

"The pack saved me," he said. "Didn't save me from falling, obviously, but from getting hurt worse."

"Undo your pants," I said. "I need to check your kidneys."

He did as I asked. I heard him unbuckle his belt, heard his zipper go down. I didn't like the sound. It suddenly gave me the creeps. I felt like I was going to throw up.

I quickly moved away from him and pressed my back up against another tree.

The world spun slightly.

Breathe, breathe, breathe.

"Katie?"

I put my hands behind me on the tree.

"Katie?"

"Don't fucking call me that," I said.

"That's your name," he said.

"To my friends," I said. I closed my eyes.

"I've called you that since I first met you," he said. "What do you want me to call you? Katherine?"

"Shut up," I said. "Can you shut up for a moment?"

"What's wrong?" he said. "What just happened?"

"What happened?" I opened my eyes and stood, leaving my hand on the tree to steady me. "What happened is that I am remembering what happened thirty years ago today. This day. I am remembering that you and Andy and Doug had some kind of rape club. You were going to rape all three of us. And then what? Talk about it? Laugh about it? Laugh about it while you murdered us?"

"Jesus Christ," Nate said. "No, no, no! I can't believe you believe that nutcase. Sylvie's crazy! She may have killed her own children."

"Because of what happened to her," I said. "Maybe she would have never gone around the bend if it wasn't for Doug raping her, if it wasn't for Andy killing Amanda. You're trying to tell me that you were some kind of saint hanging around with rapists and murderers? Birds of a fucking feather, Gunderson."

He grimaced.

"What's wrong?"

"It hurts," he said.

"Take off your pants," I said, "so I can check."

"No," he said. "You can't do anything even if I am bruised."

I went over to his back and pushed him forward, so I could look at his back.

"I can't see your fucking kidneys," I said.

"That's because they're in my body," he said.

I went around to the front of his legs and began pulling on the ends of his pants.

"Katie—Kate," he said. "Stop. That hurts."

I kept pulling. "I said to take off your fucking pants. I need to make sure you're all right."

"No!" he said. "You don't need to look. Christ. That hurts."

I jerked on his pant legs, and Nate fell on his side. I kept pulling and his pants came down past his hips. He grabbed onto his underwear as they started to come down, too.

"Goddamn, Kate," he said. "What the fuck are you doing?"

I was suddenly so angry. I could barely see. I felt humiliation and anger rising in me.

I saw red.

I wanted to scream.

"Katie!" Nate cried.

The world seemed to snap into the focus again. I had Nate's pants down below his buttocks. Nate was desperately trying to hang onto his underwear while trying to keep his pants on, while trying to stop me from—from doing whatever I was doing.

I let go of the ends of his pants and sat on the ground.

What the fuck was I doing?

Nate's eyes glistened with tears.

What the fuck was I doing?

"Shit, Nate," I said. "Jesus. I am so sorry."

He lay with his cheek against the ground.

Fuck me.

I got up and went over to him.

I reached out to help him sit up. He waved me away. So I stopped. But he couldn't do it.

"May I?" I asked. He nodded.

I crouched down and helped him sit up.

"I guess you hurt your arm some, too," I said quietly. He nodded.

He tried to hike up his pants, and he couldn't. So I gently pulled them up for him as he leaned first on one hip and then another until we got them up above his hips again.

"Can you please lean over?" I asked, before he zipped up again. "So I can check your kidneys."

He leaned forward.

I looked down at his lower back.

"May I touch you?"

He nodded.

I gently pushed on the kidney area.

"Does it hurt?" I asked.

He shook his head. And wiped his eyes.

I looked at his head. "May I touch your head?"

He nodded.

I gently ran my fingers across his scalp to check for bumps or bleeding. It all seemed fine.

"OK," I said. I patted him on the shoulder. "I don't see anything else." I left my hand on his shoulder for a moment. Then I moved away.

He zipped up his slacks and buckled his belt. I turned my head away, didn't listen, tried to hear the breeze in the trees.

"We should eat something," I said. "And then I'll try to get help."

Nate got fruit bars out of his backpack and tossed one to me. I listened to crows calling out in the trees.

"I want you to know," Nate said finally, "that I never knew what Andy was planning. Or Doug. I swear on my children that I never had any intention that night—or any other night—of hurting you. Are you kidding? I thought you were the smartest and funniest person I had ever met. I was amazed you would spend any time with me."

"Smartest and funniest?"

He shrugged. "I was young and hadn't met a lot of people yet."

I laughed. He smiled, and I kept laughing until my laugh hiccupped into a sob. And then a giggle.

"Kate, I loved you back then," he said. "The way a teenage boy loves a girl. I thought we would ride off into the sunset together. I wouldn't have dreamed of hurting you."

"You loved me? We fought all the time."

"I just thought we were having good discussions," he said. "You were so out of my league, to my way of thinking. So I tried to keep up with you. By arguing. Andy and Doug were just summer people I hung out with. I would have hung out with anyone to be closer to you. That's what mattered to me."

"Well, now you're sounding all needy and desperate," I said. I smiled at him.

"Yeah," he said. "See. You were just always so . . . you. You never seemed unsure. You were going places, and I wanted to go to those places with you."

"Jesus," I said. "That's how you saw me?"

"You fill a room," Nate said. "You did then, you still do."

"Maybe I was like that once," I said. "After Amanda was raped and murdered, everything changed. I can't remember who I was before then. All women understand that we are just one moment, one mistake, one accident, one moment of chance, one twist of fate from being Amanda—from being raped and or murdered. Do you have any idea what that is like? No, you don't. That's why I became a cop. To even up the odds a little."

I sighed. I did not want to talk about this. But I could not stop saying all of it. And I could only say it to Nate. He was the only person in the world who could hear it.

"I've felt guilty for thirty years for what happened to Amanda," I said. "I-I knew Andy was looking at me. He was just creepy. I was glad Amanda ended up with him that night. Because I would not have wanted to be alone with him. But I didn't warn her. Why didn't I make sure she was safe? I wanted to spend time with you. I didn't really give a fuck about what was going on with any of the rest of them. Amanda was sweet, but she was young. Sylvie was weird. Doug was just nothing. And Andy was . . . himself. You were vaguely interesting."

Nate shrugged and smiled. "Sometimes I think I became a cop to make up for not protecting Amanda. Now I protect everyone I can. Except you. You don't need protecting. You don't need anyone."

"Damn straight I don't need protecting," I said.

"What do you need?" he asked.

What did I need? What a question to ask here, now, under these circumstances. I looked down at the ground.

"I need to feel at home. I need to be able to take a deep breath again. I don't think I've had one in thirty years. I need to live without guilt. Without hope. I need a world where love is more important than greed. I need my child to be safe and happy." I looked up at him. "That's all."

"What about love?" Nate asked. "Most people say they need love. Not you?"

I shrugged. "Sure, I want my kid to love me."

Nate laughed. "You're always so fucking cagey. You don't trust anything."

"OK. Sure, love would be great. If someone came along who could love me. Me, as I am. Love me fiercely, just as I am. Not in spite of who I am, but because of who I am. Someone who has absolutely no expectations of who I should be because I happen to be a woman. But am I looking around for that? Fuck, no. Life's too short. I've got things to do."

"Aren't you gonna ask me what I need?" Nate asked.

"I already know what you need," I said.

"What?"

"Peace," I said. I looked at him and grinned.

"So you pay attention when I talk. Ain't that sweet?"

"I try not to pay attention, but some of it seeps through, in spite of my best efforts."

"Yeah."

"Just think," I said, "if it hadn't happened, we wouldn't be here now. Those girls wouldn't be in jeopardy."

"I know," he said.

"I wish I could remember what I was like before," I said.

Nate nodded. "Oh, and let's be clear before we end this conversation. I don't love you now. Now I think you're an asshole."

I laughed. "Well, I think you got that right."

We were silent for a few moments.

"It's not your fault what happened to Amanda," I said. "Or Sylvie. Or what's happened today. Shit happens. And then we have to deal."

"So what are we doing here?" Nate asked. "I mean, we should have both known better. What the fuck? We're out here alone." He rubbed his face. "I should have done something different with Johnson so that search and rescue was here. I just didn't want bloodshed. And he was so friendly to me. That was creepy. He agreed to whatever I asked—except letting anyone else come. I don't really understand. It's this fucking day. It screws with my head."

"The smart thing to do now is to get some help. I'll try to phone again. We'll get you out and get search and rescue here. We can't do this alone. Which we should have known, I agree. My ex says I get a kind of flu every June 25: I go a little crazy. I guess this year is no exception."

"This year is even worse," Nate said. "The thirty year anniversary. Andy trying to get a hold of all of us."

"Yeah, what's with that?" I asked. "He never tried to get in touch with me, thank god. I would have told him to go fuck himself. I'd tell him to go rape and murder himself."

Suddenly the woods got very quiet. I looked at Nate. I opened my eyes wide.

"Sorry," I said.

"I know I can't understand what you went through," Nate said, "or what you go through. But I have a daughter. And it pisses me off she still has to worry about this kind of shit."

I said, "There's a little ridge at the end of these woods. Let me go see if I can get a signal from there."

"Looks like the storm might be coming early," Nate said,

nodding toward the west where black clouds arched over the horizon.

"Shit," I said. "That's all we need." I got my phone out and walked through the trees until I came out the other side, near where I'd found the crutch for Nate. I punched in 911.

"What's your emergency?"

"Yes, yes, this is Kate Kelly," I said. "I'm here with Sheriff Gunderson, in the lava beds. The sheriff has been hurt and needs medical attention. He's hurt his leg and can't walk out. Deputy Sandy Dean knows where we started walking in. We've been walking a couple of hours."

I didn't hear a response.

"Hello?" I called. "Did you hear me?"

Nothing. I called the cop shop. The phone rang.

"Deputy Dean here."

"Sandy!" I cried. "It's Kate Kelly. The sheriff is hurt. We're in the lava beds. He can't walk out. Can you track his phone?"

"How badly is he hurt?" Sandy asked.

"He's conscious," I said. "It's not life-threatening. But he can't walk."

"Did you find the girls?" Sandy asked.

"No," I said. "We should have never come out here without more search and rescue. It's crazy."

"I can barely hear you," she said. "You keep breaking up."

"We went in where the blanket is," I said. "We walked for about two hours. Nate is in a copse of trees up on a hill. I think we were walking east most of the time."

"Sylvie has been going crazy," Sandy said. "She won't shut up. She talks about this being a day of reckoning, for all of you. For everyone who was there that night."

"Did she say anything else about her girls?" I asked.

"No, just that they were now in heaven," Sandy said. "That storm is coming in fast and fierce. It's knocked out power in

Portland and Vancouver. We won't—" I couldn't hear what she said.

"Sandy!" I called.

"We won't be able to get a helicopter out there if it's storming," she said. "We'll try to figure something out. Why—"

Nothing again.

"Sandy?"

Nada.

Crap.

I started to go back to Nate when the flash of silver caught my eye again. I walked over to the small puddle of water near the two stones. I leaned down. In the mud, where the water was evaporating, was a footprint.

My stomach lurched.

A child's footprint.

Fresh and clear.

Beauty had been here!

I stood. "Beauty!" I called. "Are you there? It's Kate Kelly. I won't hurt you. We've come to protect you."

I listened.

No response.

I hurried back to Nate.

"I found a footprint." I knelt down next to him. "It's a child's footprint. It's fresh. And I got through on the phone. The connection ended before I could find out what they're going to do. I talked to Sandy. That storm is coming, so they're not sure they can send anyone out until it passes."

"You've gotta try to find Beauty and Joy," Nate said. "I'm fine here. I'll have my phone. I've got the locator on. They'll find me."

"What if it storms?" I said. "You can't stay here."

"Sure I can," he said. "I live in the Pacific Northwest. Rain is nothing. I won't melt."

"What if the wind shifts and the fire comes this way?"

He laughed. "Then I guess I'd be toast."

"And you're essentially a sitting duck," I said.

"What?"

"You're prey."

He shook his head. "Lions, tigers, and bears, oh my. This is a new side to you. A worry wort. What the fuck do you care about me? Go find her."

"Here's my phone, the one you gave me. I have my other phone. And my gun." I handed the gun and phone to him. "Crap. And I need my shirt." I went down to where Nate had fallen and picked up the stick and my backpack and walked up the hill again. I dropped the pack next to Nate, put on my shirt, and then held out the stick to him.

"I don't know if the firearms will stop a bear," I said as I buttoned my shirt, "but you could always poke it with a stick. I've heard they like that, makes them playful."

"Funny," he said. "How will you find your way back?"

"Bread crumbs, of course."

"Take your pack," he said.

I shook my head. "I won't be gone long."

"That's what every person who gets lost in the woods says."

"I won't get lost," I said.

"That's another thing every person who gets lost says."

I unhooked my water bottle from my pack. "I will take this," I said. "I'm not completely stupid. But the pack is too heavy, and it's too hot out."

I held out my hand to Nate. He reached up and shook it. We both held on for a moment as we looked each other in the eyes.

"You'll be all right," I said.

"Of course," he said.

I nodded. "Promise me."

"OK," he said. "I promise."

"Because—because no one else knows, Nate. No one else in the world."

He nodded. "Ditto."

We let go of each other's hands.

I walked away from him.

"You've got this, Katie," he called.

"I told you not to call me that," I said.

"OK, Katie bear."

"We are not friends," I called.

"Tell it to someone who cares," he said.

"That's what I'm doing."

Thirteen

I glanced at the small footprint in the muddy puddle one more time, and then I headed down the narrow trail. I saw another footprint, this one in the dust. I was on the right track. I looked up behind me. I couldn't see Nate, could only see the tall lodgepole pines, looking like teenage boys again, and the black clouds behind them.

I was walking away from the lava beds. This was a relief. It might mean my compass and phone would work. As I got further from the lava beds, the ground leveled off. I walked for a while in the merciless sun, trying not to trip over pieces of stray lava. Then the path I was on curved, and I walked out of the sun and into the forest again.

I heard thunder and looked behind me, back in the direction of the lava beds. Lightning sliced the black sky, and then I heard thunder again.

Crap. Nate was gonna get drenched. Unless the helicopter turned up sooner. Probably not. They usually needed at least two hours lead time. It hadn't even been an hour yet.

I stopped once I was amongst the trees to let my eyes adjust to the lower light. I breathed deeply. These were old growth Doug firs. I squinted as I looked around. The forest floor was relatively uncluttered, Oregon grape and salal grew up amongst the ferns and Doug firs, along with vanilla leaf. This was—at least in part—an old growth forest. It had probably been spared the blade because it was deep inside the lava fields.

It was so quiet. I didn't hear a single bird, not even one alarming on me. Maybe they were all watching quietly, waiting, looking down at the intruder.

"Beauty!" I called. "Beauty! My name is Katie Kelly." I wasn't sure what to say next. I couldn't say her mother sent me. Her father? Did she have a good relationship with her dad?

"Beauty! You're safe now. Everything is all right."

Well, that was just bullshit. Everything was not all right.

Everything was relative.

I listened to the silence.

It was difficult to believe anything was amiss as I stood on the soft forest floor, surrounded by the huge old Douglas firs. I thought of Scott and Kirti. I liked knowing they were having a good day in and out of my ramshackle house. This day that felt like it had lasted a week. And what a cluster fuck. We should have never come out here alone. What the fuck had I been thinking? It was this day. This stupid anniversary.

I closed my eyes and took a deep breath.

I had to find those kids. I was fairly certain they were alive. But it could get cold out here, even in the summer, especially after a rain. Plus lions, tigers, and bears. And wild fires.

And psychopaths.

I needed to find them now.

I heard running water.

I opened my eyes and looked around. I put my hands behind my ears and pushed them forward—deer ears my dad used to call them. I listened.

Yes, water!

I hurried toward the sound, skirting the shrubs and ferns until I found an animal path through the trees. The ground sloped down, and the sound of water got louder. I went up and then down.

The ground was shaking beneath my feet, and I could hear rushing water. I slowed and walked up a rise. I stopped when the ground dropped away into darkness along with water from a river and a waterfall. I stepped back, a little overwhelmed by what I was seeing. A two-tiered waterfall fell down a flat wall and into the darkness below. Mist rose up around the waterfalls. Next to the falls was a river—or a creek. The level was down, even though it was flowing strong. A series of flat rocks crossed the creek to the water fall. Standing on one of these rocks, in a pool of sunlight, hands together at her heart as though she were praying, was . . . Beauty.

I recognized her from the photo her father had shown us, even though her face and arms were dirty, her shirt ripped, bloody scrapes on her legs. She looked as though she'd been in these woods for days rather than hours.

"She is alive," I whispered. Thank every divinity on the planet. Now where was her sister?

I backed away so I wouldn't startle her. Didn't want her falling into the abyss which was just feet away from her.

I walked upstream a bit, and then walked over the rise to come down the narrow shoreline toward Beauty.

When I was about fifty feet from her, I said softly, "Beauty."

She turned her head slowly, opened her eyes, and dropped her hands to her sides.

"Your mother can't hurt you," I said. "I'm here to help you."

She reminded me of a fawn. A fawn getting ready to bolt.

"Where is your sister?" I asked.

Beauty blinked.

And then . . . she bolted.

She leapt from the flat stone she was on to another one and then headed straight for the waterfalls.

No, no, no!

I couldn't have found her only to lose her.

"I won't hurt you!" I cried.

She ran straight into the falling water and disappeared.

I ran along the creek until I got to the line of stones, and I hopped onto one and then another. I didn't know what was on the other side of the falls. Maybe it went straight down. It was completely crazy to follow her.

But I did. I leapt into the void.

As the falling water hit me, I felt momentarily breathless. And then my feet hit ground. Slippery ground. I somehow steadied myself and kept from falling in the darkness. I blinked, waiting for my eyes to adjust. The waterfall sounded strangely muffled even though it was an arm's length from me. I was in a kind of alcove on the other side of the falls.

"I'm here to help," I said. "Your father is back in town, and your mother is in jail."

Deep dark silence vibrated around me, and then I heard, "What about Princess?"

Ah, thank god. Her voice sounded small and strong all at the same time. The light coming through the waterfalls showed me Beauty standing near the back of the cave.

"I'm sorry to tell you this, but she didn't make it."

I listened for Joy but heard nothing. Maybe the sound of the waterfall was drowning out her sounds.

But I could hear Beauty breathing.

I suddenly felt sick to my stomach.

"Where's your sister, Beauty?"

"She's here," Beauty said. "I brought her here, to Beauty Falls. I thought this was Beauty Falls. Now I don't think so. Are you sure my mother is not out there?"

"I'm sure," I said.

I saw her lean over. She picked up something and then carefully walked over to me. It was her sister. I felt a rush of relief. She cradled her in her arms.

She stepped into the light near the waterfalls, and I could see Joy. For a sickening moment, I thought I was looking at a doll.

Beauty held out what was in her arms. "My mom said Beauty Falls could cure anything. So I brought Joy here."

I took the infant from Beauty and sank to my knees.

Joy wore a cream-colored dress. And her face and arms were light blue, or slightly purple.

I quickly felt for her pulse. But her body was already stiff.

"I put her near the falls," Beauty said. "Close enough so that she got some of the drops on her. But it didn't cure her."

"You can't cure dead," I said.

"But Mom said…"

"Did she do this?"

Beauty stared at the ground. She looked so small, so pale.

"Mom had the gun," Beauty said. "She was gonna kill us all. So I picked up Joy and ran. I heard the shot. Heard Princess yelp. And Joy was screaming and crying. Mom yelled at us to come back. I heard her following us. I held Joy against me, for her to be quiet. And she was. After a while I couldn't hear Mom, and then I tripped and fell on those rocks. I fell on top of Joy. When I got up, she wasn't breathing. I tried everything. I shook her. I breathed into her mouth. I brought her here, and I prayed." Tears streamed down her face. "I prayed! I was trying to save *us*."

"I'm so sorry, Beauty," I said.

I didn't know what else to say.

It wasn't her fault. But she would remember killing her sister for the rest of her life.

"You didn't cause this," I said. "It is not your responsibility."

"I'm her big sister," Beauty said. "I should have kept her safe."

"Come on. I'll take you back."

"I don't want to go back," she said. "Maybe if we stay longer, Joy will get better. God will save us."

"No," I said. I felt angry that her parents had indoctrinated her with such bullshit. "God cannot bring the dead back to life."

"But Jesus came back from the dead," Beauty said.

"That's a story," I said. "It's not real life."

Beauty suddenly looked desperate. And a million years old. I had seen this look before, on the faces of other children who suddenly realize they are alone in the world.

"We have to go back," I said. "There's a wildfire not far from here and a storm coming. We need to get to safety."

I slowly stood. How was I going to carry this baby?

"Did you carry Joy all the way here?" I asked.

Beauty nodded. "I put her in my backpack." She went into the darkness again and came back with a pink backpack. She pulled out a small fuzzy blue blanket and held it out to me.

"My mom wanted a boy," she said.

What?

"OK," I said. "Put the blanket on the ground there."

"That's why it's blue," she said. "Mom said life is harder for girls. So she wanted a boy."

Oh, the blue blanket.

"Blue is a boy's color," she said.

I was holding a dead infant, and Beauty was talking about blue being a boy's color.

"Someone made that up," I said. "Blue for boys and pink for girls."

"And purple for girls," she said.

"Beauty, that's nothing real or true. Color doesn't have a gender."

She cocked her head slightly.

"Color is not boy or girl," I said.

"Does that mean life isn't harder for girls than it is for boys?"

I looked down at the dead baby.

I could not have this discussion now.

I gently lay the baby on the blanket and wrapped her in it.

"You shouldn't cover her face," Beauty said. "She can't breathe."

"Darlin'," I said, "She has taken her last breath. Now the blanket can protect her until we get her back."

"And then they can fix her?" Beauty asked.

"No," I said. "She can't be fixed."

I took the backpack from Beauty. I retrieved from it a water bottle and a couple of fruit and nuts bars. Then I carefully put Joy into it. I zipped it up as best I could, and then I put the pack on my back.

"What about me?" Beauty asked. "Can they fix me?"

"What do you mean?" I suddenly felt panicked. "Did you get shot? Hurt when you fell?"

"I killed my baby sister," she said. "That means there's something wrong with me, like Mom."

"No, it's different," I said. "It was an accident what happened to Joy."

Beauty looked like a deer about to bolt again.

And then I smelled smoke.

"Can you put these bars in your pocket?" I asked. "Have you eaten anything? What about water?"

"I'm not hungry," she said.

I handed her the water bottle. "I want you to drink some water," I said. "And take a bite or two of one of those bars."

She uncapped the water and took a swig. Her hands shook slightly. Then she unwrapped the bar, too slowly, and took a bite. She looked at me as she chewed. She was used to doing what she was told. Taking her sister and running was probably the first time she had ever defied her parents. She took another bite and then another, as though suddenly realizing she was starving.

"Is my mom mad at me for running away?" she asked.

"Your mother is ill," I said. "She's not thinking right. But running away is probably the best thing you've ever done."

"Even though I killed Joy?"

"You didn't kill her," I said. "You told me it was an accident. Isn't that right?"

"Yes," she said. "But it was still me who did it."

I didn't say anything.

"Maybe God wanted her in heaven," she said.

I wanted to say, "That is complete bullshit."

"Maybe he wants me in heaven, too," she said.

"Don't believe everything you hear," I said, "or everything you think. Come on. We need to go. Can you take my hand, and we can walk out of here together?"

I didn't want her to suddenly decide to go to heaven by jumping into the abyss.

I held my hand out to her. She put her tiny hand in mine. My breath caught in my throat. Her hand was icy.

"Are you cold?"

She shook her head.

We ran through the falls and out onto the rocks on the creek. Then we hurried across until we were on firm ground again. Beauty let go of my hand and began walking up the hill. She knew the way back.

I definitely smelled smoke. The wind had picked up, but part of the sky was still blue, part was covered in clouds, and part was tinged with smoke. It was a west wind, and we were traveling mostly west, so I hoped that meant the wind would push the smoke and fire away from us.

The way back went quicker than the way down, it seemed. I kept looking over my shoulders, but I didn't see any flames. And the smell of smoke went away. Maybe that meant we had left hell, and we were headed for paradise.

Not that I believed in hell or paradise.

Beauty moved quickly ahead of me. Despite the trauma she had experienced, she seemed full of vigor and grace.

And then I could see Nate up ahead, still sitting against the tree. How long had I been gone. Five minutes? An hour?

Beauty saw him at the same time I did. She stopped until I caught up with her. Joy felt heavy in the pack, and I suddenly remembered I was carrying a dead infant on my back.

"It's all right," I said to Beauty. "I know him. He's the sheriff. He was looking for you, too, but he fell and hurt himself."

Nate turned his head just then and saw us. He waved. Beauty reached for my hand again, and we hurried up the hill.

"You must be Beauty," Nate said. He looked pale and in pain. "I'm glad to see you."

Beauty moved so that she was behind me.

"Where's the baby?" Nate asked.

"She didn't make it," I said. "I have her . . . body."

Nate and I looked at each other. I pressed my lips together. I felt like I was going to fall down. How long had this day been?

"How's your leg?" I asked.

"It hurts," he said.

"Did my mom do that?" Beauty asked, peeking around from behind me.

Nate pulled himself up a bit and said, "No. I fell. This is a dangerous place. Your mom is in jail. She can't hurt anyone anymore."

"God is in jail," Beauty said. "He still hurts people."

Nate and I glanced at each other again.

Nate cleared his throat and said, "What do you mean, Beauty?"

"God is in jail," Beauty said again. "He calls our house and asks for my mom."

"And she calls him God?" I asked.

Beauty nodded. "God was the one who told her to bring us out to the woods."

"Does God have another name?" I asked.

She shrugged. "I don't know. Are Jesus and God the same?"

"Was his name Andy?" I asked. "Did you ever hear her call him Andy?"

"I don't think so," she said. "I asked Dad why God was in jail."

"What did he say?" Nate asked.

"He said as far as he knew God wasn't in jail. He said she was talking to someone she knew in high school. But Mom said he was God."

Oh crap.

Beauty squeezed my hand. I looked at her and then followed her gaze.

To the east of us, flames were licking up the side of several second growth Douglas firs.

Just then I heard a helicopter coming out of the west.

"The calvary has arrived," Nate said.

Fourteen

Fortunately, the helicopter was able to land not far from us. One of the rescue workers was a doctor. As far as she could tell Beauty was physically fine, and Nate needed an X-ray. They carried him to the helicopter on a stretcher. We gently put Joy into a bag that they tucked into a corner. Beauty and I sat close to each other on the helicopter.

When the helicopter rose high enough, I could see flames topping the trees.

I kept my arm around Beauty as the chopper flew us over the Gifford Pinchot National Forest toward the town of Beauty Falls. A strong wind rocked the helicopter, and Beauty threw up.

I nearly did. I was glad when we finally landed on the grounds of the elementary school half a block from my house.

Nate and I glanced at each other now and again. It was too loud to talk, and I wasn't interested in putting on headphones.

It was strange to see Nate on his back like that. He looked . . . bigger. And too vulnerable. I didn't like it. It was difficult to be pissed at him, or angry, or disgusted when he was down and out.

I hated this day. I hated this date.

When the helicopter landed in the elementary school soccer field, an ambulance was waiting to take Nate to the clinic that they'd opened especially for this emergency. The doctor wanted Beauty to get a more thorough check-up. Beauty and I got out of the helicopter and stood near the ambulance. The sound of the helicopter made my head hurt.

Dr. Winslow, Beauty Falls' coroner, was there to receive Joy's body. Beauty kept an eagle eye on the bag that contained Joy, watching as one of the rescuers handed the body to Dr. Winslow who walked it over to his van and then put it in the back. Winslow mostly did home visits after someone who was terminally ill had died, to pronounce the death. Murder was rare in Beauty Falls.

Deputy Hill, Sandy, and several other deputies stood near their cruisers in the school driveway. We hurried over to them. No one said anything—it was nearly impossible above the noise of the helicopter. We watched as the rescue workers and EMTS transferred Nate from the stretcher onto the ambulance gurney.

Then the sounds from the helicopter increased, and it began to lift off the ground. It hovered above the old oak tree for a moment, and then it headed west again.

"Sandy," I said. "Can you take Beauty down to the clinic?"

"Sure," Sandy said.

Beauty kept a firm grip on my hand.

"I need to go get your dad," I said. And talk to her mother. If Sylvie had been communicating with Andy, if she considered him God, had he convinced her to kill her own children?

Beauty still hung onto my hand.

"I'll come down to the clinic in just a few minutes," I said. "Or Sandy will bring you up to the sheriff's office. Sandy will protect you. You won't see your mother."

Beauty reluctantly let go of my hand and went with Sandy, who took her to one of the cruisers. I watched them drive away. Thunder rolled overhead.

I walked over to Deputy Hill.

He nodded. "Good job finding the girl," he said.

"Bringing one back dead doesn't feel like a good job."

"By the way, the stand-off is over," he said. "They just got up and left."

"The FBI let them go?" I asked. "Danny Johnson kidnapped us."

"Yeah," he said. "They arrested him, and they've taken Elias Johnson in for questioning. But it's over. I think Johnson et al were afraid of the fire. City folk, ya know."

I laughed. "Yeah, us country bumpkins aren't at all afraid of a roaring inferno."

"I don't think you're a country bumpkin *yet*," he said.

"Has Sylvie said anything else?"

Hill shook his head. "She's writing some things down in between bouts of babbling."

I glanced over at the ambulance. Nate was waving to us. We hurried over to him.

"This shouldn't take long," Nate said. "Katie, I want you to talk to Sylvie. Find out if Andy had anything to do with her trying to kill her kids. Hill, you can inform Mr. Smith that Beauty is alive and that Joy has died and that the coroner will determine the cause of death."

I nodded.

"You want a ride?" Hill asked.

"Katie—Kate," Nate said. He held out his hand to me.

"I'll be right there," I said to Hill. He headed back to his cruiser.

I looked down at Nate's hand. I hesitated, and then I took his hand and shook it.

He laughed.

"I just wanted to say thank you," he said as we shook hands and then quickly let go. "And good job. I'm sorry about the baby, but you found Beauty. I don't know if anyone else could have done it."

"Probably *anyone* else could have done it," I said. "And I wish it had been anyone else. My son and his fiancé are waiting for me. Have been waiting all day. He is gonna be pissed."

"My son is on a plane to India," Nate said. "I'm not sure what that is all about. And my daughter just texted to say she's at my house. I wasn't expecting her, but she's there. So I've got someone to go home to, too."

"It's not a competition," I said.

Nate shook his head.

"Talk to Sylvie and then go home," he said. "This is over, I think."

"Let's hope that fire doesn't reach Beauty Falls," I said.

I glanced in the direction of my house as I hurried to the squad car. Maybe I should just run in and tell them I was back.

No, I'd be home soon.

I got in the car, and Hill screeched out of the parking lot and headed for the cop shop.

I texted Scott, "I'm back in BF. Be home soon."

I didn't get an answer. I hoped he wasn't mad at me.

"You and the sheriff close?" Hill asked.

"You know we knew each other when we were kids," I said. "So about as close as you and I are."

"I wasn't out in the woods with you when Amanda Stenson was murdered," he said.

"Yeah," I said. I looked out the window as we pulled in the parking lot of the cop shop. "We've got that one horrible day in common. And that's about it."

Inside the cop shop, Hill told me Sylvie was still in Interview Room 1.

"Good luck with the father," I said.

I took a deep breath and then knocked on the interrogation room door. I opened it a crack. Sylvie still sat at the table. She was writing on a yellow legal pad. A sheriff's deputy stood at the back of the room, her arms behind her back. The deputy looked at me and nodded.

I opened the door and stepped inside. I nodded to the deputy to stay.

Sylvie looked up, startled.

"Why are you here? You shouldn't be here. You should be out in the woods."

"Why?" I asked. I stood on the other side of the table.

She shook her head. "Did you find my girls?"

She didn't wait for an answer. She began writing again. She had her other hand up, at the end of the pad, and I couldn't see what she was writing.

"Did Andy tell you to take your girls out into the woods and kill them?" I asked.

Sylvie laughed but didn't look up. "Not Andy, God. He said we all must pay for what happened to Amanda."

"Why? We didn't do anything to her."

"Doug raped me," Sylvie said.

"He shouldn't have done that," I said. "But what does that have to do with Amanda?"

"And what about you?" Sylvie asked, still looking down. "Did Nate rape you?"

"No," I said. "Nate never raped me. He never tried to rape me. He was not a part of Andy's rape club."

"Ha!" She looked up at me. "They're all a part of God's rape club." She bit her lip. "I mean Andy's rape club. Why isn't there a clock in here? What time is it?"

"Why does it matter what time it is?" I asked. "Where you're going, time won't matter."

I don't' know why I said that. I was tired. I had carried a dead baby on my back for part of the afternoon.

"I want to know if Andy put you up to all of this," I said. "And if he did, why."

"God, god, god," Sylvie said.

I pulled out a chair and sat across from her.

"What is it you're not telling me?" I asked.

She turned the pad of paper over and looked at me.

"I knew what Andy wanted to do to Amanda," she said. "He told me he wanted to have sex. Not with me. He said I was too ugly." She laughed. "He was fixated on you. But I told him Amanda would be easier." She smiled. "All these years you didn't want anything to do with me, but I saved your life. You owed me everything."

"What did you mean Amanda would be easier?" I asked.

She shrugged. "She was smaller, younger. I just thought it would be easier."

I felt dizzy.

"Why didn't you tell someone?" I asked.

"I didn't think he'd force himself on her," Sylvie said. "I thought he wanted a girlfriend. I didn't hear about the rape club until later. I didn't know he would kill her. But later, not too long ago, he revealed himself to me. He said I was forgiven for getting the abortion. He was God, and everything he did was for the good of everyone. He said the only way I would feel better is if I stopped taking my medication and helped him."

"Helped him how?" I asked.

She shrugged. "You'll see." She turned the pad back over. "Is it six yet?"

"I dunno," I said.

Someone knocked on the door. It cracked open a bit and Deputy Hill motioned to me. I got up and went out into the hall and closed the door behind me.

"The FBI called," Hill said. "Elias Johnson is aka Elias K. Linderson. He served time in prison, here in Washington state. His cell mate was Andy Weston, Amanda Stenson's killer."

"What?"

He nodded.

"Do you think he and Andy planned this together?" I asked. "But why?"

"I don't know," Hill said. "The FBI is talking to him and coordinating with the sheriff while he's at the clinic."

I glanced at the clock. 5:50.

"Did you talk to the father yet?" I asked.

"No, I'm going in now to tell him," he said. A young woman in her twenties came up to us. Hill said, "Hello, Katie."

"Where's my dad?" she asked.

"Uh," Hill looked back at me. "This is Nate's daughter. Can you tell her what's up?" And then he disappeared down the hall.

The young woman held out her hand. "I'm Katie Gunderson," she said. "Do you know where my dad is?"

Katie?

I shook her hand. "I'm Kate Kelly," I said. "Your father fell while we were out on a search and rescue mission. He hurt his leg, and he's at the clinic right now."

"Then he's not fine," she said.

I laughed. "Well, fortunately, he fell on his ass, and we all know how hard that is."

She didn't want to, but she did smile.

"Ha! I'm glad to see you didn't get your father's sense of humor," I said. "Which is virtually nil. But he is fine. He said you had come home to see him unexpectedly."

"He emailed me to come to the house today," she said. "I thought it was strange because it wasn't from his regular email. But I came anyway."

A strange email.

Wait.

Wait.

Wait.

Scott had sent me an email about coming out today, and he said he had received one from me, inviting him. But I hadn't invited him.

I figured we had just gotten our communication wires mixed up. And I hadn't cared because I'd get to see him.

"Katie," I said, "you need to stay right here until I find out what's going on."

I felt suddenly panicked.

I ran into the interrogation room.

"It's 5:55," the deputy was saying.

Sylvie looked at me and then in one swift clean move, she stabbed the pen into her neck. Blood immediately began squirting out.

"God is dead!" she screamed. "God is dead!"

The deputy radioed for help as she and I jumped on Sylvie. Sylvie screamed and screamed. Two other deputies burst into the room. Between the four of us, we got Sylvie on the floor, with the pen still in her neck.

"Get a medic!" someone yelled.

One of the deputies pressed a hand against Sylvie's neck.

Sylvie looked at me and smiled.

"Why did Andy have Elias Johnson take over the ranger's station?" I asked.

"He wanted you and Nate out in the woods by yourselves, just like you were 30 years ago."

"Why?"

She began screaming again. And then she passed out. The medics arrived, and the rest of us moved out of the way. They carried Sylvie out of the room just as Deputy Hill came in.

"What happened?" He shook his head. "It doesn't matter. Just got word that Andy tried to hang himself, just now, just minutes ago."

"Did he succeed?"

Hill shook his head. "He's alive now. I don't know if that'll last. You've got blood on you."

"Shit," I said.

I headed for the bathroom as they carried Sylvie away. Katie was sitting on a bench near the bathroom door. She looked shell-shocked.

I went into the bathroom and washed my hands and face, quickly, scrubbing them with soap. What was happening? What was going on?

I went back out. Katie was standing now, waiting for me.

"Can I go see my dad?" she asked.

"We haven't figured out what's happening," I said. "For now, it's safer for you to be here."

"Why?" she said. "Can you tell me what's going on? Everything's strange. I was at my dad's house before I left, and this man from the gas company came. He tried to get into the house, but I wouldn't let him in, and he finally left. But that's why I came here. It just seemed strange."

"The gas company?" I asked.

She nodded.

Kirti and Scott had said someone from the gas company had been at my house.

I hurried back to the now empty interrogation room and looked at the pad Sylvie had been writing on.

She had written over and over, for page after page, "The sins of the father and mother shall be visited on their children." Until at the very bottom she wrote, "God is dead. 6:00 p.m."

The sins of the father and mother shall be visited on their children.

Our children.

"Hill!" I hollered as I ran out of the room and toward the front door. "Send someone out to Doug's house to check on his wife. Keep Katie here."

And then I was outside.

No, no, no.

That was why Sylvie asked about my son, about Nate's children. It was why she had tried to set a fire in my house weeks earlier. She was testing the easiness of it. Or the response time. Something.

Andy blamed us all for him being in jail.

So he would punish us by killing our children.

The gas man. What had he done?

As I ran, I pulled out my phone and tried to call Scott. The phone rang and rang.

Where was he, where was he?

Had the gas man turned on the gas so that it was leaking into the house now, killing my son and his fiancé. Had he set a bomb?

Answer, answer, answer.

Why wasn't he answering?

I ran around the corner. Couldn't see my house just yet, but I didn't hear a bomb. 6:00 must have been the time they had set on to coordinate it all.

Then, then, then I heard an explosion. It was too far away. Wasn't my house. Not yet, not yet. Maybe that was Nate's house. Where did he live?

I turned the corner. My house, my house was still standing.

"Scott!" I screamed. "Scott!"

Why hadn't I spent more time with him? Who gave a shit about my job? About anything except spending time with my son. I wanted another chance, another chance.

"Scott!" I screamed.

I was at my driveway. I could smell gas.

No, no, no!

"Scott!" I screamed again.

"Mom!" He came around the corner, from the back of the house, Kirti next to him.

"Oh my god!" I said. I flung my arms around him and held him close, closer than I had since he was a baby. I began sobbing. "My boy, my boy. You're safe, you're safe."

I could feel Kirti's hand on my back.

"We need to move away from the house," she said softly. "There appears to be a gas leak."

I let Scott go, and I began to laugh. I wrapped my arms around Kirti and embraced her. "Yes, yes, yes. Let's move away." I let her go and caught Scott's hand in mine.

"We've called the gas company," Scott said. "Mom, what's going on?"

"I-I don't know completely," I said, "but let me call the fire department. And come with me to the police station. You'll be safe there."

"Safe from what?" he asked.

"Everything," I said.

Fifteen

It was a long night.

Once Sylvie was medicated, she told the interrogators—not me—that she had been following Andy's—God's—orders for about a year. He believed everyone who had been in the woods the night of in Amanda's murder should be punished, just as he had been. The best way to punish us was to hurt our children. He had wanted Sylvie to take her children out to the place where he killed Amanda, but she changed her mind and set them loose in the lava beds—or they escaped while she was trying to kill them. She wasn't sure.

A gas leak was introduced into my house and Nate's, as well

as bombs for good measure. Nothing happened to Doug or his family. Maybe Sylvie wasn't able to figure out where he lived. So the person who had harmed her the most got off unscathed.

Nate's garage blew up, but his house was fine. The bomb squad dismantled the bomb at my house.

Andy survived his suicide attempt, and he later told authorities that Sylvie had made up the whole thing. He wished nothing but good things for all of us.

I don't know if we'll ever figure out the truth of it all.

After a while, the police cleared Scott's car. Scott and Kirti were allowed to go back to the house and get their car. Before they left the police station, I held them both for a long while.

"So your car is safe," I said, "and Sylvie says there's nothing else they planned. Drive carefully."

"Mom, please come to Portland with us," he said. "We can all stay at the house together. It'll be like old times."

I smiled. "I'm sure your dad would like that."

"I already asked," Scott said. "He said the couch is yours. And then you could sneak into his room when you are sure I am asleep."

"You knew we did that?" I asked.

"Of course," he said. "I'm not stupid."

I nodded. "You get started home," I said. "I'll call you."

Deputy Hill had driven their car from my house to the cop shop. I stood outside and watched Scott and Kirti get into the car and drive away. I wanted to run after them and beg them never to leave my sight again.

Just then, Sandy drove up in a cruiser. Nate got out of the passenger side. His right foot was in a boot, and he had a cane.

"What a drama queen," I said.

Nate smiled. Sandy nodded to me as she went into the cop shop. Nate limped over to me.

"Scott leave?" he asked.

"Yes," I said. "Man, that was tough seeing him go."

"Katie is going to stay with her mom," he said. "She's pretty shaken up about the whole thing."

"That reminds me," I said. "Your daughter's name is Katie?"

He smirked. "Don't be getting any ideas. My ex-wife's mother's name is Katherine."

"Why not Kathy?" I asked. "Or Cat. But Katie? Come on. You named her after me because you *love* me: you've been pining for me for 30 years." I was laughing so hard I almost couldn't talk.

"Yep, you found me out," he said. "And your son Scott. That's my middle name. I know you named him after me."

"Really?" I asked. "Is that your middle name?"

He laughed. "No. Hey, we can't go back to our homes until the bomb squad and detectives give us the all clear. I checked the Econo Lodge. There are two rooms left. We could each get a room. Sit out on the porch there and count the cars going by."

"Watch the flames get closer to town," I said.

"Play cards," he said.

"Get drunk," I said. "Well, in my case. You could just watch me get drunk."

"Yeah, man, I hate this day."

"It's the next day," I said. "We can't hate the next day, too."

Another squad car drove up. This time Mr. Smith and Beauty got out of the back. I thought they had left for home a long while ago.

Mr. Smith came to shake our hands. "Thank you for bringing my daughters back to me," he said.

"I am so sorry about Joy," I said.

He shook his head. "God will bring her back to us." I let go of his hand and looked down at Beauty. Her father and Nate walked away from us.

I squatted so that I was nearly face to face with Beauty.

"He thinks God will make Joy live again," she said, "as long as we don't bury her. Is that true?

"No, darlin'. That won't happen."

She nodded. "I didn't think so." She tilted her head. "Everything is different now."

"It is," I said.

"I can smell the smoke," she said.

"Can you? I don't smell it."

"Do you think the fire will burn down Beauty Falls?" she asked.

"I don't know," I said. "I hope not."

"But fire can't burn the real Beauty Falls, right?" she said. "Fire can't burn water."

"I think you're right about that."

"Poor daddy," she said. "He keeps saying he is so glad I'm alive."

"I bet he is."

She leaned down so that her mouth was close to my ear. "He doesn't know that I'm already dead."

Oh. No, no, no.

I instantly thought of myself the day after Amanda was murdered, the morning they found her body. Everything changed. Everything. It was as if I had been murdered that night, too.

I withdrew from life.

I held Beauty's hands.

"Beauty," I said. "I can feel your hands in mine. I can feel your blood coursing through your veins. If I put my ear to your chest, I could hear your heart beating. When I was just a few years older than you are right now, someone I knew was murdered. I blamed myself for that most of my life. After it happened, everything changed. I let that terrible moment be the highlight of my life. Don't let that happen to you. It's horrible what happened. It's unforgivable what your mother did. But you did nothing wrong. You saved your life." I squeezed her hands. "You saved your life. You almost saved your sister's. You did a great and beautiful thing. You stay here in this world, and you live your life. Your life! You don't have to prove yourself, you don't have to justify your survival. You just live your life, and try to do it with beauty and joy."

"Even though the world is burning," she said.

"Even though."

"Even though there are so many terrible things happening," she said.

"Even though," I said. "And for as long as I am on this Earth, you can call on me. I will be there, and I will remind you that there is beauty in this place. Because you are still here."

She put her arms around my neck. I pressed her tiny body against mine as I stood up. I held her while we both sobbed. And when it seemed our tears were spent, we let each other go.

I borrowed a pen and paper from someone and wrote out my phone number and address and gave it to Beauty.

"Goodbye, Katie," she said just before she and her father left. One of the deputies was driving them back to Vancouver. "Thank you for finding me."

"Goodbye, Beauty," I said. "Call me any time."

They got into the car and drove away.

Nate and I stood alone in the parking lot.

"Is someone going to check on him and Beauty?" I asked. "She said he's not going to bury Joy's body because God is gonna bring her back to life."

"They're staying with someone who has been vetted by the authorities," Nate said. "Tomorrow social services will be out. Or today, I guess. You ready to go to the Econo Lodge?"

I looked out into the darkness.

"Beauty said she could smell the fire," I said. "Can you?"

Nate shook his head. "No, not yet at least."

I looked down at the phone as it vibrated. Scott texted, "Hope to see you soon."

"Look at this," I said. "My son wants to see me. Now that is a miracle."

Nate nodded.

"I'm not going to the Econo Lodge," I said. "In fact, I'm leaving June 25 behind me for now and forever. I'm going to spend some quality time with my family."

"OK," Nate said.

We were silent for a few moments, and then Nate held out his hand to me. "Hello, my name is Nate Gunderson," he said. "I don't think we've met before."

I hesitated, and then I shook his hand.

"Hello, I'm Katie Green," I said. "Nice to meet you."

We held hands for a moment. And then we moved slightly away from one another, our hands dropping to our sides.

"Nice little town you got here," I said. "But it seems to be burning down, so I'm leaving." I started to walk toward my car.

"Naw," Nate said. "Stay. Don't you know? You can't kill beauty."

I wanted to turn around and shout, "Bullshit. Don't you understand that beauty is usually the first thing to die?" But I didn't. I kept walking. Let him keep his delusion. So much depended upon it.

About the Author

Kim Antieau's novels include *Church of the Old Mermaids, Butch, The Jigsaw Woman, Whackadoodle Times*, and many others. She lives the the Desert Southwest of the United States. www.kimantieau.com